A Passage to Siam
A Story of Forbidden Love

A Passage to Siam
A Story of Forbidden Love

A novel by
V. Vinicchayakul
Translated by Lucy Srisuphapreeda

First published and distributed in 2024 by
River Books Press Co., Ltd
396/1 Maharaj Road, Phraborommaharajawang,
Bangkok 10200 Thailand
Tel: (66) 2 225-0139, 2 225-9574
Email: order@riverbooksbk.com
www.riverbooksbk.com
@riverbooks riverbooksbk Riverbooksbk

Copyright collective work © River Books, 2024
Copyright text © Lucy Srisuphapreeda,
except where otherwise indicated.

All rights reserved. No part of this book may be reproduced or transmitted in any form or by any means, electronic or including photocopy, recording or any other information storage and retrieval system, without prior permission in writing from the publisher.

Editor: Narisa Chakrabongse
Production supervision: Suparat Sudcharoen
Design: River Books

ISBN 978 616 451 100 2

Cover image after a painting by N. N. Karazin from the book
The Tsarevitch's Journey to the East.

Printed and bound in Thailand by Parbpim Co., Ltd

Contents

Translator's Preface	6
Prologue	7
Chapter 1	The Seed of a Dream	10
Chapter 2	The End of the Horizon	27
Chapter 3	The Blue Sky of Siam	52
Chapter 4	The Dilemma	69
Chapter 5	In the Shade of the Palace	81
Chapter 6	Bua	100
Chapter 7	The Crossroads	110
Chapter 8	On the Wings of Love	130
Chapter 9	Blown Away by the Wind	164
Chapter 10	Bitter Love	197
Chapter 11	When Love is Doomed	213
Chapter 12	The Wind from the Past	236
Chapter 13	New Life	252
Chapter 14	On the Other Side of the World	278
Chapter 15	The Sands of Time	288
Chapter 16	When the River Runs Backwards	308
Chapter 17	The Glowing of Such Fire	315
Epilogue	329
Background	332
About Khunying Vinita (Vinicchayakul) Diteeyont	334

Translator's Preface

'*A Passage to Siam*' is an award-winning novel by leading Thai novelist V. Vinicchayakul. It is a historical fiction that tells the story of the tragic romance between Catherine, a young Englishwoman, and Justin, or Prince Vijjuprapha of Siam, during the reign of Rama IV and the beginning of the reign of Rama V. Although the two main characters are fictional, they were inspired by the true story of Prince Chakrabongse and his wife, Katya, who lived during the reign of Rama V. The novel weaves in other characters based on individuals who lived in Siam at the time and the story is intertwined with actual historical events. The clash of civilizations that occurred during this period, when traditional Siamese ways were challenged by the arrival of Western ideas and culture, is reflected in the conflicts that arise between the headstrong young Englishwoman and Justin's conservative relatives inside the palace. Above all, it is a magnificent and compelling love story that transcends the boundaries of time, religion, race and custom.

I am immensely grateful to V. Vinicchayakul, the novel's author, for sharing her work with me and to Mom Rachawongse Narisa Chakrabongse, for giving me the opportunity to introduce the author's work to English-speaking readers and help bring modern Thai literature to a wider audience.

I hope that this translation will captivate English-speaking readers as much as the original work has enthralled Thai readers from the time it was written until today.

Prologue

The story you are about to read was compiled from primary sources, such as photographs and letters, and as many historical documents as I could find, both in Thai and English, which I pieced together to write the story of Catherine Burnett Lindley, an Englishwoman who lived in the mid-nineteenth century, and a Siamese man from the same time. He was my ancestor, and his name was Prince Vijjuprapha, or as he was known by the palace nobles, 'Prince Saifa'.

Catherine's story is known by his descendants in the 'Vijjusena' clan because it has been passed down by word of mouth through the generations, but it does not appear in Thai historical chronicles. It is simply the story of a life entwined with Thai society during the reign of Rama IV.

I am more fortunate than my relatives in that I know more of Catherine's story than they do because my father, Vachara Vijjusena Na Ayuthaya, is a direct descendant of Prince Vijjuprapha and I am his only son. All the sources that he had collected were, consequently, passed down to me.

I did not see the original records of Saifa, but I saw the parts that had been copied into his biography in the memorial book for his funeral. In that book was a photograph of Saifa taken when he was around seventy years old. In addition, several of his personal belongings were passed down to my father.

To be honest, I had heard the story since I was a child, but I only became interested in it when I had the opportunity to go to England two years ago. I was free for a month, so I decided to travel around the British Isles by myself armed with several maps.

I visited the village of Longstock in Hampshire without expecting much, except that I wanted to see what Catherine's cottage was like and to take some photographs to show my father. But owing to my inquisitive nature, I miraculously found, not only Catherine's cottage, but also one of her descendants who still lived in the village.

Her descendant was called Kenneth Lindley, and he was the owner of a small antique shop in the village. He willingly invited me to stay at his home and showed me Catherine's photographs, letters, and records, which he had carefully collected. His documents were flawless, and I felt as if I had unexpectedly stumbled on a gold mine.

I saw photographs of Catherine from when she was a child until she was a young woman and I can say that she was, without a doubt, an English rose as lovely as Saifa had described her. When I saw Jane, Kenneth's daughter, who worked in London but had come home to visit her parents while I was there, I understood how Saifa must have felt when he first met Catherine.

Jane, like Catherine, was an 'English rose' with wavy golden hair and blue eyes, and if she had dressed in Victorian costume, she could have easily been taken for Catherine's sister.

Jane was as interested in Catherine's story as her father, and she and I became as close as relatives who had known each other for ages after knowing each other for just a few days.

I photocopied all the documents and took them back to show my father. Just as I had expected, he was very happy and excited and began to goad me into writing this story.

I kept in touch with Jane Lindley over two years and we exchanged news and information about our common ancestor. Finally, a month ago, Jane accepted my invitation to Thailand where I gladly welcomed her into my home and arranged for her to meet all my relatives. With Jane by my side to fill in the gaps in my knowledge, I was motivated to finish the book.

As I drove along the elevated expressway, I looked out at the skyscrapers all over the city of Bangkok and the congested traffic, and contemplated how much Thai society has changed since the days when Catherine first sailed past the mouth of the Chao Phraya River and saw Rattanakosin for the first time during the reign of Rama IV.

The last thing I saw was a man, on the other side of the world, who was the most important person in Catherine's life.

I understood how Catherine must have felt when she wrote on the first page of her diary, "...when I first heard the name, The Kingdom of Siam, all I knew was that it was a small country in the East, or as the Siamese say, in Burapha..."

Asanee Vijjusena Na Ayuthaya
17th July 1998

1
The Seed of a Dream

The person who first mentioned the word 'Siam' to Catherine was Arthur Lindley.

It was also the first time she had met him.

Arthur, like Catherine, was blonde and, when he smiled, his brown eyes sparkled. He had just returned from India, as the aide-de-camp to General Gilbert Burnett, Catherine's uncle. Her uncle had completed his term in India and had moved his family back to England while Arthur was still deciding whether to return to India or take up a post somewhere else.

Arthur had been invited to a garden party, which Catherine's aunt Mabel had arranged at the home of Catherine's uncle in the town of Breamore in Hampshire.

Catherine enjoyed the lively atmosphere of the party, which she found a fascinating change from the tedium of her life that had been the same from the day she was born until now. She had just turned eighteen.

Catherine tried to find a topic to talk to Arthur about so as not to bore him or make him think she was unsophisticated compared to the other girls who had been invited to the party.

"India is far, but there are other smaller countries even further east like Burma, Siam and Singapore," he told her.

"What strange names. They sound so interesting," Catherine replied earnestly. "And are those small countries more like India, or more like China?"

Another Eastern country that Catherine had only ever heard the name of was China. She had seen the blue and white Chinese porcelain in King George's summer palace in Brighton, when her parents had taken her there several years earlier, before her father's illness and subsequent death, but that was the extent of her knowledge about the East.

"They're nothing like either," Arthur replied after pausing for a moment as if he was trying to remember.

"I met a Siamese fellow at the military college in India. He was smaller than an Indian with yellower skin. Can you imagine a place so hot that you must bathe several times a day, or where you can swim in the river all day?"

He stood up as if to show her his tanned skin more clearly, his face glowing with pride.

"A lot of people can't bear the heat, but I don't mind it. I think faraway lands have a lot more to amaze us with. If you're too concerned with being as comfortable as you are at home, you'll never go anywhere."

Catherine began to agree with him.

When her father was alive, he used to say, "East or West, home is best." Therefore, he had hardly ever left his home except for when he went to work at his law firm in the town, and as soon as he had finished work, he returned home. His life had continued in this way year in year out until he had become seriously ill and passed away two years earlier. Even after her father's death, her mother and older sister, Pauline, had held fast to the same mantra.

Only Catherine felt that there was so much more to learn and see in the world outside. She did not want to simply look out of the window at the fence and the road that passed through the village of Longstock until the day she died without ever having seen so much as the English Channel.

The conversation turned to other topics as several others had joined in. When Mary, her uncle's youngest daughter spoke, Catherine became quiet.

Catherine's hair was golden, curling naturally in ringlets, and her skin tone was even, while Mary's hair was straight and hay-coloured, and her skin was freckled. Most noticeable were Catherine's blue eyes that sparkled like the morning sky, along with her rosy cheeks, full lips, and round chin above her long neck, which made her appear as fresh as spring in comparison to her cousin.

When they had first returned home, her aunt had complained that

Mary had not had a chance to meet a 'suitable young man' because they had lived in India, lamenting that if they had returned to England earlier, by now, she would have been married.

Catherine was amused to see Mary flirting with the men at the party, which included Arthur, but she could tell it was to no avail. Arthur was just twenty-three and, for another thing, if he had liked her, he would have already proposed to her in India.

The question of marriage, however, was far from Catherine's mind, even though eighteen was considered a suitable age to get married.

Her sister, Pauline, on the other hand did not mind following in her mother's footsteps. She had enjoyed busying herself around the house ever since she had been old enough to help her mother with the housework, while Catherine had always liked to walk outside in the fresh air as far as the River Thames, where she would sit and read until it was dark before walking back home.

Pauline seemed as if she would be content with her new life, no different from her old life, because a 'suitable man' had proposed to her, and she was preparing for her upcoming wedding.

When Catherine saw Mary flirting with the young men around her, in a bid to exchange her dull existence for a life just as tedious as her mother's and her sister's, Catherine was amused and inexplicably puzzled.

Catherine sat quietly at the table until she was sure that nobody was paying her any attention before she discreetly got up from her chair and wandered over to the flower garden.

If I were a man, I would leave Hampshire, not just for London, but to travel further – to see what's beyond the horizon, which is more than just a silver line that I see from my bedroom window.

But – she was not a man, and her dreams were nothing more than fantasy.

"Miss Burnett…"

A deep melodious voice behind her made her turn around, and she saw Arthur Lindley hurrying towards her.

When he came close, he blurted out, "Miss Burnett, I know we've only just met. There's not much time for us to meet, but I have even less time because, in two months, I have to go abroad again..."

Catherine was puzzled at first, but then her heart suddenly began to race when she looked into the eyes of the young man, which had a strangely agitated, but tender expression.

"What do you mean?" she asked softly, realising that her cheeks were burning.

"I want to see you again," Arthur answered at once. "I wish I could get to know you better. If I lived in Hampshire, I could wait, but I live in London and coming to ask you is difficult..."

"I don't understand."

"Miss Burnett, ordinarily, I would come to see you and get to know you, but I don't have that much time...I..."

He paused as if holding his breath before blurting out, "I know what I'm doing. I never believed in love at first sight until I met you. Miss Burnett...May I tell you that I fell in love with you from the first moment I saw you, and I want to marry you!"

***

Emma Burnett was Catherine's mother.

She had been widowed in her early forties after her husband had passed away at the age of forty-six.

Her husband's death was a signal to warn her that she might also leave this world in a few years' time, and her two unmarried daughters would find life difficult with no one to support them.

They no longer had their father's income to depend on, and all that was left was a small sum of savings and no debt. Fortunately, Emma owned their small house in Longstock, but she recognized the need for Pauline and Catherine to get married.

When she heard from her daughter that the young officer, Lieutenant Arthur Lindley, had proposed, Emma felt that her prayers had been answered.

***

Catherine woke early when the pale rays of the morning sun began to shine through the window onto her bed. Her bedroom was in the garret under the thatched roof of the white cottage that had been built in the sixteenth century and modified through the years. There was a low stone wall in front of the cottage and red roses climbing up to Catherine's bedroom window, their brightness contrasting with the grey road that ran past the cottage and disappeared at the bend.

From her window, Catherine could dimly see the silver line of the River Thames, which meandered through the village, its trout-filled waters and picturesque scenery creating an idyllic atmosphere, but at the same time, reminding Catherine that nothing ever changed there, even the roses outside her window, which had bloomed every summer since she could remember.

Catherine's heart lurched – she wasn't sure if it was in alarm or sorrow – when she told herself this might be the last summer that she would look out of her bedroom window at the familiar view of Longstock.

In two-days' time, she was to marry Arthur Lindley and accompany him to the East. It had been less than two months since she had first set eyes on the young officer.

Catherine had kept his proposal a secret the whole time she was staying with her uncle until the day after she arrived home in Longstock with her mother and sister and Arthur had returned to London. She had not accepted or rejected his proposal because, at that moment, she had been too confused to think. Even several days later, when she received a letter from Arthur urging her to decide, she still could not answer because all she knew was that Arthur's confession of love had thrilled her, but marriage was still too far off to contemplate when they had only just met. All through the week, Catherine considered the possibility of marrying the young officer and decided that it was indeed possible.

The first reason was that she would be able to leave her narrow life in the village. The second was that she would be able to see faraway lands that she would otherwise never get to see, like India, China, or any of the other countries that Arthur had told her about. Which country it was did not matter, only that she would get to experience what was beyond the horizon.

And was there a third reason? Did she like Arthur Lindley enough to spend the rest of her life with him? This was something she could not answer, since she had only met him once, and it was far too soon to decide.

In the end, Catherine had no other option but to tell her mother and sister, since time was running out and Arthur needed an answer.

Her mother was pleased, even though she tried to hide it, and Catherine could tell. In fact, Emma was over the moon.

"Invite him here, Catherine. He should get to know our family."

"I haven't given him an answer yet, Mother," Catherine replied with a lump in her throat. "I don't know what to say."

"He said he has to go to India, or somewhere even further," Emma mused, the excitement fading from her voice. "Aren't you afraid of leaving your home to go and live so far away?"

"No, Mother," Catherine answered at once. "Not at all."

Nothing filled her with as much fear as remaining in Longstock until the day she died.

Now at least – she would see life outside of Hampshire!

* * *

Arthur set out from London to see Catherine as soon as he received her letter telling him she was honoured that he had proposed and inviting him to visit her that weekend.

After Catherine had accepted Arthur's proposal, he returned to London to prepare for the wedding and their passage to the East in just over a month. Catherine busied herself preparing for her wedding as it turned out that she was to get married before her sister, so Pauline had to put her preparations aside to help her get ready.

Arthur wrote to Catherine to tell her his news before coming to see her at the end of the month.

"...I have some good news. This time, I've decided not to go to India because I've been posted to the Kingdom of Siam. One of the officers, Captain Thomas Knox, has resigned from his post and been appointed by the Second King of Siam to give British military training to his soldiers. Knox sent word to his friends in England that he needs an assistant.

The Seed of a Dream 15

I volunteered, and so I informed the Ministry of Defence that I was resigning from my post in India. Since the Foreign Office has assigned Sir John Bowring, the governor of Hong Kong, on a diplomatic mission to Siam on the orders of Her Majesty the Queen, and the boat will leave at the beginning of next month, we must get married even sooner than planned. I hope you will be ready in time."

"On, no!" Catherine exclaimed, springing to her feet with the letter in her hand and hurrying over to her mother and sister.

"What am I going to do, Mother? Arthur says we'll have to bring forward the wedding!"

Arthur planned to arrive two days before the wedding. He did not want to have to hurry there on his wedding day because travelling between counties, whether by train or by horse-drawn carriage, was uncertain. Moreover, he wanted to see his bride before the wedding, since they had not had a single opportunity to be alone together.

He arrived that afternoon.

Since they were to be married, Catherine's mother didn't prevent her from being alone with the young man and going for a walk along the River Thames with him that evening.

***

Catherine had enjoyed being outside from the time she was small.

She loved to walk along the River Thames behind the village, where the grass was green, and she could see a small white fence on the other side of the river with the church steeple rising above the treetops. This was the first day she had walked there with a young man at her side. She was going to marry him the day after next, but she knew almost nothing about him, except that his parents had passed away, and he had an older brother in London with a secure job.

"I like to come for walks here and read."

Arthur frowned. "You like to read? Then you should take some books with you. At least you won't be lonely if you've got books to read."

Catherine's thoughts suddenly turned to the Far-Eastern kingdom.

"Can you tell me more about the East?"

Arthur was only too pleased to regale her with stories.

He told her of the first time he had travelled to India when he was only nineteen, since he loved adventure and had not wished to work in his family's tobacco business. He had joined the army there and climbed up the ranks until he became a lieutenant in the battalion commanded by General Gilbert Burnett. Arthur liked to travel, and had journeyed through Burma to Siam, telling himself that it would be a good place to be stationed.

"The capital of Siam's like London in that it has a big river that runs through the centre, just like the River Thames. You might like it. They live in floating houses."

"What are they like, these floating houses?"

"They're on both sides of the river, and they use bamboo poles, which are light because they're hollow, so they float. They tie the bamboo poles together and build the houses on them. Siamese homes are light and airy. They don't need to use bricks like us because it's so hot there. It's too hot to sit in the sun and it's even hot in the shade."

"What's it like living there?"

"The Siamese find us strange. Children run after me and point everywhere I go, and the women stare at me from windows and doorways, but you don't need to worry. The Siamese are peaceful and unhurried. You might even call them lazy."

"Does that mean they don't mind being colonized?"

"Siam hasn't been colonized yet, but it won't be long before…"

Arthur considered for a moment before quickly continuing.

"But if it comes to war, you don't need to worry. You'll be safe with me."

***

On the morning of her wedding day, Catherine awoke with a fever and a throbbing head. In fact, she had felt unwell since the previous afternoon when she had asked Arthur to take her home when they were walking beside the river. She had tossed and turned all night, feeling hot and cold, drifting in and out of sleep. She couldn't understand it because she was usually so healthy. In fact her head throbbed so much that, as soon as she got up from the bed, the room began to spin, and she was forced to lie back down.

When Pauline came inside the room and saw her sister, she hurried to help her up, but when Catherine tried to walk over to the screen in the corner of the room her knees almost gave way. Pauline felt her brow and hesitated.

"What are we going to do? You need to get ready to go to church, and Arthur's taking you to London this afternoon. This is a fine time to be ill!"

Her sister's words made her realize that she would have to force herself to do what she had to do, and that she couldn't allow anything to stop her from getting married.

* * *

Arthur was beside himself when he heard the unexpected news.

All his plans were set in place as firmly as a brick wall, making it very hard to change anything. After the wedding, Arthur was to take Catherine to London where they would stay with his brother Alfred for three nights before travelling to Dover to board the ship that would depart for the East. The ship they were to sail in had been commissioned by the queen on a diplomatic mission to Siam, so it was a vast vessel, sturdier, safer, and more comfortable than most passenger ships. It was to be the most special honeymoon that Arthur could provide because, after that, Catherine would be living in a strange new land, far from the life she was accustomed to, and she would have to remain there for several years before she would have another opportunity to go home.

But, in the blink of an eye, the brick wall came crashing down.

There was no way that Arthur could take his sick bride to London without making her even more ill. If they were to postpone the wedding until Catherine was better, the ship would have already sailed, and it had already been arranged for Arthur to report to Captain Knox. If he postponed his departure, he might have to wait another six months or a year before another passenger ship set sail for the East.

It was Catherine who came to a decision before anyone else.

"I can manage to go to church. The ceremony won't take long. I'll be alright."

She forced herself to smile at Arthur to reassure him, but he was too agitated to smile back. He clasped her soft hand, which was burning, and his heart ached for her.

"Alright. At least then you'll be Catherine Lindley."

Alfred Lindley, Arthur's brother, arrived later that morning. At thirty-three years of age, he was ten years older than Arthur and an imposing-looking businessman from the capital with long sideburns.

When he found out about Catherine's illness, Alfred Lindley frowned.

"Are you mad, Arthur? How can you take her to London in such a state? You'd better stay here with her until she's recovered."

"But I have to prepare for my journey to the East…"

"You'll just have to postpone it."

"I can't!" Arthur cried. "I must go on the next ship, or I'll have to wait for months until another ship sails for Singapore. I have to go no matter what."

"Let's not argue about it now," Alfred resolved. "You'd better get the wedding over with first."

Captain Gilbert Burnett had travelled from Breamore to walk the bride down the aisle and give her away.

During the wedding ceremony, Reverend Rigg's voice drifted in and out of her consciousness as if it was coming from far away.

"Arthur Augustus Lindley, do you take this woman to be your wife, to love, honor and cherish…"

Arthur answered firmly.

"I do."

"And do you Catherine Lavinia Burnett take this man to be your husband, to love, honor and obey…"

Catherine's lips were dry as she forced herself to answer.

"I do."

Reverend Rigg's voice seemed to be coming from afar as he pronounced them man and wife. They turned to walk back down the aisle, but the moment Catherine stepped outside the church, everything went black, and she collapsed.

***

The Seed of a Dream 19

Nobody had warned her that in the days that followed, her symptoms would become so severe that she wouldn't even be able to get out of bed. She had a high fever, and her throat was so swollen she couldn't even swallow.

She wasn't aware that Arthur and his brother had been arguing heatedly as she drifted in and out of sleep in the bedroom.

"Are you mad?" Alfred asked his younger brother hotly. "How can you just go and leave your wife? You're responsible for her now. You can travel anytime or, if you're so worried about giving up your job in the East, you can always come and work for me."

"That's exactly what I don't want to do. You know how I hate sitting in an office all day. I'd sooner go back to India."

"I don't know what you find so objectionable about having a secure job. You'd earn a lot more than you would gallivanting half-way around the world."

But Arthur's mind was already made up. He had his reasons for taking up a position on the other side of the world. He had always dreamed of going to live in a faraway land, but he could not tell his brother that. Alfred could not imagine that anywhere was better than England. He had been to France once to visit the beautiful city of Paris and had no desire to go again.

Arthur had to admit he loved Catherine. He had fallen in love with her from the first moment he saw her, but if he stayed with her in England, he would have to wait for months before he could travel to Siam, which would cause problems, not to mention the fact that he had only a small amount of money left for them to live on.

That being the case, he would have to go and work for his brother in order to survive, and he could not bear the thought of being stuck in an office all day under the strict gaze of his brother.

He told Alfred, "I've made up my mind. I'm going ahead of her, and I'll find a way for Catherine to join me later."

Alfred gazed at him incredulously.

"You're raving mad!" he cried. "How can a woman travel by herself to the other side of the world?"

"I won't let her travel alone," Arthur replied irritably. "I'll find someone to chaperone her, or I'll come back for her."

***

Catherine didn't know what to say when Arthur told her of his decision. All she could do was lie on the bed, her throat dry and sore, her skin burning, and the fever melting away her tears.

"I know it's hard for you. It's hard for me, too," Arthur whispered. "But we don't have any other choice. If I don't go ahead of you, I'll be too late. And if I stay, I'll have to work for Alfred, and I'd rather die than sit in an office all day."

Catherine reached out to touch his hand and squeezed it. She understood how Arthur felt and thought that she would also hate to be stuck in an office all day, just as she hated kneading dough, cooking stew, and sewing. They were alike in that they both wanted to spread their wings and fly. But she couldn't help feeling hurt that his freedom was more important to him than she was.

"There's no need to worry," Arthur reassured her. "I'll find a way for you to join me as soon as possible. Trust me."

Catherine lay her head back down on the pillow wearily and fell asleep, still holding Arthur's hand.

Although Catherine's mother and sister were not too thrilled that Arthur was travelling East to take up his new post, there was nothing they could do except swallow their disappointment and resign themselves to Catherine's fate.

The day that Arthur left for London, all Catherine could do was to see him off at the window and watch as the carriage that had come to take him to the train station disappeared as it turned the corner. After that Catherine staggered back to the bed, where she lay face down on the pillow and wept.

She couldn't say for sure whether it was because she was sorry to see Arthur go, or because she had missed the opportunity to see what was beyond the horizon. All she knew was that she felt as if her whole world had become an empty void. She had no idea of how many months or even years she would have to wait before she would see Arthur again.

***

"How are you feeling? You're looking much better this morning," Pauline greeted her as she entered the room to find her sitting up in bed looking at her reflection in a hand mirror.

Catherine smiled weakly. The ugly red spots had almost all disappeared, and her skin was almost as clear as before, but she still looked pale. She had been ill for over a month and had lost more than five pounds.

"It's a good job Arthur decided to leave you here instead of taking you abroad. You might not have survived the trip. John went to France once and he said there's nothing worse than seasickness."

"Except for measles," Catherine smiled.

***

Four months later, Catherine received her first letter from her husband.

"…I'm on my way to the East, and I can't help but wonder if it was a mistake to leave you by yourself. When I asked the captain, he told me it would be a long time before another ship like this sets sail. If you travel by ordinary ship, you might have to wait in a foreign land while you're waiting for the next ship.

I'm tired of being stuck in a cabin. I can't walk on the deck because the waves are so strong. I've been through a storm in the Bay of Bengal, and I know how terrifying it is. The waves are as big as mountains, and the ship feels like a toy being tossed about by a giant.

I must sign off, so I can post this letter from our next port of call.

I'll find a way for you to join me in Siam as soon as possible, so that you won't have to wait for me to come and fetch you, which won't be for another two years at least.

May God protect you until we meet again, darling."

Catherine tried to imagine what it would be like. From what he had said, embroidery and sewing would not be sufficient to keep her occupied for months on end at sea. Even reading would not be enough, so she decided it would be a good idea to keep a journal of her travels.

***

Towards the end of autumn, Catherine received a letter from Arthur's brother inviting her to stay at his home because he had met a Scotsman who had lived in Siam.

"…So I want you to meet him because he'll be able to advise you before you go. Send me a telegram before you come, so that we can prepare for you."

Catherine was elated and accepted the invitation without hesitation. Even though she had never taken a train by herself before, she told herself that she was now a married woman and could go wherever she pleased just like her mother. She quickly sent a telegram to Alfred to let him know that she would arrive in London the following Friday.

Alfred Lindley's home was in Leicester Square. It was a large, terraced house with steps leading up to it from the iron gate in front and pillars on either side of the door.

Alfred was wealthier than Catherine thought and, as soon as she stepped inside the door and saw the large staircase, the sparkling chandeliers, the chairs covered in red velvet, and the blue and white Chinese porcelain, she felt small until the lady of the house came to greet her. Martha, Alfred's wife, was a woman of around thirty years of age. She was dressed in a crinoline with a brooch at the neck, even though she was at home. She smiled at Catherine approvingly and bent down to kiss her cheek.

"Do go and rest. I expect you're tired after your journey. Dinner will be served at eight o'clock, but we always have tea first."

Catherine was shown to her room where she rested for a while before a maid knocked on the door to tell her it was time for tea. Martha was sitting in the living room, and appeared more relaxed as she asked Catherine about Arthur.

"Alfred has found someone who's lived in the East. Where was it again?"

"Siam."

"That's it. Arthur must have arrived there by now. I don't understand why he wants to go even further than India. Alfred and I met a Scotsman by the name of Hunter. His father traded in Siam for years. I can't remember where we met him, but Alfred said to me…

The Seed of a Dream 23

Martha, Siam's the country where Hunter was born."

"Has he settled back here now?"

"I believe he's here on business. He went to school here a long time ago. Alfred found out that he's still in London, so he invited him for dinner."

Martha lowered her voice.

"His mother's Siamese."

***

Robert Hunter was around thirty years old with dark brown hair and eyes, and his skin was even more tanned than Arthur's. He was smartly dressed and when he spoke, there was a hint of a Scottish accent.

"Mrs Lindley, I've heard ye're travelling to Siam."

He eyed the young woman solicitously.

"Ye'll find it very different there, but as an officer's wife, ye'll have an easier time of it than other foreigners."

"How does Siam compare to India?" asked Alfred, feeling uncomfortable about the way the young man was looking at his young sister-in-law.

"I've never been to India, so I can't tell ye. All I can say is the locals are lazy and sluggish. Ye'll find that nothing ever changes there from one year to the next."

Martha looked anxiously at Catherine.

"I expect it's like the countryside."

"It's worse than that. The Siamese are content just to have enough to eat. My father can't understand why they don't trade. All the trade is in the hands of the Chinese."

"But your father was a tradesman, wasn't he?"

"He traded with the king and the nobility. When the king wanted something from abroad, my father got it for him, but as soon as he became rich, he was exiled, and his business fell into someone else's hands."

"I expect you'll be staying in England for good now, won't you?"

"I have to return," he replied after a pause. "I'm going to see my mother. She didn't come to England with my father."

"When will you be leaving?" Catherine asked.

24 A Passage to Siam

"Soon," he replied, smiling. "I don't want to wait until the spring. I'll let ye know when I'm leaving, so ye can travel with me. A woman shouldn't travel so far alone."

The glimmer of hope that had been lit began to falter at his last sentence. She didn't know why, but she didn't completely trust Robert Hunter. Even though he was polite and friendly, perhaps it was the way he looked at her that made her uneasy.

Alfred invited Catherine to meet him in the library, which also served as his study.

"I commend you for your intention to join Arthur in the East, but I don't approve of you travelling alone."

He paused before continuing carefully.

"Hunter has offered to chaperone you, but we barely know him, and the journey takes almost six months. I hardly think that Arthur would approve if I allowed you to travel with a stranger."

"I agree."

"I'm going to write to Arthur and ask him to come and fetch you himself."

Catherine thanked him and took her leave, promising to write to him as soon as she heard from Arthur.

***

Catherine's home seemed especially welcoming when she returned. She sat down next to the fire and looked out at the reddish-brown leaves that were falling from the trees, the autumn colours contrasting with the cold grey sky.

"Catherine, there's a letter for you."

Her mother handed her an envelope before disappearing back inside the kitchen to prepare their evening meal. Catherine took the letter from the envelope and was surprised to find it was from her uncle, whom she hadn't seen since he gave her away on her wedding day.

"Dear Catherine,

My friend, Colonel George Rowland, will be coming to stay with me. He'll be travelling to India shortly and has a friend who will be travelling to Siam, so I'd like you to invite you to come and stay with me next week to meet him.

If you can come, let me know as soon as possible, and please give my regards to your mother."

* * *

The carriage that her uncle sent to collect her from the station rolled along the winding lanes and stopped outside a wide lawn in front of a house as grey as the sky, which was surrounded by maple trees that had still not shed their red leaves.

Her uncle had returned from India a wealthy man and could afford to keep several servants as well as a carriage driver and a stable boy. Mary greeted her cousin eagerly, glad of the company to relieve the monotony of her daily life, in which her only hope of change lay in the chance of meeting a suitable husband.

She was obviously disappointed by her father's guest, telling Catherine, "Colonel Rowland's forty years old, but he's bringing a guest with him from Siam."

"Really?" exclaimed Catherine. "I'd like to meet him."

"I expect you will, but I don't know if he even speaks English."

"Who is he?"

When officers returned from India, they sometimes brought locals back with them as servants, but they would not have been considered guests, so Catherine was curious.

"He must be a friend…or someone he's looking after…I don't know. He'll be staying in the room next to Colonel Roland's. When I was in India, I never spoke to the locals."

Mary had lived in India for several years, but all she had to say about it was, "It's so tiresome, and the sun's so hot, and the only people I had to talk to were officers' wives," stopping short of adding, 'You'll see for yourself when you travel to the East.'

26 A Passage to Siam

2
The End of the Horizon

Catherine was not in the house when her uncle's guest arrived. She had gone for a walk in the back garden but saw the horse-drawn carriage roll up outside the front door. Her uncle's butler was waiting with two other servants in tow to help carry the luggage to his rooms.

The roses had dropped their petals and the garden where she had first met Arthur looked dry and barren. Everything seemed to confirm that he was gone. It was strange that, although he had only been gone for a few months, the picture of his face had faded from her memory.

Catherine stood daydreaming under one of the large maple trees as the sun began to sink, the golden rays that shone through the red leaves casting shadows on her flaxen hair. She was suddenly engulfed by a feeling of emptiness that she had never experienced before, and tears began to roll down her cheeks, so she wiped them with a handkerchief.

There was no sound from behind her, but Catherine felt instinctively that someone was there, so she slowly turned around.

A pair of eyes was looking at her! They were the strangest eyes she had ever seen, coal black like a starless sky, almond-shaped, and sparkling like a torch in the darkness.

Her wide blue eyes stared back and she must have looked astonished because he lowered his eyes and bowed his head.

"Forgive me if I startled you."

He spoke English clearly with only a slight accent and his voice was deep and resonant.

Without needing any introduction, Catherine realized that this was 'the man from Siam'.

Only his clothes were like an Englishman. His build was smaller than the average Englishman and his skin was the colour of honey-brown wood, complimenting his jet-black hair and eyes. Catherine gazed at his high cheekbones and nose, which was neither pointed nor flat, his full lips and his angular chin. His face, although exotic, was well-proportioned and was not unattractive.

She must have stared at him for too long. The 'man from Siam' bent his head to regard himself before gazing back at her with a smile adding, "And made you puzzled…"

"Not at all," she answered quickly. "I wasn't startled…"

The tears had dried from her face, and she forgot her sadness for a moment as she searched for the right words.

"I know that you're a guest…from Siam."

He looked at her as if he could not take his eyes away and she noticed his full lips break into a warm smile.

"You're the first Englishwoman I've met who's heard of Siam."

"I've only heard the name."

Catherine paused for a moment before adding in a voice that she forced to steady, "My husband's gone there to work."

A puzzled look crossed his face as if he had not expected such a statement.

"Your husband…Then you must be Lieutenant Arthur Lindley's wife."

A glimmer of hope flickered in Catherine's heart.

"You know my husband…?"

"I met him in India several years ago, and I heard he'd gone to work for the government…"

He paused for a moment as if he was thinking of the right English word.

"…The Second King of Siam wants English soldiers to train his guards. I know from Colonel Rowland."

Catherine thought back to what Arthur had told her about the 'man from Siam' whom he had met in India. It must have been none other than this man.

She nodded sadly.

"I was supposed to go with him, but I was taken ill, so I couldn't travel. I don't know when I'll be able to go. My uncle promised to find a way for me to…"

Catherine stopped, suddenly embarrassed that she was talking to a stranger. A flicker of understanding appeared in his black eyes.

"I see. That must be the reason for your sadness."

"Well…" she began, searching for an explanation. "I suppose so."

The young man smiled as if he understood how she felt before continuing, "We haven't been properly introduced. I'm Justin. It isn't my real name. My Siamese name's too difficult for English people to pronounce, so Colonel Rowland gave me an English name."

Catherine smiled, not wanting to appear unfriendly.

"Did you live in India for long, Mr Justin?"

"Several years. I was sent there for military training at a British military base. Colonel Rowland has been assisting me, so when he returned to London on business, he brought me with him."

Catherine noticed his straight back and square shoulders, indicating his strict training.

"You're an officer…"

"I'm a captain."

She could not guess his age but thought he must have been about the same age as Arthur. Although she would have liked to have asked him about his country, she suddenly remembered something when she noticed the sun sinking behind the trees.

"Oh, I almost forgot! I'm sorry, I must go. Mary will be waiting for me."

Mary wanted Catherine to help her choose a dress for dinner, so she hurriedly took her leave, telling him, "Pleased to meet you, Captain Justin. I'll see you at dinner."

"It will be a pleasure."

She hurried up the steps to the patio without turning back, his dark penetrating almond eyes watching her every step.

The candles in the large silver candlestick cast a warm glow on the fresh flowers that had been arranged in a vase by her along with the wine glasses and the silverware on the table.

Aunt Mabel had arranged the seating and Catherine was seated between Dr Shaw and Captain Justin, with Mary on his other side, who flirted openly with Colonel Rowland.

As far as Catherine could see, Colonel Rowland was a middle-aged man with thick hair and no belly, but he was hardly as handsome as Mary had described him. Nevertheless, he was well-mannered and tried to include the young man from Siam in the conversation. Mary, however, was determined to secure his attention for herself, so she ignored Captain Justin completely.

Catherine, tired of remaining silent, was sure that the young man felt the same way, although he was too polite to show it, so she turned to speak to him.

"Tell me about Siam."

A smile twinkled in his dark eyes, as if he understood her awkwardness, and he replied softly, "If you're afraid I'm uncomfortable, don't worry. I'm used to it."

"What do you mean?"

"I mean…" he said in a low voice, "I'm used to Westerners like you greeting me out of politeness and then ignoring me."

Catherine was shocked. He spoke with an amused tone, his voice untinged by animosity or resentment.

"I mean it," she answered softly. "I want to know about Siam. If I'm going to live there, I want to learn as much as I can."

His face softened at her enthusiasm.

"I haven't been back there for years, but I expect it's still the same. Life there is peaceful. There are no religious or tribal conflicts. Foreigners are free to practice their own religions. We believe in tolerance and compromise…"

His lips formed a smile and Catherine noticed that he was happy to talk about his homeland.

"You might find that it's a land in which it seems 'always afternoon' like in 'The Lotus Eaters'. It's hot and the sun's always shining. The people that live there would rather sleep under the trees than do work, but I don't think Siam is as bad as the land in the poem…"

He stopped, noticing her blue eyes growing round with astonishment.

"Did I say something wrong?"

"No," Catherine replied hurriedly. "It's just that…"

She smiled bashfully before continuing, "I didn't expect you to be able to quote Tennyson."

His face became serious, although the twinkle in his eyes remained. "When I first went to India, the officer that assisted me thought the best way for me to learn English was to read poetry, and Tennyson was the easiest to read. I didn't know then that it was a hundred years old!"

Catherine laughed for the first time since Arthur's departure, and she was struck by the sound of her own voice, which sounded as light and clear as when her life had been carefree, unlike today.

Just then Colonel Rowland spoke.

"I'm leaving for India at the beginning of next month. I know winter isn't the best time to travel, but I want to get there before the monsoon when the seas are rough. Captain Justin will continue to Siam."

Several pairs of eyes turned to the young man, and he said, "That's right, Colonel."

Aunt Mabel looked at Catherine sympathetically.

"Is it far to Siam from India, Colonel?"

"It will take about a month if they don't have to wait in Singapore for a boat to Bangkok. I understand that they won't have to delay because there will be a special passage for Justin from Singapore to the capital of Siam. Travelling by boat is easier than by land as it's all jungle."

"A special passage?" Catherine's uncle asked.

"A boat commissioned by an important Siamese dignitary. It will be there to collect Justin on the orders of the Second King of Siam. Mrs Lindley…" he said, addressing Catherine for the first time, "if you want to join your husband, I can promise you that you'll be safer and more comfortable travelling with Justin than if you travel alone, or with anyone else."

***

Catherine was careful to avoid the flower garden, not wanting to impose on Mary when Colonel Rowland proposed, so she walked past the lawn behind the conservatory and past the yew trees to the edge of her uncle's garden.

A small stream ran alongside the lawn next to a wood. Since the weather had been dry, the water was so shallow that the pebbles on the bottom were visible, and Catherine would have been able to lift her skirt and jump across the stones that appeared above the water to the other side without getting it wet, but she wasn't in the mood, so walked alongside it by herself.

Suddenly feeling that she was not alone, she turned around. Once again, the same pair of dark eyes watched her from the other side of the stream, some distance away, since he had just appeared from a clearing in the wood. Justin stepped deftly across the stones above the water to meet her, his eyes sparkling with excitement.

"I've important news to tell you."

He continued as soon as he had reached her.

"I've asked George…I mean Colonel Rowland to travel to Siam with me instead of stopping in India. I've written to the Second King of Siam asking permission for Captain Rowland to stay in Siam as my guest. I think he'll agree. He's always had good relations with the British. It will be easier for you if George is there to chaperone you."

"I'll tell my uncle. If I'm coming with you, I'll have to get ready."

"There's no need to hurry. The colonel and I are going back to London, and we'll be there a few days."

He gazed at her as if he was satisfied that she had made her decision quickly without hesitation.

"I'll send more news to you. You'll be able to go to Dover straight from Breamore without stopping in London. We'll cross the channel to France and travel to Malta. Have you ever been to France?"

"I've never been further than Brighton. This will be much more exciting…"

At that moment, it suddenly dawned on her that she had begun a new chapter in her life. And the person who had handed her the opportunity was a stranger from Siam. Not Arthur as she had expected.

Her uncle was in the library, which he used as a study, and when she stepped inside, he greeted her cheerfully.

"George is travelling to Siam with Justin. That's a stroke of luck. I can trust him if you go with him. It's better than going with anyone else."

He was referring to Robert Hunter, whom Catherine had told him about, and even though he had never met him, he did not trust him.

"I was just about to ask you about it," Catherine said with relief, suddenly feeling confident that things were going to turn out right.

As Catherine was coming out of the library, she caught sight of Mary's crinoline moving in the pergola outside. She was about to turn and walk the other way, not wanting to thwart her efforts to charm the middle-aged officer when Mary saw her and waved excitedly.

Catherine walked towards her.

"I've got good news..." she began.

"I've got good news," Mary interrupted happily. "George has proposed to me. We're getting married before we travel to India. Isn't it wonderful? I won't have to stay in Breamore any longer."

* * *

Mary got married four weeks later in Breamore, and the wedding fulfilled her hopes in every way. As Catherine watched the bride and groom standing before the vicar, her thoughts turned to her own wedding day several months earlier.

Her recollections were as faint as if it had been someone else instead of her, and she couldn't even recall what colour the groom had worn. The only thing she remembered was how she had felt hot and cold with the fever and had wanted to get the ceremony over with.

Suddenly, she became aware of a pair of eyes staring at her, and when she glanced over, she saw that it was those eyes as black as night. She met their gaze, and he bowed his head and smiled slightly without drawing anyone's attention.

Justin looked strange in the British army officer's uniform due to his small build, jet-black hair, and golden skin. He was standing alone, apart from the others, making him appear even more like an outsider. She could not help feeling sorry for him but was relieved when she noticed his calm and unperturbed demeanour, as if he was interested in observing the unfamiliar wedding ceremony.

Later, when she had got to know him better, she came to understand that, in Siamese culture, it was considered bad manners to openly express dissatisfaction, so the Siamese would hide their discomfort to avoid making others uneasy. This was encapsulated in the word, *kreng jai,* for which there was no English equivalent.

* * *

Alfred welcomed Catherine warmly, as if she were his own sister. She told him she was writing to Arthur to tell him about her journey. Justin would send her letter along with his letter to the Second King of Siam, and Arthur would be sure to receive the news before her arrival. He was interested to learn that the Siamese man would be travelling with her.

"He must be a nobleman of some importance in Siam," he remarked, satisfied that she would be travelling with someone reliable, increasing his confidence that she would reach Siam safely.

* * *

The crossing to France across the English Channel took about five hours. In the chilly December air, Catherine stood on the deck looking up at the ship's masts towering above her against the overcast sky and watched the white cliffs of Dover recede further and further in the distance as the large sailing ship ploughed through the white foam. At last they faded from view completely and the vessel seemed like a toy boat drifting in the grey sea.

The sea was not as rough as she had feared, but Mary had retired to her cabin as soon as they left the shore, despite Catherine's cajoling.

"I'll have months to see the sea. Come with me, Annie!"

She had found a maid at the last minute before they left. She was Scottish with red hair, and appeared robust as if she was used to hard work.

Colonel Rowland didn't mind that his wife had retired to her cabin and stood chatting with those passengers who were unperturbed by the cold wind. Although the winter had been mild without any snow, the wind under the grey sky was biting.

Catherine became aware that someone was approaching her and, before he had even stood next to her, she knew that it was Justin.

She turned to him and smiled.

34   A Passage to Siam

"This is the first time I've seen the sea…I mean away from the shore."

"We're fortunate the sea isn't rough today," he replied, staring out at the sea in front of him.

Only a few other passengers remained on deck, most having returned to their cabins, not wishing to brave the wind and the cold. Justin found that talking to Catherine was preferable to joining Colonel Rowland and the others.

"You mean this isn't rough?" Catherine asked, feeling that the waves were growing stronger with every passing moment.

"No," he smiled. "Wait until we get to the monsoon zone. The waves are as high as mountains."

Catherine laughed cheerfully, the bracing sea air lifting her spirits.

"I can't wait to see that."

"Most people pray they won't."

"You must have travelled through many seas, Captain Justin."

"The Siamese are born on the water. We live on the water, and practically learn to swim before we can walk…"

He stopped suddenly when a harsh voice cut through the howling wind.

"Mrs Lindley. Here you are."

A dark-haired young man in an overcoat was hurrying towards her. He smiled and took off his hat before bowing his head.

"I'm glad to see ye again. I saw ye before we set sail."

Catherine ought to have been pleased to have met someone she knew among all the strangers on the ship, but since it was Robert Hunter and he would not take his eyes off her, she began to feel uncomfortable.

"Mr Hunter," she mumbled.

"What a coincidence that fate would have us travel on the same ship," he said, standing in front of her with twinkling eyes.

He turned to the man next to her with undisguised bewilderment.

"If I didn't know there were no Siamese in London, I would have sworn…"

Hunter appeared to have been drinking, and Catherine noticed his face was flushed and his eyes were bloodshot.

"I am Siamese," Justin answered coldly.

"Well, well!" he blurted in amazement. "I never knew there was a

The End of the Horizon   35

Siamese in London. As far as I know, no Siamese has ever been there before."

Justin did not answer, indicating that he had no wish to talk to him. He tapped Catherine's arm gently.

"Mrs Lindley, the wind on deck's getting stronger. I'll see you back to your cabin."

Catherine felt relieved that Justin had found a way to end the conversation, making it clear that he did not wish to be introduced to the other man.

She bowed her head slightly before taking her leave.

"Good day, Mr Hunter."

Robert Hunter's expression turned sour, but he could not argue because almost all the other passengers had retired to their cabins. Only those with Colonel Rowland remained, so he could only watch as Catherine and Justin disappeared down the staircase before deciding to walk towards the older officer.

"Colonel Rowland, I didn't know you would be on this ship," he said abrasively. "I just met…"

"I am aware," he interrupted. "The young lady is the wife of Lieutenant Arthur Lindley, and she's also my wife's cousin."

"I already know her. I met her in London. And who's the Siamese? What's he doing here? He seems an arrogant fellow."

Robert Hunter made no attempt to conceal his dislike, even though Colonel Rowland was glaring at him disapprovingly.

"Captain Justin has been undergoing military training in India, under my supervision."

"Justin?" he repeated. "His name's Justin?"

"Yes."

"Then I've never heard of him. I only know of a Siamese prince that trained in India, but that was years ago."

They walked down the staircase before retiring to their cabins, and Colonel Rowland, having no wish to talk to him further, ended the conversation.

"Good day, Hunter."

***

Justin was sitting in his cramped cabin and stood up when Colonel Rowland entered after knocking.

"What is it, Colonel? You look as if we'll have to change plans."

Colonel Rowland's taut expression relaxed as he regarded the younger man.

"Oh, it's nothing like that, Your Highness. It's just that there's a passenger travelling with us to Siam whom you might not like."

"I met him on the deck," Justin replied. "He doesn't know who I am."

"I didn't tell him who you were. You didn't introduce yourself to him, so I assumed you didn't want him to know, sir."

Justin raised his long black eyebrows slightly.

"What good would it do? I don't want everyone to know I'm a prince. I thought that was understood."

"But Hunter might disparage you. It wouldn't do, sir."

"It isn't as if I'm a prince of much importance. There are others of far more distinction."

"You're still a prince," Colonel Rowland pressed. "No one can deny it."

Justin chuckled softly.

"Thank you, Colonel Rowland. I appreciate that you're doing your duty, but the Second King of Siam believes that if princes are extravagant while abroad, it will create a great deal of expense for a small country like ours."

Colonel Rowland did not argue.

"Siamese princes aren't that wealthy, so I'm happy to remain Captain Justin for the rest of the journey. When the ship from Siam comes to collect me, I'll remove my mask…"

"I'm not sure I understand, sir."

The young man laughed.

"I mean I'll reveal that I'm a prince."

Colonel Rowland shook his head slowly.

"As you wish, sir. I'll see that no one knows except Mary."

"Does your wife know yet?"

"Yes, sir. But I've instructed her not to tell anyone."

Justin was quiet for a moment.

The End of the Horizon 37

"And what about Mrs Lindley. Does she know?"

"I've instructed Mary not to tell her, sir."

"I know it will be difficult for her to keep it secret, but I must insist that she doesn't tell her. It's better that way."

***

Catherine knew that, after crossing the English Channel to France, they would travel to Marseilles, where they would board a ship that would take them across the Mediterranean and through the Suez Canal.

By meeting the same five people every day of the journey, Catherine learned a lot about each person's character. Colonel Rowland was the opposite of his wife, which was fortunate for Mary. He was calm and wise befitting his forty years, making him the undisputed leader of the group. If there was anything that made him seem distant to Catherine, it was the fact that he spent nearly all his time playing cards, sometimes through the night, until he had very little to do with the women, even his own wife. Annie was hardworking, cheerful, and showed amazing forbearance in the face of Mary's overbearingness.

The last person was Justin.

He was impenetrable, Catherine had decided to herself before they even reached Marseilles. At first, he had appeared uncomplicated, but as she got to know him better, she found that there was something about him that she couldn't quite explain. He was sometimes relaxed and cheerful, but at other times he was aloof, such as when he was with Robert Hunter who had been separated from them as soon as they had set foot in France.

Justin's true character was as mysterious as the land of Siam, where he came from. She could say for certain that he was curious about everything he saw, but he never betrayed his excitement, and she noticed he wrote things down in a notebook he carried.

She was relieved when their journey by horse-drawn carriage ended in Marseilles three weeks later.

***

Catherine sat in front of the globe in the small library on board the ship that was headed for Malta. Mary tended to remain in her cabin until the ship docked, but Catherine could not bear to be confined to her cramped cabin, so she would come outside and read. She turned the globe thoughtfully, and discovered to her puzzlement that, while the countries of Europe were clearly marked, only China and India appeared in the East as if the person who had drawn the map had no idea what other countries were there.

Siam is not there!

She closed her eyes, which had become blurry from staring at the small place names on the map.

She looked up after hearing the door open and sat up abruptly when she saw the young man, whom she had assumed she would not have to meet again.

"So this is where ye are."

Robert Hunter sounded pleased, as if he had been looking for her.

"I was waiting for ye on the deck, but ye weren't there."

"I didn't know ye were on the ship."

He moved towards her, looking her up and down from her flaxen ringlets to her shapely figure in the navy dress with the nipped-in waist.

"It'll be hard for us to avoid each other," he chuckled. "I've been waiting for a chance to be alone with ye."

"What for?"

"Ye're a beautiful woman, Mrs Lindley. That man of yers is a fool for letting ye travel alone. If I were him, I wouldn't let ye out of my sight."

"I'm not alone," she said coldly, smelling the alcohol on his breath. "Colonel Rowland and his wife are travelling with me, and Captain Justin…"

"Oh, them!" he scoffed dismissively. "I mean ye're alone in yer cabin. Does anyone even know ye're here?"

He moved closer as she took as step back.

"I'm concerned about ye," he crooned. "Ye can trust me."

"Thank you, but I can look after myself. Excuse me…"

She stood up and pushed past him, but stopped when he took hold of her arm, despite her attempts to shake him off.

"Mr Hunter!" she cried, her voice trembling, "Let me go!"

The End of the Horizon 39

"I haven't finished talking to ye, Mrs Lindley."

At that moment, the door opened and a middle-aged man with a black beard entered. He stopped abruptly on seeing the room was not empty before walking to a table in the corner, where he picked up a feather quill and began to write a letter without paying them any more attention.

Catherine seized the opportunity to rush out of the door and hurried along the passageway without noticing who was coming down the staircase from the deck.

"Mrs Lindley," he called.

She stopped suddenly and saw Justin hurrying towards her, having noticed her flushed cheeks and frightened expression.

"What's the matter? You look as if you're running away from someone."

She hadn't intended to tell Justin but felt strangely relieved to see him.

"I met Hunter in the library and he…"

She turned around and her heart lurched when she saw Robert Hunter coming towards her, but when he noticed Justin, he stopped and walked the other way.

"Did he touch you?" Justin asked in a low voice.

She took a deep breath.

"He was drunk."

"Then he could do anything. And you're staying by yourself."

"He knows that!" she cried.

"Don't forget to always lock the door, and don't open the door to anyone at night. My room's close to yours. You can call me at any time."

＊

Colonel Rowland entered the young man's room and saw the Siamese servant sitting on the floor while the prince sat on a chair. He didn't understand what Justin was saying but noticed his tone was serious. The Siamese servant prostrated himself on the floor and crawled away backwards past Colonel Rowland to the door, where he stood up and walked outside.

"Please have a seat, Colonel," Justin offered. "It'll only take a few minutes."

The colonel sat down.

"Robert Hunter has behaved improperly towards Mrs Lindley. She's afraid of him. How can you help her?"

"I'll have a word with him. Lieutenant Lindley won't be happy when he hears about it. Why on earth would he let his young wife travel alone? If anything happens to her, he'll be sorry."

Catherine forced herself to eat dinner in the ship's dining room.

It wasn't that she disliked the Italian food, but she was uncomfortable because Robert Hunter would not take his eyes off her.

She heard Justin's voice next to her but didn't catch what he said.

"I'm sorry. I didn't hear you."

"May I see you to your cabin after dinner?"

"Yes. Thank you."

She talked to him cheerfully about Siam as if nothing was the matter.

He had told her about Siam before and, although he had been away for several years, his memories remained vivid, especially when he talked about the Second King of Siam, whom he had accompanied all over the country when he was a boy. Catherine suddenly realized that he had never spoken about his family, so she introduced the topic.

"Your parents must be happy you're coming home."

"I've never lived with my parents. They gave me to the Second King of Siam when I was a child, so I lived in his palace before I went to India."

Catherine tried to take this in.

"You mean you're his adopted son?"

Justin laughed.

"No. I could never be considered of equal status to the king's own children, but the reason I was sent to the palace was because of what a fortune teller told my parents when I was born – it's normal in Siam. They were afraid I wouldn't live long if I stayed with them, so my father decided to give me to the king to protect me – that's what they believe. He was still a prince then, and I was less than a month old when I was sent to live in the palace."

As if reading her thoughts, Justin continued, "He let one of his *chao chom* take care of me, so she became my adoptive mother. She doesn't have any children of her own. She's waiting for me to come home."

He used the Siamese word, *chao chom*, because he couldn't think of the right English equivalent.

"*Chao chom*...was she a concubine?"

He paused uncomfortably before telling her frankly.

"You could say that, but a *chao chom* isn't a mistress like Mrs Jordan."

Although she had never seen the woman, her parents, who had lived through the reign of William IV before Queen Victoria was crowned, had spoken of the pretty actress who had been the king's secret mistress and borne him ten illegitimate children, all of whom took the surname Fitz Clarence.

She heard Justin continue.

"A *chao chom* is respected and honoured. When we get to Siam, you might have a chance to meet some of them in the palace where your husband is working. I'd like you to meet Khun Chom Klee, the woman who raised me. She's very kind."

***

Catherine was becoming accustomed to the vast ocean. The Mediterranean was warmer than in France if the wind wasn't too strong and she could stand on the deck and look at the view until sunset. Sometimes she stayed there until it was dark, and she could see the stars sparkling across the black velvety sky.

That night, the air was still, and Mary stood next to her for a while before returning to her cabin. Justin had been walking by himself, but when he saw Mary walk away, he strolled over to her.

"You shouldn't be by yourself. I'll keep you company."

She expected him to talk about Siam but was puzzled when he said something else.

"You've never told me anything about yourself. All I know about you is that you're Mrs Rowland's cousin."

She wondered why he wanted to know about her, but swallowed

her question, telling him instead about her life in Longstock and her marriage to Arthur. She told him the reason that they had been separated but was too embarrassed to tell him that they had been apart since their wedding day. She admitted that, if it hadn't been for her marriage to Arthur, her life would have been no different from that of her sister's, and her mother's, and her grandmother's before her.

"If I wasn't for Arthur, I'd still be knitting by the fireside until the day I died…"

Catherine laughed, but her laughter dissolved when she noticed his dark eyes fixed on her lips.

Coming to his senses, Justin turned away when he noticed her puzzled expression.

"It's a pity your husband isn't travelling with you. It would have made things easier."

She assumed he was referring to her safety, since she had still not been able to lose her fear of Robert Hunter.

Catherine woke with a start in the middle of the night.

She was certain she'd heard something out of the ordinary. It wasn't the sound of the ship's engine, which hummed from far away, but was closer. There was a rattling at the door as if someone was trying to turn the handle.

Her heart lurched and she grabbed her shawl to pull over her nightdress as she crawled out from under the covers. A dim light shone in through the round cabin window, making it possible to see faintly in the dark, and she stood silently in front of the door. Someone had pushed a piece of metal in the keyhole and tried to force the lock open, but when their efforts had failed, they had shaken it more forcefully and woken her.

Catherine tried to scream, but her throat was dry with fear and no sound came out.

At that moment, the door handle turned, and the door was pushed open. A dark shadow loomed in front of her, and she screamed at the top of her lungs, stepping back, and bumping into her trunk full of clothes. She could hear the intruder's heavy breathing as he tried to lunge for her, but she lurched towards the bed.

The next thing she heard was Justin's voice,

"What's going on?"

The black figure retreated and disappeared out the door. A moment later, someone moved towards her, and she felt a strong hand on her shoulder.

"Catherine, are you alright?" he stammered.

Catherine's knees buckled and the next thing she knew she was in the young man's arms as he helped her to the bed. He asked her repeatedly if she was alright.

"Yes…I'm alright," she forced herself to answer.

She breathed deeply in relief that Justin had come in time.

"Mrs Lindley, what happened?" a deep voice boomed from the doorway.

A moment later, the cabin was full of people. The lamp on the table was lit and Colonel Rowland stood in the middle of the room. Mary stood behind him, her face agitated, a large shawl over her long white nightdress. She looked at her cousin and the man from Siam in confusion.

Justin explained that he had been woken by Catherine's screams, so he ran to her cabin and saw a figure run out, but he did not run after him because he was afraid Catherine was hurt, so the intruder got away.

Colonel Rowland examined the door for traces of the intruder.

"I'll have to report this to the captain," he said gravely before hurrying out of the cabin.

He returned with the captain, a stocky middle-aged man with a black beard, who apologized to Catherine and questioned her for more details.

"One of the passengers was probably drunk and thought your cabin was his, so he tried to put his key in the lock and, when he heard you scream, he got scared and ran away."

"I thought the key to every cabin was different," said Justin coldly. "How would he be able to open the door with his own key?"

The captain looked uncomfortable and bowed apologetically.

"You're right, sir. I'll carry out a thorough investigation. I'll get you a chain for the door, madam, and I'll send someone to stand guard at night."

Colonel Rowland appeared satisfied with his answer, unlike Justin who still looked worried.

"Something like this has never happened before, has it?" he asked the captain.

"Never," the captain replied, glancing at Catherine, "but then we don't have many female passengers. Most are with their families."

"What's that supposed to mean?" Justin barked, rather uncharacteristically since he was normally calm and composed.

"The captain means he's concerned for Mrs Lindley's safety," Colonel Rowland cut in soothingly.

Justin turned to Catherine.

"Did you see who it was? Can you remember anything about him?"

Catherine considered and shook her head.

"It was dark. I couldn't see his face. I only know it was a man. He didn't say a word."

"Was he tall?" Colonel Rowland asked.

Catherine shook her head wearily.

"It all happened so quickly. Oh! He was wearing a cloak."

"A cloak…yes," Justin replied. "As I ran out, I remember seeing the edge of a cloak as he turned the corner."

"We'll investigate," said Colonel Roland. "I think we should all return to our cabins now."

"Thank you. Goodnight," Catherine replied, forcing a smile, even though her heart was still racing.

Justin remained after the others had left and looked hesitant before telling her softly, "Don't be afraid. I'll leave my door ajar and, if anyone walks past, I'll hear them. You can call me at any time."

"Thank you, Captain Justin."

***

Colonel Rowland saw Catherine the next day when she went up to walk on the deck after breakfast. The weather was getting warmer as they moved further east, and the passengers no longer needed to retreat to their cabins to escape the cold.

She was standing next to the rails looking out at the blue sea that stretched as far as the horizon. Golden ringlets had escaped from the bun at the nape of her neck, and her long pale blue skirt billowed in the breeze.

Before Colonel Rowland could approach her, he stopped when he saw a young man walk up to her first.

"Hunter," he said to himself.

Hunter said something to Catherine that made her suddenly stiffen and reply in irritation, but he laughed and continued talking as he stepped closer to her. Colonel Rowland was about to step in but was beaten to it by someone else who had been standing on the other side of the deck.

"Mrs Lindley," Justin said. "I wanted to see you."

Catherine had been enjoying the view when Hunter had appeared, grinning and gaping at her.

"We can't get away from each other. Ye're as lovely as a water nymph emerging from the sea."

"Mr Hunter, I was about to leave."

"Why the hurry?" he drawled, blocking her.

When she heard Justin's voice, she breathed a sigh of relief.

"Captain Justin, I wanted to see you, too," she remarked, turning to Justin.

"I have some news about the intruder last night. My servant brought me some evidence that he found in the passageway."

He glanced at Hunter, whose face became taut.

"I think we should tell the captain."

Justin turned to Hunter.

"Good morning, Hunter. Did you sleep well last night?"

Hunter looked at him disdainfully from head to toe, but when he saw the black eyes fixed on him, he shrugged.

"Last night, I was playing cards with the ship's navigator, so I didn't sleep…Why? Did something happen?" he asked, turning to Catherine.

At that moment, Colonel Rowland stepped in.

"An intruder went inside Mrs Lindley's cabin. Finding him shouldn't be difficult. There aren't that many passengers on board."

Hunter looked shocked.

"An intruder! Were ye hurt, Catherine?" he cried, turning to her,

46   A Passage to Siam

the familiarity with which he called her 'Catherine' jarring on the other two men.

"I'm perfectly fine. Captain Justin heard me scream and came to help, so he ran away…"

"What a coincidence that Justin…" he remarked, deliberately omitting the title 'captain', "came in time. It's rather surprising he was up so late."

"How do you know it was late?" Justin snapped. "We didn't say what time it was."

Hunter started, before continuing casually, "It's common sense. It wouldn't have happened in the evening. It had to be late."

"Strange," Justin replied calmly. "You said you were playing cards all night. Didn't you hear anything? You would have passed Mrs Lindley's room on the way back to your cabin."

Hunter became furious.

"Colonel. I don't know who this man is, but I refuse to be spoken to so impertinently by an Oriental."

The colour rose under Justin's brown skin, but he maintained his composure.

Colonel Rowland's tone became stern.

"Captain Justin is a man of high esteem. If you refuse to answer his question, then I'll ask you myself. Did you or did you not hear anything last night at around two o'clock?"

"I didn't hear a thing," Hunter barked. "Like I said, I was playing cards. There's nothing more to say. Catherine, I'll see ye again."

He stormed away leaving the others looking at each other in confusion.

Justin spoke first.

"He wasn't willing to talk. You'd think he'd be concerned for Mrs Lindley's safety."

It was clear he suspected Hunter and, from the look on his face, Colonel Rowland appeared to share the suspicion.

"There's something else I remember. The man that came into my room smelled of whiskey," Catherine explained. "I remembered when I saw Hunter. He's smelled of whiskey before, but he didn't today."

"If Hunter was playing cards with the ship's navigator, I'm

The End of the Horizon 47

curious as to when he returned to his room. Why don't you ask the ship's navigator, Colonel?" Justin asked.

At that moment, Catherine was struck by the feeling that this man from Siam was not an officer below Colonel Rowland, and that he sounded like someone who was used to giving orders rather than receiving them. And Colonel Rowland seemed to have forgotten that this man was of a lower rank.

"Yes. The three of us should go and ask him. And Mrs Lindley might think of something else."

They had only walked a few steps when Catherine remembered.

"Captain. You told me your servant found something in the passageway."

Justin stopped and pulled something out of his coat pocket before holding it out in the palm of his hand.

It was a metal rod, sharpened at one end.

"This was used to unlock your door."

The captain and the ship's navigator listened attentively.

The ship's navigator confirmed that he had been playing cards with Robert Hunter, and that they had been drinking whiskey.

"What time did you stop playing?" Colonel Rowland asked.

"It was quite late, sir. Around two I'd say."

Catherine noticed Colonel Rowland's eyes meet the captain's while Justin whispered to her, "If he went back to his room, he would have walked past your room, and two o'clock was when it happened."

The ship's navigator looked at the metal rod that Justin held out to him.

"That's from the curtain rail inside one of the cabins."

"Then we should check the passengers' cabins," Justin declared.

"We should start with Hunter's," Colonel Rowland decided.

Although she had guessed that Hunter wouldn't want his cabin inspected, she did not expect him to react with such fury. His face flushed with rage.

"How dare ye insult me by making such a preposterous suggestion! Besides, I have an alibi who can tell ye where I was."

"Then where were you?" the captain asked gravely.

"I was playing cards with the ship's navigator for God's sake! Didn't he tell ye? We were playing until dawn."

"He said you stopped playing at around two," the captain said.

"It was later than that. It was almost four when I got back to my room. I hadn't been back for long, and it was light. And for another thing, Captain," he said, his voice becoming softer. "I've known Catherine since we were in London. I've been looking out for her. Catherine, tell them we've known each other for ages."

The familiar way he spoke to her made her very uncomfortable.

"We haven't," she replied coldly. "I've only met you once before. My brother-in-law invited you to his house to ask you about Siam."

Hunter was dumbfounded, and the captain pushed past him inside his cabin.

"I'd like to see your room."

One of the curtains was missing, and the captain asked, "Where's the curtain gone?"

"How should I know? It's been missing since I got here," Hunter replied with a frown. "Ye should have replaced it. Ye're lucky I didn't complain."

"The cabins are always checked and repaired each time we dock," the captain said sternly.

Hunter shrugged.

"Then repair it. Ye shouldn't be blaming me for the fact that this cabin's so shabby. It isn't my fault ye didn't bother to replace the curtain."

"We're not blaming you, Mr Hunter, but a curtain rail has been found that was used as a skeleton key."

"Who found it?" Hunter barked.

"Captain Justin," Colonel Rowland said angrily.

Hunter eyed the Siamese man suspiciously.

"First again, I see. What a coincidence! Why aren't ye questioning him?"

"Don't be evasive."

"Me? Evasive?" Hunter scowled. "Ye're accusing me without any proof. There must be someone behind this. I won't let ye get away with it."

Catherine could see that Hunter would not relent, but the look on every face told her that everyone suspected him, but they had no evidence. When they had all returned to the captain's cabin, he found a way out.

"Are we going to let him get away with it?" Justin asked anxiously.

"No," chuckled the captain. "When we get to Malta, I know which ship will be going through the Suez, so I'll tell that skipper to make sure Hunter misses the boat. Then the lady will be able to travel to Siam safely."

The captain kept his word. Catherine only saw Robert Hunter for a moment when the ship docked in Malta, but after that, she didn't see another trace of him.

The next part of the journey passed more smoothly than the first and, even though Catherine sometimes woke up at night and stared at the ceiling in her cabin, she no longer felt afraid.

The journey through the Red Sea opened her eyes to a new world. The houses, the people, the way of life, the languages and everything else felt as strange as if she had fallen into a fairy-tale. Then as soon as they had passed through the Red Sea to the vast Arab Sea, there was nothing to see for days on end except for the sea and the sky.

The incident with Hunter had taught her to be careful about going out alone, and Justin tried to watch over her as much as he could, particularly when she went for a walk on the deck each morning and evening.

One day, as she stood on the deck watching the sun go down, Catherine mused, "I should learn Siamese, don't you think?"

She glanced at him and saw his black eyes were fixed on her in surprise, so she repeated her assertion.

"I'm serious. If I can understand Siamese, it will make life much easier."

"Would your husband allow it?"

"Why wouldn't he allow it?" she asked. "Arthur's adventurous. I expect he knows a lot about Siam by now. He'd be pleased if I learned about the Siamese way of life."

Justin was quiet for a moment before he smiled and said thoughtfully, "If you'd allow me to teach you, it would be an honour."

***

The Siamese language was difficult for Catherine at first. It had tones like music, with each tone giving the words a different meaning, and getting the tone even slightly off would change the sense completely. Catherine got the tones wrong at first, much to Justin's amusement, but he persevered in his efforts to teach her.

"At least I don't have to learn to read and write," she told him after she had learned to pronounce a few words correctly.

"It isn't necessary," he replied. "Siamese women don't learn to read and write. People think it will do more harm than good."

"Why?"

"They're afraid that if women can read and write, they'll play courting songs with men. Siamese women, especially the upper classes, are kept apart from men until their wedding day. Most of the marriages are arranged."

"Will a marriage be arranged for you?"

The expression on Justin's face changed suddenly, and Catherine was startled.

"I'm sorry, I didn't mean to…"

Justin composed himself and smiled.

"There's no need to be sorry. You did nothing wrong. I don't know what my elders have planned for me, but men have more freedom to choose than women."

And he quickly changed the subject, indicating to Catherine that he did not wish to talk about marriage. She guessed it was because he did not want to be forced to marry someone without even knowing if he liked her.

Catherine asked herself if she liked Arthur. The first thought that came to her mind was that yes, she did, but a moment later, a question rose from within her.

Don't I?

3

The Blue Sky of Siam

Justin had warned her that when they had passed Sri Lanka, south of the Sea of Bengal, they would be faced with tropical storms, since by now it was June, and they were entering the monsoon season.

Catherine had experienced a storm once before when they had come out of the Red Sea, but it was not too severe. The sea had simply been too rough to leave her cabin, so she had expected the tropical monsoon to be no different. But when she came face to face with this storm, it shattered her confidence completely.

It began in the afternoon when the sun suddenly disappeared, and a wall of dark clouds spread quickly across the sky. The sailors were caught off-guard and almost failed to take down the sails. The howling wind competed with the crashing waves and the roaring thunder, and they were engulfed by a heavy sheet of rain, which prevented them from seeing even the towering waves outside the boat.

Catherine was writing her journal in her cabin, and almost jumped out of her skin when she heard a booming clap of thunder, and the lights outside her cabin window went suddenly dark. All at once, the boat lurched downwards as if it was about to roll over before swinging back in the opposite direction.

Catherine tried to make her way to the bed, stumbling before she reached it, and the floor of the cabin was tipped upwards before dipping back down again. The heavy rain poured inside the cabin through the cracks around the cabin window with no relent. The floor began to flood, and her belongings were scattered around the room, and over bursts of thunder, she could hear the voices of people shouting as they stampeded up to the deck.

Someone banged on her door and shouted, "Mrs Lindley,

are you alright?"

Even over the roar of the storm, she recognised Justin's voice.

She fought her way to the door, her skirt soaked with water, tripping on the way, but managing to open the door. The force of the boat tipping hurled Justin inside the room straight into her and they were both almost pushed to the ground. Justin held onto her with one hand, while grabbing hold of the doorframe with the other.

"Let's go up," Catherine stammered, "or we'll be stuck inside the boat and drown."

Justin held her tight amid the confusion and she could tell that he was calm.

"If you go on the deck, you'll be thrown in the sea. It's safer to stay in the cabin…You're not hurt, are you?"

Catherine shook her head.

"I'm afraid…I don't want to die."

His arms held onto her more tightly, and, although it was too dark to see his face, she heard his voice in her ears.

"No one will die and there's no need to be afraid. In another hour, we'll have passed through it."

Justin had experienced such storms before, and his resolve lessened her fear. A flash of lightning lit up the room and was followed by another crack of thunder.

Justin straightened up, attempting to prevent them both from falling, but the force of the boat swinging sent them both flying. They were almost hurled against the wall, but he grabbed onto the leg of the bed in time and pulled himself and Catherine onto the bed, holding onto her tightly to prevent her from falling.

Although time moved on as usual, in Justin's arms, Catherine felt that time had stopped still. The storm continued, but, to Catherine, it seemed far away, and the warmth she felt in his arms drove away her fear.

At that moment, a force more potent than the tempest that raged in the middle of the sea consumed her, making her both bold and scared, repelling and attracting her simultaneously, her emotions as conflicting as the flashing lightning and the darkness that enveloped the sea.

The Blue Sky of Siam 53

In the darkness, all Catherine could feel was Justin's warm caress and his hot breath on her face, chasing away the cold from her wet clothes and replacing it with a heat that she had never experienced before.

"There's no need to be afraid, Catherine," she heard him whisper in her ear. "We won't die. We'll reach Siam together."

His voice was calm, unlike the storm that shook the boat. A flash of lightning lit up the cabin, followed by a crash of thunder as if the boat was being ripped apart.

"I'm afraid of the thunder," Catherine whispered.

"Thunder and lightning are normal in the monsoon. The ship's big enough. It won't sink."

He lifted her chin with his finger.

Another streak of lightning lit up the cabin, and Catherine saw he was smiling.

"My name in Siamese means lightning. There was a storm like this when I was born. I've never been afraid of storms. I believe they're lucky for me. I want you to believe the same when I'm with you, so you won't be afraid."

"I'm not afraid," she heard herself whisper. "I'm not afraid when you're with me."

"Good girl," he breathed, bending to kiss her hair. "I'll be with you all the way there. There's no need to be afraid."

Justin released his arms from around her frame and, almost at the same time, Catherine backed away from him. The spell was broken, and she came back to reality with a jolt. Her face became numb with embarrassment.

"I'm alright now," she blurted.

The ship began to stabilize and was not swaying as violently as before. Justin slid off the bed and stood up on the soaked floor.

"Catherine," he said softly, but resolutely. "If you weren't already married, I'd tell you right now…"

"Don't! Don't say it…" she said at once. Justin stopped suddenly.

He paused for a moment before saying in a voice he tried to steady, "Will you be alright by yourself now?"

Catherine could only nod, not trusting herself to say any more. The door was difficult to open because the floor was submerged, but Justin managed to push it open. The ship continued to sway for a while until it gradually lessened, and the captain steered it through the gale. But the storm that raged in Catherine's heart had only just begun.

***

The next day dawned clear and sunny and soon the cabin was tidy and dry with everything put back in its place, and her wet clothes had dried.

Catherine was busy in her cabin all day, too preoccupied to think of anything else. But that night, with nothing to do, she was too restless to sleep, even though she was exhausted.

"I was scared to death! I was praying the whole time. You must have been terrified!" Mary gushed.

Catherine glanced at Justin, who was standing on the deck next to the railing, and his eyes as black as the night sky met hers.

She looked away and muttered, "Well, who wouldn't be afraid?"

"George wasn't afraid. He said it's normal in the monsoon, but I couldn't stand it, even though I've seen it before going to India."

"Storms like that are normal in the monsoon," Colonel Rowland remarked. "I've seen worse."

"In Siam, the monsoon begins in May and continues until October," Justin said quietly. "People often get fevers."

Since the day of the storm, even though he joined the group like before, Catherine felt that Justin was quieter. Sometimes, she noticed him looking at her without speaking, a hurt expression in his eyes as it was obvious that she had been avoiding him.

"Oh, Catherine!" Mary exclaimed. "I'll tell Arthur to make sure he looks after you. In India, so many Englishwomen die of fevers. Oh! What have I said? You've gone pale!"

In truth, the colour had suddenly drained from her face when Mary mentioned 'Arthur', and not because she feared getting sick with a fever.

"Excuse me, I think I'll go back to my cabin."

She didn't know that he was following her until she had gone down the stairs and was standing in front of her cabin. She stopped suddenly

The Blue Sky of Siam 55

in front of the door when Justin touched it, and her heart began to race.

"Catherine. We can't keep avoiding each other. Unless you don't want to see me. Tell me and I'll understand."

She heard herself answer in a voice that sounded like a stranger, "Between you and I, it can never be!"

She dared not look at his face but heard him take a deep breath.

"I know. You're another man's wife. I'm sorry I met you too late."

Catherine closed the door softly behind her before sinking down in a chair and burying her face in her hands as the tears rolled down her face.

* * *

Three days later, the weather was hot, and the sky was clear. The sun was so intense that it even hurt Catherine's eyes to look out of the cabin window, and it shone all day until sunset when everyone was able to go up on the deck.

The ship was to dock at Singapore before they sailed through the Gulf of Siam to the capital. Arthur was to travel to meet her in Singapore, but if he couldn't, due to his work, he would meet her in Siam's capital, which Colonel Rowland called 'Bangkok'.

When Colonel Rowland mentioned Arthur, Catherine's heart sank. She recognised that she had wronged him, but she dreaded facing him – the young man who had stood next to her at the altar had become a dim shadow in her memory. What would he say if she told him the truth?

'I don't love you. It happened too fast between us. And it's over. We've never lived together as man and wife. I want to divorce you, so I can start a new life with the man I love.'

She knew it was out of the question. For one thing, Arthur would never let her go to be a Siamese man's wife. It would not only bring shame on him but would humiliate all his countrymen. For another thing, divorce was almost unheard of, and couples would rather live together in misery until the day they died than suffer the shame of divorce. And the worst of it was that Catherine had no grounds on which to ask Arthur for a divorce. He had not abandoned or abused her, but she wanted to leave him for another man, which was unforgiveable, even to herself.

56 A Passage to Siam

***

Singapore was a small country with a hot climate, but it was green and shady. The orderly streets and European-style houses made Catherine feel at home as soon as she stepped on dry land.

The ship dropped anchor about fifteen miles from the shore, and they travelled by small boat to the harbour, where a young Englishman, who introduced himself as the secretary to the Governor of Singapore, was there to meet them.

"I've been assigned to meet Prince Vijjuprapha, and to welcome Colonel and Mrs Rowland, and Mrs Lindley."

At first, Catherine didn't understand who he meant, but when he bowed to Justin, she almost fainted.

Justin was a prince!

She should have realized before. From the way Colonel Rowland was respectful towards him, his refined manners, and the way he was able to write a letter to the Second King of Siam, she should have known Justin was a man of importance in his homeland, not just a Siamese student who had trained in India. At the same time, she also realized that the gulf between them was wider than ever.

The house that the governor of Singapore had arranged for them was a modest-sized bungalow with enough rooms for them to stay by themselves comfortably. Justin resided alone in the right wing, while the others stayed in the left wing.

Catherine had a small bedroom with her own sitting room. The English-style furniture made her feel at home, except for the nets attached to the posters of the bed.

"They're mosquito nets. They'll prevent you from getting bitten," Mary explained.

Catherine liked to walk in the garden in the mornings and evenings. She enjoyed the large trees with their dense green foliage. Some of them had bright crimson flame-like blossoms and others had large round fruits with thick skins as if someone had tied bunches of pale-green balloons to their branches.

***

One evening, after they had been there about ten days, she went out for a walk after waiting for the sun to go down when she could enjoy the cool evening breeze. After a while, she suddenly became aware that someone was watching her. She turned around and her heart lurched when she saw Justin walking down the steps of the veranda in front of his room towards her. There was nothing else she could do except to curtsey, her heart thumping.

"Mrs Lindley," he said with a polite nod.

The tension between them was palpable, and Catherine realised that it was her fault. She had been avoiding him.

"We haven't had a chance to talk," Justin said, after gazing at her for a moment, "since we arrived here."

She glanced at him before looking away, saying softly, "You're a prince."

"I'm not a prince of any importance, Catherine. And that isn't the reason you've been avoiding me. You don't want to see me because you know how we both feel."

"Please forget what happened. It isn't right. It was just a moment's emotion."

A hurt expression flickered in his eyes.

"Is that how you regard my feelings for you?"

"I'm sorry…" she said softly. "But I'm already married."

"Do you love him?"

She avoided the question, not wanting to raise his hopes.

"Please think of me as a friend. And I'll think of you in the same way."

Justin took a deep breath.

"As you wish, Mrs Lindley."

She wanted to walk back to her room with composure but, after a few steps, she lifted the hem of her skirt and ran up the steps of the bungalow to her room, her eyes blurred by tears, which prevented her from seeing Colonel Rowland, who was watching from the veranda in front of his room, a concerned expression on his face.

"Your Highness," he began gravely. "May I speak with you a moment?"

The prince glanced at him, and his face tightened.

"I know what you're thinking. There's no need to worry."

But the middle-aged man would not leave it, considering it his duty to nip the impending complication in the bud.

"I'm concerned about your feelings, sir. I do understand the intensity of forbidden love."

The prince was speechless for a moment.

"Can you help me?"

"I can help you by putting a stop to it. It's for the best. If you were both English, or both Siamese, then I wouldn't interfere. But I'm afraid, if this continues, it could become a spark ..."

"You don't seriously think it could start a war?"

"A British officer would consider it an affront to his dignity if you were to fall in love with his wife. It could cause a great deal of damage if he were to report it to Captain Knox."

The blood rushed to the prince's face.

"Rest assured, Colonel. The Siamese have no less dignity than the British."

Feeling that he had been too harsh, he added, "Siamese men can have several wives, all of them legitimate, but the Five Precepts forbid a man from taking another man's wife."

Colonel Roland breathed a sigh of relief, even though a part of him was still concerned.

"Quite right, sir. In a few days, Lieutenant Lindley will be arriving in Singapore. It was most gracious of the Second King of Siam to allow him to leave the kingdom."

***

Nobody had told Catherine that Arthur was coming to meet her in Singapore, since Mary had thought it best to surprise her. But it wasn't difficult for Catherine to guess, especially when her cousin invited her to take a carriage with her to the harbour. When they arrived, Arthur was there waiting. He was standing talking to the governor of Singapore's secretary, his tall frame and blonde hair conspicuous amid the smaller raven-haired locals.

"Oh! Look who it is! Are you surprised?" Mary cried in excitement.

Catherine stepped down from the carriage as if she had been hypnotized, her legs and arms feeling as heavy as lead.

The Blue Sky of Siam 59

Arthur had spotted her from afar and was walking towards her.

"Catherine!" he cried excitedly before sweeping her up in his arms. "Catherine, darling! I'm so happy to see you!"

Arthur's exuberance helped to ease the emptiness in her heart, and she muttered, "Yes, me too," although her voice was muffled compared to Arthur's excited cries. Arthur's skin had been tanned darker than before and he had lost weight. His face was gaunt, and his blonde hair had been cropped close to his skull. He seemed like a stranger who was nothing like the sturdy young man that had stood next to her at the altar six months earlier.

"What happened to you? You look ill," she blurted.

Arthur smiled, thinking she was concerned about him.

"I've just recovered from a sickness, darling. It almost did me in. But I'm alright now. Now that you're here, I've never felt better."

He gazed at her contentedly.

"Catherine, you're still as beautiful as ever."

Catherine had nothing to say, so she remained silent, not knowing what else to do except smile. He introduced her to the Siamese nobleman who had accompanied him. He was a small man about the same age as Justin and he greeted her with an unfamiliar accent.

"Darling, this is Mr Suriyawut. He's a friend of mine and an attendant of the Second King of Siam."

It was the first time she had seen a Siamese who appeared different from Justin. She had been used to Justin's Western clothes and haircut, assuming that all Siamese would be the same. Now she realized she had been mistaken. This man's head was shaven at the sides, leaving only short, cropped hair on the top. He wore a long-sleeved shirt with a long piece of cloth knotted to look like baggy calf length pants.

But the strangest thing was that when he smiled, his mouth revealed teeth as black as coal.

Then she remembered what Justin had told her.

"The Siamese chew betel like some Europeans chew tobacco. It has a spicy taste and makes people feel good. And it stains the teeth black."

Justin's teeth were as white as an Englishman's, so she could not imagine what it would look like, but now she understood.

Then the governor's carriage took them back to the bungalow.

"I've missed you so much, Catherine. I should never have left you. I wanted to go back for you."

Catherine knew that Arthur felt guilty.

But what would he say if he knew that she was guilty of something she could not tell him? Something much worse.

"Well, I'm here now."

Arthur clasped her hands and brought them to his lips.

"When I got your letter, I was so relieved to know you were alright."

"I was fine. I had Mary with me."

Arthur was too happy to notice that her voice was dry. A moment later, he moved closer and wrapped his arms around her.

"Catherine, I've missed you terribly. Let's make Singapore our honeymoon, darling."

Catherine caught her breath. Arthur had no idea that Catherine had been dreading this moment for the past month. When she had boarded the steamboat in England, she had never dreamed that this would happen, and was intent on being faithful to Arthur. But on the boat, several months later, she realised that what she had felt for Arthur was not love, but simply friendship and nothing more. Love had turned out to be something else that had suddenly attacked her, like the storm that had shaken the boat, and even though she had fought it, she knew that she would never be the same.

She knew that she should starve her feelings for Justin and be faithful to her wedding vows.

But at the last minute, as if she had managed to shake herself free from the net she had been caught in, she made an about-turn.

"Arthur, there's something I must tell you. You'd better sit down."

She pulled away from him, her heart thumping with fear.

Arthur looked puzzled.

"I don't know how to tell you. The truth is…we hardly know each other. We only met twice before our wedding. And then you left suddenly."

Arthur assumed that she was embarrassed to be intimate with him and smiled.

"I understand, darling. There's nothing to be afraid of. This is your first time. I'll be gentle, I promise."

She tried again.

"There's something I need to confess, Arthur. The reason I married you...was because I longed for adventure."

Her voice began to tremble as she continued to explain.

"The only way I could leave Hampshire was to marry you. I've never loved you."

Arthur remained silent, listening intently.

"You're a stranger to me. The reason I came wasn't because I loved you, but because I wanted to see the world. Does that make sense?"

Arthur did not speak for some time and the excitement disappeared from his face.

"I'm a stranger to you," he repeated.

"Yes, Arthur. And if you're angry with me, I understand. But that's how I feel."

"You're afraid of a stranger..."

"Yes. I'm sorry."

He forced a smile and patted the back of her hand.

"I didn't know until now. But I understand. You're tired from your journey. I shouldn't rush you."

Catherine knew that Arthur was disappointed and that even though he said he understood, he was puzzled. He blamed the circumstances and tried to put her at ease.

"I tell you what," he said, "I won't force you. I'll let you rest, and I'll sleep on the sofa until you're ready."

* * *

Catherine hoped that her face belied her distress throughout the dinner that the governor of Singapore had arranged to welcome Arthur and the Siamese nobleman. And as for Justin, if she had not known him so well, she would not have noticed the difference in his manner.

Arthur remembered him as the 'man from Siam in India' and was not surprised when he later learned that Justin was a prince. Living in Siam for the past several months had taught him that the Siamese were keen to open the country to foreign progress, so it was only natural that a Siamese prince would be sent to India for training. He took the opportunity to talk to Justin because, although the other Siamese nobleman could understand English, he could only speak a little.

"When I take Catherine to Siam, I hope we'll have an opportunity to invite you to our home," Arthur said.

Justin glanced at Catherine, and although his expression remained unchanged, Catherine noticed a glimmer of sadness in his eyes.

"Thank you. It would be an honour."

* * *

Catherine arrived in Siam nine days later.

The seven-day journey passed smoothly, and it was fortunate that Catherine and Arthur's cabin on the ship had two rooms, so they were able to sleep separately without anyone knowing. She learned that Arthur did not like to stay in one place and was like Colonel Rowland in that he enjoyed socializing with the other men. If he was not up on deck, he was chatting with Colonel Rowland and Justin. She did not once meet Justin alone, and although he was never out of sight, he avoided being alone with her.

By now, Justin seemed a different person to the officer with just one servant and had become the most important person on the ship. Besides the Siamese nobleman, there were numerous other attendants, and she hardly had an opportunity to speak to him, even in front of her husband.

Catherine had expected the journey to the capital of Siam to be as easy as the journey to Singapore, but in fact, it was quite difficult.

The ship had to drop anchor when it reached the mouth of the river, since it was such a large vessel, so they disembarked in the estuary town of Samut Prakan before changing to a smaller boat with a roof and curtains on either side to sail up the Chao Phraya River, which ran through the capital.

Catherine saw crowds of Siamese people for the first time standing on both sides of the river. She was shocked to see that the Siamese did not wear any clothes on the top halves of their bodies. Even the Siamese noblemen wore only a long piece of cloth on their bottom halves while their brown chests were bare. Their heads were shaved at the sides, leaving only the hair on the top of their heads. At first, Catherine didn't understand where all the women were, since she could only see men carrying children on their hips.

She asked Justin in a whisper, forgetting herself, and he laughed softly, "The women are there holding the babies. I'll ask for them to be brought closer, so you can see."

He gave the order in Siamese and, a moment later, two or three locals were brought to the prince. They did not stand or sit but crawled towards him on their hands and knees before prostrating themselves on the ground without looking at his face. The Siamese women appeared no different from the men, except they were smaller. Their hair was cut short like the men's and their clothes were like the men's, except that they wore a strip of cloth wrapped around their chests, except for those with children, who were bare-chested.

To an Englishwoman used to the restrictions of a corset, the bodies of the Siamese women appeared enviously free, even though she found them unshapely. This remained her opinion until she went inside the Inner Court and had a chance to see the ladies of the Inside.

Particularly the young woman betrothed to Justin.

* * *

The boat sailed on up the Chao Phraya River that evening. Catherine could see nothing except for dense forest on both sides of the river. There were no buildings or houses and the vast river appeared empty and quiet, without any large boats. Further back from the river was flat land that stretched as far as the eye could see beneath the dark blue sky. But as soon as it was dark, the most beautiful sight appeared in front of her eyes.

After dinner, Justin invited her and Mary to stand at the helm of the boat and look out on either side of the river.

"Look at that row of trees, and you'll see…" he said.

In the darkness of the trees on the riverbank, small lights shimmered in an unbroken row alongside the river. The yellow lights were not fixed in one place like lanterns or flickering like candles, but were full of life, moving up and down like the wings of thousands of tiny water nymphs in a fairy-tale.

It was the strangest and most magnificent sight that Catherine had ever seen, and she stood transfixed, without realising that she was clinging onto Justin's arm.

"What are they? It's so beautiful," she whispered.

"They're fireflies. They perch in the mangrove trees and emit light. Have you heard of fireflies?"

"No, I've never seen anything so lovely before."

She suddenly realized she was holding Justin's arm and quickly let go, but it did not go unnoticed by Mary, who cleared her throat before saying, "We should fetch Arthur."

Catherine felt the colour rise in her cheeks and replied, "You forget, he must have seen it before. I'm sure he'd rather play cards with the colonel."

"Well, I'm going downstairs. Good night, Your Highness."

The two of them were left alone in the darkness with only the breeze, just as it had been on the big boat. Catherine glanced at the young man by her side and saw him looking back at her as if he was thinking the same thing. Catherine took a deep breath. The opportunity for them to meet like this had become increasingly limited.

She heard him say, "You must be glad to have reached your destination."

It was a perfectly normal question, but Catherine knew it carried a deeper meaning.

"I've reached my destination, but I've come to a crossroads, Your Highness."

"Justin," he corrected her. "Why? Aren't you happy to see your husband?"

"Justin…Arthur and I have reached a crossroads. We haven't reached our destination."

Justin looked at her, puzzled for a moment, before an expression of understanding gradually appeared on his face.

"Catherine," he said softly, but urgently. "Do you mean you share my feelings for you?"

Justin reached out to clasp her hand and the warmth of his hand

The Blue Sky of Siam 65

made her realise that her own hands were cold, despite the sultry weather. Before Catherine could answer, Justin noticed someone was coming out of the corner of his eye, and gently stepped away from her.

Arthur walked towards her and remarked, "Mary said you were waiting for me, darling."

"I was just about to go back to the cabin."

The row of fireflies began to dim, and Catherine turned away from them before her eyes met Justin's in the darkness.

"Good night, Your Highness."

"Goodnight, Mrs Lindley."

Arthur bowed to the prince before taking his leave and walking away with his wife.

"Catherine, we'll be arriving at about midnight. It's too early to go back inside the cabin."

"Yes, I know, but I want to pack."

It was an excuse, he knew. If he invited her to go up on the deck, she wanted to stay inside the cabin, and if he tried to talk to her in the cabin, she would politely say that she needed some fresh air. Things between them were decidedly awkward and he didn't understand why she was giving him the cold shoulder, but he assumed her mood had been affected by the long journey and blamed himself, so he tried to be patient with her, although his patience was beginning to wear thin.

***

Just after midnight, the boast sailed past a beautiful pagoda bathed in silver moonlight, towering majestically beside the river.

"This is Wat Arun, the Temple of the Dawn. We'll be arriving soon."

The bright half-moon illuminated the houses on both sides of the river, which appeared to be built on stilts, reminding her of what Arthur had told her about the 'floating houses'.

A small boat took them from the larger boat to the harbour. In the darkness, Catherine could see little, except for a white wall along the water's edge, where many people were waiting.

For the past few months, Justin had always been with her, and she had grown accustomed to having him around. Tonight, was the first night that she would be separated from him, and she would not have another chance to be close to him. Instead, she would have to live with a husband who was like a stranger to her. As she bent down to curtsey, his voice revealed that he was no less distraught than she was.

"Goodbye, Catherine."

He paused before adding in a seemingly ordinary way, but letting her know that he meant it, "We'll meet again."

* * *

Arthur's house was outside the Front Palace, close to the residence for guests of the Second King of Siam. Catherine saw it was a small two-storey house like houses in England, except that it was more open, and the stairs were outside the house.

After she had lived in Siam for some time, Catherine learned that the Siamese believed that stairs should be outside the house, even in the palace.

When she walked up the stairs to the first room, she found a large balcony and three doors that opened into the room inside. Arthur ordered the Siamese servant to put her chest of clothes down in front of the room.

He turned to her and asked gruffly, "The room on the left is mine and the room in the middle is the guest room. Which room do you want to stay in?"

Although she knew that the servant probably couldn't understand English, her face reddened.

"I'll stay in the guest room. Until…everything's clear."

Arthur pursed his lips, and an angry expression clouded his face.

"The guest room isn't comfortable. You can stay in my room, and I'll have the guest room."

He opened the door to his room and motioned for the servant to bring the chest inside. Then he lit a kerosene lamp. The lamplight illuminated the small room with whitewashed walls. The two large windows made it look spacious and there was a door leading to the next room. The room was simply furnished with a large four poster bed and a thin white mosquito net hung over it. A chest of drawers stood against the wall with a mirror above it, and a washbasin and jug on the top. The room had wooden floorboards and a rug made of strips of cloth was placed in front of the bed.

Arthur turned to Catherine and asked testily, "Catherine, how long must we go on like this?"

Catherine's heart sank.

"Let's not discuss it now. I'm tired."

"You've always got an excuse to avoid me!"

He could not contain his anger any longer, and walked towards her, grabbing her by the shoulders and shaking her.

"Tell me what's going on…What's the matter with you? Last year, you took a vow to love, honour and obey me, and now that we're together, you're treating me like a leper? Why?"

He raised his voice in fury, and when Catherine tried to break free from his grip, he would not let go.

"We can't live like this! I don't want to force you, but I don't know what I've done wrong! Why are you doing this to me?"

"Arthur, let go of me! You're hurting me!" she cried.

At that moment, the door connecting the bedroom to the guest room was pushed open. The blurry voice of a woman came from the doorway.

"Are you back? I've been waitin' for you."

Arthur suddenly jumped and loosened his grip, so Catherine broke free, and turned to look.

She could hardly believe her eyes. A woman was standing in the doorway. She was European, but her skin was tanned, and the lamplight revealed her red hair and ample bosom, clearly visible through her thin nightdress, which hardly hid a thing.

4
The Dilemma

Arthur hurried to the door to push her out of his wife's sight, but they both knew full well that Catherine had already seen her.

"Charlotte! What are you doing here?" he barked.

The young woman looked up and smiled nonchalantly.

"Why wouldn't I be 'ere? I've been 'ere for the past few days since you went to Singapore. This 'ouse is more comfortable than mine. I told you before. Don't you remember?"

"But it isn't your house," Arthur cried. "And you've no right to come in here without my permission."

The young woman shrugged.

"Calm down, darlin'. John asked your permission already. 'Ave you forgotten?"

She stifled a yawn.

"I'm sleepy…I 'eard a noise that woke me up. Oh!"

She gasped when she looked past him, and her eyes met Catherine's.

"I didn't know…Oh, Lord! This must be Mrs Lindley!"

Catherine turned to Arthur. She could not believe that all this time Arthur had not been alone, but with this woman.

"It's not what you think," Arthur stuttered.

Catherine didn't answer, but her cold gaze silenced him.

He turned to the other woman and ordered, "Go home, now! Get your things and get out!"

The woman showed no sign of alarm and when he grabbed her arm as if he was going to drag her inside the next room, she shook herself free.

"John's not back. 'Ow can I go 'ome?"

"I'll have a servant take you. You must have a key. I don't want

Catherine to misunderstand."

Charlotte laughed.

Catherine glanced at Arthur and saw his face was red. The woman lifted his chin with her finger and pulled back before he could brush it away. Then she blew him a kiss.

"Alright. Then your wife won't misunderstand. I'm goin'. Shame, though. I don't like stayin' by myself. You know what I mean, don't you?"

She directed the question at Catherine, and Arthur was furious.

"Charlotte! I told you…"

"Alright, I 'eard. Bye, Mrs Lindley. I'd like to say it was nice meetin' you, but I don't s'pose you feel that way…"

Arthur dragged her back inside the room she had appeared from and opened the door to the balcony. Catherine heard him call for a servant and give an order in Siamese, which she guessed was to take the woman away.

"But I left my clothes in the bedroom!" she cried.

"Then get them and go!"

It was a while before Arthur came back inside, the angry expression on his face replaced by a troubled frown.

"I know what you're going to say."

In fact, she had no idea what to say.

"I'll explain everything in the morning. It will soon be light. You should go to bed. If you need to bathe, I can have a servant bring you some water."

"Thank you," she whispered.

Arthur sighed as if he was relieved that she had not asked him any questions.

***

A strange noise outside the window woke Catherine just before dawn. As golden rays shone inside and illuminated the room, the noise outside increased until Catherine had to pull back the mosquito net and walk over to the window.

It was the sound of birds chirping. There were all kinds of strange

70   A Passage to Siam

birds, including black crows clamouring so loudly it was almost deafening as the large trees that surrounded the house made good nesting places.

Catherine had never seen so much dense foliage as in Bangkok. Not even the parks in London had so many trees, and every tree was covered in so many leaves that you could hardly see the branches. She leaned out of the window until she could see the long river not far away bathed in the yellow rays of the morning sun. Several small boats sailed up and down, the busyness on the river contrasting with the stillness on the land.

There was a knock at the door, and Catherine called out, "Who's there?"

Her husband's voice replied.

"If you're up, I'll send a servant girl to you. Kham doesn't speak much English, but she understands."

"Thank you."

Kham was a sturdy Siamese woman who wore a long piece of cloth pulled up between her legs and tucked in at the back, and a strip of cloth wrapped around her chest. Although Catherine did not find her pretty, she was taken with her bright black eyes, which shone with intelligence and warmth.

"The master told me to prepare water for your bath, Mem," she said in Siamese, pointing to a bath in the corner of the room behind a large screen.

It was so hot that Catherine had been bathing twice a day since Singapore, even though she wasn't used to it. After bathing, she picked out the thinnest white cotton blouse she could find from her chest and a black skirt but found that she still felt hot when she walked out to the balcony. Arthur had set up a breakfast table there and he stood up to greet her.

His face appeared tired as if he had hardly slept, and he had not shaved.

"Did you sleep well?" he asked.

"Yes," she replied, and added, "I was tired."

Arthur searched her face, trying to ascertain her mood. He didn't know whether he should be relieved that she was not angry or upset

The Dilemma 71

that she didn't seem to care.

"What are you going to do today?" he asked, attempting to make conversation. "I'll be off to train the soldiers in a moment, but this evening, we could go out…There aren't any roads to walk on, but we could take a boat."

"I've had enough of boats. If you don't mind, I'd like to go and see Mary."

She was just the same as before, Arthur thought resentfully. She was obviously avoiding him.

"Catherine. There's something I need to tell you," he blurted. "We need to straighten things out."

As soon as he had spoken, he realised he had chosen the wrong moment when Catherine suddenly put down her glass of milk.

"If you don't mind, I'd like to have breakfast in peace."

Arthur was dumbstruck. They finished breakfast in awkward silence. Then Catherine excused herself.

"I'm going to unpack. And I want to do some laundry."

"If you didn't have laundry, you'd have something else."

Catherine started a little and turned to face him.

"Are you trying to start another argument?"

Arthur came to his senses.

"I don't want to argue, but I think we should talk in my study today. Please, Catherine."

Catherine did not want to talk, but she had no other option. Arthur's study was on the far side of the centre room where he had slept and had an adjoining door. Inside was a large desk and a chair, as well as an armchair and a bookshelf with papers on it, but not a single book. She sat down on the armchair while Arthur walked up and down in agitation. He was waiting for her to ask him what he wanted to talk about, but when she was silent, he spoke first.

"About that woman…If you think Charlotte's my mistress, I can tell you she isn't. I've never supported that woman…"

Catherine listened with an expressionless face. Even if that woman was not Arthur's mistress, it did not make things any better.

"In Siam, there are few people who speak English, so we have no choice but to associate with each other. Charlotte's about the only

72   A Passage to Siam

woman among us…besides the American missionary wives. But we don't mix with them."

In trying to make excuses, Arthur was only digging a deeper hole for himself.

"I didn't invite Charlotte as a guest. Charlotte came with John Fowler, a navigator on the trade ships. He's still not back, so she took advantage of the opportunity to come and stay in my house because it's more comfortable than hers. I wanted to tell you that Fowler told me not to let her stay here again."

"You mean she's stayed here before?"

Arthur stopped, realizing he'd put his foot in it.

"I told you she came with Fowler."

"If you hadn't let her stay here before, she wouldn't have had the nerve to come again. And she was drunk."

"I promise she won't disturb you again," he said softly, looking at her with a guilty expression.

"As far as I can see, she's already disturbed me quite enough," she said coldly.

* * *

Arthur got up and hurried down the stairs since he had to go and train the soldiers in the Front Palace not far away.

Catherine sat down wearily and put her head in her hands. She decided to call for the servant girl.

"I'm going to Captain Knox's house. Can you call for someone to take me there?"

The Siamese woman understood, or at least she recognised the name Knox. She gave a wide smile revealing black teeth and quickly replied politely in Siamese.

"Yes, you can sit in a *khan ham* to the consulate, Mem."

Justin had taught her that the Siamese used the word 'mem' to describe a white European or American woman, and she understood the Siamese words for 'sit' and 'consulate', but she had no idea what the word '*khan ham*' meant. But when she descended the stairs and saw the '*khan ham*' for herself, she could hardly believe her eyes. Four

The Dilemma 73

mucular men were standing still in the stone courtyard, having placed the contraption on the ground. It was a small seat attached to two long bamboo poles, which had a cushion and a small back that was not high enough to lean on, and when she saw it on the ground, she could not imagine how it would move, since it did not have wheels and there was no animal to pull it. She did not want to believe that these men would carry her to Knox's house.

But Kham confirmed that her supposition was right, explaining in broken English.

"Mem sit on *khan ham*. Men will carry you."

"I can't!" Catherine exclaimed. "I'd rather walk."

"No path. Cannot walk!"

Catherine realised that, beyond the clear courtyard, the ground was dense with grass as high as her waist, and she could not see any sign of a footpath. She had not noticed how Arthur had left the house that morning, since the previous night they had travelled from the harbour in a horse-drawn carriage. Since there was no other option, Catherine stepped between the poles and placed herself on the narrow seat. The mid-morning sun was scorching, but luckily, she had remembered her parasol, so she opened it hastily.

The four burly men lifted the poles carefully, but the thing began to rock as soon as they started walking. Catherine grabbed hold of the side of the seat with her one free hand, but it did not make her feel any safer.

The ground was bumpy, but beneath the dense foliage, Catherine could make out a brick path, which the men seemed accustomed to, and they walked quickly as if she weighed only a few pounds. In almost no time at all, they had reached the house where Captain Knox lived.

Mary listened to Catherine's story in excitement, but when Catherine had finished and she saw her cousin's unhappy face, she became serious.

"You mustn't be hasty. Arthur was just lonely, and that woman means nothing to him. No man would be foolish enough to choose such a hussy over his wife."

"Mary, if I wanted to stay with Arthur, then I'd follow your advice, but the thing is, I don't want to stay with him anymore. I don't know

74 A Passage to Siam

what to do."

Mary's jaw dropped as she suddenly realised that Catherine really meant it.

"If you leave him, whatever will you do here? Bangkok isn't like London where you can find a job. When women here get married, they have no other option except to be a housewife. You can't possibly divorce him."

"Why not?" Catherine asked.

"Oh, really! You know as well as I do that nobody gets divorced," Mary cried in irritation. "No one will accept you, even if you're not in the wrong, and the law isn't on your side. If Arthur doesn't want to marry that woman, you can't possibly divorce him. And this is Siam, not England. Who would decide except for the consul? Consul Hillier isn't interested in trifles. And Captain Knox and Arthur are thick as thieves. They'd never allow it. And Arthur would never forgive you."

"I knew you wouldn't agree," Catherine sighed.

"As a woman, I sympathise," Mary said, patting the back of her hand gently. "If George did the same, I'd be angry too. But I'd grit my teeth and let it go. Look, why don't you give Arthur another chance? After all, we all make mistakes. Even you. If you'd strayed, you'd want him to forgive you, wouldn't you?"

The blood suddenly rushed to Catherine's face, and when she saw that Mary's eyes were fixed on her with a knowing expression, she felt hot all over.

"What do you mean? If you've something to say, then say it."

"I can tell how that Siamese prince feels about you, and I can see you feel the same way. It's only natural when you were in such proximity on the boat. But it can never be. Even if you were unmarried. An English woman could never marry a native of a colony."

"Justin isn't a native of a colony. Siam has never been colonised."

"What nonsense!" Mary barked. "Sooner or later, Siam will be colonised. Such a small country can't possibly survive by itself. And when it is colonised, Captain Knox will be promoted, and so will Arthur. And you should know that if there's one thing that no man can stand, it's to be cheated on. So you'd better make sure that you have nothing more to do with that prince."

***

Prince Vijjuprapha spent the whole of his first day in Siam in his father's palace. He felt like a stranger when he first woke up there, especially when an attendant led him to his father's room, where a young woman was fanning him, but as soon as the prince entered, she crawled away. The first time he stood in front of his father, Prince Vijjuprapha noticed that he had lost weight as if he had just recovered from an illness and his hair had turned white, even though he was not that old.

Prince Vijjuprapha was born on the same day as King Pinklao, the Second King of Siam. They had been ordained at the same time, and the young prince had followed him everywhere.

"Some people say you look like me. I don't think so. You look more like my father."

This was a compliment since his grandfather was known to have been good-looking right up until his death at the age of just thirty-seven.

"I gave you to the king…"

His father meant King Pinklao, the Second King of Siam.

"Be sure to do your duty faithfully, and don't do anything that might cause trouble. You've travelled far and wide to gain knowledge. Be sure to bring honour to your family. Don't pursue your own happiness at the expense of others. And always show gratitude."

Although he did not know it at the time, his father had been more astute than he realised. According to custom, Prince Vijjuprapha could say nothing except to answer his father's questions. The only person who was able to ask him questions was his mother, Mom Yad.

A moment later, the meeting with his father was finished. The main hall, which was used for meetings, was by now full of siblings who had come to welcome him, whom they all called Prince Saifa, after his long absence. His two elder brothers were now grown men with wives and children, and had their own homes close to the palace. Of his sisters, the only one that remained in the palace was the youngest, who was sixteen years old.

His mother had gained weight as was normal for a woman of

76 A Passage to Siam

middle age, but she still appeared fit and healthy. She looked at her son happily before turning to her daughter to scold her.

"What are you laughing at? Where are your manners?"

Princess Kanika, who was known by her family as Princess Ying, had grown into radiant young woman, but she was still rather immature, since she was the youngest and had been indulged more than her siblings.

"I've never seen anyone with such white teeth before. Prince Saifa looks like a foreigner. If Bua sees, I don't know what she'll say."

"Who's Bua?" Prince Saifa asked, puzzled.

The other siblings looked at each other, but no one answered, so his mother replied evasively, "Bua's the daughter of Phraya Rachayotha. Her mother sent her to live with Khun Chom since she was a child. She and Ying have always played together."

"She's very pretty. Everyone loves her," the princess added. "Aunt wants her to...ouch!"

Before she had finished speaking, she cried out when her mother pinched her and quickly changed the subject.

"And when are you going to see Khun Chom?"

"I want to give her some gifts," Prince Saifa answered, "I can't go inside the Inner Court to see her, and I don't know when she'll come out. When will you be going inside, Mother?"

The rules relating to the Inner Court caused Prince Vijjuprapha some irritation after his return to Siam, since he could not go to see Khun Chom Klee because she lived there, where only women were allowed, and he did not know when she would come out, so his mother was the go-between.

"I can go any day. Bring me the gifts to take," Mom Yad replied. "It won't be a problem. Now...we need to talk about the house that your father wants to build for you. Where would you like it to be built?"

According to custom, building a house meant marriage, but Prince Saifa did not understand, assuming his father wanted to build him a house because he was old enough to have his own home.

His father's palace consisted of a group of Thai-style houses and was not extravagant because most of the nobles in his palace

The Dilemma 77

were not wealthy. However, Mom Yad, his principal wife, was the daughter of a Thai nobleman of Chinese ancestry whose father had amassed his wealth through trade since since the reign of King Nangklao, so he had helped to provide for his daughter's comfort.

"I like living next to the river. If nobody lives on the raft, I'd like to live there."

Building a house there would be easy because the craftsmen had already built it and would simply have to reassemble it on the raft next to the river. Only the main pillar needed to be installed on an auspicious day.

All the princesses there knew what 'building a house' meant, and Princess Kanika asked mischievously, "Have you brought a guest with you?"

As soon as she had spoken, her mother pinched her and she cried, "Ouch!" again. Prince Saifa looked confused.

"What guest?"

His elder brother laughed.

"Ying's teasing you. It's a good thing you haven't brought a wife back with you."

This time, he understood and smiled as his mind turned to a certain young woman. At the same moment, thinking of Catherine made his heart sink and he felt hot all over.

***

The evening was cooler, even though the breeze was still warm, but it felt pleasant to Catherine when she opened all the windows in Arthur's study. She tried to gather her thoughts as she asked herself how she would face Arthur for the second night.

In the end, the answer appeared unexpectedly. She heard Kham's voice outside the room, and the agitated tone and broken English indicated that she was not talking to a fellow Siamese. She decided to open the door and froze when she saw Charlotte standing with her hands on her hips on the balcony, while Kham was trying to block her.

"What's going on?" Catherine blurted out.

Charlotte spun around. In the evening light, Catherine noticed that

Charlotte was not as attractive as she had appeared the previous night. Although she was young and shapely, her skin was coarse, her eyes were bloodshot, and there were dark shadows under her eyes.

"That's 'er…Mrs Lindley!" Charlotte cried angrily. "I've come to get my clothes, and she won't let me in!"

In truth, Catherine did not want to let her set foot in the house, but if she were to find Arthur out, she would need this woman's help.

"What clothes did you leave here? I'll have Kham bring them to you."

Charlotte's eyes twinkled.

"My underwear. It must be in the drawer next to Arthur's clothes."

"Come inside. Where is it?"

Charlotte was puzzled at her calm demeanour but walked over to the chest of drawers and knelt to open the bottom drawer. She pulled out a garment and held it up against herself.

"'ere it is! My corset! It's a nightmare in this weather, so I take it off at night. I wouldn't be without it mind…a girl needs a corset."

"May I ask you a question, Miss…"

"Palmer. Charlotte Palmer,' she said brightly.

"What's your relationship with Arthur?"

Charlotte's mouth dropped open. Then she grinned.

"My, you don't mince your words, do you? Your 'usband and I are good friends. There aren't many of us over 'ere, so we stick together. Arthur's been good to me. We often 'ave dinner together. 'e's never mentioned you. I didn't know 'e was married."

"And John Palmer?"

"Oh," she said nonchalantly. "'e's another friend of mine. 'e's going back to Singapore."

"And can you tell me, Miss Palmer," Catherine continued in a voice as cold as steel, "if you intend to contact Arthur again now that you know his wife is here?"

Charlotte Palmer's curiosity was aroused. She had faced other men's wives before, and none of them had been as collected as this woman.

She giggled again.

"If you're askin' me straight, then I'll tell you straight. It's up to Arthur. It's not up to me. But Arthur 'as money, and if 'e wants to

The Dilemma 79

share it with 'is friends, it's up to 'im."

If Charlotte was telling the truth, Arthur was not the man she had thought he was.

"Thank you, Miss Palmer. I have nothing more to say to you."

At that moment, she heard Arthur's voice shout, "What did you say?"

Kham must have told him about the visitor, and he stormed into the room, his face white as a sheet.

"Charlotte!" he bawled, grabbing hold of her arm. "I told you not to come here again!"

"Miss Palmer left her undergarment in you drawers, so she came to collect it."

Arthur froze and his face reddened with fury.

"You did this on purpose!" he barked.

Catherine walked out of the room. She did not want to witness the two of them arguing. Their dispute was trifling compared to the turmoil she felt. A moment later, everything went quiet, and Arthur came into his study where Catherine was sitting. He was silent for a while before blurting out, "I'm sorry..."

He wished Catherine would foam and rage or burst into tears. Anything would have been better than her cold reply.

"I know you're sorry, but it's too late now. Please don't mention it again until I've decided on a way out."

Arthur hung his head and muttered, "I've never wanted any other woman. Except you."

He changed the subject to ease the tension.

"We've had an invitation from the Second King of Siam. He's invited us to dinner at the palace tomorrow. Please don't refuse his invitation. Other matters can wait."

The heaviness she felt in her heart began to lighten as soon as she heard. Justin would be there for certain. He would find a way out for her, she was sure, even though she had no idea what he would do.

5

In the Shade of the Palace

King Pinklao, the Second King of Siam*, did not like to flaunt his power and only entered the Throne Hall for important ceremonies. Mostly he met with his nobles in the loft above the stables. Members of the royal family, however, would meet him in the Throne Hall. So, when Prince Vijjuprapha went to the Front Palace that evening, he met the king there.

From the first moment he entered the Front Palace, he felt as if an English house had been placed in the middle of the Siamese-style structures, but it did not look out of place. It was a two-storey house and the stairs outside led to a wide second floor balcony in front of several rooms.

The attendant who was waiting led him inside the king's study, which was next to the library. The English-style decor made Prince Vijjuprapha feel at home, but the ease he felt was replaced by reverence when he prostrated himself before the second most important person in the land.

Inside the room, there was no large entourage, but simply two attendants and Chao Chom Klee, who sat on a rug next to the king's desk with a woman behind her to attend to her.

She smiled warmly at him.

"Prince Saifa, let me look at you."

Prince Vijjuphrapa looked up and saw that, despite the several years that he had been away, King Pinklao had hardly changed at all.

---

* King Pinklao was known as the Second King or Vice-King of Siam.
He was the younger brother of King Mongkut, or Rama IV,
who crowned him as monarch with equal honour to himself.

81

He still appeared fit and strong and was as handsome as he had been in his youth; the expression in his eyes as he regarded his adoptive son remained as warm as ever.

"You've changed a lot. If I hadn't seen a picture of you in India, I wouldn't have recognised you. Klee..."

He turned to Khun Chom.

"Klee, do you recognise your son?"

Khun Chom looked up at the young man she had raised as her own son and supressed a smile, although her eyes sparkled with joy.

"I can hardly recognise him. When he went to India, he was just a boy. Now look at him. He's as tall as a foreigner, and his hair's cut like a foreigner, too."

Khun Chom had changed considerably as was normal for a woman approaching middle age. She had been a beautiful and shapely woman with radiant creamy skin, but now she had grown plump, although her cheerful countenance remained. When she was young, she had been one of the king's favourites, but sadly, she had been unable to bear him any children, so when one of the nobles gave his new-born son to the king, he gave the child to her.

"Are you happy now that your son's home? Your mother's been waiting for you these past few years."

Then he continued.

"I could only find one son for Klee, so when you left, she took in Chan Rachayotha's daughter to keep her company."

Chan Rachayotha was Phraya Rachayotha, whose name had been Chan, a nobleman who was now in charge of the Interior Ministry. Prince Vijjuprapha vaguely remembered his mother mentioning him.

"She takes her everywhere. When Bua gets married, will I have to find you another girl to keep you company?"

Khun Chom bowed her head and smiled.

At that moment, Prince Vijjuprapha noticed a young woman sitting quietly behind her. She raised her head slightly on hearing her name and her eyes met his.

The young ladies inside the palace were nothing like the villagers he had passed on the river, whose skin was tanned and who were as sturdy as the men. The women inside the palace were the beautiful daughters of the nobility who had been well taken care of and had never had to endure the harsh rays of the sun. Therefore, it did not surprise him that this young woman was as pretty and graceful as Khun Chom had been in her youth and could easily have been taken for her daughter. Her pretty red lips and smooth cheeks were as dainty as a statue, and when she looked up at him before quickly looking down again, her bright eyes sparkled like jewels. Below her neck, one smooth shoulder and slim arm was exposed, while the other side was covered by a long sash. Bua, the daughter of Phraya Rachayotha, was one of the most beautiful young women in the palace.

The king stood up from his chair and said, "I'm going to have dinner now. There's no need for you to follow. You stay and talk to your mother. You're a grown man now. You'll have many responsibilities. After you've talked to your mother and had something to eat, come and see me again tonight, and I'll ask you about what you've learned and assign you your duties."

* * *

When the three of them were alone together, Khun Chom Klee moved closer as if she wanted to caress him, but she refrained, remembering that there was a third person present, so she asked him tenderly, "You've been away for so long. Were you comfortable there, and was the food to your liking?"

Prince Vijjuprapha smiled.

"I liked the food, but I missed your cooking, Mother."

Khun Chom Klee's face lit up.

"Oh, really! Do you still remember my cooking? If there's anything you'd like, tell me and I'll have someone bring it to you."

"I like everything you cook. All the time I've been away I've only eaten Indian food and European food. I'm glad to be eating home cooking again."

"I've made something for you today," she said eagerly. "I'll have a servant bring it to you. Let's go downstairs and I'll keep you company. I haven't heard from you for so long. I've missed you."

She turned to the young woman.

"Come along, Bua. The past few years, I've had Bua to talk to. She's been keeping me company."

This was a subtle introduction to make sure that the young prince looked at the young woman again. Bua was silent and did not make eye contact with him according to her upbringing. She reminded Prince Vijjuprapha of a doll who wouldn't move unless Khun Chom Klee pulled her strings.

Downstairs was where the palace officials worked. All of them knew Khun Chom Klee and held her in high esteem. When they found out that she was cooking for her son, they busied themselves preparing the room for him with a rug, a small table, and a screen so he could eat his meal in privacy.

Khun Chom Klee asked him about his travels. Although she knew nothing about politics, she was astute enough to be aware of the affairs inside the palace, so she told him confidently, "Now you're back, the king will need you to liaise with foreigners. When foreign diplomats arrive, he meets with them. Their numbers are increasing every year, so I expect you'll have to work hard."

"I intend to work hard to repay his kindness to me."

"Good. And if there's anything I can help you with, tell me. Where do you plan to stay? Will you be with your father, or will you have your own house? Tell me and I'll have one built for you."

Khun Chom Klee had been wealthy since before she entered the palace, and now she good-naturedly called herself 'discharged from duty', although she was still held in high esteem.

"I've asked to build my house on the raft. My mother's having it repaired."

"Then I'll send some of my people to help, and I'll find furniture for you," she said sincerely. "You won't be second to anyone."

Then she chatted about other matters.

"You probably know that the king's keen on foreigners. He says we must learn their ways to survive, so inside the palace, we've all had to get used to foreign food."

The prince looked at her in surprise and amusement.

"You've been eating foreign food?"

84 A Passage to Siam

"Goodness!" she cried. "I can eat the angel hair that the Portuguese brought during the reign of King Narai, but I can't tolerate milk and butter. I'm too old to get used to that. But the young girls in the palace don't seem to mind it."

The prince laughed when he saw her glance at Bua as if to indicate that she was one of them. Bua bowed her head and suppressed a smile.

"They've been saying they want to learn to cook foreign food, and some of them want to speak foreign languages. The king says he'll let one of the missionary's wives teach them, but he hasn't found anyone yet."

"He wants the missionaries to teach in the palace?"

"It's already happening in King Mongkut's palace. The American consul's wife has been teaching the ladies inside."

"Do you mean she's teaching them how to cook?"

"Well, I don't expect they're training to be soldiers! You must have seen plenty of foreign ladies. Do they teach them to fight?"

"No," he smiled, but then he was silent.

His thoughts turned to a certain young woman whose blue eyes looked at him sadly for the last time before she climbed into the horse-drawn carriage with her husband.

Was Catherine still thinking of the young man who had held her in his arms when the storm had almost destroyed the boat?

Or now that they had both reached their destinations, would the storms of life tear them apart and cause them to go their separate ways?

***

King Pinklao did not go to bed as late as the previous king, but it was always past midnight by the time he retired. Before that, if he was not outside the palace, he was riding horses. But tonight, he returned earlier than usual to meet Prince Vijjuprapha in his study.

He asked him about his studies and the things he had seen in India and in England, concluding by saying, "I've set up palace guards from both the army and the navy. You trained in the army, so I'll put you in charge of the armoury. You'll know all about new weapons from abroad."

"Yes, sir."

"Now that they've arrived on our shores, the king believes the only way is to forge friendships. If we use force, they'll destroy our forces with their guns and colonise us. If we want to know what they're up to, we need to befriend them so we can keep an eye on them. That's why I want you to be a mediator and make friends with the English. The missionaries are from America. We'll let them teach their religion. We mustn't threaten them, or there'll be trouble."

After informing him of the details, he concluded, "You must keep everything I'm telling you secret. Don't even tell your parents or siblings. Your father gave you to me, so I consider you as my son. Remember that whatever you do, you're using my name. Whether you do good or bad will reflect on me."

***

Arthur was waiting for Catherine to finish dressing for dinner at the palace.She looked fresh and lovely in her prettiest summer outfit. It was a pale pink cotton dress with white roses on it, and her flaxen hair was swept up at the back with ringlets falling at her long neck. Her radiance and innocence were a complete contrast to Charlotte's coarseness. Tenderness mixed with remorse filled his heart.

He handed her the thing he had been holding. It was a white lace parasol, much daintier than the small black one that she owned.

Catherine looked at it and glanced at him questioningly.

"It's a gift I kept for you when you arrived," he explained gently. "To protect you from Siam's scorching sun."

She should have thanked him, but by now, everything he did aroused her suspicion, especially after he had lied about Charlotte.

The words that came out instead of expressing thanks were, "Where did you get it?"

"I bought it in Singapore."

It was clear that Arthur was trying to make it up to her, but all she could say was to mutter, "Thank you."

This was enough to make him heave a sigh of relief. He did not know that in the small cloth bag she held, there was a letter to Justin folded into a tiny square.

She was waiting to give it to the man to whom she realised her heart belonged.

* * *

Captain Knox sat in a separate horse-drawn carriage to Colonel Rowland and Mary, but his Siamese wife did not join him.

Knox was a man of refined manners with a cut-glass accent, but Catherine felt that he was aloof compared to Arthur and Colonel Rowland. He was not the consul, but since the consul, C.B. Hillier, had been called to Singapore, Knox had temporarily been assigned as acting consul.

Colonel Rowland and Mary stepped out of the carriage at almost the same time as Captain Knox. Mary wore a dark blue taffeta gown with a silk rose in her hair. She felt a twinge of envy when she saw Catherine step down from the carriage and noticed her willowy frame and tiny waist.

She turned to Arthur and saw him gazing tenderly at his wife as he helped her down from the carriage, while Catherine hardly looked at him and lightly brushed his hand with her fingertips before stepping down unaided.

Catherine forgot about Arthur for a moment as she gazed excitedly at the Siamese-style structures that she had never seen before. Everything looked more remarkable than in a fairy-tale – from the elephant stalls to the Western-style house that was glowing with lanterns. She could see people, whom she assumed were the Second King of Siam's attendants, standing in a line to welcome them. Her heart beat faster when she saw a man step out in front as if he was coming to greet them. But she was disappointed when the lamplight illuminated his face and revealed that it wasn't Justin as she had thought.

He was a polite young man, who appeared confident as if he was used to meeting foreign guests.

"My name's Captain Dick. I'm the king's attendant. Welcome ladies and gentlemen."

Catherine had forgotten that when Justin arrived in Siam, his status was higher than when he had lived as a commoner in India and

England, so he did not come out of the Throne Hall to greet them but was standing behind King Pinklao.

The room below the Throne Hall was tastefully decorated with Western-style furnishings that made Catherine feel as if she was in an aristocratic Englishman's home. Except when she looked up at the ceiling, she noticed a large fan.

A bell was sounded, and everyone was quiet. When the door opened, King Pinklao stepped into the room, followed by several men.

Catherine fixed her eyes on the person walking behind him, and her heart suddenly began to race.

It was Justin! He was still the same Justin as before. Tonight, he was not dressed like the other Siamese nobles, but was wearing a dinner jacket like he had worn on the boat. Suddenly, their eyes were pulled towards each other as if by a magnetic force.

His eyes met hers for a moment before he looked past her composedly so that no one would be suspicious, but Catherine could discern the tenderness and longing in his black eyes, and she knew that nothing had changed.

Prince Vijjuprapha had to force himself to maintain his composure when he noticed the fair-haired young woman in the pale pink dress that made her appear as lovely as a rose. It was not just her beauty that captivated him, but the sparkle in her luminous blue eyes, her radiant smile, and the dignified way that she carried herself. The more he looked on these things, the more he sensed the vitality pulsating through her veins.

Catherine's zest for life and her eagerness to experience all that life had to offer, whether good or bad, meant that nothing could dampen her spirits, and her every glance and movement communicated the energy that bubbled up inside her. Catherine made everyone else in the room become nothing more than dim shadows, devoid of meaning. The graceful way that she curtsied was flawless, and she caught the eye of everyone in the room, but the attention did not faze her, and she maintained her calm and composure.

'If only she were my wife…' the prince thought to himself.

And his heart sank.

***

The Western-style dinner was impeccable. The silver candlesticks and tableware sparkled, and the candles flickered in the breeze from the fan. The fresh flowers that decorated the table were all new to Catherine as were the fruits arranged on a silver platter. Arranging the seating plan had not been difficult when the person in charge of organising the dinner was Prince Vijjuprapha himself. So Catherine found herself seated next to him – the man who was constantly in her thoughts. There were only six people seated at the table, with the Second King of Siam at the head, and besides Justin, there were no other Siamese nobles present.

A Siamese gamelan played throughout the meal with the musicians in the next room, but the music wafted on the air.

The meal was American-style rather than English, but the soup and the main course were tasty, and Catherine assumed the chef must have been American.

When she asked Justin, he laughed.

"There are no American chefs in Siam. The chef learned to cook from American missionaries, but perhaps he'll start making English dishes soon."

"Do you mean you've found someone from England to teach him?"

"I mean my attendant. Won's a very good cook. When we were in India, he used to cook for the English officers."

Won had kept himself to himself for the entire journey, but she had thanked him several times when he had assisted her in various ways, although she had never had the opportunity to talk to him any more than that.

"I expect you'll like the fruits. There are many kinds you won't have tried before, and crystalised fruits, too."

They talked about small matters of no significance, since neither of them could speak their true feelings because everyone else at the table would have heard.

But Catherine knew their hearts were intertwined. She could tell that they both knew from the tone of the other's voice and the expression in their eyes that there was as much meaning between

In the Shade of the Palace   89

them as before. It was a bittersweet feeling that brought both bliss and torment.

As everyone stood up from the table, Catherine took advantage of the opportunity to take the folded piece of paper from her bag and slip it into Justin's hand unnoticed.

Justin, my love,

I hope this letter finds you without anyone else seeing, so that you know what I'm facing and might be able to help.

First, I must tell you something that I've never told anyone else. No one except Arthur and myself, my mother and my sister know that, after we were married in church, our marriage was never consummated because I had measles and Arthur had to leave for Siam right away. He asked me to join him later, and you know what happened after that.

All the time that Arthur and I were apart made me realise that I've never loved him. I married him because I wanted to escape the monotony of my life. Women have no chance of choosing a new way of life unless they marry. And whatever Arthur's reason was for marrying me, it wasn't love because, when I arrived in Bangkok, I found another woman had been living with him in his house.

My marriage to Arthur is over. Even though we are not divorced, I have no desire to live with him anymore. We are two strangers living under the same roof.

I have no one else to turn to. You are the only one who can show me a way out. Please help me, but it must be kept secret.

I shall wait for you with hope.

Catherine

***

King Pinklao went to bed late as did many of the Siamese nobles at that time. If he was not visiting the city, his attendants knew that, after dinner, he liked to go to his study by himself, or with only two or three attendants.

Prince Vijjuprapha had the special privilege of being allowed to meet the king without an invitation, and since he had arrived back in Siam, he had met the king every day because the king had many matters to discuss with him.

The attendant on duty that night led him into the king's study. King Pinklao was sitting alone at his desk with Suriyawut in attendance. When he saw the prince, he smiled.

"I was just thinking about you...And here you are. I have something to tell you."

Prince Vijjuprapha prostrated himself before the king.

"Now that you're back, I was going to have you to train the palace guards, but now we have both Knox and Lindley, you might be treading on their toes, so I'd like you to be my private secretary until Lindley goes home. Then I'll give you his job."

Prince Vijjuprapha started.

"Is he going home soon, Your Majesty?"

"He agreed to stay for three years, and extend his contract after that, but after just a few months, he became sick with a fever, so I don't expect he'll remain for longer than three years."

Three years...By then, we should know about us.

"In the meantime, I want you to forge friendships with these two men. I'm counting on you because you've been associating with the British soldiers for years. I'm sure you're aware that our neighbours have all been colonised by European powers, so we need to know what they're up to. That way we won't let our guard down."

The words 'forge friendships with these two men' sent an inexplicable chill down his spine. The truth was that he could not tell the king how difficult forging a friendship with that officer would be when he was in love with his wife. But the more pressing problem was how he would free Catherine from her husband as soon as possible. If Arthur would agree to divorce her, even though it would not be easy for a Siamese prince to take an English wife, it would not be impossible.

Prince Vijjuprapha decided to ask for the king's help.

"I've been thinking. Perhaps Lieutenant Lindley would allow Mrs Lindley to teach in the palace. She could teach English, embroidery, and cooking to the women."

The king was surprised, since he had not mentioned anything about the English woman, but after a moment's consideration, he agreed.

"Good idea. But only if Mrs Lindley wants to do it. We mustn't force her."

"I'll go and ask Mrs Lindley.."

"It would be better to write to her. Then if she doesn't want to, she can let you know in writing to avoid embarrassment. If she accepts, you can talk to her then."

The king could not possibly know that, for the past few nights, she had never left the prince's thoughts.

"I want them to learn about foreign ways. Your mother says she doesn't like foreign food, but she makes Bua cook it and eat it. Perhaps she's trying to please you…"

When he hinted about the pretty young woman, he noticed that the prince remained indifferent. Perhaps he had not yet warmed to her.But whether he liked her or not was irrelevant. Chao Chom Klee had chosen the charming young woman as his wife.

***

Mary had invited Arthur and Catherine to tea, but Catherine declined with a short note.

'I'm sorry I can't come. I've arranged to visit the temples. Kham is going to take me in a boat. I'll tell you all about it.'

Although Arthur was not keen to let Catherine travel alone in Bangkok, he knew that trying to stop her would be futile, so he told her, "It's up to you. I'll have a male servant go with you and Kham. It isn't safe for two women to travel alone."

And he went to see Mary by himself. Arthur was utterly confused. He had been angry, upset, and disappointed, but now he was simply at a loss and had no idea what to do.

"Catherine wants us to separate…She's asked for a divorce."

When Arthur saw Mary's sympathetic expression, he did not hold back his feelings.

"You know, don't you? Catherine must have told you."

Mary was astute enough to remain neutral.

"I'm her cousin. Who else can she talk to? But I told her not to be impulsive."

"She's not being impulsive. She's waiting for Consul Hillier to return, and she's going to file for divorce. What am I to do?"

Mary gazed at him, concealing what she knew because, deep down, she had her cousin's best interests at heart and felt that the sooner Catherine realized the error of her ways, the better it would be for everyone.

Mary poured herself some more tea thoughtfully.

"I don't want to see Catherine get divorced. People will sympathise with a woman whose husband abandons her, but no one will support a woman who divorces her husband."

* * *

If Arthur had known that, while he was sharing his troubles with Mary, the woman whom they both considered to be in the wrong was taking in the sights without giving him a second thought, he would have been even more discouraged.

Catherine held up her old black umbrella to protect herself from the scorching sun as she sat in the boat with Kham, while an old but muscular man stood rowing the boat. The black umbrella was more effective at blocking the sun's rays than Arthur's white lace parasol, but the perspiration still seeped through her thin white blouse. Fortunately, she had packed her crinoline in her trunk as soon as she had arrived in Bangkok and wore only a white muslin petticoat under her skirt.

Catherine enjoyed going outside, regardless of the heat and was eager to sit in a boat to go through the small canals, which were all connected like a large spider's web. It was nothing like the placid River Thames, which ran through the village of Longstock. The Bangkok canals were full of life with the small boats that went up and down them as if on the busy roads of a big city. The boats in Bangkok were used for both transportation and living, and Catherine looked on in fascination.

She noticed mothers nursing their babies at the helms of the boats, while their other children jumped in the water and swam around. Both the boys and girls were naked without thinking it strange at all, but the thing that was curious to them was the light-skinned woman with blonde hair. No matter where she went, children came out to look

In the Shade of the Palace 93

at her squealing and pointing, and even the adults came out to peek.

She turned to the small houses on each side of the canal. There were no brick houses, and all were made of bamboo and set upon stilts unlike the houses on the rafts, which floated on the surface of the water in harmony with the green foliage all around.

"Kham," she asked, noticing her signalling the rower to head out to the mouth of the canal. "Where are you taking me?"

"To other side," she said, pointing to the river. "We go across river. I show you temple, Mem."

The most beautiful sight in Catherine's eyes was when they came out of the canal into the Chao Phraya River. It was wide and sparkling in the rays of the setting sun, making the boats that sailed up and down appear like little toys. And the most magnificent part was the temple and the palace on the riverbank. She could see the tip of the pagoda glittering like gold in the sunlight surrounded by a fence and small turrets, where many rafts were moored together at the water's edge.

Kham took her to the other side, which had been the site of Siam's former capital of Thonburi. The rafts were just as dense as on the banks of the capital, set amid green vegetation more abundant than on the Bangkok side, and they appeared to be larger. There were several temples, both next to the river and further back, and Catherine could distinguish them from the simple homes by their exquisitely decorated chapel roofs.

Kham instructed the rower to go deeper inside a large canal. The evening sun was setting, and the river breeze was refreshingly cool.

"Be careful, Mem," Kham warned her anxiously as the boat stopped at the pier, and she turned to the rower and said, "Mem's skirt's so long, I'm scared she'll fall in the water."

Catherine climbed up the wooden steps to the pavilion that opened onto the temple's sand-covered courtyard. There were several large trees providing shade, and it was so quiet she could hear the birds chirping and the small dogs that ran around yapping.

She turned to look around and wondered why Kham had brought her here so confidently. Catherine saw her walking quickly ahead of her, and she had no choice but to follow in confusion. Instead of taking her to see the chapel, she walked around the side of the temple and

94   A Passage to Siam

with every step the further away they seemed to be getting until they had almost entered what appeared to be a forest.

Kham quickened her pace until Catherine asked, "Kham, where are you going?"

"Wait there, Mem."

"Justin…" she said softly.

A smile spread across his face, and he held out his hands to clasp hers. "I came to wait for you," he said. "I thought you wouldn't make it."

"To wait for me?" Catherine repeated in confusion, leaving her hands in his. "How did you know I'd be here?"

He grinned.

"Won," he said, referring to his trusted attendant. "He's good at making friends, especially with women. And that includes your maid."

No wonder Kham had been so eager to bring her here. By then, she had made herself scarce and would appear again when it was time to take Catherine home.

"Let's not waste time here. We don't have long. I don't want us to draw attention. Won and Kham might not be able to keep everyone away."

It was true. She was conspicuous, while Justin blended in dressed in his Siamese noble's attire, and she almost didn't recognize him until he smiled and looked at her with the same expression that she remembered.

"Catherine," he said softly. "You don't know how happy your letter made me, after I 'd almost lost hope."

The temple grounds had some areas without any people, including another sand-covered courtyard shaded by large banyan trees, where Catherine sat on the ground while Justin stood in front of her.

"I have good news," he said.

The good news lifted her spirits. She could stay in Siam, she would not have to stay with Arthur, and most importantly, she would see Justin.

"I knew you'd help me."

Justin smiled at her, seeing her cheeks were flushed and her blue eyes were shining with happiness.

"It's due to the king's help."

"I'm so thankful," Catherine said. "You don't know how confused

In the Shade of the Palace 95

I've been. Mary and Colonel Rowland couldn't help at all."

She told Justin what Mary had said, and he sighed.

"I don't expect Mrs Rowland can see any other way."

"Do you agree with her?"

"No," he said at once. "You and Lindley are finished, but the problem is how you'll be able to stay in Bangkok by yourself. You'll be safe in the palace. Lindley won't dare to intimidate you there."

"Does the king know about us?"

As soon as she'd said it, she felt embarrassed.

Justin had never said that he loved her.

"I haven't told him about us yet," he said sensing her awkwardness. "It isn't the right time yet."

Catherine's excitement faded as a tense expression clouded his face.

"What did Lindley say? Has he agreed to divorce you?"

"No," she replied softly. "If necessary, I'll file for divorce with the consul, but hopefully it won't come to that. Arthur doesn't understand. He thinks I'll change my mind."

"And will you change your mind?"

A hurt expression flickered across her face, and Justin sat down on the ground next to her and brought her hands to his lips.

"I'm sorry. I shouldn't have said that. If I know you feel the same way, it's enough."

"When can I come to the palace?" she asked brightly.

"Is tomorrow too soon? Captain Dick's going to come to see you and Arthur about it tonight. I can't go myself. You understand, don't you?"

Catherine squeezed his hand gently.

"How are you going to get Lindley to allow you to go to the palace because you'll have to stay there. You won't be able to go home in the evenings. He has the right to stop you."

"If I have to, I'll tell him we should separate for a while," she said thoughtfully, "until I've decided what to do."

"Be careful. Don't do anything to upset him. If he thinks you might go back to him, he'll be willing to compromise, but if he thinks he's lost you, he might try to hurt you and I won't be there to protect you."

96 A Passage to Siam

***

Luang Surawiset had someone send a letter to Arthur, telling him of his visit that evening.

Few Siamese nobles spoke English, but Luang Surawiset, or Captain Dick as he was known by foreigners, came by to talk with him often, and Arthur had always found him agreeable. Consequently, when his guest explained that an English woman was being sought to teach the ladies inside the palace, Arthur did not consider it to be a troublesome request. The difficulty, he feared, was whether Catherine would agree to it or not.

"It's an honour," he said, "that the Second King of Siam would like my wife to teach in the palace, but I'll have to ask her first if she'll be able to do it or not, Captain Dick. I hope you understand."

Luang Surawiset smiled calmly.

"If you'll allow me to explain the situation to Mrs Lindley, I expect it will be easier for her to decide."

Catherine walked inside her husband's study with composure.

She answered Khun Luang politely, "It would be an honour. If I can be of use to the people of Siam while I'm here, I'd be glad to do it," before adding, "if Arthur will allow it."

Arthur was divided. On the one hand, he did not want Catherine to serve in the palace instead of staying at home with him. But on the other hand, he thought that compromising with her when their relationship was at breaking point would be a way out of the difficulty while he decided what to do.

So he replied, "It's up to you, darling. If you want to go, I won't stop you."

Catherine almost let out a sigh of relief.

***

Arthur went to see Colonel Rowland after work the next evening since he didn't know where else to go and didn't want to go home to an empty house.

Colonel Rowland planned to travel to Kanchanaburi in the

western part of Siam in the next few days. It was to be a *'study tour'* as he had just told an important nobleman by the name of Phraya Sri Suriyawongse the previous day. He was to travel with his Siamese attendant and a guide. There were to be no soldiers, no weapons, and no cause for alarm.

Phraya Sri Suriyawongse was close to Lieutenant Lindley, since he was one of the few Thai noblemen who spoke English well, even though he did not write it fluently. He came from one of the most important noble families in Siam, and his ancestors had all held important positions in the palace.

When they first met, Colonel Rowland couldn't help noticing that the modern and intelligent man with the penetrating eyes was regarding him thoughtfully as Captain Knox asked if Colonel Rowland might have permission to visit Kanchanaburi.

Phraya Sri Suriyawongse replied in English, "In the forests of Kanchanaburi, malaria is common. If you don't know the way, it could be deadly for you. I don't understand why the colonel wants to go there. If he wants to see wild animals, he can see them outside the city gates."

Beneath his friendly and polite demeanour, the nobleman sensed an ominous undercurrent between the two countries. Colonel Rowland knew that, since the previous reign, the king and the nobility had been wary of British ambitions to colonise Siam as they had done Burma, while the ordinary folk knew nothing of it.

Phraya Sri Suriyawongse was aware that on the far side of Kanchanaburi lay the border between Siam and Burma, and that if they were to attack, British forces would be able to enter by boat or on land especially if this British officer were to survey the route. For this reason, Phraya Sri Suriyawongse did not accede easily until Captain Knox interceded for his countryman by assuring him that the trip was purely recreational and that only a servant and a guide would be necessary. In the end, he agreed.

"If the colonel wants to go, I will not stop him, but let one of my men go with him."

That would mean that one of this nobleman's men would report everything to him. Colonel Rowland had no other option except to agree.

He and Arthur had discussed the matter, and Arthur had concluded,

"Siam has no modern weapons and it's too small to protect itself. Faced with our battleships, they'll be soon subdued."

"But we have no reason to close off the Gulf of Siam," Knox remarked.

"Oh, that won't be difficult," said Arthur excitedly. "All we must do is force them to open it up some more. Look at the French. They claim they want to trade, and the Siamese always give in to them."

Colonel Rowland was confident that Siam's days as a free country were numbered as a small tree must yield to the shadow of a bigger tree. The question was which large tree would win the contest. He agreed to travel to Kanchanaburi to survey the land and draw up a map, believing that it would be useful in the days ahead.

* * *

Arthur's anxiety was of no consequence to Catherine.

She was full of excitement from the moment Luang Surawiset, or Captain Dick, came to meet her at the palace gate.

Captain Dick explained, "I can only take you as far as the door. No men are allowed inside the Inner Court. Klon will take you inside to meet Khun Chom Klee at your house."

The door lead inside the Inner Court, where the royal consorts, princesses, and young princes lived. The buildings were mostly wooden, with only a few built of bricks and mortar, and it was shaded by many large trees.

Klon, a sturdy dark-skinned woman, led Catherine to a large wooden villa with a Thai-style roof and stairs leading to a wide veranda shaded by large trees with pale yellow flowers whose heady scent was carried on the breeze.

Khun Chom Klee was not waiting to meet her as Catherine had expected, but instead there were several teenage girls giggling excitedly as they peered at Catherine out of the windows and from behind pillars. Nobody came out to greet her, and Catherine stood awkwardly on the veranda. She could see no sign of a chair and wondered how she would sit down. Then one of the girls walked towards her, followed by another with a fresh face and a cheerful countenance.

It was the first time that Catherine met Bua.

In the Shade of the Palace 99

6

Bua

Bua was a beautiful young woman, confirming for Catherine that a woman's beauty was not determined by her race, and that a woman who had grown up on the other side of the world could be as lovely as any English rose.

She was small, typical of a Siamese woman, and could not have been more than five feet tall, but she was shapely and in proportion. Her butterscotch skin was as smooth as silk, and even though her hair was cropped short like a boy, her oval face was too pretty to have belonged to a boy. Her dark brown eyes sparkled, and her red lips smiled shyly when she spoke some words to Catherine that she did not understand.

It was a pity her teeth were stained black like most other Siamese, Catherine thought. If they had been white, she would have been even prettier. She turned to the other fresh-faced young woman who was also very charming, although less so than the first. Her features were sharper, her skin was a little darker and she bore a striking resemblance to Justin. The second girl was bolder than the first and she spoke brightly behind giggles.

'Oh, dear! I've forgotten everything my brother taught me! How will Mem know where to sit?"

Catherine realised that communication would not be easy as she could see that none of the women here spoke any English. The girl who looked like Justin was quicker than the other.

When she spoke and Catherine didn't understand, she laughed guilelessly and took her by the hand to lead her to the sitting room, which was walled on three sides with one side open and was raised above the ground with polished wooden floorboards. The two young women sat down on the floor with their legs to the side as if signalling Catherine to do the same. She looked at their way of sitting, puzzled, having never sat on the floor and having always thought that the floor was for feet. When she had seen Kham and the other servants in Arthur's house crawling on the floor, she had never once thought that she would be expected to do the same inside the palace.

Catherine tried to remember the Siamese word for 'no' that Justin had taught her.

"*Mai,*" she said awkwardly.

Bua looked confused before supressing a smile when she guessed that Catherine didn't want to sit on the floor.

"Bua," Princess Kanika whispered. "Mem won't sit on the floor. We'll have to bring her a chair like my brother said."

Bua looked uneasy because earlier Prince Vijjuprapha, or 'Prince Saifa' as they called him in the palace, had insisted that they brought a chair for the Englishwoman, but Khun Chom Klee had made them take it back.

"I can't sit on a chair. It gives me cramp."

Khun Chom was not in, since she had gone to visit another Khun Chom, so she had assigned Bua, her adopted daughter, to greet the Englishwoman, and Bua was hesitant.

When Princess Kanika reminded her of what they had been told to do, even though she could not imagine why the Englishwoman refused to sit on the floor, Bua saw no other way except to comply. A moment later, several servants brought some chairs, but Catherine felt awkward when she found that she was the only one sitting on a chair, while the other two women sat on the floor.

She motioned for them to sit on chairs, not wanting to be the only one on a chair, and at that moment, became fully aware of the gulf between Siamese and English customs.

* * *

The next thing Catherine learned was that the word 'time', or to be precise 'appointment time', held no meaning for the Siamese. She couldn't help thinking to herself in amusement that time in Siam was as fluid as the water that flowed in the Bangkok canals. For one thing, it moved so slowly it was almost stagnant, and for another, there was so much of it that it could be used extravagantly and never run out.

The Siamese used their time leisurely and were never in a hurry. They considered it perfectly natural to wait for lengthy periods, and to spend extended lengths of time on small tasks. Catherine learned this when she had to wait several hours for Khun Chom Klee, and it was afternoon by the time she returned from visiting her friend.

Fortunately, Catherine decided to use the time fruitfully by trying to communicate with the girls, rather than sitting there smiling awkwardly at them. They began by teaching each other the names of the items around them in English and Siamese.

kao ee = a chair *na tang* = windows
sua kraprong = a dress *rom* = an umbrella

They pronounced the words falteringly, but fortunately, Catherine could remember some of the words that Justin had taught her.

Bua was shy compared to Princess Kanika, who seemed more eager at first, but after a while Bua showed no less enthusiasm in her desire to learn. The tension gradually eased and was replaced by giggles as one by one the other girls came to join Bua and Princess Kanika

By midday, Catherine was hungry, but she didn't like to say anything because Khun Chom had still not returned.

Bua noticed it was almost noon and whispered to the others, "We should bring something for Mem to eat."

"I've heard that foreigners don't eat the same things as us. They don't like shrimp paste or fish sauce," one of them said.

"Then leave out the shrimp paste and fish sauce, and don't bring her anything spicy," Bua suggested. "I'll go and see what I can find."

She quietly crawled out of the room and half an hour later a servant brought in a tray of food. The only Western dish that Bua could think of was soup, although it was more of a broth. There was also a glass of goats' milk, although Catherine had no idea where she had found it.

The soup was not bad, but Catherine had to drink it because there was no spoon to eat it with. The goats' milk was palatable, even though it tasted different from cows' milk. But the uncomfortable thing was that she had to eat her meal alone watched by several pairs of eyes. Nonetheless, those eyes were friendly. The Siamese regarded the strange ways of foreigners with amusement rather than with derision or hostility.

That afternoon, Khun Chom Klee returned.

The woman, whom Justin had told her was his adoptive mother, saw no need to apologise for making Catherine wait, since the young woman was less senior. Indeed, she was young enough to have been her daughter.

Khun Chom Klee was reluctantly forced to sit on a chair, since it would have been improper for her to sit on the floor while Catherine sat on a chair because Catherine's head would have been higher than hers. But once she had sat on a chair, she had no idea what to say, so she called on Bua.

"Bua, go and get the letter that Prince Saifa sent. It's in my bedroom."

Justin had written the letter in English and put it in a sealed envelope in case it found its way into someone else's hands. And as an extra precaution, he had addressed Catherine with formality to prevent her from getting into trouble.

Madam,

Khun Chom Klee asked me to tell you she is honoured that you have come to visit her. If you are willing to teach the ladies of the Inner Court, she will be glad to provide a house for you, so that you can teach English, embroidery, and cooking without being disturbed by outsiders.

I apologise for being unable to contact you directly. I am occupied with repairing a temple in Bangkok Noi Canal in accordance with my father's wishes, and I must go there every Tuesday. Luang Surawiset will contact you on my behalf.

The Second King of Siam has kindly offered to recompense you for your services, so I would like to offer you the sum of fifty pounds a month for your consideration.

Yours sincerely,
Prince Vijjuprapha

Catherine folded the letter neatly and put it back inside the envelope as her heart raced with excitement. Justin had let her know that she could meet him at the temple next to the canal where they had met before. As for the pay, when she considered that a governess's salary in London would have been no more than five hundred pounds a year, six hundred pounds was incredibly good, and would enable her to support herself without having to depend on Arthur.

The letter that Catherine gave to Captain Dick to pass on to Arthur, contained a short message in neat handwriting as if she wanted to be sure that he would understand every word clearly.

Dear Arthur,
I have decided to take up the position inside the palace. Since I need to get ready, I would like to remain at Khun Chom Klee's house for the time being, and for Captain Dick to bring my trunk of clothes for me.
Please don't worry about me. I'm fine.
Catherine

She had not signed her name 'Lindley'! Arthur inadvertently clenched the letter in his fists, feeling both angry and hurt. After a long pause, he remembered that Luang Surawiset was still there in his study, and was looking at him waiting for an answer, so he forced a smile.

"I'm sorry, Captain. I…"

"Mrs Lindley has asked me to bring her trunk of clothes to the Front Palace. I told her I'd be glad to."

If he refused to allow her to stay overnight at the palace, the difficulties between them would have been evident to an outsider. At least, he thought, within the Inner Court of the palace, she would have no contact with men.

"Thank you on behalf of my wife," he replied flatly.

Prince Vijjuprapha sat with his sister on on the wide veranda of his splendid new house, which had been a gift from King Pinklao. Perched elegantly on the raft, the house had been crafted from rich golden teak and had a steep tiled roof edged with exquisitely carved wooden gables.

The sun had set, and the full moon was shining against the deep purple sky. The old city across the river was dark except for the glittering lamps of the floating houses on the Chao Phraya River. On the side of the capital, the Front Palace wall was a striking sight, which was visible from the house on the raft not far away.

Even though he could not see her, he was comforted to know that Catherine was behind the wall in a small house further back from Khun Chom Klee's villa. Princess Kanika brought him the news excitedly, unaware of what was really happening.

"Mem's as pretty as your doll."

The porcelain doll she was referring to had been brought back from London. When she saw Catherine, she was excited.

"Tell me about her."

She eagerly told him of how Catherine had taught English to her and Bua, of her flaxen hair and blue eyes, of how white her teeth were, and of the strange clothes she wore, concluding, "She's like a doll, but she's real."

"Do you like her?"

"I like her a lot."

Her brother smiled and asked playfully, "Would you like her to come and live with us?"

"No."

"Why not?"

She tried to think of an explanation before replying, "Because Mem's a mem. How can she live with us? She must live with her own people."

Seeing her brother was waiting for further explanation, she added, "Like I live with Bua and Choei and Chan. I like to learn with her, but I don't want to live with her. You're not going to send me to live with her, are you?"

At that moment, Prince Vijjuprapha suddenly became aware of the gulf that existed between East and West. Even if it wasn't an issue now, it could become one later if Catherine became his wife.

"If you get to know Catherine better, you'll be able to speak English, and bake cakes, and do embroidery better than anyone else."

"I'm afraid…"

"You're not even afraid of Mother. Why are you afraid of the pretty mem?"

She smiled and said, "Bua said she's not afraid of Mem because she's pretty. Bua wants to learn to cook Western food."

When he heard the name Bua, he recalled the attractive young woman he had seen sitting still and silent. She was indeed lovely but was as lifeless as a doll, he thought.

"Is Bua Mother's favourite?"

"That's what they say. When you went to India, Aunt took her in. Her father gave her away. She's betrothed to...oops!"

Her brother could guess the rest. He couldn't say it surprised him since arranged marriages were the norm. Bua was the daughter of an important nobleman in King Pinklao's Front Palace. She had been raised inside the palace and it was only natural that she would be expected to marry a prince.

"Tell me the rest."

"I can't. I'll get into trouble with Aunt and Mother."

This made it clear. Princess Kanika smiled and refused to divulge any more. A moment later, she returned to her father's palace, leaving her brother alone on the raft with his thoughts. He leaned against the rails and looked at the ripples on the surface of the river glimmering in the moonlight.

At least there was no immediate hurry for him to be married because he had still not been ordained as a Buddhist monk, but he would not be able to put it off for much longer.

Bua would have the status of his principal wife and, even if he had other wives, they would not be equal to her in status. And what about Catherine? Would she accept being one of several wives, even if she were his favourite?

He knew it was impossible. Monogamous marriages were customary for English men and women, and a third party was considered adultery, as Catherine had believed when she found Arthur with Charlotte. How could she accept another woman, or perhaps several, to come between her and Justin? That being the case, Catherine would be his only wife as soon as she had divorced her husband, he decided.

***

The house that Khun Chom Klee had arranged for her had one room with a bed and a small table with a basin and a white porcelain jug. Catherine relaxed when her trunk of clothes arrived, and the first night she slept peacefully because she was not woken up in alarm by

Arthur pacing up and down in the next room.

Even better, when she awoke the next morning, she saw Kham.

"Kham! How did you get here?" she asked happily.

Kham smiled and answered in broken English, "Lieutenant send me."

She didn't know if Arthur was being kind, or if he had sent Kham to spy on her, but nevertheless, Kham would be useful for contacting Justin through his attendant. Catherine smiled at her.

"There are some things I need. I'll write a letter for you to take to Won, the prince's attendant."

Kham blushed when she heard the young man's name and her eyes sparkled.

"Yes, Mem."

She continued to explain in broken English, "He wait at door in afternoon. He send boat for you."

Catherine smiled gratefully.

"Thank you. I'll be busy for the next few days. Ask Won to send a boat to collect me on Tuesday."

* * *

Life inside the Front Palace was not extravagant. From the decor to the clothes that the inhabitants wore, everything was simple. Catherine couldn't help thinking that even the home of Arthur's brother Alfred was more luxurious than Khun Chom Klee's villa.

Only the Throne Hall and the temple were magnificent Siamese-style structures unlike those anywhere else in the world, and Catherine thought it was a shame that an Englishwoman like herself would never have an opportunity to go inside.

However, even though it was not opulent, she was comfortable because of the abundance of labour. Everything was completed by the servants inside the palace, from cleaning, laundry and cooking to making the beds, and this labour was also provided for Catherine since she was a special guest. Although Khun Chom Klee had a relaxed attitude towards time, she was strict about not allowing Catherine to do any chores herself, other than the duties she had been assigned.

Bua 107

And her duties did not include anything more than trying to communicate as she had done on the first day. Arithmetic was not necessary, since the Siamese were as good at it as the English, and art and music was not something that these girls understood. All that remained was to teach them about foreign foods, and some needlework.

Catherine wrote in her journal:

The difficult thing about cooking is that milk smells bad to the Siamese, so if I teach them to cook with cream or cheese, one of them might faint.

But they do not mind the strong smell of fish, since their rivers and canals are full of them. Even worse than the smell of fresh fish is the smell of fermented fish, which they don't mind at all, but I can't abide it.

But the good news is that I was able to teach them to make lemon pie without anyone fainting and some of them found it quite delicious.

They are familiar with some deserts that were brought by Portuguese traders several hundred years ago.

Siamese women are illiterate, even the women inside the palace. This is because the Siamese are afraid it would be a way for them to communicate with men, and communication between the sexes before marriage is strictly forbidden, particularly among noblewomen. For that reason, I am not allowed to teach them to read, and can only teach them to speak.

It is a shame. I had hoped to have time to read them some poetry.

Fortunately, they are keen to do needlework. Otherwise, I would have no idea what to teach them.

Catherine had brought some of her needlework with her, such as embroidered white linen pillowcases, broderie anglaise, lace-trimmed handkerchiefs, and small crocheted dressing-table cloths.

The Siamese girls were excited with the needlework that Catherine showed them, and their black eyes sparkled when they held them carefully in their small hands as if they thought they were something precious and were afraid they would rip.

"I'll teach you how to do it," Catherine said brightly.

At least the needlework lessons were a success after her stalled attempts at teaching them other things. Of all her students, Catherine found that the one she got along best with, instead of being the lively princess whom she discovered was Justin's sister, was the pretty young woman named Bua. Bua was quiet and shy at first, but once they got to know each other, she proved to be quicker at learning than the others, including Princess Kanika.

She succeeded in communicating with Catherine by using Kham as an intermediary and learned how to cook and do needlework, as well as gradually beginning to pick up English words and phrases.

"What do you like, Mem? Tell me and I'll make it for you," she offered generously.

When she had finished making a lace border, she stayed up making a long strip of lace for Catherine as a gift, smiling shyly with pride when Catherine thanked her for it.

"Thank you, Bua. It's beautiful."

Catherine learned later that the Siamese liked to do things for people they respected without expecting anything in return. Sharing was a common custom and, even in the palace, food and other small things were shared all the time without anyone considering themselves above receiving acts of kindness.

Khun Chom Klee did not interfere with Catherine's work but observed with interest from afar since a huge gulf lay between them.

"No, I can't possibly!" she told the girls who had crowded around her. "How can I meet her? Sitting on a chair gives me cramp, and we can't understand each other. It's better if you girls talk to her."

Nevertheless, Catherine believed that Khun Chom liked her, or at least was not hostile towards her. The best thing, however, was that on Tuesdays, she would meet Justin, even though they had to change the location each time.

He warned her, "We can't meet in the temple anymore. People are starting to notice."

This was another obstacle for Catherine that she had not thought of. Whether inside or outside the palace, she was conspicuous even from a distance since her blonde hair and white skin could not blend in with the black-haired and brown-skinned people around her. Although they did not regard her with hostility, they found her both strange and amusing.

And the worst thing was that this made Justin conspicuous too.

7

The Crossroads

Today, Kham took her along small canals through dense plantations, far from the houses built along the large canals, to find an isolated place where she could meet Justin.

Next to the canal were the houses of noblemen, but a few hundred metres away, were plantations as far as the eye could see with all kinds of fruit. The land in that area was abundant and any kind of fruit would grow without the need for much tending. Justin explained that many of the fruits had grown without being planted, and that the owner did not mind if anyone picked and ate them.

But Justin never let her eat the fruits straight from the trees. He would always pick them and tell her, "Take them back to the palace. The girls will prepare them for you."

Although Catherine could not stand the smell of the savoury foods, she loved the fruits. Whether it was star fruit, mangosteen, mango, rose apple, rambutan, or custard apples, the girls in the palace would peel them, stone them, carve them beautifully, or crystalise them and arrange them on a tray.

Life in the palace was exciting for Catherine, but it could not compare to the stolen moments with Justin when he held her hand as they stepped over rickety wooden bridges that ran across the furrows.

The first time they had to cross, Catherine stopped and cried, "How can I walk across?"

Justin laughed.

"I'll hold your hand. Be careful you don't step on your skirt."

Catherine's dress was cumbersome compared to the simple clothes that the Siamese wore, and she hitched up the top of her skirt to her waist as she warily climbed across.

She laughed in relief when she had crossed the furrow and, after that, was no longer scared.

"I know! Next time, we should bring a picnic."

Justin turned to her and smiled, his black eyes twinkling.

"Why should we wait until next time?"

In front of her, the land came to an end next to a long clear canal that ran through the middle of a plantation and was connected to a bigger canal that flowed into the Chao Phraya River. Since it was far from the large canal, there were hardly any houses, and everywhere was green under the vivid blue sky dotted with fluffy white clouds.

Under a coconut palm on the canal bank was a piece of land that Won had swept clean, where he had put down a mat, and on top of it was a blanket covered with a white English-style tablecloth and picnic food that had been taken out of a basket and neatly arranged.

"Oh, Justin!" Catherine exclaimed. "Where did it come from?"

He smiled.

"From the same place that you live. Won can make English food. I sent him to help in the palace kitchen. The cook often bakes bread for the king, so Won got bread to make sandwiches for a picnic."

She should have known. Khun Chom Klee was fastidious about food and made sure a servant took her bread and soup for every meal. When she had found out that Catherine liked fruit, she never forgot to provide an ample supply for her.

They sat down on the white tablecloth and handed tasty morsels to each other. Won had even made limeade with Siamese limes and sugar.

"Did you ask Khun Chom to prepare food for me?"

"I wrote to tell her what you like, and I sent Won to tell the cook."

He chuckled as he added, "My mother's a good housekeeper. She makes sure everyone eats and sleeps well. If you don't eat anything, she'll worry. Siamese women measure the happiness of the people around them by how much they eat."

No wonder Khun Chom would always peep at her from afar when she was eating. She never joined her for meals, but always had a special table placed outside her house with a maid to serve her. Catherine realised that Justin was trying his best to help both her and his relatives adjust to each other, so that she would not feel alienated from them.

The Crossroads   111

***

After that, their weekly meetings became a matter of course.

Justin would choose places far from the eyes of anyone they knew, but they could not always avoid meeting villagers, even though Won tried to keep them away. Catherine did not mind meeting the villagers, and was getting used to being stared at, since she was fascinated by their way of life. She was amazed at the simplicity of their lives, along with their seeming contentedness, which stemmed from the fact that nature had provided them with all they needed. There was an abundance of food, their homes were built of timber from the trees, and they exchanged the things they grew with each other, so there was hardly any need for money.

Justin was not haughty with the villagers, which Catherine learned was something he had absorbed from King Pinklao, who was keen on visiting villages and meeting with the village leaders informally.

Once, he told Catherine something that made her start.

"Wherever he goes the villagers love and respect him, and they often present him with their daughters."

Catherine's eyes grew wide.

"And must he take them?"

"It would be an insult to refuse them."

Justin had explained on the boat that Siamese men could have several wives, but she did not know the methods by which it came about. And she had never connected it with Justin.

"Do you mean a father will willingly give his daughter to be one of several of a man's wives, and that the man can't refuse?"

"Both sides agree to it. The girl will gain honour and status, and it isn't illegal."

"And what if someone gives their daughter to you? Would you accept her?"

Catherine caught herself, realising she had sounded harsh.

Justin was quiet for a moment before he smiled and replied, "Nobody has so far. People don't give their daughters away that easily. They must make sure the man is dependable. I'm not that important."

Catherine wondered, *'And what if they did?'*

112 A Passage to Siam

As if reading her mind, Justin reached out to clasp her hands. "Don't worry about something that hasn't happened yet. We need to concentrate on you. What does Lindley say?"

The previous times they had met, they had avoided mentioning Arthur, even though they both knew he was like a large shadow that loomed over Catherine no matter where she went. But today, Justin decided it was time to face their difficulty instead of avoiding it.

"I heard that Consul Hillier's back. He's the only one who can decide."

Consul Hillier had returned to Bangkok and was the sole person to whom Catherine could file for divorce.

"I'll go and see him and file for divorce."

They both knew it would not be easy. Divorcing Arthur was the difficult first step, but divorcing Arthur to marry Justin was several times harder.

* * *

Charlotte Palmer smiled sweetly at the young man when she came into his study. She was not perturbed by his displeasure and greeted him brightly.

"'Ow are you, Arthur? I ain't seen you lately. You know John's been in Singapore for weeks, don't you?"

"What do you want?" he asked coldly.

She laughed. She was not drunk at this time of day, and she looked fresh with her red hair piled up in a bun, revealing her long neck. Her white shirt was rolled up at the sleeves and unbuttoned at the top, revealing her ample bosom.

"Calm down. Don't get snappy," she said, smiling. "I'm 'ere as a friend. That's all, I promise. You must me lonely without me."

One good thing about Charlotte was that she always managed to dispel the tension with her easy-going manner, and Arthur mused approvingly that she was like a man in that she wasn't touchy or easily offended. Even though he had been angry with her for coming between him and Catherine, Charlotte bore him no ill will and was the same as always. When he didn't ask her to take a seat, she remained standing, but she smiled at him teasingly.

The Crossroads 113

"I've got a new friend. At first, I was goin' to Singapore, now that John's not 'ere, but Robert 'unter's 'ere, so I'm stayin' a while longer."

Arthur frowned in annoyance.

"Good for you. Why are you telling me?"

"I thought you might be interested," she replied with a twinkle in her eye, "'cause Robert 'unter was on the boat with your wife."

Arthur was silent, wondering what she was getting at.

"Robert told me somethin' interestin' about Mrs Lindley and a Siamese prince who was on the same boat, but if you don't want to know...I won't say anymore."

***

Robert Hunter's house was close to a Chinese neighbourhood in Thonburi. It was a half brick and half wooden house that his father had built before he was exiled. He had taken most of his assets with him to London, and only the house remained in Siam. Now it had fallen into disrepair. Arthur was uncomfortable about coming to see him, but Charlotte's story had left him with no other option. He was relieved that Robert Hunter made him welcome, meeting him in his study, which had hardly any books and was furnished shabbily.

"Throughout the voyage, Captain Justin...I mean the prince... took a great deal of interest in Mrs Lindley. I can't say I was surprised. A woman travelling alone is an easy target."

"Catherine wasn't travelling alone. She was accompanied by her relative. And I don't know what you mean by interest."

Robert Hunter grinned.

"I can't say how close they were. I wouldn't want to cast doubt on Mrs Lindley's virtue. I don't suppose she's told ye about the night a man tried to get into her room, has she now?"

A look of alarm spread across Arthur's face.

"Is that true?"

"I don't know if it's true," he said casually. "Nobody saw anything except Catherine, but the prince was found inside her room. He said he heard a scream, so he went inside. The captain didn't want a scandal,

114   A Passage to Siam

so he hushed things up."

Robert Hunter's words were like a slap in the face, and Arthur felt a sudden loathing for the man well up inside him.

Hunter continued breezily, "After that, it was obvious the prince had taken a liking to her. They stayed in separate cabins, but they were always together. But don't take my word for it. Ask Mrs Lindley."

Arthur regained his senses and snapped, "I was there to meet Catherine in Singapore. I didn't see anything suspicious between them."

Hunter shrugged.

"I'm just telling ye what I saw. Why would I lie?"

"Catherine knows to behave with propriety around men, especially an Oriental."

Hunter chuckled.

"The prince is no ordinary Oriental. If it were his servant, Mrs Lindley would no doubt never speak to him, but he was a British army officer in India, and he's good-looking. More to the point, he's unmarried and yer wife's a young beauty."

Arthur was sickened to hear his wife being derided in such a way.

Even though he was suspicious of his wife, as her husband, it was his duty to protect her honour.

"I believe my own eyes," he said coldly. "I trust my wife. If she was friends with the prince, it was because she thought him more trustworthy than the other men on board."

He did not give Hunter another opportunity to speak.

"I think we've talked for long enough. Good day."

He walked out of the room with Hunter's derisive laughter ringing in his ears, shaking with anger. He told himself he would have to take decisive action. He could not leave the situation as it was for any longer.

Arthur wrote a short letter to Catherine asking her to come outside the palace to meet him about an important matter. He hoped that, after several months apart from him inside the palace, Catherine might be ready to reconcile with him. He did not believe what Robert Hunter had told him. There might have been some truth in the fact that Catherine had been friendly with the prince, but his instincts told him that Robert Hunter was not to be trusted.

He was even less trustworthy than the Siamese prince.

Catherine replied that she would be able to meet him the following Friday, since it was a Buddhist holiday, and her students would be listening to a sermon in the Throne Hall.

Arthur could not know that Catherine was no less disturbed than he was. She took his letter to Justin. Meeting him was becoming increasingly difficult because of his many duties. King Pinklao had been upcountry for a fortnight and Justin had been responsible for the military in his absence.

The Second King of Siam preferred not to remain in the capital for too long so as not to interfere with government matters and compete with King Mongkut.

Prince Vijjuprapha was aware of all Arthur Lindley's movements. He knew that Charlotte Palmer had been to his house. He also knew that he had been to see Robert Hunter.

Therefore, Catherine found that Justin advised her to have a frank discussion with Arthur before filing for divorce with Consul Hillier. If Arthur was willing to divorce her, they would simply have to report the matter to the consul, which would be preferable to contriving against Arthur without speaking to him.

He concluded, "I want to go with you, Catherine. I'm worried Arthur will hurt you…"

"Don't go. It will only make matters worse. And for another thing, Arthur's never lifted a hand to me," she said, forcing a smile.

Justin sighed and gazed at her anxiously.

"I can't let you face things alone."

She knew he was worried that Arthur had the right to stop her from leaving the house, and that no one in Siam would dare to take her away from her husband, and that, if Justin were to do it, the matter would reach King Mongkut, the First King of Siam, not just King Pinklao.

"I'll take Kham and have a horse-drawn carriage wait for me. Don't worry about me, Justin. I'll come straight back to the palace if he becomes aggressive."

She hid her fear so as not to make Justin even more anxious, even though she knew that she had come to a tipping point. Not even Justin's encouragement could assuage her.

* * *

Siam's strong sun had not damaged Catherine's skin at all and living in the palace had been so congenial that she had not lost any weight. Arthur glanced at her and found her as lovely as before – or even lovelier. She looked fresh and healthy with only the expression in her eyes cold and distant.

"What is it that you wish to speak to me about?" she asked as if talking to a stranger.

"I want to talk about us…you know that. We can't leave things like this."

Catherine listened in silence.

"I've asked you before to start over with me, but you've never answered. I let you go inside the palace to give you time to cool off. And now it's been months…"

Catherine shifted uncomfortably, and Arthur decided to get straight to the point.

"Can you tell me straight? Is there anyone else apart from me?"

Catherine took a deep breath. The dreaded moment had arrived.

"If you're asking me if I have a lover like Charlotte Palmer, then the answer's no, but if you're asking me if I'm in love with another man, then…yes, I am."

Arthur almost fell over backwards. By now, he knew she was more determined and stubborn than he had first thought, but he never dreamed that she would have the audacity to declare that she was in love with another man. He still believed that Catherine was a virtuous woman, not a harlot like Charlotte, and he could not understand what had possessed her to go astray.

"Then what Hunter said is true!" he barked.

Catherine was relieved that the truth was out.

"You can't believe what he says!"

"But it was true about you and the prince, wasn't it?"

"He was just guessing," she said firmly. "The prince and I are good friends, and all the time we were on the boat gave us a chance to get to know each other. And yes, I fell in love with him…As for Hunter, I suppose he told you that someone tried to get into my cabin."

Arthur's head was spinning.

"He told me…It was the prince, wasn't it?"

"No. It was Hunter," she shot back. "He's tried to take advantage of me before. If it hadn't been for the colonel, and Mary, and Justin… I don't know what I'd have done."

The way she said 'Justin' grated on his ears, but she was in the middle of the story.

"Tell me the everything. I want to know."

He listened as she told him the whole story, and it was like a slap in the face, even though it had happened months ago. But he felt responsible for allowing another man to get close to his wife, and then for destroying her trust. Although he was disappointed in her that she had been as unfaithful to him in spirit as he had been to her in reality, he still felt that it was his fault that he had caused her to stray.

He collected himself before asking her, when she had finished her story, "If that's the reason you want to divorce me, have you never thought of how difficult your life would be? You don't know the ways of the world. Being the wife of a prince is not a life you'd want, believe me. You'd be one of many…confined to the palace…cut off from society without any friends. Even the other Westerners in Siam would see you as an outsider. How long could you stand it?"

His voice became hoarse.

"Did you know that when Charlotte first came to Siam, a Siamese nobleman wanted her as a wife, but she refused. She chose a drunkard like John Palmer instead…At least he's English."

Catherine jumped up at once. His last sentence felt like a low blow. "How dare you?"

Arthur was silent, realising he'd said the wrong thing.

"Sit down. Please," he said in a softer tone.

She sat back down, watching him pace up and down in agitation.

"What do I have to do…" he cried, "to make you understand I have your best interests at heart? You don't love me…you want to divorce me. That's one thing. But the other thing is worse. You're making a big mistake."

"I can decide for myself."

"No, you can't," he said firmly. "It's different for a woman. If I'm

118 A Passage to Siam

unfaithful, it won't destroy my life. But if you have relations with that prince, your life will never be the same."

"That's your opinion," Catherine replied coldly.

"You can ask anyone. Ask Knox, ask Colonel Rowland, ask Consul Hillier, or even the captain and the sailors on the ship. They'll all say I'm right."

"You've forgotten someone."

"You mean you? I know you won't listen."

"Not me. Justin. He'll tell you what he thinks."

He was dumbstruck.

"It concerns him," she said cooly. "Why would you ask people who have nothing to do with it."

Catherine returned to the palace.

She got into a boat at the pier. It was a royal barge for ladies of the Inner Court shielded by curtains on either side. Although, it was simply a mark of respect, to Arthur's eyes it appeared that she had already become one of them.

He did not sleep for several nights after that. The first night he was angry and disappointed – angry at the man who had come between him and his wife, and disappointed that Catherine had been unfaithful. But by the second night, his anger had turned to concern for Catherine. He could not erase from his memory the picture of the innocent young girl in the garden whom he had fallen in love with at first sight.

On the third night, he decided to act. At that moment, the only person he felt he could trust in Siam was Knox. He would find out sooner or later, so Arthur decided to tell him the facts. Knox had gained the king's favour to such an extent that the king had presented him with a young Siamese woman named Prang as a wife, and he was allowed regular audiences with the king. If Knox were to ask the king to forbid the prince from having anything to do with his wife, it would not be too difficult. In addition, Consul Hillier was old-fashioned and strict, and Arthur was certain he would not approve of allowing Catherine to divorce her husband.

He decided to take the matter to Thomas George Knox.

Knox had heard the rumours, although he did not know the details. In the small society of Siam, nothing escaped the eyes of others, and even Captain Knox, who had no interest in gossip, had noticed that Catherine had not been living with her husband for several months. Knox already knew that Arthur had become entangled with Charlotte and was not surprised since he was good-looking, agreeable, and gullible. He had been relieved when Catherine had arrived in Siam, because a woman like Charlotte was not a suitable partner for any respectable Englishman, but the situation between the couple had turned into an unexpected difficulty.

He listened politely while Arthur described his troubles, asking him at last, "And will you divorce your wife?"

"I'm concerned about Catherine. I don't want a divorce," Arthur said firmly.

"I understand," Knox agreed, nodding. "And I commend you for accepting responsibility for what happened between you and Miss Palmer and what's happened between Mrs Lindley and the prince."

Arthur smiled bitterly.

"If Catherine files for divorce with Consul Hillier, would you help me persuade him not to allow it, Knox?"

"Even if we don't talk to him, Hillier would never agree. It's an affront to the dignity of the British. It would be better if you and your wife could sort things out yourselves."

"I've tried to talk to her, but she won't listen…" he blurted and stopped, realising he was blaming Catherine. "She's…young, you see, and she doesn't understand Siamese society."

"I tell you what," Knox said, "Don't take the matter to Hillier yet. If it comes to that, the whole of Bangkok will know about it, and no matter what he decides, you'll be humiliated. I'll take the matter to the Second King of Siam. He'll tell the prince to stay away from your wife. That way Mrs Lindley will know it's over between her and the prince, and you and she can make amends. That would be best for everyone."

✳ ✳ ✳

The evening began with no sign of anything amiss, and Prince Vijjuprapha had no idea that something was about to happen concerning him. The only thing out of the ordinary was that the king had not been out riding but had been meeting with Captain Knox in his study. When Knox took his leave, Prince Vijjuprapha was invited to meet the king as usual.

King Pinklao was sitting at his desk and when he saw who had crawled in, he said, "I'm glad you're here. I've just been reviewing the book on canons I translated years ago in order to revise it since you brought me a new one. Read it and see if there's anything that needs updating."

He handed over the book and regarded the young prince. Although his eyes were full of affection, they held an expression of concern.

"Your father's sick. He didn't tell me. I met Chao Nuam yesterday, and he told me he went to see your father because he was sick."

"He's been ill for the last two years, Your Majesty, but he's got medicine that helps."

"A sickness that lasts for years is chronic. Your father isn't a young man anymore. I'm getting older myself."

He paused before continuing, "Your brothers have all been ordained as monks. You're the only one that hasn't. If you become a monk for your father, he may recover, and if he doesn't, at least he'll be comforted to know you've been ordained and that he has seen you in a saffron robe."

This meant that the king wanted him to be ordained. He prostrated himself in response.

"You've been schooled in worldly knowledge much more than others, but in spiritual matters, you're still far off. You need to learn to be calm and level-headed, so you'll be able to lead your family with wisdom and discretion."

This time, Prince Vijjuprapha forgot himself and glanced at the king, meeting his gaze.

"You're intelligent. You know what I'm talking about. But let me be direct. Captain Knox told me you're involved with Lieutenant Lindley's wife...Is it true?"

The prince had no other option but to tell him the truth. He told the king of the first time he had met the young woman in England,

The Crossroads 121

of their passage to Siam, and of the things that had happened between them to cement their relationship until there was no turning back. His despair when he found out that Catherine was already married had turned to hope when he heard from her own lips that she was 'Mrs Lindley' in name only and had separated from her husband the moment she found out he had been unfaithful.

He concluded by saying, "Whether I've been right or wrong, I ask for your mercy."

The Second King of Siam was silent for a moment before replying wearily, "Oh, Prince Saifa! You've been both right and wrong. I've never heard a story as complicated as yours before."

Prince Vijjuprapha listened to the king's sermon in silence.

"…What you did wrong was to fall in love with a married woman. Whether the marriage had been consummated or not is between her and her husband. Your reputation will be ruined no matter what. And you can't prove it. But what you did right was to restrain yourselves, so Lindley can't blame you for anything more. If you took his wife, he would file a charge against you, not to me…but to King Mongkut. There'd be a scandal, and my reputation would be ruined because you're my son."

He paused before continuing, "How could you marry her? I don't see a way."

"Catherine…Mrs Lindley will file for divorce from Lieutenant Lindley."

"Since Lindley asked Knox to petition me, it's clear that he doesn't want to divorce his wife. He wants you to end your relationship with her instead."

He stopped thoughtfully.

"Western culture's monogamous, I know. If a couple hasn't divorced, they're still considered married. You'd better withdraw until they've decided what to do before things get any worse."

∗ ∗ ∗

It was unusual for someone like Prince Vijjuprapha to call on a foreign officer at his home, especially when he had not been invited, but both men accepted that there was no other way. Arthur's voice and manner were cold when he bowed to the prince.

"Your Highness," he said curtly.

Since their first meeting, he had never felt antagonistic towards him. On the contrary, Arthur had always found the good-looking Oriental to be almost as civilized as any Englishman. But when he found out what had happened between the prince and his wife, that feeling had vanished in an instant. Prince Vijjuprapha was 'just another Oriental' who had the audacity to disrespect a civilized person like himself.

"Lieutenant Lindley, I realise that this is uncomfortable for both of us, but it's best if we discuss it man to man. I came here to affirm my devotion and my sincerity towards the woman I love."

"My wife," Arthur corrected, in a tone even colder than before.

The prince looked him in the eye.

"I understand that the marriage between you and Catherine was never consummated, and that she wishes to end it."

Arthur hid the twinge he felt.

It was true. She must have told him everything by now. Why would she lose the upper hand? It was reason enough to leave him. He ought to have let a woman like that go. She had disappointed him even more than Charlotte, from whom he had expected nothing. But... A thin bond still connected him to Catherine. He could not say if it was love, sorrow, regret, or concern.

"I've told my wife," he said, emphasising the word 'wife', "that divorce is difficult, but starting a new life with a Siamese is even more difficult."

The prince smiled.

"Knox and Hunter's father would disagree with you. They both have Siamese wives."

"It isn't the same. An Englishman can marry a woman of whatever race he chooses, but an Englishwoman can't do as she pleases."

"Have you asked an Englishwoman about that?"

Arthur fired back angrily, "Even if I wasn't her husband, I'd still say the same thing. An Englishwoman can't be kept in a harem, cut off from the world outside. She wouldn't even be your only wife. Just one of many that must compete for the same man's affections. Catherine doesn't know how unbearable it would be. Love wouldn't be of any use to her then."

"I can guarantee that Catherine wouldn't have to face that situation. Just because Siamese men are allowed to have more than one wife, it doesn't mean they have to. A man can have only one wife if he so chooses. If I marry Catherine, she'll be my only wife. And I won't keep her at home and not allow her to meet people. She can meet whomever she chooses. Is there any other reason you won't allow Catherine to divorce you?"

'Is there any other reason you won't allow Catherine to divorce you?'

Oh, there are plenty, Arthur thought. Prince Vijjuprapha was a Buddhist, like virtually all the Siamese, and Catherine knew nothing about his religion. Arthur knew very little himself, except that Buddhism permeated every aspect of Siamese life. Every morning, Arthur would see the monks in saffron robes going out in boats to receive alms from the people on both sides of the canal. Monks were invited into people's homes to perform ceremonies after the birth of their children, when their children came of age and cut off their top knots, and when they got married, right up until the day they breathed their last breath.

Arthur had heard some of the American missionaries say, *"The Siamese won't convert to Christianity because they don't want to be excluded from society."*

Prince Vijjuprapha would be expected to participate in royal ceremonies and where would that leave Catherine? She would not be able to participate because she was a Christian. And if she married a man of a different religion, who would perform the marriage?

There were other reasons still. Arthur could not tell the prince that it would be humiliating to allow Catherine to become the wife of a Siamese because it would have been disrespectful to the prince and would have created too much hostility, so he kept quiet.

***

Nevertheless, after that day, Arthur realised that the matter could no longer be kept secret, and that word would spread.

Knox acknowledged the matter more calmly than he had done at first. As far as he was concerned, he had done his part by taking the matter to the king, and since the king had told Prince Vijjuprapha to become ordained as a monk, he was clearly not taking sides with him. That should have been of some comfort to Arthur. But whether they were to reconcile, or divorce, was between the two of them and was not his concern.

"The prince seems serious about Mrs Lindley," was all that Knox would say on the matter.

Consul Hillier was opposed to the relationship, but in his opinion, the cause of all the trouble was Catherine. He sympathised with Arthur for having the misfortune to have a wife who was no different from Charlotte Palmer. She had not only brought trouble on her husband and her lover, but on him as well.

"I understand that you don't want to divorce Mrs Lindley, but if you prolong the matter your reputation will be ruined unnecessarily."

Then he advised Arthur to do something he'd never considered.

"The best thing to do would be to take her away from Siam. Whether you take her back to England, or to India with Colonel Rowland and his wife is entirely up to you. I know your contract in the palace isn't up yet, but Knox can explain the matter to the king, and if you wish to return to Siam in the future, I'd be happy to help you. Take her away from the prince, so you can resolve matters between the two of you without his interference. Having no one else to turn to but you will soon cool her ardour."

***

When Catherine went to see Consul Hillier to file for divorce from her husband on the grounds that he had been unfaithful, she was refused with cool politeness.

"Mrs Lindley, divorce isn't easy, even when both sides agree to it. I suggest you think things through because Lindley is about to leave Siam and you're going with him."

This was Arthur's way out. She clutched the arms of the chair tightly to prevent her knees from buckling beneath her.

"I don't wish to go home with him. I'm staying in Siam. Please let me divorce him."

"If only one side wants it, you must have proof of the other's wrongdoing. Do you have any?"

"You can ask Miss Palmer."

"Miss Palmer will deny it, and she isn't a reliable witness, anyway."

"How can you say that?"

Consul Hillier regarded her cooly.

"Excuse me?"

"I'm sorry," she stammered, "but I thought as the consul you'd…"

"My job is to protect the rights of British citizens in Siam," he interrupted. "If you are threatened or harassed in any way by a Siamese, you can bring the matter to me, but this matter is between you and your husband, and a third party. There are no secrets in Siam."

The moment Catherine stepped inside Arthurs's study she challenged him directly.

"How could you do this to me?"

Arthur looked up and his eyes met Catherine's.

"We've talked about it already," he replied steadily. "I've decided not to remain in Siam. It's bad for my health. I'm going to work with Alfred like I should have done before."

"That's just an excuse," she said bitterly. "You know it is."

"Yes," Arthur said. "But you don't know that a man must maintain his dignity. I can't remain in Siam as if nothing has happened and face your new lover every day. We both work in the palace."

"But if you're going back to England, you won't have to face him anymore. You don't have to force me to go with you."

"Since you're my wife, Consul Hillier wants you to go back with me."

"That's what you want. Why can't you accept that it would be best if both of us were free? We're not meant to be together."

"I've made my decision," Arthur said without looking at her. "We're leaving with Colonel Rowland and Mary. They'll disembark in India, and we'll return to England. We can forget about this nightmare in

126 A Passage to Siam

Siam and start over."

"Arthur," Catherine cautioned. "We can't start over. It's finished between us. In fact, it never even began."

"Please…give me a chance to start over."

"Why do we have to start over instead of going our separate ways?"

Arthur jumped up suddenly, grabbing her by the shoulders and shaking her.

"Because I still love you!" he cried hoarsely.

Catherine was silent, not knowing what to say.

"I should let you go, but I can't. I feel responsible for you. You're my wife. We took vows in church before God.

"And you broke them a long time ago," Catherine said in a low voice. "You've had no right to remind me of those vows from the moment you took Charlotte into your bed. Our relationship ended then. You're no longer my husband."

Arthur released his grip on her shoulders.

"You've left me with no other choice," she said resolutely.

Arthur was quiet for a moment before asking hesitantly, "Do you mean you'll come with me?"

Her blue eyes stared at him with an expression that was hard to read. They both knew she was cornered. If she was still his wife, she had no right to remain in Siam alone and Consul Hillier would not allow it. If she refused to comply, she would be cut off from the British community with no work, no money and no one to turn to.

"Goodbye, Arthur," she whispered.

She walked out of his study with her head held high and did not turn back.

***

Justin was preparing for his ordination in a few days' time.

A Siamese man did not have to be ordained for a lengthy period and was free to leave the monkhood and resume normal life whenever he wished, but during his time as a monk, he would be bound by a strict moral code, and even his mother and sisters would not be allowed to visit him alone. For this reason, Catherine would not be allowed to see him or even contact him by letter, and she would not be allowed to participate in ceremonies because she was not a Buddhist.

They both knew the reason that he had been required to become a monk unexpectedly. In this way, King Pinklao had hoped to avoid a scandal and believed that three months as a monk would be enough time to resolve the difficulty, and that Arthur Lindley would have taken his wife away from Siam by then. But Justin had not entered the monkhood yet, and there lay a glimmer of hope for Catherine.

* * *

"Arthur insists on returning to England and he refuses to divorce me. I believe he and Consul Hillier planned for Arthur to take me away from Siam because, as his wife, I can't remain here alone. You must enter the monkhood for three months at least, so the chance of us meeting again is unlikely.

I hope to have the chance to say goodbye, but if I don't, may this letter affirm that I love only you. Goodbye, Justin, my love."

Catherine handed the letter to Kham in the morning. That evening, Kham brought a reply.

She whispered, "Won's boat is waiting at pier in front of palace, Mem. You must hurry before palace gate shuts."

Then she handed her a length of black Chinese silk.

"Here. Shawl and sarong."

Catherine unfolded the cloth, and looked at it, puzzled.

"What's it for?" she asked. "You don't expect me to disguise myself as a Siamese, do you?"

"You must, Mem. I help you put on. No one must see you at prince's raft."

That evening, the sky was dark and gloomy as if conspiring with her. In Siam, the monsoon season lasted around six months, and it was now the monsoon when it was getting dark by the afternoon. Kham covered Catherine's head with the Chinese silk shawl with another one around her shoulders and gave her a bundle of clothes to carry over her shoulder so she would look like a worker and avoid arousing Klon's suspicions.

Klon was only interested in the people coming inside the palace and did not pay attention to those leaving, especially when it was almost time for the gate to shut and people were hurrying to leave. Kham led Catherine through the gate with haste, not looking anyone in the eye.

It had begun to rain, which made walking out of the palace much easier, and the boat that came to collect her was shielded by curtains on both sides. Catherine stepped onto the boat in relief.

Because of the rain it was pitch dark when she arrived at Justin's house on the raft and there were no lights on. Kham pulled back the curtain for Catherine to step out of the boat onto the raft and at that moment, someone bent down in the shadows and held out a hand to pull her up onto the raft. Won rowed the boat away from the raft into the darkness.

The evening air was cool, and droplets of rain fell softly onto the raft. Justin held her tightly in his warm embrace – like that night on the boat when they had faced the storm together.

"Justin," Catherine whispered as she lay her cheek on his broad shoulder, "I don't know if we'll get through this storm."

She heard his voice in her ear as he pulled her flaxen hair free from the bun on her head and let it cascade down her back.

"Don't be afraid, my love. We have each other."

8

On the Wings of Love

Catherine woke up drowsily when she felt a soft warm touch on her cheek and the weight of an arm pressing down on her body.

In the dim moonlight that shone through the white mosquito net, she could see Justin's handsome face above hers. He was lying on his side his upper body half raised and she could see his smooth golden chest. One arm was resting across her and the touch of his lips and his arm woke her.

Their eyes met in the moonlight, hers blue as the morning sky and his black as night, and he smiled – a smile that lit up his entire face.

"Sleeping beauty," he whispered softly. "It's time to wake up, I'm sorry to say."

Her drowsiness vanished and reality set in as she realized she wasn't dreaming and sat up suddenly, but she was pushed down again.

"There's no need to hurry. We still have some time left together. The Front Palace gate won't be open yet, anyway."

Catherine listened to the sounds around her. Besides the soft undulations of the waves against the raft, she could hear the faint crowing of roosters. Some of the women in the palace said they mistook the moonlight for the sunrise, and that if it was dawn you would hear the birds, so she listened and was certain it was almost morning.

She lay in Justin's arms contentedly, having slept well for the first time in many weeks, and woke up to find that all that had happened had not been a dream, although she had forgotten everything, even the question of what was going to happen to them the next day.

Justin lay down beside her, his arm still tenderly resting across her.

"My love," he said, breaking the silence that had enveloped the room. "Are you really going to leave me?"

Catherine lifted her head to look at him and saw him lying on his side gazing at her in the dim light.

"You didn't say that last night. You said…"

"It was you that told me it would be our first and our last night together before you left Siam."

Reality sent a stabbing pain rippling through her chest. Tears rolled down her cheeks without her realising until she heard herself sobbing. When Justin heard, he enfolded her in his arms.

"Don't cry, my love," he breathed shakily. "Did you think I'd let you go? You're mine. You're not Lindley's wife…you never were…and you never will be…"

Catherine felt as if her prayers had been answered.

"You can't go," Justin affirmed. "No matter what."

In the dim moonlight, she saw his face was tense.

"Who can you depend on?…Let's see…there's Knox…and there's Captain Dick…Yes, Luang Surawiset will be able to find you a house. We must keep things secret. The king mustn't find out."

"What will happen to you?" Catherine asked, her heart sinking.

"I'm going to be ordained in three days' time. I won't be able to see you for three months. The king will be travelling to the south, but you can continue working in the palace. Don't be afraid, my love. Love will find out the way."

The line from the old English poem made her smile through her tears.

The morning-star was shining in the sky when Justin led her by the hand to the front of the raft. Everything was bathed in silver rays that touched the surface of the river like a firefly perched on the water. The back of the raft was dark as it swayed in the breeze, and everywhere was quiet and empty.

"Can you swim?" he asked her with a chuckle.

"Yes."

"Then let's swim!"

Catherine held onto his hand more tightly.

"What do you mean? How can I swim in the river? Women can't…"

Justin laughed, his face as happy as that of a teenage boy.

"If you're too scared, sit here and scoop water from the river. No one will see, my love. There's only us…Put a dry cloth here. You've got a lot to learn about the Siamese way of life."

Catherine knew Justin would not touch a woman's sarong as it was taboo for Siamese men, so she picked up the cloth and put it next to her before scooping water from the river to pour over herself.

Justin immersed himself in the water. The ten years that he'd been away from Siam had not changed him and he quickly adjusted to his old way of life, unlike Catherine who was still unfamiliar with many things. He floated contentedly close to the raft watching Catherine dangling her legs in the water. The cloth wrapped around her chest was wet and her hair was swept up on her head revealing her long white neck and shoulders shimmering with water droplets in the moonlight like diamonds.

"I once went to see the ballet, Undine, at Covent Garden. You remind me of the water nymph," he told her softly as he swam towards her, and she splashed him with water.

She had never seen the ballet, but she knew the story of the beautiful water nymph who had fallen in love with a young man who was unfaithful to her.

"It's sad," Catherine sighed. "I don't like sad endings."

Justin took her by the hand.

"You should come in the water, my love. It's refreshing. Don't be afraid. I'm here."

The previous evening had been cool because of the monsoon but it had stopped raining during the night. Now it was almost dawn, the air was warm again and a soft breeze caressed her skin. The ripples on the water looked inviting and she tested the water with her hand before lowering herself cautiously into the river.

"That's my girl!" Justin laughed contentedly.

After she had been in the water for a while, the Chao Phraya River felt strangely warm. Justin enfolded her around the waist and a moment later her initial awkwardness had vanished. At that moment, all their differences of race, status, and everything else, could not come between them, alone in the warm river under the glittering morning-star.

In the morning, the gates of the Front Palace were opened to outsiders. Klon was strict about who entered from the outside and, in the harsh light of day, Catherine could no longer pass for a Siamese woman, so she had brought along her own clothes to walk through the palace gates dressed as an Englishwoman.

Justin knocked on the door and walked inside when she had finished dressing. He paused to gaze at the young woman in the green cotton dress spotted with white flowers, her hair pulled back in a bun at the nape of her neck.

"I shouldn't have made you disguise yourself as a Siamese woman. You could have walked out of the palace dressed like that, but I was being overly cautious because my head was spinning."

Catherine turned around and said gently, "Better safe than sorry. I hope no one from Khun Chom Klee's villa sees me going back in."

"You should be alright because they go to bed late and wake up late. My mother gets up early to give alms to the monks, but then she goes back to her room until late morning and, even if she sees you, she'll think you've been back home."

Catherine was quiet for a moment before asking, "Will we have another chance to see each other?"

"Kham will bring you again tonight. Tell everyone you're going back home. We've got three days left together."

Then he smiled and said, "Close your eyes. I've got something for you."

Catherine closed her eyes. She felt her left hand being lifted and something cold and hard being slipped over her finger.

"You can open your eyes now."

She lifted her hand to look. She had removed Arthur's wedding ring the night she met Charlotte Palmer and put it away in her trunk without touching it again.

Now there was a ring on her finger. It was a ring encrusted with different coloured stones all round the band, and no stone was the same. There were gems of red, green, yellow, blue, brown, and some colours she had never seen before. It was the most beautiful ring she had ever seen.

"Justin," she whispered. "It's lovely."

On the Wings of Love 133

He put his arms around her and turned the ring for her to see each stone.

"There's a diamond and eight other precious stones, and it can only be found inside the palace. King Pinklao gave it to me when I went to India. It's a symbol of safety to protect you from danger. I've never taken it off until now…"

He kissed her forehead gently.

"I learned in London that a ring with stones all along the band is called an eternity ring, so I want you to have it to remind you of our everlasting love."

Catherine felt a lump in her throat and lay her head against his chest as if she wanted time to stop still. Golden rays stretched across the sky and crows began to caw. Justin released her from his arms and took hold of her soft hands in his and squeezed them.

"Don't be afraid. I'll go and see Lindley myself."

Catherine put her arms around him and held back tears as she whispered, "No matter what happens, I want you to know…I love you alone."

Justin held her more tightly until he could feel her heart beating.

"I know. I knew since we were at sea on the night of the storm. I knew you loved me, but you had a husband. Now, I'm your husband."

***

Arthur stared at the face of the Siamese man who was standing in front of him as if could not believe his ears.

"You…" he blurted. "You mean Catherine will be your mistress!"

The colour rushed to Prince Vijjuprapha's face, but his voice was steady.

"Don't insult her. She'll be my wife. I've already told you."

The third person in the room was Colonel Rowland, who put his hand on Arthur's shoulder to restrain him.

"Steady, Lindley. Losing your temper won't help."

Rowland had returned from Kanchanaburi and, instead of preparing to leave Siam for India, he had to witness this debacle. He could not leave the two men alone together since Arthur was angry

134   A Passage to Siam

and his pride had been wounded, while the prince was so enamoured that he would not even listen to the most important person in the land.

Rivalry over a woman could easily become a spark that could ignite a rift between Siam and Britain.

Even though it would not have surprised Colonel Rowland if fighting broke out between Siam and Britain, as had happened in Burma, he felt that if people were killed for personal reasons, there was no honour on either side. Moreover, Colonel Rowland had a great deal of affection for the prince, as an older brother feels towards a younger brother, and Catherine was one of his relatives, so he wanted to nip the matter in the bud.

Arthur pushed his hand away angrily.

"Get your hands off me! I know you're on his side!"

He broke free and faced the prince.

"I must protect my honour…"

Colonel Rowland grabbed his hand before he could strike Justin.

"Are you mad?" he cried. "You can't kill a Siamese prince. All hell will break lose!"

"Try me!" Arthur yelled. "If I don't die, then he must!"

"I accept your challenge!" Justin shot back.

They're just as bad as each other, Colonel Rowland thought wearily. Hitherto he had thought the prince clever and reasonable, even though he sometimes appeared sensitive. But when it came to love, Colonel Rowland realised there were men like Shakespeare's Romeo in every corner of the world, and their unbridled passion never made their lives easy.

"Stop it both of you!" he exclaimed. "No good will come of either one of you getting killed. If an Englishman gets killed, the British might close off the Gulf of Siam, and if a Siamese prince gets killed, even if you don't have to be tried in a British court, Consul Hillier will have to punish you. And Catherine would never forgive you, Lindley!"

The last sentence stopped Arthur in his tracks.

"And as for you, sir…" Colonel Rowland said turning to the prince. "I know you're in love with Mrs Lindley but announcing it to her husband like this is too humiliating. There's a way out…"

"I'm listening," the prince replied.

"Let Mr and Mrs Lindley leave Siam. If Mrs Lindley finds a way to get a divorce…in the future, she'll return to Siam herself."

The prince bit his lip.

"You know as well as I do that it's almost impossible to get a divorce if both sides don't agree, just as it's impossible for a woman to travel half-way around the world by herself. And I can't leave Siam without the king's permission."

"You have no other option but to wait for that day."

Prince Vijjuprapha glanced at Arthur.

"Lindley, I'm asking you…as a man…"

"Catherine must leave Siam. There's no other way. I have nothing more to say to you."

* * *

After that, Colonel Rowland did not see the prince again. He learned from Luang Surawiset that the prince had been ordained as a monk and was not allowed to leave the temple to meet anyone, especially Catherine. The Colonel informed Catherine of the schedule for leaving Siam since she had refused to contact Arthur directly and she wrote him a short letter in response.

"I will continue to work in the Front Palace until the day of departure. Please send a carriage to collect me and take me to the harbour on the Chao Phraya River."

Since men were not allowed inside the Inner Court, Colonel Rowland used Mary's Scottish maid, Annie, as an intermediary to take a letter to her. Annie was only too pleased to have an opportunity to go outside the house, since she was normally busy attending to Mary and could only leave when she needed her to go somewhere, or at night when her work was done.

* * *

Colonel Rowland did not tell his wife about the love triangle, leading Mary to understand that Catherine had agreed to accompany Arthur back to England. The day before they were leaving, he discovered that Mary was also facing an unexpected problem.

"How could Annie do this to me?" she cried when her husband entered the bedroom to find her trunks open with her clothes still hanging up in the wardrobe instead of being neatly packed.

"What did Annie do?" he asked, puzzled.

"Annie's resigned," Mary huffed. "She's getting married."

"Getting married?" Colonel Rowland repeated in surprise. "Surely she isn't going to marry an American missionary, is she?"

"No. She just told me out of the blue that she's met a sailor from a bumboat that sails between Singapore and Bangkok and they're getting married. The silly girl! What am I supposed to do now?"

Colonel Rowland shook his head wearily. There was nothing to do except leave Mary to grumble to herself while she packed her things.

***

It was towards the end of the monsoon season when they set sail. There had been drizzle from dark clouds since the morning, but by afternoon it had stopped raining and the sky was streaked with gold, the smell of rain-soaked earth and foliage permeated the air. Consul Hillier, Knox, and many nobles from the Front Palace came to see Arthur off, including Luang Surawiset or 'Captain Dick'. He said goodbye to Arthur and shook his hand with an anxious expression when he noticed the British officer appeared tense.

"Isn't Catherine here yet?" Arthur asked Colonel Rowland when he stepped down from the carriage and saw no sign of her.

"Mrs Lindley's already on the boat," Luang Surawiset replied. "She asked to board early because she wasn't well. She wanted to go to her cabin and rest."

Arthur looked towards the harbour and saw a paddle boat pulling up alongside the large boat in the middle of the river. The figure bathed in golden sunlight was dressed all in black and her hair was covered by a straw hat of the same colour. When she turned to face the harbour, he noticed a black veil hanging from the rim of her hat as if she were a widow in mourning.

Arthur felt a sharp stab of pain in his chest. He should have accepted the fact that Catherine did not love him, and even if he dragged her around the world, he could not force her to stop loving that man. When he had boarded the ship, Arthur left Catherine in the cabin and did not disturb her, his heart still as heavy as the first day he had learned of her relationship with the prince.

As the boat slowly moved away, Arthur remained at the edge of the boat watching the view of Siam by evening on both sides of the river slowly fade out of sight, the white walls and the dazzling roofs of the Front Palace gradually disappearing along with the small boats of the locals.

He knew he would never return to this land of rivers and canals, and that the thick fog and damp cold of London awaited him on his return after a short stop in India.

"We'd better stay up here," Colonel Rowland said to Arthur. "We'll have more than enough time inside our cabins."

The sun had sunk behind the trees and stars slowly appeared across the dark purple sky before everything was swallowed by darkness. There was no restaurant for them to share dinner in, so they each ate alone in their cabins. Catherine had still not come out but opened the door for someone to bring her food.

When the boat finally reached the estuary and they were preparing to board the larger boat to sail out of the Gulf of Siam to Singapore, Arthur decided to knock on the door.

"Catherine, open the door. We need to change boats."

There was a rustling inside the room before the door opened gradually as if the person behind it was unsure. The figure in black appeared as a shadow in the light from the lantern behind, but the uneasy freckled face framed by red hair was still visible. The moment he saw her, he felt as if the boat had been turned upside down.

"Annie!" he cried as if he couldn't believe his eyes. "Where did you come from?"

Annie's expression was tense, and she swallowed before replying, "I'm sorry, sir, but Mrs Lindley said…"

Arthur grabbed hold of the door frame to steady himself.

"You mean Catherine made you pretend to be her, and she's still in Bangkok?"

The only other people who knew apart from Arthur were Colonel Rowland and Mary. Colonel Rowland spoke to him outside his cabin, but his attempts to ease the tension were to no avail.

"I'm going to ask the captain to turn back. I'm going to get Catherine."

"The boat has a schedule to follow. It can't turn back just for you. And do you really think she'd come with you?"

"She's still my wife. I have the right…"

"Stop trying to overcome that obstinate woman," Colonel Rowland barked. "Suppose you were able to force her onto the boat. When you got to Singapore, she'd likely run away back to Siam as soon as your back was turned. And even if you took her to England, don't you think she'd find a way to go back to that prince?"

The colour drained from Arthur's face. He could not deny that Catherine did not love him.

Colonel Rowland concluded, "You'd better let her go. She's made her bed, and she must lie in it."

"But it's humiliating…for her…and for me."

"Everything happened in Siam. No one in England will ever know about it. Consul Hillier considers it to be a personal matter and won't report it. And if you don't want to return to England, you can take up a post in India. Wait two or three years and then tell your relatives that you and Catherine have separated. And it's up to Catherine to tell her relatives."

Arthur seemed despondent for a moment.

"I'm worried about Catherine," he confessed. "I don't want to leave her alone in Siam like I left her alone in England. I feel as if I'm repeating the same mistake."

Colonel Rowland put his hand on Arthur's shoulder.

"I understand and I sympathise. I suggest you write to Knox and ask him to send you news about Catherine. Then, if she's ever in trouble, you'll be able to help her."

***

Khun Chom Klee was in a quandary when she learned that the

foreign teacher had not returned home as she had thought, even though her husband had left Siam. She knew about the relationship between the woman and the prince, even though they had tried to keep it secret, since there were no secrets in Siam due to the closeness of families and friends.

But this dilemma presented her with a difficulty because she was not able to question the pair concerned. Prince Vijjuprapha was bound by the monk's precepts, so she was not allowed to disturb him until he left the monkhood. And she could not speak to the other party due to the language barrier, not to mention the awkwardness she felt, which prevented her from being able to summon her for questioning.

In the end, the only person she could turn to was the prince's mother. So she sent someone to invite Mom Yad to visit her at the Front Palace and discuss the matter inside her room.

"What shall we do, Yad? The foreign teacher won't go home, and your son will be leaving the monkhood in a few days. If they get together it will cause a scandal. And nothing worries me more than news of it reaching the…"

She paused, leaving Mom Yad to infer whom she meant and lowered her voice.

"If he gets angry, there'll be trouble. He sent your son to the temple as soon as he found out. But this time, I don't know what will happen."

Mom Yad was no less concerned, after expecting the matter to have resolved itself once the teacher was gone. Since the chain had not been broken, Mom Yad suggested the only way out she could think of.

"My son's still young. He's easily led," she reasoned. "But if he gets married, I'm sure he'll turn around. I tell you what. As soon as he leaves the monkhood, let's find an auspicious day for the wedding. The house on the raft can be his wedding nest. It's all ready."

"Do you mean to my Bua?" Khun Chom asked, knowing exactly who she meant.

"Well, who else? Bua's the perfect match for him."

Khun Chom considered for a moment.

"You can't rush into these things. I've cared for her as if she were my own daughter. Her parents have put their trust in me. If she gets married, I must make sure she won't be disappointed. If Saifa were single, it would be different, but now he's got that foreign woman, where does that leave Bua?"

"She'd be his principal wife, of course," Mom Yad replied at once. "Anyone else is a secondary wife. They're not equals."

"Oh, dear!" Khun Chom sighed. "A foreign woman wouldn't put up with being a secondary wife. And she was Bua's teacher. How will Bua keep her in line? Bua's as timid as a mouse. I don't know what to do. That's why I invited you over."

Mom Yad was at a loss. She could see that Khun Chom Klee was disappointed since she loved them both dearly and thought they would make a wonderful couple.

"I want Bua." Mom Yad declared. "My son will have to meet a lot of important people. He needs a capable wife who'll be able to manage the servants and host foreign guests, and Bua's up to the job."

"It's such a pity," Khun Chom sighed. "They're a perfect match. But what are we to do? Your son's in love with that mem."

"I tell you what," Mom Yad suggested. "Let's wait for him to come to his senses. Eventually, he'll realise Bua's better."

***

The fact that Catherine had remained in Siam did not remain a secret for long. Knox was called to the Front Palace urgently since King Pinklao wanted to know the whole story before deciding what to do. In Knox's opinion, the best way forward was not to punish either party, or to wash his hands of the matter as Consul Hillier had done, but to help the couple find the smoothest way out of their dilemma. It was not that he agreed with them, but simply that he believed attempting to separate them was not his responsibility.

So he told the king, "As far as I know, Lieutenant Lindley and Mrs Lindley have separated. A reconciliation is unlikely. Mrs Lindley chose to remain in Siam, and he isn't likely to return. He's going to work in India or in England. I expect I'll hear from him in due course."

The Second King of Siam was still not satisfied.

"People will still gossip. Saifa took another man's wife. How many people know the truth that…"

On the Wings of Love 141

He stopped, realising he ought not to say any more.

"If I let them get away with it, it will look like I consent. And for another thing, I forbade him from seeing her and sent him to be a monk, but he disobeyed me. There must be a consequence of some sort."

Even though King Pinklao was deeply fond of Prince Vijjuprapha, he could not be biased.

"And what do the other foreigners think about it?" he asked carefully.

"The British considered the matter closed when Lindley left the country. And the American missionaries think it's a British matter and none of their concern."

"If I continue to hire Mrs Lindley to work in the palace, will it cause gossip?"

After a moment's consideration, Knox replied, "I think…if you sent for Mrs Lindley, it would be easier for you to decide, Your Majesty."

When Catherine was summoned to meet the king, it was not unexpected, but she could not help feeling far more anxious than she had been the first time she had met him. Catherine knew that this meeting would determine her future. If the king was displeased with her and did not want her to work in the palace, she would no longer be allowed to remain in Siam. She chose to wear a plain black dress with a white lace collar and cuffs and pulled her hair into a bun at the nape of her neck.

The Throne Hall was silent with only the palace guards and Knox who took her to see the king. Although Knox was polite, his manner was reserved and solemn. The meeting was in the king's library, which was decorated like those in the homes of wealthy Englishmen. Shelves full of books covered the walls and there was a large desk and a leather upholstered chair imported from England. There was even a small folding ladder for reaching books on the top shelf with a globe and a pencil box on the polished wooden desk.

She was reminded of England except for the heat, which was mitigated by a fan that hung from the ceiling, and she found the familiar atmosphere comforting. A moment later, her heart began to race again when the second most important person in Siam entered the room followed by Luang Surawiset, or Captain Dick, and two Siamese attendants.

Catherine curtseyed and looked up to find the king gazing at her thoughtfully.

He smiled slightly and said, "Please sit down."

His English pronunciation was clear with a slight American accent since his teacher had been American. Catherine sat on a chair with her hands, as cold as ice, folded in her lap. But a moment later, she began to relax. King Pinklao did not appear hostile towards her, even though, beneath his cool politeness, she sensed he was not pleased with her. It seemed that he was weighing her up before making his mind up about her.

"I've met you before, Mrs Lindley. The last time, I didn't get a chance to talk to you, but the ladies in the palace say they've learned a lot from you."

Catherine mumbled something in reply but found herself feeling so reticent that she could not remember if she had thanked him or told him she had done her best.

"Apart from embroidery, what else do you know?"

"I can read and write, Your Majesty. I like reading and I've learned some arithmetic."

The word 'reading' caught the king's attention.

"You like reading? Have you read the works of Charles Dickens?"

"Yes, Your Majesty," Catherine replied.

"I've read 'Pickwick'. It was very entertaining. Are there any other works you'd recommend me to read?"

"I like 'A Christmas Carol' and 'Oliver Twist', Your Majesty. My father used to read 'A Christmas Carol' to us at Christmas time when all the family was together. We used to have a small celebration at home…"

Catherine stopped, a lump in her throat. She had been so preoccupied with the difficulties of the past few months that she had almost forgotten the warmth of her family when she was young, and she was filled with nostalgia. She came to her senses when she became aware of the king gazing at her with a kind expression.

"I haven't read them. But from what you've said, I think I should. Captain Knox…"

Knox, who had been sitting listening in silence spoke.

"I should be able to find them for you within a couple of months, Your Majesty."

"Thank you, Captain Knox."

And he nodded to Luang Surawiset to pass Catherine a book that had been placed on a nearby table.

"Mrs Lindley. I have a new book. It's a book of poetry by a writer whose work I don't often read, but I think some of the poems are impressive. Would you read one and explain it to me?"

It was a book of poetry by Lord Byron. She chose a short poem at random and began to read.

"When we two parted
In silence and tears,
Half broken-hearted
To sever for years,"

Catherine's dulcet voice made the poem sound like a sad song, and she read it verse by verse until she came to a verse near the end.

"In secret we met
In silence I grieve,
That thy heart could forget
Thy spirit deceive."

Catherine's voice trailed off as the poem's poignancy shook her to the core. She had deceived Arthur. She read to the end in a voice barely above a whisper and came to her senses when she heard the king say, "You read it beautifully."

Knox exhaled slowly as if he had been holding his breath. Catherine explained the poem, relieved that no one had made the connection between the poem and her own situation.

When the meeting ended, she was pleased when Captain Knox told her, "The Second King of Siam is keen to gain knowledge from England. I think you'll be able to continue working in the palace."

***

When Catherine went back to work at the palace, the atmosphere was completely different from before. Catherine thought that word of her relationship with Justin must have spread. The girls regarded her with a mixture of curiosity and suspicion, and even though they were respectful, they seemed distant and not as friendly as before.

Only one remained forthcoming and that was Bua who was as agreeable as always. Although she had been shy at first, once she had got over her reticence, she had come to be the one to whom Catherine was closest.

So Catherine was surprised when, one evening after they had been talking about ordinary matters, Bua plucked up the courage to ask her shyly in Siamese, "Please don't think me rude for asking, but is it true what they're saying about you…" she paused before continuing in a voice barely above a whisper, "…and Prince Vijjuprapha?"

Catherine was silent for a moment, not knowing what to say.

"What are they saying?" she answered in English, but Bua understood.

"I'm…I'm…worried," she stammered, her face anxious. "Please don't be angry with me. I'll still respect you no matter what. Because you're my teacher."

"Why would I be angry with you? And why do you say you'll still respect me no matter what?"

Bua looked puzzled and thought for a moment before replying, "Because…I don't know how to explain. You're a teacher. You're not like a royal consort."

She was not. Before, Catherine had been in a respected position since, after their parents, the Siamese held their teachers in the highest regard, in stark contrast to how teachers were viewed in England. Every day after class, no matter what she had been teaching, her students would prostrate themselves at her feet and crawl away from her backwards without turning their backs to her before standing up and walking away reverently. Even when they sat down, they would not sit too close to her, but would maintain a respectful distance, or would sit on the floor. If Catherine wanted to show them something, such as an item she had crocheted, they would place their palms together before taking it from her.

On the Wings of Love 145

But now, everything had changed. The girls had begun to disappear one by one with various excuses, leaving the few who remained feeling even more uncomfortable. She heard their whispers and, although she did know what they were saying, she knew it was not positive.

"Can I ask you something?" Catherine asked. "Why do you not approve of me marrying a Siamese prince?"

It was a hard question for Bua to answer, and she almost evaded answering by replying, "I don't know."

But when her eyes met the imploring blue eyes, they filled with tears.

"Because…you're a mem."

She had said it. Bua stood up suddenly, which was out of character for someone with such a gentle manner, as if she could not face the embarrassment of any further questions.

* * *

A parcel from Mary arrived the following day. She had written a long letter complaining about the journey from Singapore to Bombay for two whole pages, so Catherine decided to turn it over and read to the end for news of Arthur.

"As for Arthur, he's decided to resign from the military due to health reasons, but he's still staying with us for a while to see if there's any work for him in India. Personally, I think he should go back home to work for his brother.

Arthur hasn't mentioned you. While it's a relief that he's decided to let you go, I'm still worried about the two of you because you're not legally divorced, so Arthur won't be able to remarry unless he divorces you. And it's the same for you.

I'm concerned about you because you're like a sister to me.

I don't expect your clothes are suitable for Siam's climate. There is a lot of thin cotton in India, of better quality and more colourful than any you'll find in Siam, so I'm sending you some cotton and you can have some dresses made of it. Keep them as a reminder of me…"

Mary had sent two lengths of cotton. One was pale pink and flowered, while the other was pale blue. She had also sent a white cotton nightdress framed with lace and a cream silk shawl.

A letter from Justin had arrived two days' earlier and she had tucked it into her blouse, not because she was afraid someone would read it, but because it comforted her to keep it next to her skin.

Catherine, my love,
To tell the truth, writing to you is a breach of a monk's precepts since I'm not allowed to contact you. Although I'm following all the other precepts, I can't force myself to stop thinking about the woman I love.
Between the two of us, there is no 'prince' or 'Mrs Lindley', only 'Justin' and 'Catherine'.
Your letter reached me safely. I'm glad you're alright.
I don't know when the king will give me permission to leave the monkhood, but I understand that his decision to send me to be a monk will put a stop to the gossip about us.
I'm going to ask my father to go and see the king to ask permission for me to leave the monkhood and return to work in the Front Palace. I think he'll allow it and then we can be together.
Wait for that day. It won't be long.
Love Justin

Shortly after that, Catherine heard that Justin's father had been to see King Pinklao, despite bring unwell. And a few days later, Prince Vijjuprapha left the monkhood and returned to work in the Front Palace as before.

At the same time, there was news that Siam would be sending an envoy to Europe for the first time in Siam's history to deliver a message from the king to Queen Victoria.

***

Catherine's second marriage was nothing like the first.

There was no church ceremony, no witness, and not even a bouquet of flowers, and Catherine's life as the wife of Prince Vijjuprapha began quietly without a ceremony of any kind. The fact that King Pinklao had given his permission for Justin to leave the monkhood implied that he would forbid their relationship no longer. The next day, Khun Chom Klee sent Kham to tell Catherine to move out of the Front Palace that evening.

"I help you pack, Mem."

Kham was the only one whose face showed relief that she would be leaving the Front Palace. Lately, Catherine had felt the girls inside the palace had become even more distant until some days there were no students left at all. At least, King Pinklao assigned her to explain words that were unfamiliar to him from history books and novels that he read, and even though he did not call her to see him, Catherine sensed his kindness in the notes he wrote.

It was due to their awareness of the king's kindly nature that Khun Chom Klee and the other women did not show open hostility towards Catherine, although their coldness made it perfectly clear.

The fact that she looked different and had been born on the other side of the world meant that she would not be accepted, no matter what kind of person she was or how much she loved Justin. Being of a different race was a barrier as Justin would also have discovered if he had settled with her in Longstock.

Catherine knew that the neighbours in the village would have raised their eyebrows, and even if they were polite to his face, they would have talked about him behind his back and would never have invited him into their homes. She sighed and helped Kham put the rest of her belongings inside her trunk.

Catherine did not have a chance to say goodbye to her students as none of them were there. She did not know that Khun Chom Klee had instructed them to remain inside their rooms and not come out on any account. She considered it an embarrassment that the foreign teacher was leaving the palace to go and live with the prince without a ceremony, which was a breach of custom akin to elopement, and she did not want the girls inside the palace to follow her example.

So Catherine did not have a chance to see Bua, which she was sorry about, because once she was married, she would have to stay at home and would not be able to teach in the palace any more.

***

Catherine imagined that Justin's house on the raft would be as quiet as the first time she went there, but she discovered that it was full of his servants waiting for her from the moment she stepped out of the boat. They all looked at her as if they thought her strange, but when she looked back at them, they quickly looked down and did not meet her eyes, according to the Siamese custom of not making eye contact with someone of a higher status.

Only Justin's smile put her at ease. He stood up from the low bamboo table and clasped her hand, gazing at her with an expression full of love and happiness.

"Welcome to our home, my love." He led her by the hand to sit next to him on the low bamboo table. "First of all, you must get to know my servants."

Justin had so many servants that Catherine could not remember who was who. She was beginning to understand that, although Siam was not rich in money like England, it was rich in labour, but she still could not understand what all these men and women did from dawn until dusk. Justin guessed what she was thinking and laughed.

"Don't worry. At first, you'll only have to give orders to Won and Kham. I called all of them here to let them know that they're your servants. You're in charge of them just as I am. You can assign them anything you want."

"I'm perfectly happy with just Kham, Justin."

"No, Catherine," Justin replied. "You're not Mrs Lindley anymore. You're the wife of Prince Vijjuprapha. You're in charge of them."

But when he saw her looking bewildered, Justin's face relaxed.

"You'll get used to it in time. And soon, we'll go to see my parents. But for now, it's just the two of us."

He nodded to Won, who understood at once and hurried to prostrate himself at Catherine's feet before crawling away backwards followed by all the others. A few minutes later, the two of them were left alone on the raft together.

Catherine stood up and walked over to the veranda in front of the raft. She peered through the darkness at the flickering lights in the houses on both sides of the river. It was a crescent moon that night and the stars gleamed brightly across the sky. The river breeze blew her cotton skirt and wisps of flaxen hair that had escaped from her bun, and she felt Justin's hand stroke her hair before he enfolded her in his arms from behind.

"Catherine," he whispered in her ear. "At last, we're together."

She put her hands on his and closed her eyes.

"I'm glad…" was all she could say since there was a lump in her throat.

Justin's touched the ring on Catherine's finger before whispering, "Remember, no matter what happens, my love for you will never change."

She did not know what he was thinking and had no idea that his words meant more than a simple declaration of love. He did not tell her what his father had said to him two nights earlier.

"I had people carry me to see the king. I apologised to him on your behalf. You've got off lightly this time because the king knows I'm sick and I won't live much longer. When I'm no longer here, your brothers and sisters will depend on you because you've had more education than they have, and you have a more important job. Don't give more importance to that foreign woman than to your own mother and siblings. If you want her as a wife, I can't stop you, but don't make her your principal wife. Khun Chom has raised you as her own son and found a suitable wife for you, so show her gratitude. You're still young. You won't understand how valuable a capable wife is until you're older.

***

Catherine's life after that was much the same as any married Englishwoman. She hardly left the house, even to walk across the bridge that connected the house on the raft to the group of Thai-style houses in her father-in-law's home. She did not have an opportunity to meet Justin's father and she had only seen his mother coming down the steps of the house followed by servants. She was an elegant woman who appeared younger than Khun Chom Klee. Sometimes she was followed by Princess Kanika and once, Catherine saw the princess turn as if to come towards the raft, but her mother called her sternly.

"Ying, where are you going?"

"I'm going to see Mem. She's been here for ages, and I still haven't been to see her. My brother will say I'm being mean."

"There's no need," her mother said firmly. "I'm going to the Front Palace. You should come with me."

She hesitated for a moment before following her mother obediently. Catherine was watching from the bedroom window and sighed.

* * *

A date was set for the Siamese envoy to set sail for Great Britain. Phraya Sri Suriyawongse was to be the ambassador that delivered the message and gifts to Queen Victoria with Mom Rachothai as an interpreter. And the special emissary to deliver gifts from King Pinklao was to be none other than Prince Vijjuprapha.

Catherine was excited by the news, hoping that it might be possible for her to travel with Justin and visit her mother and sister in Longstock. But two weeks before the day of departure, Catherine woke up feeling inexplicably tired. She stood up to supervise Won making her husband's breakfast as usual and her knees gave way beneath her.

Prince Vijjuprapha was alarmed.

"Catherine, don't get up. I'll lift you back onto the bed."

He lifted her onto the bed and hurried out to find Kham. Catherine felt dizzy and thought she was going to be sick. Kham brought her a bowl in time and stroked her back.

"I'll get a doctor," Justin decided. "I'll go and find Dr Bradley."

Dr Bradley was an American missionary who had lived in Siam since the previous king's reign. He knew people from all levels of society and was a familiar face inside the Front Palace. Catherine had met him a couple of times and found him agreeable. Even though he was set in his ways, she had felt he was friendlier that many of her fellow countrymen. Kham mumbled something to another of the servants who had come to check on Catherine.

"What did you say, Kham?"

Kham looked down and stammered, "I think…your wife is pregnant, Your Highness."

Catherine was asleep on Justin's bed. She had been sleeping in the same bed as him since she came to live on the house on the raft. Prince Vijjuprapha did not sleep in a separate room to his wife, which was considered strange by those in the palace since most princes had their own bedrooms. This was due to the custom of having several wives.

Catherine rested her hand on her stomach. Her corset had become tight over the past few days, and she had slackened the laces, but besides that, she still showed no sign of the life growing inside her. Catherine felt a strong hand on top of hers. She opened her eyes and looked into the black eyes that were filled with love and concern.

"My dearest, you mustn't dress like this anymore. It isn't good for our baby."

"I'll take it off soon, and I won't wear it when we're travelling."

"Travelling?" he repeated. "What do you mean?"

Justin squeezed her hand as if to warn her that she might be disappointed by what he was going to tell her.

"You won't be able to travel, my love."

"But Dr Bradley said I was in good health. I was never seasick on the boat. Don't you remember?"

Justin shook his head.

"You weren't pregnant then. Dr Bradley doesn't agree with you travelling while you're pregnant."

"But what will I do if you leave me here by myself?"

Justin was quiet and his face fell. There was no way that he could avoid going to England, and he knew that the journey there and back would take at least a year.

The American doctor, who was a thin old man with a white beard, stepped off the boat onto the raft deftly, indicating his familiarity with his surroundings, and after giving his hat to a servant he bowed politely to Catherine.

"Ma'am," he addressed her kindly, "Your husband asked me to come back and talk to you. Even though you're young and healthy, traveling by boat for six months during your first pregnancy is too risky. You'd be extremely lucky if the child made it through. And just think about how tough it would be to bring a newborn halfway around the world. Even if the child survives until you give birth in England, you'd have to wait at least two years before you could bring the child back to Siam."

Catherine was alone in the bedroom since Justin had not yet returned from meeting King Pinklao in the Front Palace. She knelt in front of Justin's trunk and tried to remember if she had packed everything he would need. Finally, she closed the lid and rested her head on it despondently, the drowsiness overcoming her. She came to her senses once more when she felt a hand touch her arm and help her up.

"Justin," she said opening her eyes. "I didn't hear you come in. I must have fallen asleep."

"Go to bed, my love. It's very late. It will soon be morning."

"You should sleep. Tomorrow, you must go to the palace. You must be exhausted."

She let him lead her to the bed and lay in his arms until he fell asleep. Catherine could not sleep since every minute was too precious to lose. She gradually slid away from him and sat up to gaze at the lovely face on the pillow next to her as if she was trying to imprint his face in her memory. There was a lump in her throat as she recalled all the nights that she had looked on his face. But tonight was the last night.

Tears soaked her cheeks as she slid off the bed without making a sound, not wanting to wake Justin. She stepped outside, the river breeze soothing her agitation, and leaned against a post, her hands resting distractedly on the rails as the cool evening breeze blew her hair across her back. She was wearing only a white cotton nightdress trimmed with lace, since it was too hot for a dressing gown and pregnancy had made her more sensitive to the heat.

Catherine heard a voice calling her from inside the bedroom before Justin followed her outside.

"I woke and didn't see you. Why did you get up?"

He took hold of both her hands and gazed at her face in the moonlight.

"I was hot, so I came outside."

He put his arm around her and led her to the edge of the rail, stroking her hair tenderly.

"Remember this, my love. Every day that passes is a day closer to the day I return. As long as we're in each other's thoughts, we're never apart."

He sighed and looked at her stomach, which still showed no sign of the life growing inside her.

"My mother knows you're pregnant. She's thrilled. I expect she'll come and see you or send for you. Our child will be the bridge that connects you. I've asked Ying to come and see you as often as she can, so you won't be lonely."

Catherine leaned her head on his shoulder, forcing herself to suppress her sorrow.

"Don't worry about me. May God protect you," she whispered. "When you return, I'll be waiting for you with our child. I promise."

* * *

Kham knelt in front of the chair where Catherine was sitting, her face anxious as she held out a small silver tray with a glass of milk on it.

"It's goat's milk. You haven't been eating lately, Mem."

Catherine put down her crocheting. She was making a tiny sweater for her child who was due in less than five months' time. Preparing for the birth was the only thing that kept her going.

"Thank you," she smiled, taking the glass of milk to drink. It was about all she could tolerate since everything else made her nauseous.

She was almost in the fifth month of her pregnancy and her nausea was gradually diminishing, but she still had no appetite. Justin's mother had not been to visit her on the raft, which was only natural since it was not customary for elders to visit younger relatives, nor did she send for her, but she was not so unkind as to forbid Princess Kanika from calling on her from time to time.

Princess Kanika was keen to call and was excited to see Catherine.

"Your stomach isn't showing," she said when she saw Catherine before stopping herself in embarrassment. "Oops…I shouldn't have said that. If my mother heard, she'd scold me."

The princess had a lot to tell her, and she spoke a mixture of Siamese and English, but it did not impede communication. The openness and sincerity in her pretty face that bore a striking resemblance to Justin's seemed to bring him closer.

Once the princess asked, "Is there anything you want? My brother told me that if there's anything you want, if isn't too hard to find, I should get it for you."

Catherine smiled gratefully.

"I'd like some books."

"Books," the princess repeated in English. "What kind of books?"

"Novels to help pass the time. The days seem so long."

* * *

A few days later, the servant of Thomas George Knox brought a letter to the raft and gave it to Kham.

It was a short and formal.

"Madam,
I am sending you a letter from Lieutenant Arthur Lindley.
Respectfully yours,
Thomas George Knox"

Catherine caught her breath when she saw a cream envelope tucked inside the first and almost opened it, but she stopped herself. What was the point of reading Arthur's letter? It was over between them, and whether he had agreed to divorce her or refused to change his mind made no difference to her. She was no longer Mrs Lindley but the wife of Prince Vijjuprapha and the child growing inside her had made them a family. She put Arthur's letter inside her trunk without touching it again.

On the Wings of Love 155

***

The news reached Siam that the Siamese envoy had arrived at the court of Queen Victoria. They had been well received and were to remain in London for several months before returning to Siam.

Luang Surawiset informed Catherine of the news, and she did not know whether to laugh or cry. He had asked Princess Kanika to talk to her as an intermediary before his visit.

"My aunt told me Luang Surawiset's coming to see you tomorrow, so you should be ready for him."

"Luang Surawiset? Oh…Captain Dick," she remembered. "Why does he want to see me?"

"He has news from my brother, and he's bringing you a book. My eldest brother will come with me tomorrow when Khun Luang arrives."

At first, Catherine did not understand why Justin's siblings needed to be present when Captain Dick arrived, but then the princess explained.

"My mother wants us to be there because you're here alone and it isn't appropriate for a man to visit you."

Mom Yad thought the matter so important that she had called for her eldest son to be a witness as it was not customary for a Siamese man to visit another man's wife when he was not home. Luang Surawiset had no choice because Prince Vijjuprapha had asked him to take books to the king and to bring a letter to the Englishwoman, and he was the most fluent in English of all the nobles in the Front Palace.

He had also brought a book by Sir Walter Scott and told her, "Khun Chom Klee said that you like to read, so I asked Mr Knox if I could borrow this book for you. Take your time. He's in no hurry to have it back."

At that moment, he noticed her swollen stomach, and his awkwardness turned to concern, so he asked, "Have you seen adoctor?"

"Yes. Dr Bradley's been to see me."

"Ah, Dr Bradley," he repeated. "I don't think the palace will allow a man to deliver your child. Prince Vijjuprapha's wife must be seen to by a midwife."

"Are there English midwives in Siam?"

156   A Passage to Siam

Luang Surawiset's awkwardness returned.

"No, madam. I meant a Siamese midwife."

"I can't allow it."

How could she leave her child in the hands of a Siamese midwife who did not speak the same language? Although Catherine had never seen a Siamese birth, Dr Bradley had told her about the custom of lying by the fire after giving birth which he had witnessed in the palace. Mother and child would lie on a low bamboo table with a fire beneath it day and night for a whole month.

"I couldn't stand to see it. I pitied the young woman. It was terrible," he grumbled, since the old American doctor was firmly against the practice.

"I can't allow it," Catherine repeated, realising that another unexpected obstacle had presented itself.

* * *

The white wicker cradle stood beside the bed covered with a mattress and a tiny pillow framed with lace. Everything was white, including the crocheted blanket folded on top. Catherine reached out to tenderly pick up the cotton baby dress framed with lace before putting it back on the side of the crib.

Kham sat on the floor and gazed at the items excitedly before saying softly, "I'll put them away, so they don't get dusty."

It was true. There was more dust in Siam than in England and the houses had to be swept constantly. Catherine turned from the baby items that Justin had sent from England with his letter and replied, "I'll put them in the trunk, but I'll leave the crib there."

Catherine didn't know, and Kham dared not tell her, but in the palace, they believed that preparing things before the birth of a baby was unlucky, and that if you did, the baby would not live to use them. Kham feared that Mom Yad must have already heard about it because, when Luang Surawiset came to bring the items from the prince, the young princess and the eldest prince had been there and seen everything. Two days later, Princess Kanika was sent by her mother as a mediator. Catherine was crocheting a hat for her child so that the child would not catch a cold when taken outside.

When the princess caught sight of it, her eyes widened.

"What are you doing?" she exclaimed. "Stop! It's unlucky!"

"If I don't prepare, how will I be ready in time?"

"You don't need to prepare," the princess explained. "All you need is a cloth to wrap the baby in and a simple cradle. You'll be lying by the fire."

"I shan't be lying by the fire."

The princess looked alarmed again.

"You must lie by the fire. If you don't, you'll get sick. All my sisters-in-law lay by the fire. Everyone does."

There was no point arguing. Catherine was not going to lie by the fire. She would not be able to stand it. The princess left with the understanding that Catherine did not believe her and would continue to crotchet the hat in the days the followed. And she was certain that Catherine would refuse to lie by the fire.

* * *

In March, the cool breeze was replaced by blistering heat and Catherine had to bathe several times a day until the monsoon arrived in May.

One night, Catherine woke to heavy rain pounding on the roof of the raft, which was rocked back and forth by the waves. It was safe, however, because it had been tied securely to a post on the riverbank. She listened to the rain for a moment before sliding down from the bed and tiptoeing past Kham to open the door which led outside.

The waves pounded the raft and after a while Catherine felt her insides begin to contract and a dull pain spread through her stomach. Gradually the pain increased, and she felt so dizzy she wanted to lie down but could not pull herself back inside.

"Kham! Kham!"

She called many times before Kham heard her voice above the storm.

She hurried outside and helped Catherine back inside.

"Kham, go and fetch Dr Bradley."

Kham called two of the other women asleep on the raft to attend to Catherine while she hurried to the main house undeterred by the rain. Mom Yad had told her several days before to tell her as soon the foreigner's contractions began.

Even though she did not approve of her daughter-in-law in the least, she had not forgotten that the life inside her was her own flesh and blood, no less than any of her other grandchildren. Shortly after Kham told the servants in the palace, everyone was awake. If it had been any of her other daughters-in-law, there would have been a room prepared for the birth and for lying by the fire, and someone would have been sent to call the midwife.

But this foreigner had said that she refused to give birth with a midwife or lie by the fire like other women, and Mom Yad, both angry and anxious for her grandchild, had not known what to do. Her husband had resolved the matter.

"If she wants a foreign doctor, then call a foreign doctor."

How could a man perform the delivery for the prince's wife? Mom Yad was lost for words until the last minute when she told a servant, "Go and fetch Dr Bradley."

The doctor's house was not hard to find as everyone in Bangkok knew him, but tonight the storm was heavy, and rowing a boat was difficult.

Kham and the other servant girls led Catherine to a low bamboo table against the wall and helped to massage her. Mom Yad arrived with her youngest daughter, growing increasingly agitated when there was still no sign of the foreign doctor. Catherine was not aware of who had surrounded her as the faces were dim and their voices indistinct. The pain washed over her in waves, and she writhed in agony attempting to relieve the suffering.

"Heavens above! What are we to do? The foreign doctor's still not here!" Mom Yad cried, looking out of the raft since the doctor had been sent for over an hour earlier and the rain had now stopped, leaving only drops of water dripping from the roof. The faint crowing of roosters was carried on the wind and silver rays were beginning to stretch across the sky, but there was still no sign of the doctor.

"Fetch the midwife," Princess Kanika urged her mother, her face pale with worry. "Please, mother. What if she dies? What will my brother say?"

Mom Yad decided at once and called for a servant.

"Go and fetch Fuang. We can't wait any longer."

Catherine felt numb and was barely conscious. She did not see the elderly, but strong and agile midwife look at her and shake her head.

"The first child is always hard," she muttered. "But don't worry. I've brought holy water. If she drinks this, the child will soon come out."

At that moment, Dr Bradley stepped onto the raft in agitation, holding a medicine kit. He could speak Siamese and apologized to Mom Yad, explaining that he had been delayed because he had been called to another patient that night. By that time, Mom Yad was so worried about her daughter-in-law that she forgot to protest that the doctor was a man.

"Go and see her, doctor. She's unconscious. I'm worried sick."

Dr Bradley ordered boiling water and examined Catherine. He showed no sign of alarm, but asked everyone to leave the room so that he could deliver the child undisturbed.

Only the midwife remained.

"The child won't come out. I'm afraid it's a breech birth," she whispered to Mom Yad.

Mom Yad went pale. If the midwife could not deliver the child, it usually meant neither mother nor child would survive.

"Go and help, Fuang. Never mind what the doctor says. I don't want Mem to die. My son left her in my care. He'll say I left her to die."

Catherine's child was pink all over and resembled a rose wrapped in soft white cloth. Her hair was brown and silky, and her little face round and bright. Her eyes were closed with long curled lashes and her tiny lips were red, no bigger than her mother's fingertip. She was as dainty as a doll.

"You have a daughter, ma'am."

Dr Bradley lifted her from the cradle and gave her to Catherine. He had been home to sleep and had returned to see his patient that afternoon. Catherine took her child carefully, holding her breath as she seemed as fragile as a crystal glass, and she looked up at the doctor, her eyes filling with tears.

"A daughter…" she breathed shakily. "Is she alright, doctor?"

Dr Bradley knitted his brows and hesitated before answering.

"She's small, but as far as I can see…she was delivered safely," he said, choosing his words carefully. "Her breathing's a little irregular, but it might be because…she's still a new-born. It might not be anything."

Catherine hugged the soft little body to her chest without paying much attention to the doctor's words. All she could think of was the tiny baby in her arms. She could hardly believe that she and Justin had created this new life. She was perfect in every way.

The only thing missing was Justin.

∗ ∗ ∗

Everyone from the main house came to the raft. The servants peeked in from the outside, and the relatives sat inside after hearing the news that the baby had been born safely. Even Mom Yad was excited to see the new-born.

"Bring her to see me, Ying. Let's have a look at her."

"You can't hold her yet, Mother. Dr Bradley's still inside the room. He's talking to Mem," the princess whispered. "You can go inside. I'll take you in."

"I'm not going inside if the foreign doctor's still in there," she insisted. "Why is he here again? He's a strange one. I heard them say in the Front Palace that he's against lying by the fire."

This greatly concerned Mom Yad because she had been told that Catherine refused to lie by the fire. The practice was considered essential for women since it helped the uterus to heal and return to its normal size more quickly.

Dr Bradley smiled at Catherine encouragingly.

"You need to rest. It was a tough delivery but thank God you came through okay. As for the baby…"

He glanced at the baby asleep in her arms.

On the Wings of Love 161

"There's no fever, but her breathing's irregular. Make sure she doesn't catch a cold. Keep her warm."

He stopped when he saw the young woman who had just entered the room.

"Good afternoon, Your Highness."

Princess Kanika had been reluctant to come inside and talk to the foreign doctor, but everyone agreed that she should be given the task.

She decided to get straight to the point.

"My mother's waiting outside, doctor. She wants to know when Mem will lie by the fire."

Catherine understood and looked at the doctor imploringly.

"She won't," he said slowly. "She needs nourishment. She's very weak."

"She must lie by the fire, doctor. It's already been prepared."

"Ma'am needs rest. Someone to keep an eye on her is all that's required."

Catherine did not care about lying by the fire or anything else. All that concerned her was the tiny baby in her arms. She was careful even when she bent down to kiss her and to touch her silky dark hair. She gazed at the long, curled eyelashes above the soft little cheeks. The more she gazed, the more she felt that she was like a fragile pink rosebud that could bruise at the touch.

Her heart was flooded with love for her, and she kissed her again.

"My beautiful rose," she whispered. "I'm so happy God gave you to me. When your father sees you, he'll be delighted."

The baby's cheeks were round, and her little nose was sharp. Her brown hair was wavy, and she resembled both Justin and Catherine. As soon as Catherine saw her, she knew what her name must be.

"Rosalind," she called her. "My rose."

Rosalind, after the beautiful, clever, and brave heroine of Shakespeare's 'As You Like it'.

Catherine bent down to kiss her soft hair, and she opened her eyes.

Her eyes were not blue like Catherine's or black like Justin's but were hazel like the canals of Bangkok that sparkled in the sunlight.

162   A Passage to Siam

Catherine smiled and whispered, "My Oriental princess. Now I have you, I'll never be lonely. We'll wait for your father together."

Catherine looked down at her child to see if Rosalind was awake. She slept most of the time, which was good in one way because she was easy to care for, but in another way, it was concerning because she hardly took any milk and when she woke, she was irritable. It had been raining since the morning and Catherine had shut the windows, but Rosalind was restless and would not take any milk.

She touched her forehead and was startled, finding it red hot.

"Kham," she called. "Fetch a bowl of water. I'll wipe her down."

Catherine was beginning to tire of the rain and the weather that was boiling hot one minute and cool and damp the next, making it easy for children to get fevers, especially ones as tiny as Rosalind who was less than a month old and seemed too fragile for Siam's harsh climate. She slowly wiped her, and her heart sank because Rosalind seemed to have got thinner, her tiny lips were pale, and her rose-coloured skin had turned white.

"If the fever doesn't go, I'll have to get someone to fetch Dr Bradley again."

9

Blown Away by the Wind

Rosalind's crying grew louder. It soon became a continuous scream that swelled her tiny neck. Her face was red and hot like a furnace, and her hazel eyes rolled back in their sockets.

Catherine picked her up and walked back and forth with her in between wiping her down. She was shaking with fear, knowing that the tiny life was hanging on by a thread that could break at any moment. The baby's cries were carried from the raft to the main house where they were heard by Mom Yad, who grumbled, "How can Mem leave the child crying like that?"

When the cries continued, her annoyance turned to anxiety, which grew stronger with every passing moment until she could stand it no longer. She nodded to her daughter and a servant.

"Let's go and see in case she's ill. Can't Mem even take care of her baby?"

The rain was still pelting down, but Princess Kanika was undeterred, picking up an umbrella and hurrying ahead of her mother across the bridge from the bank to the raft, unnerved by the unceasing cries. As soon as she got to the raft, she hurried inside the bedroom and saw Catherine putting the baby down on the bed. When she saw the child convulsing, she cried, "Oh, no! She's having convulsions! Mother! Do something!"

Mom Yad came inside panting, alarmed but collected.

"Ying, pass the child to me. Find some green medicine to rub her with and drop some in her mouth."

Catherine's heart sank when Rosalind was pulled from her arms as if the tiny frame had been blown away by the wind, but she could not protest. Everyone was trying to help her child, even Justin's mother

164   A Passage to Siam

who had never shown her any warmth. Rosalind's screams pierced her heart, indicating that the tiny child was struggling with all her might against this sickness and the hand of death that was trying to snatch her life away.

The cries became quieter, broken by little sobs in her throat, until finally there was silence. The tiny chest that had been heaving up and down a moment earlier became still.

The rain stopped, but the sky was still damp and grey, and drops of water fell from the roof like tears. Rosalind lay still on the bed as if she was asleep. Her pink lips were almost white, parted just a little as if to say her last goodbye to her mother, and her eyes were closed, the long lashes brushing her still warm cheeks.

Catherine knelt beside the bed, paying no heed to Mom Yad and Princess Kanika who stepped back in silence. She hugged the soft fragile body to her chest before placing her own cheek against the baby's cheek, which would soon become as cold as the earth where she would sleep forever.

Catherine kissed her child, feeling that a part of her had been broken and would never be the same again.

*** *** ***

From that day on, Catherine did not know what she was living for. She could not eat or sleep, and words of comfort made no difference to her. Although she allowed Princess Kanika to take Rosalind's tiny body from her, all she felt was numbness, even when Mom Yad dealt with her own sorrow by scolding her.

"How could she leave her child to die? She ignored all the customs. There was no ceremony of any kind. And now it's too late."

"Mother," Princess Kanika whispered. "Mem understands."

"Well, I'm telling the truth. I've lived a long time. She would only listen to Dr Bradley, but he can't bring my grandchild back, can he?"

"Oh, Mother! My brother's on the other side of the world, and her baby's dead. She's all alone. Have you no sympathy?"

Mom Yad was silent, realising she had been too harsh, but she was too proud to admit it, so she said, "If my son hadn't married a mem, this wouldn't have happened."

Catherine understood what she was saying, but it made no difference. Nothing could touch her anymore.

The Siamese did not bury their dead. The departed were cremated at temples and their ashes or bones kept by their descendants, so that they would be able to make merit for them during merit-making ceremonies. This was another obstacle for Catherine since she wanted her child to have a proper burial.

Dr Bradley agreed. But Mom Yad was opposed to the idea.

"She must stay here so we can all make merit for her. Otherwise, the merit won't reach her."

Death was not remote from her because almost every family had experienced the death of a child, and when it happened to one's own family, making merit for the departed soul could help to ease the pain. Justin's father agreed with her.

"Let someone tell Mem not to bury the child yet. She should wait for her father. Keep her in the building at the end of the orchard for now."

His palace, like other homes in Bangkok, was surrounded by orchards. Further back from the raft was a group of Thai-style houses, and a few feet away were furrows interspersed with rows of many kinds of fruit trees. There were several huts among them, some belonging to the servants, and some used for storing fruit.

Others were used for housing the bodies of relatives who for various reasons were awaiting cremation.Everyone agreed that Rosalind should be kept there for the time being.

Catherine was forced to accept the wishes of her husband's relatives.

Princess Kanika understood best, comforting her with the words, "Wait for my brother to come home. If you bury her before, he'll be devastated."

Luang Surawiset brought news that Justin had almost reached Siam, and both the Grand Palace and the Front Palace were filled with excitement that the first Siamese envoy in history had been successful.

It was a new chapter in Siam's history.

***

The white wicker cradle remained in its place with the white baby dress trimmed with lace still hung over the edge and the white woollen blanket neatly folded on top of the mattress.

The only thing missing was the tiny baby.

Catherine would spend hours each day next to the cradle, stroking the white cotton dress distractedly. She had lost weight and grown pale and the dresses that had once fitted snugly around her waist now hung loosely. Kham was worried and tried to get her to eat.

"Have some milk, Mem. There's soup, too."

Although she tried to swallow it, Catherine still grew thin.

Catherine slept late because, unless she was exhausted, she would be visited by nightmares. She waited until fatigue overcame her and finally fell asleep.

In the dim candlelight, someone sat on the edge of the bed. A familiar pair of arms enfolded her and whispered in her ear.

"I'm home, my love."

Catherine's heart almost stopped. She had never fainted before, but suddenly everything around her was swallowed by darkness. The next thing she knew, she was lying on the bed and Kham was wiping her face with jasmine-scented water. Justin was sitting next to the bed, her hand in his. When she opened her eyes, Justin smiled at her, the candlelight casting a glow on his golden skin. He had not changed at all.

There was concern in his black eyes, but he concealed his agitation by asking playfully, "Are you so shocked that I came home?"

Catherine reached out to clutch his arm and Kham crawled away before dutifully shutting the door behind her.

She brushed Justin's chin with a trembling hand and whispered, "I can hardly believe it's you. I thought I was still dreaming."

Justin gently kissed her forehead and chuckled, filling her with warmth.

"I'm here to wake the sleeping princess," he said, holding his arms out to hug her again. "I've missed you so much."

Justin looked at her again and his handsome face fell as he caressed her shoulders. The neckline of her white nightdress trimmed with lace was wide enough to reveal how thin she had become since she had lost Rosalind, and her collar bone was protruding.

"You've lost weight."

Catherine glanced down at herself despondently.

"I haven't been taking care of myself," she whispered, stroking the muscular arm under his shirt. "Not like you. You're just the same."

Justin moved back as if he had just thought of something.

"I can't stay long. I must meet my father. Listen, my love…About our child. You must let it go."

That was all it took to bring her stoicism crashing down, and before she knew it, she was leaning her head on his shoulder and sobbing uncontrollably.

"Don't cry, dearest," Justin soothed. "There's nothing in the world that's for certain, and sorrow won't bring her back."

"I still can't accept it," Catherine sobbed. "I don't understand why it had to happen to Rosalind."

Justin squeezed her gently.

"It can happen to anyone, my love. My mother had eight children and only four survived. Don't be sad. We'll have other children, and this will have been just like a bad dream."

***

The Siamese diplomatic mission was a great success and Catherine sensed the general excitement.

Friendly relations between Siam and Great Britain had been cemented and Siam would not have to engage in conflict with the superpower as neighbouring countries had done. The king of Siam chose compromise over confrontation, aware that Siam's neighbours were on a knife edge with Vietnam on the verge of a conflict with France.

If war broke out and Siam was unprepared, the wars from their neighbours could spread to the kingdom.

***

A paddle boat coursed slowly across the Chao Phraya River from the Thonburi side to the Bangkok side, headed towards the raft, unperturbed by the strong rays of the afternoon sun.

The weather in the cool season was comfortable and suited Catherine's condition. This pregnancy, like the last one, had made her feel hot and drowsy easily, so she was glad to sit on the deck of the raft and catch the breeze. All the villagers were used to her by now and no longer came to stare like before. She brought her hand to her forehead to shield her eyes from the sun as she looked out at the Western man with the long beard in the black suit who sat in the middle of the boat and smiled to herself.

Dr Bradley was coming to visit her again. By this time, they had become good friends, and talked about all kinds of topics, except the one that he had decided not to mention, which was that of Charlotte Palmer. Nobody had told her if Charlotte Palmer was still in Bangkok or if she had left to cause trouble for some other man, but she was aware that Charlotte had been involved with Robert Hunter for a time.

Dr Bradley was a missionary and considered it inappropriate to gossip. Today, he was bringing news about another British woman.

"There's a Scottish woman here who wants to see you. She married an English sailor stationed in Singapore, and now she's in Bangkok. She's been looking for you. I told her you're married to a Siamese prince, so it might be tricky for her to meet you. I came to ask if you'd be willing to see her. Her name's…"

"Annie!" Catherine interrupted excitedly, forgetting herself. "Sorry, doctor. I'd love for her to visit me."

Since Annie had left for Singapore, Catherine hadn't heard from her, but she had promised that if she ever returned to Siam she would come and visit her. She had kept her promise.

The next day, Dr Bradley had someone row Annie in a boat to meet Catherine. Annie looked more mature without her maid's uniform, but she still appeared as robust as before, and now she was brimming with joy and confidence. When she saw Catherine, she clasped her hands together in delight.

"Miss Catherine! Ye're still just as bonnie as ever!!"

Annie sat down happily and told her about her wedding in Singapore and how her husband came to Siam several times a year. There were more British people in Singapore and Annie had made several friends there.

She suddenly remembered something and said, "Oh! Ye heard about Mrs. Rowland, did ye no'?"

Catherine was taken aback.

"I haven't heard from her for ages. Why? Is she alright?"

Annie looked puzzled for a moment before her expression became solemn.

"Oh, aye! Nobody told ye, did they? Colonel Rowland must've just told his kin in England."

Catherine started to feel alarmed.

"Annie, what happened?"

"Mrs. Rowland's passed away. She took ill all of a sudden. Jack reckons it might've been typhoid. When there's an outbreak, it takes so many lives."

Annie's voice became blurred as soon as she had said the first sentence and Catherine was no longer aware of what she was saying until she heard her exclaim in alarm, "Oh, nae! Ye've gone pale! Wait... I'll fetch my smellin' salts."

Kham, who had been serving tea, quickly stepped in to help, explaining to Annie that Catherine was four months pregnant.

"Oh, aye! No wonder! I thought ye'd filled out a wee bit, but it's hard to tell. Oh, I'm so sorry for upsettin' ye. I thought ye'd heard. Mrs. Rowland passed away last year, but the colonel's still in India, as far as I know. One o' Jack's pals sails between Singapore and Bombay, ye see."

Catherine felt as if the thread connecting Siam to her homeland had been broken by Mary's demise.

"Oh! And there's another thing! I heard Lieutenant Lindley's left the army. He's gone to work for his brother's tea company, but he still has to travel to the East. One o' Jack's pals met him in Sri Lanka. They grow tea there, ye see. Have ye heard anything from him lately?"

Arthur's letter had remained unopened, and its contents were still a mystery.

"No, Annie."

Perhaps by now he had remarried and started a family.

Mary's former maid made Catherine realise how much she had missed the social connections she had been used to.

"Have ye heard about Charlotte Palmer? Her reputation's spread all the way to Singapore. She's done wi' Robert Hunter now, but she said he was just a friend. She says that about all o' them."

"Is she still in Bangkok?"

"Aye, she's always about with navigators and sailors. I saw her yesterday, but I dinnae want anything to do wi' a lass like that."

Annie left for Singapore three weeks later and the raft was quiet again. Even Justin noticed that Catherine appeared despondent without the young Scotswoman to talk to.

He asked playfully, "Are you lonely without your friend?"

"Yes," Catherine admitted. "Without her I feel cut off."

The smile faded from his face, and he studied her uncertainly.

"Are you homesick? Isn't Siam your home now? And what about me?"

"I am homesick," she replied truthfully. "But I haven't forgotten that it was me who chose to leave. Siam isn't my home, but I can live here because I have you."

Justin's frown disappeared and he smiled at her.

"I'm happy to hear that, Catherine. Sometimes I'm scared…"

"Scared?" she repeated.

"Scared that one day, you'll suddenly decide I don't mean anything to you and there'll be nothing to keep you in Siam anymore."

Whether it was because he wanted to 'keep her in Siam' or because he felt sorry for her, whenever he could take time away from his palace duties, he would take her out in a boat to visit the different temples as they used to do.

Catherine was not afraid of falling in the water since she could swim and, by now, she could step in and out of a boat adroitly, even in a long skirt, so she never refused Justin's invitations. Nothing made her happier than being alone with him away from the eyes of everyone on the raft, even if it was only for a few hours.

Lately, Justin's father's health had been in decline, and it was understood that his days were numbered. He had grown painfully thin and was now bedridden.

No matter what time Justin came home from his work, he would always go to look in on his father before returning to the raft, and Catherine noticed that he appeared tired. The boat trips did him good, she thought.

* * *

The birth of Catherine's second child was smoother than the first.

Justin was able to ensure that Dr Bradley performed the delivery without anyone protesting, including his mother, and for another thing, Mom Yad was so preoccupied with her husband's condition that she gave little thought to her daughter-in-law's delivery.

Catherine's contractions began in the early hours of the morning, and when Dr Bradley arrived in time, she felt more confident than she had the last time. She was mentally prepared for the birth, knowing that the pain would only be temporary, and the baby was delivered safely that afternoon.

"It's a boy, ma'am," Dr Bradley beamed. "He's healthy and has strong lungs. You can hear him crying."

He placed the tiny bundle in her arms and Catherine felt the warmth from the tiny body beneath the blanket spread straight to her heart. She stroked the soft dark hair above the round rubicund face and was overwhelmed with joy, which she hadn't felt for a long time.

"My son…" she whispered. "Thank God you're healthy."

What she wished for most of all was for Justin to be there with her, but it wasn't to be. He was still at the palace and wouldn't be back until nightfall.

"Does the prince know?" she asked Dr Bradley.

"His attendant's gone to let him know he has a healthy son. He'll be over the moon, I'm sure."

This put Catherine's mind at rest, and she fell into a deep sleep, which she did not wake from until the next morning. She woke to find Justin beside her, his face filled with delight.

"Kham," she called softly. "Bring the child for his father to see."

The child was asleep on the mattress and Kham picked him up carefully and brought him to her. All the others peeked in excitedly from behind the door. Her son was different from Rosalind. His hair was dark brown, and his face resembled his father's more than his mother's. Though his skin was rosier than most Siamese babies, he was not as pink as a Western child, like Rosalind had been.

Catherine glanced up at her husband and all the sadness, pain, and emptiness disappeared and her whole being was flooded with happiness.

Mom Yad came to visit that evening. As soon as she set eyes on her grandson, her haughty manner melted away, and she exclaimed, "Oh, what a relief! He doesn't look like a foreigner!"

Justin glanced at Catherine, knowing she understood, but she did not appear offended.

After a while, Mom Yad asked, "Ask Mem if she'll let us shave his head when he's a month old for the spirit-calling ceremony. She didn't do it last time and look what happened."

Catherine told her husband softly, "Whatever your mother wants."

By now, Catherine did not care if her child was taken to church or temple. Whether he was English or Siamese was no longer of any importance to her. All that mattered was that he lived.

When Catherine did not protest, Mom Yad was pleased, and her thoughts turned to all the rites and ceremonies that would be performed.

At last, she asked, "When will you take him to see his grandfather?"

This signified that the child would be accepted as his grandson.

✳✳✳✳

"We haven't named him yet. What will you name him?" Catherine asked a few days before the head-shaving ceremony.

Justin looked up from the cradle. He had just returned from the palace and was getting ready for bed, since he always looked in on his son before retiring. There was no point mentioning that he had not yet been christened. The child had implicitly become Siamese and a Buddhist.

Catherine secretly hoped that she would be able to have her child christened at some point. Although there were no Anglican churches in Siam, it did not matter. Her child might become Presbyterian like Dr Bradley. Dr Bradley would be pleased because he was greatly discouraged by the fact that, although the American missionaries had been welcomed by the Siamese, they had gained hardly any converts.

Her thoughts were interrupted by Justin who smiled and told her, "I've got good news. King Pinklao has invited us to the Front Palace. He's going to name our child."

He gazed at her, smiling as if he was waiting for her to show her excitement, but when she just appeared puzzled, he explained, "According to custom, the grandparents name the child, so it's a great honour for a child to be named by the king. He changed my name from 'Saifa' to 'Vijjuprapha' when my father gave me to him."

Catherine remembered the Second King of Siam fondly. Although she had not seen him for some time, she recalled with gratitude that he had not been hostile towards her, even though he had not approved of her relationship with Justin at first. Now she was his wife and had born him a child, the king was giving them his blessing.

"It will be an honour," she replied softly.

Justin was relieved that she was happy because their different schools of thought had caused him some consternation. Although she had never defied him, since she had been raised with the belief that that wives should obey their husbands, that was as far as it went. She had not been taught to submit to her husband's parents as well, so Mom Yad was always hesitant about matters concerning her daughter-in-law.

Prince Saifa was aware that Catherine was expected to take her son to see his grandparents regularly and to help his mother with the housework but, so far, Catherine had done neither. He could not blame either of them for these cultural differences. He could only hope that in time these differences would be smoothed over.

***

Their audience with King Pinklao was the day before the head-shaving ceremony. That day, the sky was overcast, and Catherine was relieved that her month-old son would not have to be exposed to the harsh rays of the sun, but she still shaded him with an umbrella.

"He'll be fine, my love," Justin soothed, noticing her anxiety.

"He's still so young. I don't want to take him outside unless we have to."

"Just this once won't hurt."

King Pinklao allowed Prince Vijjuprapha to bring his wife to meet him in his study and to sit on a chair without having to crawl inside like the Siamese. Khun Chom Klee was also present.

"Klee, come and see your grandson."

Khun Chom Klee appeared uneasy. The first reason was that she was not used to standing behind the king in accordance with Western customs, and the second reason was that Bua was with her. Even though her earlier hopes had been dashed, when she saw the child, she could not help being filled with regret. If only the child had been the prince's and Bua's, she would have been overjoyed.

Prince Vijjuprapha noticed his mother's discomfort, so he eased the tension by taking the child for her to see. Khun Chom Klee bent down to look and muttered, "Oh, look how ugly he is!" It was customary for Siamese elders to refrain from complimenting babies, believing that evil spirits would not cause harm to them if they were labelled as ugly.

Bua stood slightly apart from them. Although standing behind the king was strange to her, she remained composed, but when she saw the tiny baby, she could not contain her excitement. The colour rose to her cheeks, and she glanced at Catherine and smiled at her.

Bua was usually calm and did not betray her emotions, but this time her pretty face was filled with excitement. Her eyes sparkled as she gazed at the tiny baby, but she dared not touch him. The prince noticed her delight, so he held the cushion out for her to see the child better.

Khun Chom Klee looked at the dashing young man and the lovely young girl, standing next to each other with the child between them, thinking that they made a perfect couple, and sighed.

King Pinklao named the child, telling them, "I'll name your child Vijjupong. You can give him a nickname of your own. He should also have an English name. I know that foreigners have several names. You can name him after his maternal grandfather if you like, but one of his names should be Charles."

Catherine remembered that the king was fond of the works of Charles Dickens, and she suppressed a smile as she curtsied. She was pleased with the name and decided that he would be called Charles.

*＊＊

Mom Yad was delighted with the new prince's name and boasted of it to her relatives when they were assembled for the head-shaving ceremony.

"The king named him like he did Saifa. His name's Vijjupong."

She had asked the next most senior noble in her husband's palace to preside over the ceremony since her husband was unable to leave his bed.

"That's a fine name. I heard he has a foreign name too."

"Yes, he does."

Mom Yad glanced at her son to pronounce the name for her.

"His name's Charles," the prince said.

"Oh! Let's call him Chan for short. That can be his nickname," the nobleman pronounced. And so, the little prince with the dark brown eyes was nicknamed Chan.

The head-shaving ceremony began. Since it was an important ceremony, there was both a Hindu priest and Buddhist monks present. The monks chanted the prayers, and the Hindu priest blew a horn and beat a small drum, and a Siamese gamelan played for the duration of the ceremony.

Catherine joined the ceremony, but kept her hands folded in her lap instead of placing her palms together in a prayer-like posture. She looked on quietly while the ceremony was taking place, her concern for her son fading when she saw how much he had been welcomed by his father's relatives. Incredibly, Charles had become the bridge that connected her to her husband's family.

Khun Chom Klee joined the ceremony. She did not appear as excited as the others, but she did not look unhappy. She simply sat quietly, regarding her son and the young child thoughtfully.

176 A Passage to Siam

Sometimes, she glanced at Bua before glancing back at Catherine's husband. Catherine heard the whispers of two women sitting not far away from her.

"It's such a shame for Bua. Khun Chom Klee had planned for her to marry Prince Saifa."

"It depends on karma. It wasn't meant to be. That's why he got himself a foreign wife first."

Catherine's blood suddenly turned to ice.

***

Justin had told her a long time ago that Siamese parents arranged marriages for their children, and she had almost forgotten about it. Once she found out that the pretty young woman had been betrothed to her husband, she could not help watching the two of them like a hawk for the rest of the ceremony.

Bua sat behind Khun Chom Klee with her head bowed without saying a word as was expected of her. When she took her leave, Justin moved closer to Khun Chom to pay respect to her, and she gave him a benediction.

"May you prosper, my son, and may my grandson grow strong and healthy. Oh! Look at Bua here! She only needs to see a baby and she wants to pick it up."

Bua looked quickly away from the little prince, her face redening in embarrassment that Khun Chom had scolded her, albeit good-naturedly.

"I don't," she mumbled.

"When he's old enough to walk, I'll let you take him inside the Inner Court, Bua," Justin smiled. "Then you can pick him up as much as you want."

Bua didn't answer but placed her palms together and bowed her head in respect before hurriedly crawling out after Khun Chom. Catherine guessed that Bua considered Justin to be off limits just as she was out of bounds to men outside the palace.

Her relief remained with her until bedtime when Justin heard her singing softly to herself and remarked, "You're happy today."

Blown Away by the Wind   177

The baby was asleep, and Catherine put him in the cradle. She looked up at Justin and smiled. Her wavy flaxen hair rippled across her shoulders, shimmering like silk in the candlelight, and the fullness of her figure after childbirth was visible under her nightdress.

"Yes, I'm happy," she confessed. "I feel as if the dark clouds have gone. I have you…and our son. I don't want anything else."

His brown arms enfolded her, and his warm lips kissed her forehead tenderly.

"But I do, my love."

She glanced at him, puzzled, but saw his back eyes were sparkling.

"I want to have more children, so you won't be lonely when I'm away."

Catherine brushed his chin with her fingertip, and gazed at him in the candlelight, flickering in the river breeze.

"When Charles is older, I'm going to ask the king to send him to military college in India. Our son's education won't be inferior to any Englishman."

＊＊＊

Justin's father passed away three months after the head-shaving ceremony. He had grown gradually weaker and died peacefully like a withered leaf that had fallen to the ground.

His funeral was fitting for his status as a trusted relative of King Pinklao, and he was cremated at Sanam Luang in accordance with tradition. Everyone in his palace wore white, signifying that they were in mourning, and Catherine hurriedly sewed white clothes together for herself.

"There's no need for her to come," Mom Yad decided when Princess Kanika asked if Catherine would have to attend the cremation.

So Catherine remained on the raft. The uncomfortable truth was that, even though she and Justin had been married for three years, she was still viewed as an outsider.

＊＊＊

Charles grew into a chubby and vigorous little boy, larger than most boys of his age.

"He's growing up," said Princess Kanika, who came to play with the young prince every day. "Can I take him to see Mother?"

Mom Yad adored Charles, especially since he looked more like his father than his mother. Charles made Catherine's days go by quickly and kept her busy from dawn to dusk. At the same time, she was also assisting her husband with matters concerning the West.

Siam had entered a new chapter of diplomatic relations with Western powers. All through the year, the Siamese court was busy welcoming foreign guests with envoys from France, Britain, and Portugal within the space of a few months, and the king of Siam's reputation for treating Western visitors cordially increased.

* * *

"Catherine," Justin said urgently as he stepped onto the raft. "There are foreign guests coming to the Front Palace again. I need your help."

Foreign guests would visit the Front Palace of King Pinklao after visiting King Mongkut in the Grand Palace. Mostly, he would meet them in the Throne Hall.

"I'll need you to arrange a menu for the foreign visitors. And clothes for me."

This happened often and, each time, Catherine would be worn out from the preparations. The only people who were able to assist her were Won, her husband's assistant, and Bua, whom Khun Chom Klee sent from the palace to help with the food preparations, since she did not mind the smell of foreign food.

Bua was always pleased to see Catherine, and she was less shy than before, especially when they were alone.

"When will you bring your son to the palace, Mem? I want to see him again," she said.

"You love children. You should have a family of your own."

Bua's face reddened.

"I'd rather stay with my aunt. I don't want to get married."

Bua was sincere. Catherine had noticed with amazement that

Blown Away by the Wind 179

Bua did not think of the future and was content to focus on the present. She was happy making flower garlands, crocheting mats, or preparing food for hours at a time, and the thought of going outside never entered her head.

"Do you ever get homesick?" Catherine inquired.

"Yes," Bua answered. "But I seldom go home. Aunt doesn't want me to. She prefers me to stay with her."

"Don't you ever want to go outside the Front Palace?"

Bua looked puzzled.

"Go where, Mem?"

"I used to want to get away from my home to see the end of the horizon. I thought staying at home day after day was so dull."

Bua understood the words, but the expression on her face indicated that she did not comprehend Catherine's thoughts.

"I'm afraid to go outside."

Bua's answer was short, but telling, and Catherine was silent. Bua reminded her of her mother and sister. They were not as shy as Bua, but had similar perspectives, preferring a life that was narrow but safe.

***

Word spread from the palace that there was to be a Siamese envoy to France after the success of the envoy to Britain three years earlier.

"You'll have to go, won't you?" Catherine said when Justin had finished telling her about it.

"I don't know yet. It might be someone else. I'm responsible for the canons instead of Knox. I don't want to give it up."

His tanned handsome face filled with pride. The Second King of Siam had assigned him to train the artillerymen in the Front Palace instead of Knox. Prince Saifa's role in the Front Palace had become increasingly important and his mother and siblings were proud of him.

One month later, it was announced that King Pinklao had chosen Prince Vijjuprapha to go with the envoy to France.

Catherine learned of the news with dismay, even though she told herself it was to be expected. Her desire to go home, which she had tried to conceal, began to seep out like water through cracks. She missed her home, and she missed Longstock, the village she had longed to get away from. But now she had reached the end of the horizon, her home had become the place at the end of the horizon that she longed for.

As she packed her husband's clothes and belongings, she mused, "I wonder how Mother and Pauline are. My sister might have children by now. I haven't seen them for so long."

"Haven't you heard from her?" Justin asked.

"No," Catherine replied. An awkward silence followed. "I haven't written to Mother or Pauline for a long time. They don't know what happened."

Justin looked puzzled.

"Do you mean your mother doesn't know you separated from Lindley four years ago?"

"No. I didn't tell her."

"Why not? Is it because you think that one day you'll return to England, and no one will need to know you were the wife of a Siamese?"

"Justin!" Catherine gasped. "How can you say such a thing?"

Justin never lost his temper. He was sometimes irritable when he came home tired and found things were not as he expected, but such instances were rare as Catherine always saw to it that the servants had everything taken care of and that their home was clean and tidy. She had never realized that deep down, he hid a weak spot.

She gazed at him in disappointment.

"How can you say such a thing?" she repeated. "After all we've been through together."

Justin smiled and kissed her forehead gently.

"I'm sorry, my love. I didn't mean it. I know how much you love me. If you didn't love me, you wouldn't have given up everything for me."

His voice was as confident as his manner, and Catherine noticed that the robust but sensitive young man she had fallen in love with had become a resolute and self-assured man of influence. One reason was that King Pinklao held him in high esteem and had entrusted him with many important duties. And another was that, after his father's passing, he was now considered the head of his family by his siblings. After her husband's death, Mom Yad's role in the family had diminished, along with her vitality.

* * *

By now, Charles was walking, but the problem was he would not speak, even though he understood what was being said to him.

Catherine had asked Dr Bradley about it, and he had told her, "He might be confused about which language to use. Some of the missionaries' kids have the same problem. Their parents speak one language, and their nannies speak another. When he's old enough to tell the difference between languages, I'm sure he'll start talking. His development in other areas is normal."

Catherine was relieved. Charles had grown bigger than most children of his age with long arms and legs, and he looked as if he would be tall in the future. He resembled his father, but his skin was paler, and his hair was brown.

"Once he starts speaking, he won't stop, I'm sure," Mom Yad remarked.

Her close relationship with her grandson had eased the awkwardness between her and Catherine. Sometimes, the little boy would stay overnight at her palace, and she no longer treated Catherine with coldness, although they were still a long way from being close.

* * *

A few days before Justin departed, the scorching weather, which had lasted since the start of the hot season, showed no sign of relenting, even though it was already May. This resulted in an outbreak of sickness among the Siamese people, which Catherine had not expected.

"It can be deadly, ma'am," Dr Bradley explained. "Two reigns ago, they say it killed as many people as the Black Death did in Europe. The river was filled with dead bodies."

Without noticing Catherine's horror, he continued, "They couldn't cremate them fast enough, so the bodies piled up at the temple until

182   A Passage to Siam

vultures ate them. I've heard there's an outbreak coming from the North this year. You need to be careful. Make sure you drink boiled water. And don't eat anything unusual."

Although Catherine was not worried for herself, as she had hardly been sick since she had arrived in Siam, she was anxious for her son because small children were more susceptible to fevers and upset stomachs.

"Kham," she cautioned her maid. "Don't let Charles drink water from the river. Make sure you boil it first, and don't let him eat anything raw."

That evening, Kham brought the little boy back home. He was crying and had had a fever since the afternoon.

"Don't worry, Mem," Kham said confidently. "There's plenty of green medicine."

Justin had still not returned from the Front Palace. Catherine took Charles in her arms anxiously. Whenever her son had a slight headache or fever, she could not help worrying.

"I've given him some of Dr Bradley's medicine."

By nightfall, the slight fever that had seized Charles that evening had increased, and he was refusing to eat. All he did was cry and Catherine tried to comfort him in between wiping him down to reduce the fever.

Her anxiety increased when he had diarrhoea several times in a row.

"Kham, what has he eaten today?"

Kham went pale. She had heard that several of their neighbours had been sick with high fevers and diarrhoea.

"He had rice and bamboo shoot soup, Mem. Then he had coconut jelly."

"Did he eat his grandmother's desserts?" she grilled her.

There was no point in pressing her. Mom Yad would give her grandson whatever desserts he pointed to.

Before this, Charles had experienced occasional diarrhoea, but it had cleared up the next day. Even so, Catherine was always on edge until she was certain he was better.

It was almost light when Justin returned to the raft. When he heard of his son's condition, he reassured Catherine, "I don't expect it's anything serious. You rest and let the servants keep an eye on him."

"The fever won't go down," Catherine said in agitation. "And the diarrhoea won't stop. I think we should send someone to fetch Dr Bradley."

Justin did not think it was a serious matter. He had been preoccupied with preparations for his journey.

"Don't disturb Dr Bradley. He's busy enough as it is. Wait until tomorrow. If he's still no better, take him to see the doctor. Don't let him eat anything except boiled water for now."

Since Justin had lived in India for several years, he was used to tropical diseases, and was less concerned than Catherine. Nobody could have predicted that the sickness would reach Charles more quickly than those in the main house.

There might have been more concern about the boy's sickness if another important person had not also been taken ill.

That night, Kham came panting to tell Prince Vijjuprapha to go to the main house urgently.

"Princess Kanika's sick, Your Highness. She has a fever," she stammered.

Without a word, Justin hurried at once from his son on the raft to the main house. The doctor was called for urgently, but they could do little, since there were people sick in every home, and when the doctor saw them, all he could do was shake his head and hide his alarm with the words, "Take the medicine. It's probably not serious."

The princess's symptoms were severe with a high fever and diarrhoea, and she could not keep anything down, even medicine, which she vomited back up as soon as she had taken it. Mom Yad was still hopeful on the first day, but by the second day, she was filled with alarm when the princess's condition grew steadily worse. She began to burn incense and pray for her daughter's health to be restored.

At the same time, concern for Charles was side-lined because the little boy's condition was not as severe as the princess, and he simply had constant diarrhoea.

Dr Bradley came at once as soon as Catherine sent for him. He urged her to make sure that Charles drank plenty of water to bring down the fever and to refrain from milk that would make his diarrhoea worse.

"Tropical diseases are serious, ma'am. Women, the old, and the young are especially vulnerable."

The old doctor paused and sighed as he looked at Catherine's ashen face with pity. He gave her some medicine to reduce the fever and advised letting Charles get rid of all his waste rather than giving him medicine to stop the diarrhoea.

Justin returned from the main house later that morning and passed the American doctor as he was leaving.

"Didn't the doctor give Charles any medicine?" he asked Catherine as soon as he saw his son. "If this is his idea of treatment, we'll have to find him medicine ourselves."

"Dr Bradley said not to give him anything to stop the diarrhoea, He said to let him get rid of all his waste."

"Charles is still a baby. How can his body fight a sickness without medicine?" Justin protested. "I've lived in India. I know which herbs will help. Let Won bring him some."

Catherine hesitated.

"Are you sure it's a good idea?"

"Of course, I am. Don't tell me you don't have herbs in England."

When Justin was convinced that herbs would help Charles, Catherine gave in, even though she did not have the least confidence in them. She carried the little boy to the bed. In the space of two days, Charles had grown visibly thin, and his wavy hair was soaked with sweat. His chubby cheeks had become sunken, and he was pale with dark shadows under his eyes. When his mother picked him up, he sobbed and held onto her tightly. His soft little arms were burning like the rest of his body, and he had not eaten a thing for several hours after vomiting everything he ate up again.

Charles did not usually speak but pointed to things that he wanted. This time, Catherine could hardly believe her ears when her little boy held her tightly around the neck and whispered, "Mama…"

He remembered! When Catherine or Justin spoke to their son, they referred to themselves as Mama and Papa, but he had never spoken until now.

Blown Away by the Wind 185

Catherine's blood turned to ice when she realized that her son clinging onto her so tightly was a cry for help.

"It's alright, darling…" she whispered, unable to stop the tears that were rolling down her cheeks. "You'll be alright…you'll get better. I won't let you…"

She stopped, realizing she was powerless, not just in the face of the sickness alone, but in the hands of fate. It had defeated her before. When she had lost Rosalind.

The medicine that Won gave him had no effect because as soon as it was fed to him, he vomited. Prince Vijjuprapha's attendant did not give up. He tried to feed him the medicine several more times, hoping that at least some of it would be retained.

He told Catherine, "If he gets some of it, it's better than nothing."

Catherine mumbled, "Thank you," but could not say anymore because she was frozen with fear.

"Where's the prince?" she turned to ask Kham.

"He's gone to the house, Mem."

Justin had gone to the house to see his sister because Mom Yad had sent for him when her condition deteriorated.

"He should be with his son," she mumbled to herself and stopped abruptly.

If she called Justin back from the house, Mom Yad would surely scold her. She had never been welcomed there, even though she had not been expressly forbidden.

It was almost dawn when Prince Saifa returned from the house. The dim rays of the golden moon shone on the dark shadows of the trees along the path that led to the raft at the water's edge. It was silent except for the sound of the waves softly hitting the riverbank, and the air was hot and still. Not even a leaf was moving. Nature had stopped still as if in mourning.

The dim light of a candle shone out of the bedroom door, indicating that someone was awake. The prince stepped inside the bedroom, opening his mouth to ask his wife a question, and suddenly froze.

His son was lying peacefully on the bed as if he was asleep, his dark hair framing his face on the pillow. His eyes were shut, his long eyelashes brushing his sunken cheeks, and his little hands were folded across his chest.

On the floor next to the bed, Catherine was kneeling, the candlelight casting a shadow on her face against her clasped hands as she prayed for her son's soul.

"Why didn't you tell me? Why didn't you give me a chance to be with my son? You should have sent someone to fetch me…"

Catherine was silent, letting her husband's accusations flow over her like water. Kham tried to defend her.

"You were at the house with the princess, so she was afraid to disturb you."

"Enough, Kham! It has nothing to do with you!"

Kham went pale. The prince never shouted at his servants unlike Mom Yad, whose scolding they were used to. Seeing him angry filled Kham with alarm. Only Catherine remained as still as a statue, her face pale and her blue eyes staring blankly into space. She hugged the little body to her chest. By now, it was cold and soon it would become as hard as a waxwork.

"Did my son call for me, Catherine? When he was dying…why didn't you let me be with him…"

She did not understand the extent of Justin's rage. So far, his life had been filled with victory and achievements. He had won Catherine and defeated numerous obstacles to possess her, and he was proud of his distinguished position in the Front Palace where no one could rival the esteem in which the king held him. But amid all his achievements, he had been defeated.

Prince Vijjuprapha could not accept the fact that he had been unable to save his son from the hand of death. Although, on the outside, he accepted that death was natural and everyone faced it, he was confident that he could get anything he wanted and could not stand to be defeated like other mortals who did not have even a fraction of his privilege and capability.

Winning Catherine had made him confident and deep down, he

Blown Away by the Wind 187

took pride in the fact that an Englishwoman had left her husband for him. Having her lie next to him as his wife every night when he returned to the raft and having a son as a testament to their love filled him with pride and confidence.

Now, everything he had built came crashing down.

Princess Kanika died a few days later. The news of her death filled everyone with despair, including Mom Yad. The funeral arrangements were made according to tradition, along with the arrangements for Charles's funeral. It was Mom Yad's wish that Buddhist customs would follow his death as they had his birth. Catherine objected. She did not wish for her son to be cremated but wanted a Christian burial.

Her husband would not allow it, insisting that, "Charles was never baptised. He should be cremated like other royals. How can I let him be buried like the missionaries' children?"

"But Charles was my son," Catherine argued. "I went along with you before because I wanted him to fit in with your family, but now he's dead, the last thing I can do for him is to see that his soul is with God. Even though he was never baptised, Dr Bradley says he has the right to be buried in the cemetery..."

Justin grabbed her roughly by the shoulders.

"Listen, Catherine. My son was part of my family. I don't want him to be separated from the rest of us. Charles was not English. Rosalind was the same. I'm going to have them cremated together. You must understand. My relatives accepted our children as part of our family. For all our sakes, don't separate our children from the rest of us. Think of the children we'll have in the future..."

He let go of her before turning around and marching out of the room. Catherine's knees grew weak, and she sunk down in a chair, his last words ringing in her ears.

"Think of the children we'll have in the future..."

Not just one child, but two had been taken from her, and Justin was already talking about another child. How could he let her heart be broken a third time?

***

Catherine carefully opened her trunk of clothes and took a few things out to make a space deep inside. She intended to place Charles's clothes at the bottom. Mostly, they were thin cotton items that she had sewn herself.

Her eyes filling with tears, she started to shut the trunk when she caught sight of an envelope. She had put it away so long ago that she had almost forgotten about it. Arthur's letter!

She hesitated for a moment. She had never opened it, intending to keep it sealed so that it would not bother her. But now, nothing could bother her anymore. Arthur had left years ago, and she had not heard from him. Knox never spoke of him and her memories of the young man with blonde hair had faded like an old photograph until she could hardly remember what he had been like. If she opened it now, what would it matter? Nothing could hurt her now. She decided to open it.

Dear Catherine,

I think I'll return to London to see my brother. I've had enough of a soldier's life. If I can, I'm going to trade tea with Sri Lanka. It's a stable job and I wouldn't have to sit in an office all day.

I hope you don't mind, but I've decided not to tell my brother or your relatives about what happened between us. Alfred will only know that you are living with relatives in the East, as will your relatives. If they're to know, let them hear it from you, not me. I don't know how to explain why I could not prevent the difficulties between us.

I love you, Catherine, even though it's too late to tell you. I realized when I lost you.

I hope you'll be happy and that you have no hard feelings towards me, but I still believe that one day, we'll meet again. I don't think you'll remain in Siam forever. Even though we were made welcome there, it is not our home.

When that day comes, Catherine, please tell me. Even if I'm not your husband anymore, please think of me as an old friend who always wants the best for you.

Catherine hastily folded the letter before she could read Arthur's name and pursed her lips. How dare he have assumed that one day she would no longer be able to stand Justin and would eventually return to England? He must have thought her love for Justin was just a temporary infatuation, no different from his infatuation with Charlotte Palmer.

She returned the envelope to where she had found it before covering it with Charles's clothes and putting her folded clothes back on top. Then she glanced at Justin's trunk. He had been preparing to leave for France and would be gone for a year. She would be left alone in Siam with her mother-in-law who showed her no love or affection. And now her dear sister-in-law was dead. She had no one.

✳ ✳ ✳

Justin came up from the boat that night, looking puzzled when he noticed her agitation as she hurried towards him.

"Justin," she said breathlessly. "Can we talk?"

Every night when he arrived home, Justin would bathe and have a light supper before retiring. But tonight was different. He looked at her questioningly after following her inside the bedroom away from the eyes of the servants.

"I want to go to France with you," she stammered.

"What?" he cried. "I'm leaving the day after tomorrow."

"I can be ready in time," she stuttered. "I can pack in a day. I want to go with you…If I can't go with the envoy, I can go as a passenger, and I'll go to England to see my family, and wait until you go home…"

"Catherine…wait! It's not that easy."

Catherine's face fell.

"Isn't there room for me on the boat?"

"It's not that. But anyone who leaves or enters the kingdom needs the king's permission."

"I'm not Siamese. I can ask the consul. I have the same rights as any British citizen."

Justin frowned.

"You're not the same. You're the wife of Prince Vijjuprapha, and even if you don't need the king's permission, you don't have my permission. Aren't you going to ask what I think?"

Catherine was silent and looked at him in confusion.

190   A Passage to Siam

"I thought you'd be willing. Do you disagree?"

He did not answer, but simply stared at her as if he was weighing her up.

"You're going back to England, aren't you?"

"I just want to visit my mother and my sister. And I don't want to be left alone…without you…and without my son…"

His stern expression softened, and he sighed before putting his arms around her shoulders.

"Listen. This trip won't be for as long as the last one. I'll be back in a few months. I understand you miss your home, but…Catherine, you're my wife now. This is your home. My mother's in mourning for my sister. It's a chance for you to comfort her and be close to her. If you go to England, she'll feel even more distant from you."

Catherine could hardly believe her ears. Justin spoke as if his mother had accepted her.

"Your mother doesn't like me."

"It's normal for mothers and daughters-in-law not to get along," he insisted. "My mother softened when she had a grandchild. We'll have other children. I love you, Catherine. I want you to be part of my family. If you go to England…"

He stopped, realising he was about to give away too much, but when Catherine stared at him questioningly, he finished his sentence reluctantly.

"I'm afraid that if you go to England, you won't want to come back to Siam."

This was his deepest fear. Beneath his confidence, he hid a weak spot.

The night before his departure, as they lay in each other's arms, Catherine heard him tell her something she had never known before.

"After I got you, nobody thought you would stay with me. Everyone thought there were too many differences between us. That's why I don't want to risk letting you go."

"And you think leaving me here will make me stay with you forever. Is that it?"

Justin was silent for a moment.

"I'll feel safer if you stay in Siam. It's our home, my love. No matter how far I go, I'll know you'll be waiting for me at home."

"I've been your wife for a long time…"

He touched her lips gently.

"If you go back to England, you won't be my wife anymore. You'll look at me differently. I'll just be another Oriental, not a prince that everyone honours. Don't you remember when I was in Longstock? I had to stay apart from everyone else."

A picture from the past flashed in her mind like lightning. At Mary's wedding, the young man with golden skin and black hair was standing apart from the others. Justin would never be accepted by the residents of Longstock, just as his mother would never accept Catherine.

"I've never thought that way," she cried. "You're my husband. No one can divide us. I just want to go home to visit and then I'll come back to you."

He squeezed her shoulders.

"I've already decided, my love. Don't try to change my mind."

***

After Justin left, Catherine's days were dry and silent. They were more arid than dry season and more silent than the surroundings on the raft, almost empty of servants. Day after day, Catherine woke up and wondered what she was living for, but the days were not as bad as the nights which seemed endless.

The place where she taught embroidery was a pavilion with a high ceiling and no walls that stood amid shady trees. Several young women came to learn with her. Among them was Bua, and since she was the only one that spoke English, she was implicitly the leader.

Sometimes, she went to visit Mom Yad and invited Catherine to go with her to visit her mother-in-law.

"It's kind of you to come and visit me, Bua," Mom Yad would say approvingly.

By then she would greet Catherine cordially and was no longer cold towards her. Mom Yad had been depressed since her daughter's death. She had lost weight and appeared visibly older. At the same time, she was irritable with those around her.

Bua's little attentions reminded her of Princess Kanika, and Catherine was relieved that the duty Justin had assigned to her was being taken care of.

* * *

Catherine thought that the time would never pass, but at last, it came to an end.

The Siamese envoy returned from France with as much success as the previous one. Justin appeared full of vitality and the journey seemed not to have affected him in the least. When he returned to the raft, after greeting her briefly, he went to see his mother at the main house.

Mom Yad stroked his face joyfully with a trembling hand.

"I've been counting the days before you came home. I wanted to see you before I die."

Prince Vijjuprapha smiled comfortingly.

"You won't die yet. You're not sick."

"I'm not as strong as before," she said sighing. "I miss Kanika."

"While I was away, did Catherine come and see you? I asked her to take care of you."

"Now and again. But she isn't much help. We can't understand each other."

She paused before adding quickly, "I don't mind her."

"Catherine's all alone here. She needs your support."

"I feel for her," Mom Yad said wearily. "But what can I do? If she has other children, they might not survive. What will you do then? Are you only going to have one wife?"

Prince Vijjuprapha looked at his mother, puzzled, and she muttered, "I'm old. I just want a house full of grandchildren, but enough of that. You must be tired. Let's not talk about it now."

She lay down, indicating she did not wish to discuss the matter any further. She was not cruel enough to want to get rid of Catherine. She simply could not accept that Catherine would be her son's only partner for life. What would happen to him if she did not bear him any more children, and who would take care of him in his old age?

Prince Saifa had been young and impressionable when he went

Blown Away by the Wind 193

abroad, and the only women he saw had been foreigners, so it was understandable that he had fallen in love with one of them but bringing her home as his wife was another matter.

Mom Yad refused to look at the situation from any other perspective than her own and did not recognise that she was prejudiced. She had never once asked herself how she would have felt if she had been all alone in a foreign land, and someone had treated her as she had treated Catherine.

* * *

The air that day was heavy and dark clouds hung overhead waiting to burst that evening. The Throne Hall was empty and quiet with hardly any people about because the king was staying at his palace in Saraburi. Since he had started to feel unwell, he preferred to stay upcountry rather than in the Front Palace.

This time, Prince Vijjuprapha had not gone with him because the king had ordered a second Throne Hall to be built in the Front Palace and so, besides training the guards, the prince had also been assigned to oversee the construction.

But today he was there because Khun Chom Klee had sent for him using Bua as an intermediary to tell Mom Yad.

"Mom Yad's been missing me, but she's not well enough to come and see me. I sent Bua to visit her, and she told me your mother hasn't been able to eat or sleep since Ying passed away. She's lost so much weight she's like a skeleton. I'm very concerned about her. You didn't tell me."

He was silent. He had noticed she had lost weight, but she was hardly 'like a skeleton'.

"I've been concerned, and I've asked the doctor to give her medicine. My brothers and sisters visit often."

"She misses Ying," Khun Chom said. "All her sons are married with families of their own. A son isn't like a daughter."

"Her daughters-in-law…"

"Oh!" she scoffed. "Her daughters-in-law are all busy with their own families, and one's a Mem."

194 A Passage to Siam

The prince said nothing, but she was undeterred.

"I know how she feels," she continued. "If she had someone in place of Kanika, she wouldn't be so depressed. Nothing cheers an old person up like grandchildren."

"And who can replace Kanika?" he asked.

"If you found another wife, she could take care of her."

"Another wife?" he repeated. "What about Catherine? I can't just abandon her."

Khun Chom looked at him and smiled.

"Nobody's asking you to abandon her. Not after all these years. What I'm saying is…"

She opened a tub of wax and patted her lips with it as she considered her words.

"I can't think of any other way. The king told me that foreign women are not expected to take care of their husband's parents, so you can't force her to look after your mother. And you're not a youth anymore. You're older now, and you've become an important man, so you should have a suitable wife. It concerned your father and that's why he didn't want you to make Mem your principal wife. Don't you remember?"

He remembered, but he would have forgotten about it if she hadn't reminded him.

"I've never thought about it."

"Well, it's time you did. You still haven't given your mother any grandchildren. Both Mem's children died. You should have children with a suitable wife."

"I want children," he admitted. "We'll have other children."

"You can have children with her. But you should also have children with a Siamese wife."

In a softer tone, she continued, "Nobody makes a foreigner their principal wife. You can keep her as a secondary wife, but your principal wife must be someone suitable. You brought Mem home before you'd even had a chance to get to know anyone."

She saved her best shot until last.

"If you love your mother and you want to show your gratitude, consider what I've said. I'm not forcing you. I'm just asking you to make your mother happy before she dies."

***

It had been raining every evening for days and today was no exception.After the heavy rain, the Chao Phraya River was full and drops of water fell on the surface. A rainbow was arching across the darkening sky and a cold river breeze was blowing as Prince Vijjuprapha sat in a boat on his way back to the raft.

He caught sight of a slender figure in a light-coloured dress leaning against a wooden post distractedly. It had become a familiar sight and, even when they were together, Catherine seemed lost in her thoughts.

When he stepped onto the raft, he greeted her attentively.

"I've been able to come home early lately, but the king will be back in three days, so I'll have to stay until late."

Catherine smiled at him and went to greet him as usual. Kham had prepared a bowl of water sprinkled with jasmine for him to wash his hands and face as usual. Nothing had changed. The only thing that was not the same was that something had been extinguished like a lamp that had gone out. Justin sat down and made conversation.

"I'll tell you about the new Throne Hall. We've got craftsmen from China. The old one was hot. This one has better ventilation."

"Really?" she said.

She was grateful to him for trying hard to chat to her like before, but sometimes even Justin appeared distracted as if a dark shadow had come between them. A current of fear was gradually taking hold of her. Catherine had not tired of her husband, but since the death of their child, the bond between them was no longer indestructible.

10

Bitter Love

"I want a companion, not a servant."

It was the first time in months since the tragedy that Mom Yad had sounded lively.

"Who you choose is up to you."

"I don't have anyone else in mind except Catherine."

"It doesn't matter to me. I might die tomorrow, but you need a suitable wife, and there's no one more suitable than Bua. Khun Chom has been grooming her for the role. She's a perfect match for you. Whenever she comes to see me, she reminds me of Kanika."

Bua – the girl as fair as a statue. Prince Vijjuprapha was not surprised. He knew his elders had chosen her as his wife, but he had not been sorry to let her go because he had no feelings for her. The only woman in his heart was Catherine, and the obstacles they had faced had only made their love stronger.

"And how would Bua accept being my secondary wife, Mother?"

"Oh, really!" she cried. "Khun Chom and I are going to ask her parents to decide on the bride price."

"If you expect Bua to be my principal wife, where does that leave Catherine?"

Mom Yad had prepared an answer ahead of time.

"I'm not that cruel," she purred. "Mem has been your wife for many years now. She's your first wife and she can stay on the raft with you like before. You can build another house for Bua close to mine and further away from Mem, so she won't be disturbed."

When she noticed that the prince was quiet as if he was considering the matter, she continued to coax him.

"And for another thing, I chose Bua because I know from Khun

Chom that Bua and Mem get along."

"Bua won't argue with her elders," the prince said. "But foreigners have only one wife. What if Catherine won't agree?"

"You're not an impetuous young man anymore. You can control an army of a thousand men. Surely you can control one woman."

When he did not reply, she pointed out,

"It doesn't matter how many wives you have. The important thing is that you treat them equally. Inao could manage ten wives, after all. All your siblings look up to you, so why wouldn't you be able to manage two wives?"

* * *

Prince Saifa made no mention of the matter to Catherine. He asked himself if his feelings for her had changed and answered with certainty that no woman had ever captured his heart as she had. And if he had another wife, how would she react? If it had been five years ago, he would have flatly refused, but now that had been back in Siam for so long, he wondered if it might be possible.

Would it matter if I don't abandon you, and still love you like before?

Bua is just someone to help you with the duties that you can't do. I'm doing this to show gratitude to my mother and to please my family. They'll all be relieved that I finally have a wife whom they consider suitable.

I know that Bua won't argue with you or be jealous of you, and she'll be your friend. That's why my mother chose her.

He was confident that Catherine loved him enough to go along with him. She might be angry and resentful at first, and was sure to oppose the idea, but it was up to him to help her understand the differences between Siamese and English customs, and to reassure her that nothing had changed.

* * *

In the past, when Catherine's husband went to work, he took a boat, but since returning from France, he preferred to ride a horse along the small path behind the main house that cut through dense forest all the way to the Front Palace.

Young Siamese princes preferred to travel by horse when traveling alone or with only one or two attendants in tow. So Catherine was not surprised when Justin ordered stables to be built behind the raft, close to the main house, and later told her with a smile, "I've ordered a horse for you, too, so we can go horse-riding together."

Catherine was touched that he had been so thoughtful. The horse that Justin found her was a mare called Den, so docile that she could ride side-saddle with confidence that she would not fall off. Catherine was pleased with her. She bent down to pat her mane as a signal for her to start walking, and appeared relaxed as she rode along the path behind Justin, her face flushed with excitement.

Riding made Catherine happy, and whenever Justin was free, he would take her riding to see Captain Knox, or Phraya Suriyawongse, and Mom Rachawongse Kratai, both of whom spoke English well and understood enough about Western customs to make her feel welcome.

Throughout this time, Justin never mentioned the Thai-style house that was being built on the empty plot of land behind the main house where the small hut that had been used to house Rosalind's body had been torn down to make room for it.

Catherine first noticed the new house after it was finished. She did not see the pillars being put down, or the house being assembled because Prince Saifa had ordered for it to be built in an area where it would be concealed from the raft by the main house.

The first time she saw it, she had walked from the raft to the stables to see Den, since the stableboy had said she had not eaten any hay for two days, and Kham and Won went with her. It was then she noticed the new Thai-style house, which was joined to the main house by a long veranda.

"Did Mother build a new house?" she asked without paying it much attention. "Who is it for?"

Won hesitated and Kham turned to glare at him.

"I…I don't know, Mem," Won stuttered, looking down to avoid meeting her gaze.

Catherine was perplexed at their behaviour, which made it seem as if there was something they knew but didn't want to tell her.

Bitter Love 199

"What is it?" she asked, "What is it that you're not telling me?"

"Nothing…It's just that Den's been unwell."

Catherine could see that Won would not tell her, and she wondered if they knew something about Justin that she didn't know. She decided to ask him about it. She mentioned the new house to Justin that night and he frowned.

"Why did Won take you to the stables? I told him I didn't want you to…"

He stopped, suddenly realising he was about to let the cat out of the bag. Catherine looked at him questioningly, but he looked the other way to avoid meeting her eyes. Realising that he had been trying to keep her away from the new house for some reason, she asked him directly, "Has something happened?"

He started a little.

"Why would you ask?"

Catherine laughed, attempting to ease the tension that had suddenly filled the air.

"I'm your wife! Do you think I can't tell when something's bothering you? I know you've got a lot on your mind, but if there's no one else you can talk to, you can talk to me. I'm not only your wife, but I'm also your friend. I know I'm not as clever as you, but you can trust me."

Justin relaxed and put his arms around her.

"Thank you, my love. You're too good to me. No matter what happens, I want you to know I love you…You're my first love, and I'll never feel the same about any other woman."

Justin had not spoken so sweetly to her in a long time, and she was both moved and puzzled.

"No matter what happens…What do you mean? Do you have to go abroad again?"

"No, I won't have to go anywhere again."

Catherine sighed with relief.

"If you're not going away, then I'm not worried. Even of you go upcountry, I can wait because I know you miss me."

He pulled her even closer.

"I miss you so much. I always count the days until I see you again."

"I love you," Catherine whispered. "So many things have happened

200   A Passage to Siam

between us, but I want you to know my love for you hasn't changed."

Catherine sensed Justin's relief when he sighed as if as weight had been lifted from his shoulders.

"I believe you," he said firmly. "I believe love will overcome every challenge, my dearest. Even if we face pain and disappointment, we'll get through it together."

He clutched her hands and squeezed them tightly as if he was afraid that she would slip from his grasp.

"We can overcome our problems, my love. We must accept that there are many things you can't do, but I love you just as you are, and I don't want you to change. But I have a duty to my parents and my family."

Catherine looked at him, puzzled. She had never seen such a strange expression on his face and the feeling of warmth and contentment that had flooded her heart a moment earlier suddenly turned to ice. He had never appeared so hesitant before as if what he was about to tell her was the hardest thing he had experienced in their life together so far.

"Tell me what it is," she said, trying to keep her voice steady.

"I mean…I have a duty…to my mother and my family."

Justin was going to get married!

He was going to take another wife to please his mother and his family because a foreigner like her was unsuitable, even though she had been his wife for the past few years.

She could not crawl in front of his mother or help her with the cooking and the housework, she could not give her a grandchild that would look like the rest of the family, she could not welcome guests with a tray of betel, and she could not participate in ceremonies at the temple because she believed in a different religion. But his new wife would be able to do all those things because she was Siamese.

"She's like one of my relatives. She won't disturb you at all, and I'll never love her like I love you. You'll still be my wife like before, but my mother and my relatives won't bother you anymore, I promise."

He concluded by telling her firmly, "I've never broken a promise to you. If I tell you I'm going to do this to resolve the problems that

Bitter Love 201

have been building for the past few years, I mean it. I'm doing this for us, Catherine. If I give in to my relatives, they'll have to give in to me sometimes."

Catherine did not answer. The figure in the middle of the room appeared as white as marble and the blue eyes that stared ahead did not see the pleading black eyes gazing at her.

She was staring out from the raft, past the Chao Phraya River, past the Gulf of Siam out to a stormy turquoise sea when someone had held her for the first time.

"It's a pity I met you too late."

"Catherine!"

She came to her senses when he shook her by the shoulders. His face was pale.

"What's the matter? You're not responding. Sit down. Don't do this again. You gave me a fright."

She sat down on the low table close by, but she was numb. He sat down next to her and squeezed her shoulders.

"Are you feeling alright now?"

She did not have the energy to answer, but if she had she would have answered that she would never 'feel alright' again.

Justin frowned and his face appeared suddenly drawn and weary.

"Oh, Catherine…" he cried, and Catherine found herself being hugged tightly.

"Forgive me. I shouldn't have told you so suddenly. I should have let you know a bit at a time. But I want you to know that when you're upset, I'm upset, too…"

Catherine went limp as he held her and tried to convince her that he still loved her. But it had no meaning for her when the truth was like a poison arrow.

*** ***

"I'll be home early, Kham…"

When Kham crawled in to take her orders, Catherine's husband told her resolutely, "Take care of my wife and don't let her out of your sight."

Catherine was not sleeping inside the bedroom but was sitting on a low table at the front of the raft where she used to sit with her son. She did not have any needlework on her lap as she usually did, and she did not even get up to say goodbye to her husband when he stepped off the raft onto the bank where his attendant was waiting with his horse.

She sat motionless, staring into space without paying any attention to what Justin said to Kham. Kham glanced at her anxiously and crawled into a corner to keep an eye on her. She knew that Justin was worried about her, but it did not solve the problem. What she wanted from him was a clear decision.

"You can't have two wives. You must choose between her or me," she had told him icily.

"If I could choose, of course I'd choose you. You know I don't love anyone apart from you."

"But you're going to take another wife when you don't love her."

"It's my duty."

"Justin…Oh, Justin," she cried wearily.

"How could you let this happen? Your mother and your family are asking you to do something terrible. What right do they have to come between us and claim it's for the sake of tradition?"

"Don't blame my mother. She grew up with the custom of men having more than one wife…"

"It's because they don't like me for who I am, not because of anything I've done. When you took me as your wife, you knew I was different from you in every way, but it didn't matter because we loved each other. But now I know that even love isn't strong enough to overcome the differences between us…"

She stopped suddenly, the truth of what she had said piercing her heart like an arrow.

"Oh, Catherine!" Justin cried, taking hold of her shoulders. "That's not true. Just because our love hasn't been smooth, it doesn't mean it isn't strong enough. All I ask is that you stand by my side, and we'll get through this together."

Catherine stared at him before speaking in a voice slow and firm.

"I would stand by your side even if you lost everything and became a beggar, but I can't accept you having another wife."

After that, she did not say another word.

Bitter Love 203

We are like two boats going in opposite directions with the captain of each boat trying to signal to the other that it is going the wrong way, but each is confused as to which way is the right way.

Or are we both right, each going in the direction we're supposed to go? Or are we both wrong?

* * *

Justin's wedding was in July, and even though nobody mentioned it to Catherine, she could sense the excitement coming from the main house. Nobody came to disturb her, and Mom Yad was being unusually nice to her, ordering Kham to bring her fresh milk every day, since she had heard that Catherine was not eating.

Noticing she had lost weight, Justin ordered Kham and Won to fetch Dr Bradley. Kham told the American doctor what had happened, and he was full of sympathy. Indeed, he was the only person she would talk to.

"I feel hopeless."

"No matter what happens, you can't give up. God won't let you down if you don't give up."

She looked up at the old doctor.

"I'm searching for a way out, doctor. I won't give up. Thank you, doctor."

Dr Bradley nodded sadly.

"If there's anything I can do, just let me know. I'm here for you."

"Thank you, doctor. I might need to ask for your help…" she said before lowering her voice. "But until then…What shall I do? I can't bear to stay here alone."

"You should have a change of scene. Take a boat ride and visit some people you know," the doctor advised, relieved that he was able to offer her some temporary relief. "It'd be better than staying home alone."

Justin tried to take her out as much as he was able, but it had no meaning for Catherine when he was going to marry another woman in a few days' time.

"Please tell my husband that I should go out for fresh air and that Kham will come with me."

204 A Passage to Siam

"I'll be glad to, ma'am."

* * *

Catherine watched the water flowing past the helm of boat dreamily. She was on her way to the Inner Palace to see Bua. It was her last resort. She had sent Kham to give her a short note telling her of the day she would come. Justin did not know that she was coming to meet Bua, but she was sure that he would not have approved of her coming to see her without consulting him.

She stepped onto the pier and walked through the gates that led to the Inner Court, her blonde hair and billowing skirts no longer a strange sight to those who saw her. Bua was waiting for her anxiously amongst all the people walking in and out.

When she saw Catherine, she came towards her and pressed her palms together gracefully, before telling her, "Come this way, Mem."

She led Catherine along a path through some bushes to a small pavilion where there were no people about. The pavilion had no chairs, but it was raised above the ground, so the two women sat down on the edge. Bua signalled for her maid to leave them alone and she wrung her hands anxiously without looking Catherine in the eye.

"You know why I'm here, don't you?" Catherine said.

Bua bowed her head, and the colour rose to her smooth ivory cheeks.

"Yes, Mem," she whispered.

"Are you willing to be my husband's wife when you know that he already has a wife?"

Bua looked up hesitantly and her black eyes met Catherine's.

"It's up to my elders, Mem," she replied softly. She was paused for a moment before continuing, "I'm young…My aunt thinks it's appropriate."

"But it's your life," Catherine cried. "How can you give up your life to please someone else?"

Bua did not answer. She continued to gaze into Catherine's eyes as if she wanted to say something but was too shy.

"My aunt thinks it's appropriate," she repeated. "It's up to her. She has more experience, and she can see…"

"See what? You and the rest of them think I won't be able to stay with my husband, don't you?" Catherine cried. "Because it isn't my duty. Why can't you think for yourself, Bua? Don't you know how painful it will be to stay with a man who doesn't love you? He already has a wife, and you'll have to compete for his love? It will be torture!"

"I don't expect anything, Mem. I just want to show gratitude to my aunt. I've never thought about love. I don't have the fortune to be with the man I love, so I accept my fate. It's my karma."

"The man you love…Have you been in love?" Catherine asked in astonishment.

Bua's eyes filled with tears as she confessed that she had fallen in love with a young man from her village, whom she had known since she was a child. When she had come to live in the Inner Court, he had become an attendant in the palace, and they had been able to meet when she went outside or went home to visit her parents. But fate would not allow them to be together because Bua had been betrothed to Prince Vijjuprapha.

By now, having lost hope of ever being with her, the young man had entered the monkhood and determined never to leave, while Bua had no other option except to do her duty to the best of her ability. She did not love Catherine's husband, but it was her duty to marry him. For that reason, she did not mind that he loved someone else.

Catherine did not understand the Siamese concept of marriage. It was a duty that had to be performed at a certain time by both men and women who cooperated to make it as smooth as possible. From what she had seen, women like Bua did their duty of attending to their husbands and their husband's relatives and supervising the servants, and if their husbands decided to take another wife, they considered it another pair of hands to help with all the tedious duties.

This was what Justin had tried to explain, but she had not understood. Instead, it was Bua who had helped her to understand what her husband had tried to tell her.

Bua promised not to tell anyone about their meeting, so Catherine took her leave and returned home with a heavy heart.

***

"I won't let you to go back to England!"

Catherine had never seen such an expression on Justin's face before. His face and lips were pale. He grabbed her by the shoulders.

"How can you leave me? You're my wife! You're not going anywhere!"

"It's been over between us since you took another wife. You can't force me to stay with you."

"You're staying with me even if I must lock you up day and night. I won't let you go! You can be angry with me, but you can't leave me. You're my wife. Even if I have Bua or a hundred more wives, I'll never love anyone else like you!"

Catherine had never seen him so furious before as Justin was not prone to losing his temper. But this time, he had unleashed his fury as soon as she had told him she was returning to England on his wedding day. The more she tried to convince him to let her go, the more furious he became.

"Let's part on good terms. This is the best solution. I've made my decision."

"I don't care what you've decided."

His reply was harsher than he had ever been before.

"How many times do I have to tell you? I'm not letting you go anywhere. Do you hear me, Catherine? You can be angry with me, you can hate me, but you can never leave me. I'll never let you go!"

Catherine had never imagined that Justin would be so resolute.

When he said he would not let her out of his sight, he meant it, telling her forcefully, "If you go out, I'm going with you. I don't permit you to go out with Kham. If I can't go with you, you must stay on the raft."

Catherine slumped down the low table against the wall despondently, her hands trembling.

"Why are you doing this to me when you don't even want me anymore?"

Justin got down on one knee in front of her and clasped her hands tightly.

"It hurts me more than it hurts you. I'm doing this because I can't live without you."

Catherine was speechless. Her silence made Justin's expression relax and he pulled her to her feet before enfolding her in his arms and pressing her wavy hair down on his shoulder.

"That's life, my love. Nobody's fortunate enough to have everything they want all the time. Remember, no matter who I'm with, I'll always be thinking of you."

Through her tears, Catherine saw the walls closing in around her and a door shutting her behind it forever. A door that Justin had locked and chained with his love.

* * *

Golden rays shone in through the window and the fresh breeze that signalled the start of the cool season came in through the mosquito net. Flocks of birds chirped in the trees next to the riverbank and the scent of jasmine wafted from the next pillow. Justin had carefully placed a branch full of sweet-smelling white flowers that he had picked on the lace-trimmed pillow. He did not want her to wake up and find he was no longer lying next to her.

Catherine had shut her eyes tight and breathed slowly in and out, so that he would not know she was awake, and when he thought she was asleep, he had slowly tiptoed out of the room.

Justin did this about once a week. He would lead her to the bedroom and hold her in his arms until he thought she was asleep before sliding quietly off the bed and leaving the room. He had never stayed the night with Bua, even though he visited her regularly, and always returned before dawn, and he never forgot to pick a fragrant flower to leave on the pillow for Catherine.

"While I was walking, I saw this fragrant flower and thought of you," he had told her the first time she had sat up and looked at him questioningly after finding a flower on the pillow.

Neither of them mentioned Bua who kept herself to herself in the Thai house behind the main house and never ventured near the raft. All of them acted as if, so long as nobody mentioned it, Catherine would forget that another woman had come between her and Justin. Catherine felt the weight of her husband when he sat on the mattress and placed the sweet-smelling jasmine on the pillow. She felt his hand stroke her silken hair that spilled across the pillow and his warm breath as he bent down to touch her hair before carefully slipping away so as not to wake her.

When Justin had left the room, Catherine sat up before going to have a wash and get dressed before he had breakfast. She sighed when the scent of jasmine filled her nostrils, and quickly recoiled as if it was poison.

Oh, Justin! You want to tell me that, even when you're lying next to another woman, you're still thinking of me, but you don't realize that all these flowers only serve to remind me that you're no longer true to me.

The dew of the morning
Sunk chill on my brow
It felt like the warning
Of what I feel now.

Even though you've kept your word never to stay the night with her and you hurry home so that you're here when I wake up, and even though you tell me your feelings for me are still the same, it makes no difference now because the promise you once gave me is broken.

✳✳✳✳

On the surface, Catherine's life had not changed.

Her life was peaceful, she had servants to attend to her, and there was no longer any need for awkward meetings with her mother-in-law. Mom Yad no longer required her to do anything and if she found out that Catherine wanted anything, such as seasonal fruits or fabrics from abroad, she would arrange for it to be brought to her at once, and Justin's relatives were more cordial towards her when they came to visit him.

Only Catherine knew that nothing was the same.

It would never be the same.

✳✳✳

Catherine woke with a start, her heart thumping in her chest and a cold sweat soaking her skin. She sat up and calmed herself for a moment, realizing she had been having another nightmare. The sun was shining outside and a cool breeze blew in through the window to her mosquito net. The waves hit the raft gently and the birds were twittering in the trees like every morning. But something was missing.

She looked beside her, and her heart lurched when she saw the empty space next to her. The dent on the pillow told her that Justin had come to bed with her but had got up and left during the night as he had done before. But this was the first time that he had not returned by dawn.

Catherine pulled back the mosquito net and put a robe over her nightgown before walking to the window to look out at the path on the riverbank, but she could not see it clearly from the bedroom. To see the path that Justin used, she had to go to the back of the raft, and although she did not usually go outside in her nightgown, her agitation made her decide to go out of the bedroom onto the veranda. She stopped suddenly when she caught sight of something she had never seen before on the next pier, which was used by the people from the main house.

The gentle rays of the morning sun shone on the saffron robes of the monks who sat in boats as they collected offerings for their alms bowls. In the golden light, she saw her husband sitting on the pier as he carefully placed an offering in the bowl. A beautiful young woman sat just behind him, passing food to him with several servants sitting quietly in a line behind her. The couple offering alms in the morning was a heart-warming sight, and even though they did not speak to each other, the gentleness in their manner was evident as they made merit together, united by their common faith.

Catherine clutched the rails of the veranda to steady herself and her heart lurched again.

Thy vows are all broken
And light is thy fame;
I hear thy name spoken,
And share in its shame.

You broke your promise. You promised you would never stay the night with her.

You might make excuses and say it was necessary, or it was your duty, or it was appropriate, but I call it untrue.

You've started to see what your family wanted you to see – that a suitable wife is better than love born out of differences.

Prince Vijjuprapha finished making his offerings a moment later. He stood up quickly and looked up at the brightening sky before hurrying away from Bua and her servants and hastening towards the raft. Catherine would be awake by now. It was the first time he had returned later than he had intended, but there was nothing he could do since Bua was pregnant and had told him the previous night.

When he heard the news, he was naturally pleased and instructed her, "Follow the precepts to make merit for our child, Bua."

"Yes," she whispered. "Tomorrow I'm going to offer alms to the monks."

"Very good."

This was the reason he had stayed to offer alms with her that morning and by the time they had finished, the sun was already up. He quickened his step as he walked across the bridge to the raft and stopped suddenly when he caught sight of the veranda behind the raft. Someone was standing there like a strange white vision silhouetted against the dark foliage, standing motionless, her blue eyes staring vacantly into space. Devoid of the zest for life that had once captured his heart.

Prince Vijjuprapha was both despondent and relieved when he arrived back at the raft and found that his English wife did not chide him, or even ask him where he had been. She did not mention the matter.

Although he had instructed the servants not to breathe a word about Bua's pregnancy to Catherine, it appeared unnecessary because Catherine did not seem to care about anything. He finally concluded with relief that Catherine had accepted the new arrangement and was no longer opposed to the idea.

She must have been satisfied that he had demonstrated consistency

Bitter Love 211

by never spending the night with Bua and only calling to see her after work to see how she was before returning to the raft.

So several days after that, he decided to ask her, "Do you want to go to Singapore with me?"

He was gratified to see a glint appear in her blue eyes and, before she could answer, he continued, "The king plans to visit Singapore, so he's sending me to see the consul ahead of him. It will take about a month there and back. I don't want to leave you here by yourself."

"I thought the king was sick. Is he able to travel?"

"He's much better, so he wants to go while he's still feeling up to it. All being well, he'll be going in about two months' time."

"I…" Catherine said, lowering her gaze, not wanting to arouse his suspicion, "I'd like to go."

He smiled at her in satisfaction.

"I thought you'd want to go. Singapore's clean and tidy like England. You'll be able to go for rides in a horse-drawn carriage. Oh! Does Annie still live in Singapore? Why don't you write to her? Ask her to visit you at the consul's house. That's where we'll be staying."

Catherine started. She dared not tell him that she was thinking of the exact same person, but for a different reason.

"Yes, I'll write to her. Annie still lives there."

Justin was not aware that his self-confidence prevented him from seeing that he had provided her with the opportunity that she had been praying for.

11

When Love is Doomed

On the day of their departure, all the Front Palace nobles came to see Justin off. Another noble accompanying them was Luang Surawiset whom Catherine knew well. Dr Bradley and his wife came to see Catherine off. At first, they did not suspect anything when Catherine shook their hands and said, "Goodbye Dr Bradley…Mrs Bradley. May God bless the two of you. You've been good to me." Mrs Bradley thought nothing of it, since she was not close to Catherine, but Dr Bradley stared at her with growing apprehension, although he dared not reveal his suspicion.

"May God protect you throughout your voyage, ma'am," he said gravely.

Kham was the only one who had guessed. Having served Catherine for the past several years, she knew Catherine better than anyone else, and had been alarmed ever since she saw Catherine pack all her belongings in her trunk as if she did not want to leave any reminders on the raft.

Justin was too busy to notice such details, but Kham knew, and on the day of their departure, before Catherine stepped off the raft into the small boat that was waiting to take them to the larger boat, Kham prostrated herself at her feet and burst into tears.

"Kham!" Catherine warned her, fearing that Kham would give her away. "Don't be upset that you're not coming with me. Look after the raft."

Kham sobbed until someone pulled her away. Catherine was silent. She turned away from the charming house on the raft as it gradually faded from view, and from the nights when she and Justin had swum in the cool water and stood looking at the moon together from the raft.

The boat headed out to the Chao Phraya River, passing the Temple of the Dawn. Catherine remembered that the sight of the mangroves glittering with fireflies had been the first sight of Bangkok that had greeted her five years earlier. Not long after that, Arthur had travelled by boat to the estuary as she was doing now. He had known – as she knew now – that he would never return to Siam.

Someone came and stood beside her at the helm of the boat. Catherine did not turn around until she heard a gentle voice say happily, "Do you remember the first time we arrived in Siam together? You were standing at the helm of the boat just like this, and I couldn't stop myself from coming to you."

"You remember everything."

"I remember everything about you. Are you happy, my love? This is like our honeymoon after we've been married for five years."

He laughed cheerfully, and his voice was carried away by the wind. Catherine swallowed her conflicting emotions with difficulty. She hated him because she loved him so much.

"What's the matter? You seem distracted. Don't tell me you're homesick already."

She came to her senses and turned to smile at him.

"I'm not distracted. I'm admiring the view. You know I like to travel."

"It's getting late and the wind's starting to get up. We should go inside, or you'll get a chill."

$$* * *$$

Catherine had to admit that since they had left the Gulf of Thailand for Singapore, she had struggled with her emotions more than ever before. Justin had no idea of the inner turmoil she was facing. He assumed that she was simply seasick because it had been so long since she had been at sea. His concern for her made him not want to let her out of his sight.

He did not realize that his tenderness hurt her more than if he had ignored her. If he had been indifferent towards her, it would have been easier for her to walk away from him.

Or, in the end, would she not be able to leave the man who had imprisoned her with his love?

214 A Passage to Siam

***

Singapore had hardly changed at all over the previous five years.

Justin was warmly welcomed by the consul as the representative of the Second King of Siam. The house they stayed in was a new colonial-style house with two storeys, more attractive and comfortable than the house they had stayed in on their previous visit to Singapore.

"Do you like it?" he asked, certain that she would be pleased with it, when she stepped onto the veranda.

"Yes," she replied, smiling before turning around to look at the house. "It's very comfortable."

The veranda was wide and served as another sitting room with a set of white rattan furniture. It was cool under the shade of the large acacia trees that surrounded the house which looked over a smooth and verdant lawn.

"Shall we build a house like this in Bangkok?" he asked her.

He walked to the edge of the veranda and leaned on the rail as he looked around contentedly.

"The raft's getting old and cramped. If you like this house, I'll sketch it for the builders. This is just the right size for us."

Catherine's throat was dry. She wanted to cover her ears and her eyes, not wanting to see Justin's happy countenance. Once, Justin's happiness had been her happiness, but now, who would have thought? His happiness had become her misery.

Annie came hurrying to see her the next day, having already received Catherine's letter telling her when she would be arriving in Singapore. She met Justin briefly when she arrived as he was on his way out to meet with the consul.

Annie rushed towards Catherine in excitement.

"Oh, Miss Catherine! I'm so happy to see ye. I heard the servants sayin' that the Siamese prince's English wife's as bonnie as a princess, and it's true! Ye have nae changed a bit!"

"Please sit down," Catherine smiled. "There's something I want to tell you. I need your help."

A look of alarm spread across Annie's face, but she sat down

When Love is Doomed 215

obediently with her hands in her lap.

"I want to ask about the sea routes to England. On what days is there a boat to India?"

Annie knew the answer and replied proudly, "Aye, travellin's easy now compared to five years back. Ye can get to England in just over two months. There's always boats leavin' the ports for all the sea routes. Ye dinnae have to set foot on land for days on end anymore. Singapore's a key port. There's a couple o' ships headin' for India every month. Why do ye want to know?"

"If I tell you, will you promise to keep it a secret?"

Annie's eyes widened, but she answered, "Aye."

"Please book a passenger boat for me. I'm travelling to England, but…Annie, you must promise not to tell my husband."

This time, Annie's eyes opened even wider.

"Can you help me, Annie? If he finds out, I may never have another chance to see you. My husband will never let me out of the palace again."

"A…Aye," Annie stuttered. "But…I don't understand. I thought the prince was good to ye. Ye've been his wife for years."

"Annie, you've lived in Siam. Didn't you notice that Siamese men can have more than one wife? He might love me, but I'm not his only wife. I can't accept being one of several wives."

Annie started a little, as if the idea had never occurred to her, but after a moment's consideration, her face fell, and she was filled with sympathy.

"Oh, Miss Catherine!" she cried and was silent for a while.

Catherine was also silent. She was about to step into an unknown future and for the next two months she would be completely by herself, a woman alone at sea. Whenever fear overcame her, she strengthened her resolve with the painful picture that was etched in her memory.

The picture of Justin offering alms with Bua in the golden rays of the morning sun. It was a picture she had no part in, even in her dreams.

"The prince is going to have a child with another wife," she said, trying to steady her voice. "He tried to hide it from me, but I heard the servants whispering. The three of them will be a family. The prince wants a child. I haven't been able to give him one. I don't know what my life will be like once he has a child with another wife. Do you understand, Annie?"

216 A Passage to Siam

Annie's eyes filled with tears, and she dabbed them with a handkerchief that she pulled from her cloth bag.

"Oh, Miss Catherine!" she repeated. "Ye dinnae need to say any more. I get it."

"Thank you, Annie. So you'll help me?"

"Aye, dinnae fret yerself about the journey. Jack's got pals on every boat from here to Southampton. He'll sort out the sea routes for ye. Ye'll be safe, even if ye're travellin' on yer own. May God be with ye."

Annie kept her word. Although she was talkative by nature, she did not disclose the secret to anyone from the Siamese party. Her husband helped her to plan the route for Catherine's journey, agreeing that it should not be too arduous. There would be a boat to take her from one port to another and she would arrive in England in no more than two months. Jack's friends, who worked on the boats, would look out for Catherine, but she would remain inside her cabin as much as possible for her own safety.

Justin was to stay in Singapore for about a month to prepare for the king's visit. He would be busy contacting the consul and going to the places that King Pinklao would be visiting, so it gave Annie an opportunity to visit Catherine several times without Justin's knowledge. Even the times he knew about, he was not suspicious and turned out to be pleased that Catherine had a friend coming to see her.

Justin did not forget to arrange a horse-drawn carriage for her to go out in and enjoy the view and the sea air, which made it easy for her to buy things she needed for the journey. In the end, it was easy for her to go to the port on the day the boat left without Justin having the slightest inkling, and by the time he arrived home that night, the boat had been gone for several hours.

The only sticking point was writing the final letter which she would leave in the bedroom. When he returned home, he would find nothing but emptiness.

Catherine would be gone forever.

* * *

"I met an Englishwoman at the consulate today," Justin said cheerfully.

He was dressed in a black suit and a white bow tie ready for a formal dinner at the consulate. His raven hair was brushed back from his forehead, and his dark eyes were sparkling. When Justin wore Western clothes, he looked even more handsome than when he wore Siamese costume, and Catherine could hardly take her eyes off him, even though she had seen him dressed this way before.

Especially tonight – the last night.

He did not notice that she wasn't listening to what he said, and continued talking as he buttoned his cuffs.

"Her name was Mrs Anna Leonowens. She's a widow with a young son. She's about to go and work as a governess in the palace and teach the king's children. I don't know if you should meet her."

Catherine brought her attention back in time. The last sentence puzzled her.

"Why shouldn't I meet her?"

Her husband turned from the mirror to look at her.

"She said she was English, but I lived in India for quite a while, so I can tell. Her father was English, but her mother was probably Indian. She has black hair and olive skin like a Spaniard or an Italian."

Catherine did not care if Anna Leonowens was English or Anglo-Indian. All that mattered to her at that moment was that she could not afford to meet anyone.

"I'd rather not see anyone right now. You know I haven't been feeling well. I'd prefer to rest."

Justin stood in front of her and gazed at the elegant figure in the white evening dress with satisfaction. Tonight, her hair was piled up on the top of her head and her flaxen ringlets caught the light as they hung around her long neck and shoulders above the low neck of her dress. The top hugged her figure and was trimmed with a pale blue sash around the waist while the skirt was flared with several layers of lace and trailed on the polished wooden floor. She was looking radiant and showed no trace of the sickness she had spoken of.

"You look stunning…" He wanted to enfold her in his arms, but since she was all dressed up, all he could do was lift her long white hand to his lips. "You're as beautiful as a bride."

Whatever he had meant, Catherine started.

Tomorrow, she would no longer be his bride – or his wife – forever.

It was late when she returned from the dinner at the consulate. Justin changed his clothes and got ready for bed, since he would be busy the next day and would not be back until late. They had agreed that the next day, Catherine would stay in and have dinner alone.

"Aren't you in bed yet?" he asked when he had changed into his night clothes, and walked back inside the bedroom to find his wife still wearing a robe over her nightdress as she sat writing at the small table next to the window.

"Er…no," she replied, hastily sealing the envelope. "I just need to finish writing something."

Justin put his arms around her shoulders and coaxed, "Can't it wait until tomorrow? I want to spend time with you. I'll be gone all day tomorrow."

Justin's touch was gentle and warm as usual, but she was unusually rigid. Every touch of his hand felt like the piercing tip of an arrow. Although she had never denied herself to him, he did not know that the sweetness of his embrace was followed by pain. She loved and hated this man with golden skin and penetrating eyes in equal measure. She hated his love that had enslaved her for five years, and brought her ecstasy, jealousy, and finally the misery of a broken heart.

"Justin, I want to know something," she whispered as she laid her cheek on his shoulder and let him unravel her silken hair until it rippled down her back.

"What do you want to know?"

"There's a thin line between love and hate, so if you love someone and they disappoint you, could you hate them as much as you love them?"

He chucked softly as if he was amused at her strange question.

"I'm not the sort to love anyone easily. Apart from the two kings and my family, you're the only one I love. My love will never change. Even if you disappointed me, I could never hate you. I'd just be sad."

Catherine bit her lip and wiped her tears on his shoulder before he could see.

Let me hate you until tomorrow, so that my love for you doesn't overpower my resolve to leave you.

If I don't go tomorrow, I'll be a slave in the hell you have created until I die.

* * *

The passenger boat from Singapore to India was called the Neptune. It was a larger vessel than she had ever been on before with comfortable cabins. The ship was due to depart from the harbour at ten o'clock the next morning. After having breakfast on the shore, the passengers made their way to the ship and the stewards took care of the luggage, which was a great relief to Catherine.

Catherine said goodbye to Annie and her husband at the dock. She would have to take a smaller boat to the larger vessel which had dropped anchor not far away. Although her face was pale, she was calm unlike Annie who wiped away tears as if she were the one leaving.

"Look after yerself, Miss Catherine," she cried. "Jack's pal Daniel's a steward on the ship. If ye need anything let him know. Oh! I gave your name as Mrs Lindley. It'll make things easier than usin' the prince's name."

"I know. Thank you, Annie. I won't forget your kindness."

Catherine kissed her lightly on the cheek. In her black dress and narrow-rimmed hat with a black veil covering her face, Catherine was able to conceal herself and, since there were many Westerners travelling from Singapore, she was not conspicuous.

From the moment she left Annie, Catherine felt like a lifeless puppet on a string as she stepped onto the small boat. The puppet turned to wave to her two friends before turning back. She was as cold as ice from head to toe.

She did not see Singapore again as she was blinded by tears.

Goodbye, Burapha.

* * *

It was late by the time Prince Saifa returned. He was puzzled when he went upstairs and found that the lights were all out since, usually, a lantern was lit. Normally, Catherine would wait up for him, no matter how late he was, but only the maid was there to meet him before she went home for the night, while the guard was at the foot of the stairs.

"Are you asleep, Catherine?" he called as he knocked on the bedroom door.

There was no answer and when he pushed the door open, all he saw was darkness because all the curtains had been drawn. Since he knew where everything was, he turned on a gas lamp and, a moment later, the room was illuminated, revealing nothing but emptiness.

"Catherine!"

His instinct told him something was amiss. Although the bed cover had been pulled back neatly by the maid, there was no trace of anyone having lain on it and all the curtains were shut tight. The room was shrouded in emptiness, and the brush and the hand-held mirror had disappeared from the dressing table.

An envelope standing against the lamp on the small writing table caught his eye as he looked around the room. A woman's neat handwriting was visible in the dim rays of the lamp.

His Serene Highness Prince Vijjuprapha

He froze for a moment before going to pick it up and open the envelope. He held his breath as he read the words on the white paper.

Justin, my love,

For the past five years, from the moment we belonged to each other until our last night together, I have never regretted us being together, even though it has ended with us being parted for the rest of our lives..

Thank you for giving me something precious. The incomparable joy and sweetness of love can only happen once with one man for me.

Everything has its season, my dearest. Don't be sad and don't regret that we must part. You have a duty to your wife and your child, while I must retain my dignity.

Let me go while my heart is still filled with love for you. Don't make me stay with you until love gives way to hate alone, which would happen if you refused to let me go and forced me to be the only woman in your heart, while always remaining an outsider to your family.

I will never forget you, my husband, and my dearest love.

Goodbye,

> *From your wife,*
> *Catherine*

The letter slipped from his hand without him knowing. The prince fainted and fell onto the table, knocking over the glass inkpot and the other writing utensils on the desk before it smashed and ink spilled across the polished wooden floor. The crash echoed through the silence, reaching the ears of the other two people in the house.

The first was Luang Surawiset, who was staying in the other wing and was about to go to bed. He stopped and looked around suspiciously. The other was the guard who stood at the foot of the stairs. He stood up at once and listened, but there was no sound. His sensed that something was wrong, and he was hesitating as to whether to go upstairs when he heard Luang Surawiset's bedroom door open and saw him step out looking anxious.

He hurried down the passageway to the prince's bedroom and knocked on the door.

"Your Highness, it's me, Luang Surawiset," he called out in English. "What's happened?"

At first, there was no answer. A moment later, there was the sound of a bell rope being pulled. Luang Surawiset and the guard pushed open the door at once and found the prince propping himself up and pulling on the rope that hung from the ceiling. His face was pale and drenched with sweat.

When Luang Surawiset went to help him up, he was told, "Bring the consul's secretary to me...immediately!"

The consul's secretary came hurrying in half an hour later and found the prince waiting anxiously. He had not changed his clothes and his face was taut. A few minutes later, he knew the whole story.

"If your wife's still in Singapore, I can guarantee we'll find her by morning. The only problem is, has she already left?"

"If she's already left, I need the consul to send a boat to follow her ship and bring her back."

The other man looked at him sympathetically, knowing it was almost impossible.

"If it's a small boat and she's only just left, we can send a larger boat after her, but if she's been gone for several hours, it will be difficult, Your Highness."

222 A Passage to Siam

"Please try," the prince said firmly. "Cancel all tomorrow's plans until there's news of my wife."

Suspicion immediately fell on Annie, since she was the only person who had been to visit Catherine. The consul's secretary sent for her that night before dawn. Annie and her husband appeared prepared. The sailor stood in silence, fiddling with his cap, and let his wife do the talking. The young woman answered with confidence before the three men, including Luang Surawiset.

"Aye, sir. Miss Catherine...I mean, the prince's wife left this mornin'. She's headin' back to England. I dinnae do no wrong by helpin' her to buy a ticket."

"Annie," Prince Vijjuprapha said coldly, "you knew my wife was travelling without my permission, didn't you?"

"Well, Yer Highness!" Annie cried. "Other folk's family matters are nae my affair. All I know is, I've known Catherine...I mean yer wife since we were in England, and when she asked me for help, it would've been unkind to refuse."

And she added astutely, "That's all I know. I have nae broken any laws here, and I'm a British citizen, nae a Siamese one."

The secretary replied briskly, "Tell me the name of the ship and the sea route, and I'll give you permission to leave."

Jack told him the name of the ship and the sea route readily.

"After leavin' Singapore, the Neptune's off to Sri Lanka and will dock in Columbo. The prince's missus'll get off there. She won't be headin' to Bombay like most folks 'cause there's a merchant ship goin' to Aden in the Red Sea. She'll save more time doin' that than goin' to Bombay, guv."

"What name was she using?" the secretary asked, jotting down the details in a notebook.

"Mrs Lindley, guv."

Luang Surawiset glanced at the prince and saw his face pale.

***

The Neptune, which was on its way to Bombay, had left that

morning. By now, it had cleared Singapore's waters since it was a large ship powered by a steam engine and was faster than a sailing ship. There was no way that any other boat from Singapore would be able to catch up with it.

The young British secretary reported, "If Your Highness is really going to go after her, you'll have to wait for the next ship to Colombo or Bombay. As far as I know, that will be the East Wind, which will be leaving in seven days."

"…And by that time, my wife will have already left for Aden in the Red Sea," Prince Vijjuprapha finished softly.

The other man shifted uncomfortably but said nothing.

"If the consul has a ship for me, I'll go after her myself."

The sky was growing lighter and silver rays grew gradually brighter until the green branches outside the window were visible, but for the three men the morning was gloomy. Even the secretary, who had nothing to do with the matter, was conscious of the Siamese prince's anger.

Luang Surawiset, who had been with the prince all along and spoken the least, decided to speak up for the first time in Siamese.

"Your Highness, I'm sorry…your wife is British and not bound by Siamese law. She's allowed to leave the kingdom, but you can't leave Singapore without the king's permission."

Prince Vijjuprapha froze as this fact dawned on him.

"If you leave Siam without the king's permission, you'll be escheated. You're in Singapore because the king decreed it, but if you leave Singapore, you'll be disobeying the king and will be punished. Consider it carefully, Your Highness."

It was true. In his haste, he had momentarily forgotten that he could not leave the kingdom at will. The penalty would be that all his family's property would be taken by the state, and his whole family would suffer.

Seeing the prince motionless, Luang Surawiset changed to English and told the secretary, "The prince won't be able to travel to another country without the king's permission. There's no need for a ship."

"What I can do, Khun Luang," the other man replied sympathetically, "is to write to my friend in Columbo and ask him to check the names

224   A Passage to Siam

of the passengers on the Neptune. If the prince's wife is still there, I can ask him to persuade her to return to Singapore…"

He glanced at the prince before continuing, "If the prince writes her a letter, she might come back. I can't see any other way."

Without saying a word, the prince went over to the writing table and stopped. The glass inkpot had been smashed and swept up but had still not been replaced.

Luang Surawiset was quick.

"I'll bring you a pen and ink from my room."

Everyone in the room knew that the chance of this effort succeeding was as dim as the light of a firefly.

* * *

Sometimes, being alive was the same as being dead. Catherine could not remember where she had read it, or perhaps she had thought of it herself, but it was exactly how she had felt from the moment the Neptune set sail. She had breath, her eyes could see, and she could move, but there was no life left in her. She had left her life with Justin. When he disappeared from her existence, all that remained was her body, but her life had not come with her.

She wrestled with turbulent emotions. On the one hand, when she turned around, she hoped to see him coming towards her with his arms outstretched, but on the other hand, she prayed he would not come after her. She wrestled with love and hate, and for the first few days of the journey she remained in her cabin, devoid of energy, not knowing what to do with herself. The present was empty, but the future was not only empty but dark.

She stayed in her cabin for days, asking the steward to bring her meals because she could not manage to go to the restaurant, but everything she ate made her nauseous. Half-way through the journey, she felt better and decided to get some fresh air up on the deck. She was no longer afraid of travelling alone, but for safety, she followed the advice of Annie's husband, Jack, and put on her black dress and the hat with the veil, so that she looked like a widow in mourning.

When she went up on the deck, there were many other Westerners, both British and European, so she did not feel conspicuous. But as she was walking back, her relief suddenly disappeared. She walked past a young woman who had come up after her and was basking in the evening breeze.

The golden rays in the clear sky caught her red hair. She was wearing a bright green dress that contrasted with her white skin, discoloured from her years in the tropical sun. When she turned her head, her bright red lips caught Catherine's eye from a distance.

Catherine froze. Charlotte Palmer! Who would have thought that she would meet this fortune hunter on the same ship?

Catherine hurried down from the deck at once, telling herself that being stuck in her cabin was better than coming face to face with that woman.

The sea had been calm throughout the journey and they did not encounter any storms all the way to Columbo.

After Catherine disembarked, she was to stay there for one night before boarding a merchant ship called the Southern Star to Aden in the Red Sea. The Southern Star was a larger vessel than the Neptune, but as it was a merchant ship rather than a passenger ship, there were a limited number of cabins for passengers. The clerk at the shipping company in Columbo informed Catherine politely, "The cabins are limited, madam, so you've been put in a cabin with another woman passenger. I hope you'll forgive us for the inconvenience."

"Who will I be with?"

"An Englishwoman like yourself, madam. Her name's Charlotte Palmer."

Catherine's heart lurched, but she had no reason to justify refusing, so she mumbled her thanks.

At least, she told herself, when they reached Aden, they would have to change ships again and she would be rid of her. By this point, nothing was too difficult to for her to bear. She had already faced the worst thing that could happen to her.

Two pairs of eyes met.

And the woman in the bright green dress smiled broadly, raising her eyebrows slightly in puzzlement, even though her voice was cheerful.

"Mrs Lindley from Singapore? I didn't think it was the same person as the prince's wife. Pleased to meet you again, madam."

Catherine's expression was neutral since she felt too numb to show any emotion.

"We meet again, Miss Palmer."

Charlotte Palmer scanned the cabin, which was decorated pleasantly. There were two beds against the walls on opposite sides and Catherine's trunks were placed neatly at the foot of the bed and under the bed.

"Nice room," she said breezily. "Even better than the one from Singapore. Sittin' in 'ere for two months won't be so bad. It's been years since I went 'ome. Funny, ain't it? You go 'alfway round the world only to find there's no place like 'ome."

Catherine let her talk without interrupting, but she did not have the heart to pay much attention. In the event, Charlotte was not as bad a roommate as she had feared because she hardly stayed in the cabin, preferring to go out and socialize to being cooped up inside. She would spend her days keeping company with the men, whether they were sailors or English passengers, and would stay up late drinking with them before returning to the cabin.

At first, Catherine was worried that Charlotte would bring men back to the room and that they would assume she was the same kind of woman, but she was relieved to find that they were conscious of the fact she was different and had the courtesy not to enter the cabin. The most they did was to escort Charlotte back to the cabin, knock on the door, and tell her awkwardly as she opened the door, "I've brought Miss Palmer, miss. She's...er...'ad a bit too much to drink."

Charlotte was never so drunk that she passed out. She would simply stagger in, singing incoherently, and when Catherine led her to the bed, she would fall asleep in her clothes.

Catherine was sometimes troubled by seasickness in the mornings, but Charlotte did not see because she was usually sound asleep until noon. The first time she woke up early, she was shocked when she saw how severe the seasickness was.

"Oh, Lord!" she cried as she hurried to assist Catherine. "You're as white as a sheet. Lie down, and I'll bring you some 'ot tea."

"Thank you," Catherine whispered.

Charlotte went to fetch her some tea and sat down on the edge of the bed watching her take small sips.

"I feel better now," Catherine smiled, noticing Charlotte staring. "It's just seasickness. I can never get used to the sea."

"The sea's as calm as a sheet of glass," Charlotte protested. "And you're used to the water. You've been livin' on a raft, after all."

Catherine bit her lip. Everyone in Bangkok knew where the prince's English wife had lived, but the words brought a stab of pain. Charlotte carried on talking.

"We're lucky we ain't 'ad any storms. The navigator said once we pass through the Red Sea and reach the Mediterranean, we don't need to worry about 'em. It'll just get colder."

Catherine closed her eyes, so she would not have to listen anymore.

Catherine's seasickness gradually subsided as they got closer to Aden, but it still troubled her occasionally. If Charlotte was awake, she would always come to help her, and Catherine started to realize that she had a good heart. She remained lively and chatty despite Catherine's silence, which did not make her uncomfortable. The only thing she never talked about was the reason she had ended up alone on the other side of the world. She had never mentioned a husband and seemed not to want one.

"If I were married, I'd 'ave no freedom. They say a woman's place is in the 'ome, but I wouldn't want to be stuck in front of an 'ot stove all day. That's no life, is it?"

Catherine didn't answer. She had walked far away from that issue – bruised and broken.

"Lots of girls just pretend they're 'appy. I know a girl who's 'usband beats 'er, but she's too scared to walk out on 'im 'cause she'll 'ave nowhere to go. That's why I won't marry. I'd rather be free."

It was the craziest idea Catherine had ever heard, but she felt strangely warm, knowing that she was not the only woman in the world who felt that way.

* * *

There were no storms at sea, but Catherine's seasickness remained.

After caring for Catherine several times, Charlotte remarked, "You can't be seasick. You must be ill."

"Maybe," Catherine smiled wanly. "I don't feel as well as before."

Charlotte studied her shrewdly.

"We've been roommates for a month now. Can I ask you somethin'?" She lowered her voice.

"I don't mean to be rude, but are you expectin'?"

Catherine looked at her, puzzled, before mumbling, "I don't know...I've lost track of the days...I completely forgot about it, but I haven't had my monthly since I've been seasick..."

Charlotte smiled triumphantly.

"I've never 'ad a child, but I know the signs. That's mornin' sickness what you've got. Not seasickness. The sea's as calm as anythin'. 'Ow can you be seasick? And you 'ain't 'ad your monthly."

Catherine's face became as white as a sheet and her heart turned to ice. She patted her stomach instinctively and realized her corset was feeling tight. She had been pregnant twice before and knew it was possible.

"We've only been at sea a month. It must 'ave 'appened in Siam or in Singapore. You're not showin' now, but by the time we get to England, you will be. You better get plenty of rest. 'Ere, let me 'elp you prop your pillows up. There's nothin' you can do right now, but when we get to Aden, you can get a boat back to Siam."

The sky was engulfed by dark clouds and the sun was obscured from view, leaving only dim silver rays glittering across the surface of the pale green water. Several seagulls flew up from the waves, flapping their wings and disappearing into the gloom.

A pair of eyes studied the horizon to the west as if they were searching for something – or someone – at the end of the horizon. The man they belonged to stood alone on the narrow beach, away from people and away from the bustle of the pier. A strong gust of wind chilled him from head to toe, but he remained motionless.

My love, I love you too much to be angry with you for what you've done to me, and I forgive you because I know it hurts you as much as it hurts me.

I know you're somewhere at the end of the horizon, and even if I can't

*see you with my eyes, I can see you with my heart, just as you can always
see me with your heart.*

*You only left me physically, just as I'm only apart from you physically, but
your heart will never leave me, as my heart will be with you for all time.*

Our sadness at being apart is only a reminder of the depth of our love.

He heard a horse and carriage come along the road alongside the
beach and stop behind him, but he did not move or turn around until
he heard someone call him.

"Your Highness."

He turned around slowly and saw a man striding towards him,
and when he reached the prince, he said anxiously, "You're sick. You
shouldn't be out here."

The prince was feverish, and his face was flushed.

"It's better than being stuck inside. I needed some fresh air."

Luang Surawiset shook his head wearily. Although he sympathized,
he did not agree.

"If you get a chill, it will make your fever worse. Please come back.
You've been on the beach for a long time."

Luang Surawiset knew that the prince was sick at heart. Since his
English wife had left, he had not eaten or slept for days. Although
at first, he forced himself to continue his duties, a few days later, he
became sick with a fever.

Fortunately, most of the work was done, and they had only a couple
of days left, so it was a good opportunity for the prince to rest. Luang
Surawiset had decided to postpone the journey back to Siam until the
prince was better, but as he sat down in the carriage, to his dismay, the
prince said, "Khun Luang, we return to Siam the day after tomorrow."

"You're ill, Your Highness. The doctor said you shouldn't travel
until you're well."

"I can't hang about. We must return as scheduled."

"A few days later won't make any difference…"

"I don't want to stay another day in Singapore. I'm going back to
Siam as scheduled to ask permission to go to England."

So that was the reason, Luang Surawiset thought to himself
with a sigh.

* * *

Catherine thought about Charlotte's words. Return to Siam?

Why would I return to Siam?

To tell Justin I'm with his child. He has never stopped hoping for a child with the woman he loves. He would be over the moon.

His delight would cancel out his anger that I left him. He would forgive me, I know.

I know that every day and night since I left him, Justin's pain has been no less than mine. It might be worse because he knows that he can't win this time. It will hurt his pride, I know.

If this was a fairy-tale and I returned, our story would have a happy ending like the water nymph that was reunited with her knight.

But...

That is not real life.

In real life, the cycle would be repeated.

Would my child meet the same fate as his sister Rosalind and his brother Charles? How many more times would my heart be broken as I clasped the tiny hand and felt it grow limp as the life in the body was blown away? What would I do if a tropical disease took my child's life a third time?

Or if my child lived, would he be loved and cherished as much as his siblings with a Siamese mother?

And what about me? Would I return to the hellish loop of Justin's love to suffer for the rest of my life?

Catherine inadvertently touched her left ring finger. The ring with nine stones that Justin put on her finger the first night they were together was still on her finger. The diamond and the eight precious stones caught the light and glinted.

The eternity ring…

My love for you is still eternal, so I can't bring myself to take it off.

But things will never be the same again.

Catherine buried her face in the pillow and, for the first time since the journey began, the tears that had flooded her heart spilled out.

From Aden, Catherine was to pass through the Red Sea and continue by land from Cairo to the Mediterranean, where she would get on a boat to Marseilles before travelling through France to the English Channel.

Then she would finally set foot in her homeland at Dover. The journey was smooth, and everything had been arranged as Jack had promised. Her morning sickness gradually diminished but, by this time, Catherine knew for certain that she was pregnant. Her waist had expanded such that she had had to loosen her corset, and her bust was fuller, which meant that she had to wear loose blouses and let out those that were too tight.

As they neared Aden, Charlotte packed her trunk and told Catherine sympathetically, "Once we're ashore, we'll 'ave to part ways. You'll 'ave to wait for a ship to take you back. It shouldn't be more than a few days."

"I'm not going back," Catherine said firmly.

Charlotte's mouth opened in surprise.

"You ain't goin' back? You mean you're afraid to travel by yourself?"

"No, I'm going back to England."

"I don't understand," Charlotte said, looking confused. "Are you goin' to 'ave the child in England and let the prince come and fetch you?"

"No," Catherine said, steadying her voice. "I'm never going back to Siam, no matter what."

* * *

The news of Prince Vijjuprapha's return to Bangkok reached the palace as soon as his ship reached the estuary, so everyone was excited. Even Mom Yad was agitated, telling her daughter-in-law, "Bua, go and wait for him at the pier. You should stay active when you're pregnant, or you'll have a difficult birth."

"Yes, Mother."

Bua's stomach was visible as she was now more than five months pregnant. Her nausea had passed, and she was glowing with health. Every day, she left her house to help her mother-in-law with various small tasks, such as fruit carving, which she did more delicately than any of the servants.

She was softly spoken and was a faultless homemaker, having been trained by Khun Chom Klee. She was respectful to her elders and kind to the servants, and Mom Yad was pleased with her.

She was satisfied that she had been right. Khun Chom Klee and her own efforts in securing her as their daughter-in-law had not been wasted.

'She's a perfect match for Saifa.'

She recalled Khun Chom Klee's words with satisfaction.

'They're like the sun and the moon. If only my son hadn't been misled.'

Mom Yad didn't like to mention Catherine's name to anyone unless she was alone with Khun Chom Klee in the Front Palace.

"I can't believe he's still taken with that mem. He even took her abroad with him without giving poor Bua a second thought."

Khun Chom Klee comforted her as usual.

"Don't worry. He'll come to his senses eventually. Wait until Bua has a child and he'll be smitten."

Bua stepped carefully onto the pavilion at the pier, followed by her servants, and when she caught sight of the approaching boat, her heart began to race in anticipation.

But when the boat docked, her excitement turned to alarm.

"Goodness…" she whispered.

The man who stepped off the boat was not the vigorous young man she remembered but was thin and pale as a sheet with dark circles under his eyes, so weak that he had to be supported by his attendant. Bua hurried towards him.

"Are you ill, Your Highness?" she cried in shock.

Prince Saifa looked at his wife without a trace of his usual smile, and answered gruffly, "I had a fever, but I'm better."

Won helped him onto the bridge that was connected to the bank and Bua followed behind.

Mom Yad was even more shocked by the news of his illness than Bua and sent a servant to fetch Dr Bradley, even though he told her, "I'm fine."

"You look ill, and you've lost weight. You'd better go back to the raft and wait for Dr Bradley."

She did not ask her son about Catherine, assuming she had gone straight to the raft, so she was surprised when he said, "I'm not going back to the raft. I'll stay in my father's house. Please prepare a room for me, Mother."

* * *

Khun Chom Klee left the palace as soon as she heard the news of his illness and was too agitated to sit still in the boat that took her to his father's palace. The raft was empty and quiet, but the main house was as busy as usual. Mom Yad saw her arrive at the pier and hurried to the reception room to greet her.

Mom Yad explained the situation, and Khun Chom exclaimed, "Oh, my poor son!"

However when she entered her son's room, she breathed a sigh of relief when she saw that he was not in bed but sitting by the window at a desk that had been brought from the raft and was absorbed in writing a letter. He looked up and seeing her got up from the desk and went towards her, but Khun Chom pulled him to sit down on a rug in the middle of the room.

"Yad told me, and I was worried," she said, studying her son. "You've lost so much weight! Your father's not well either."

"I haven't been to the palace yet. Is he ill again?"

"His condition improved for a while, but then his illness returned."

"I'll go and see him tomorrow."

"Wait until you're feeling better. I'll tell him you haven't been well."

"It's nothing much. I need to talk to him about the trip to Singapore next month."

Khun Chom Klee shook her head thoughtfully.

"I don't think he'll be able to go. The doctors said it would be ill-advised."

The prince was silent, his face anxious.

"And for another thing. Bua's pregnant. If you're sick it will worry her."

He did not answer, so she continued, "I realize you're sick at heart. But don't forget, you still have your duty to the king, your elderly mother, your siblings, and your wife and child. If anything happened to you, what would we do?"

Prince Saifa pursed his lips.

"That's why I don't give up."

Khun Chom Klee stroked his back tenderly.

"Good. Promise me you won't go off again. Luang Surawiset told Yad you were planning to go to Singapore with the king and to ask his permission to go to England. You should forget about it. The king isn't going to Singapore."

Prince Saifa's face immediately became taut.

"I won't be parted from Catherine. I won't be gone for long." This was what Khun Chom Klee feared the most, and she felt as cold as ice.

"Don't be so hasty, son. The king gave you the opportunity to study abroad. Are you going to repay him by leaving your home? Where's your gratitude?"

He was silent for a moment before retorting, "I'm not leaving just to go after my wife. I was planning to look at canons while I'm in England."

It was just an excuse she knew.

"The king's unwell. He needs you here by his side. You shouldn't give that woman priority."

"I can't just let her go. If you don't want me to go to England, I have one request…"

"What is it?"

"If Catherine comes back, I want only one wife."

"And what about Bua?" she cried.

"I'll provide for her as if she's my own sister, and if she doesn't want to stay with me, I'll release her to remarry if she wishes, but if she has a son, my mother should raise him and if she has a daughter, she should raise her herself."

Khun Chom Klee's heart ached for the pretty young woman and, even though she was comforted by the fact that her son would be kind to Bua, she could not abide the thought that he was still in love with another woman on the other side of the world. Later, having talked to Bua she was relieved to find that she was content and that, even though her husband favoured another woman, he was kind to her and they would soon have a young child to cherish.

12

The Wind from the Past

The air became gradually cooler as the boat sailed into the Mediterranean towards the port in the South of France. By that time, it was nearly autumn. It was still warm by European standards, but for Catherine, who had lived in the tropics for the past few years, the nip in the air was invigorating.

When she went up on the deck for some fresh air in the mornings and looked up at the sun's rays peeping through the cloudy sky in the east, Siam seemed so far away that she felt as if it had been nothing more than a dream. As if she had been asleep for the past five years and had just woken up.

She saw less of Charlotte now that they had boarded the next ship, since the passenger boat had enough cabins for them to each have their own room. Even so, Charlotte knocked on Catherine's door most days to ask how she was. One evening, she met Charlotte on the deck as she stood admiring the sunset over the deep blue sea.

"You're lookin' better," she announced. "Once we get to London, where are you stayin'?"

"I won't be going to London. I'm going to Longstock. In Hampshire."

"Oh! That's where you're from," she said. "I'm stayin' in London. I don't like the country. I don't know if I've got any relatives left. But who cares? If it ain't any fun, I'll go back."

"Go back where?"

"I might go back to Siam," she replied as if travelling halfway around the world was nothing out of the ordinary. "I can't stay in the same place for long. I do miss England, but after a while it gets borin'. My folks are dead. What about yours?"

"There's my mother," Catherine answered softly. "And my sister

236   A Passage to Siam

and brother-in-law."

"They'll be glad to see you after all this time."

"I expect they'll be more surprised," Catherine said forcing a smile. "I haven't written to my mother since I left Arthur. I don't know what I'm going to tell her."

Charlotte's eyes widened.

"You mean you ain't told 'er you left 'im?"

"I didn't know how to tell her. If she knows, she'll have heard it from Arthur."

"And what about the prince? Doesn't she know you were the wife of a Siamese prince?"

"I've never told my family."

Charlotte listened with a puzzled expression.

"I wrote at Christmas, but I never told them about what happened in Siam. It was too complicated. And I never gave them my address, so they never wrote."

Catherine stroked her stomach. After the initial shock of finding out she was pregnant, Catherine had grown accustomed to the life growing inside her, and the flame in her heart that had been extinguished by the deaths of Rosalind and Charles was reignited. This child would replace Justin. She would not be alone as she had thought. His child would always be with her.

**

For the last part of the journey, they were to travel by horse-drawn carriage from Marseilles as far as the English Channel, where they would make the crossing to England. Although the journey by land was shorter, the bumpy ride made Catherine ache all over and brought on contractions, causing her to fear for her baby child. Charlotte never left her side.

Throughout the five-hour crossing by boat Catherine had to lie down, and when they arrived at Dover, she looked so exhausted that Charlotte wouldn't let her journey on to Longstock.

"There ain't no rush. You ain't fit to travel. You don't want to lose that baby."

The Wind from the Past 237

There was nothing Catherine feared more than losing another baby. This child was her only hope left in the world.

"You should stay 'ere 'til you're feelin' better. I'll find you a place to stay and fetch a doctor. And I'll stay to keep you company," Charlotte asserted.

"Aren't you going to London?"

"There's no rush. I can go to London anytime. I like Dover."

Charlotte found them a place on the first day. It was a small hotel with a clean and comfortable room situated in a quiet street. She then went out in the afternoon and returned with an elderly doctor, having told him that Catherine was a young widow. He examined her kindly and explained that she had been affected by the journey, but no harm had been done to the child.

"Nevertheless, you ought not to travel for the next few days. I advise you to rest for a week," he said gently.

Catherine did not protest. Her health was her top priority. And besides, she was in no hurry to return to Longstock where she would be faced with questions to which she had no answer.

* * *

By the second day, she began to feel better, and by the third day she was almost back to normal. On that afternoon Catherine decided to go out for a walk to get some fresh air. It was a crisp autumn day. The trees along the street had turned yellow and red, contrasting with the silver sky. The cool wind felt like a knife on her cheeks, and she pulled her old coat tightly around her.

She stopped to rest every so often, since her weight had increased, affirming the life growing inside her. Whenever she touched her stomach, her fatigue and loneliness faded away, and her heart filled with warmth.

She walked slowly back to her hotel, stopping in front of the steps that led to the front door. At that moment, a man crossed over the road, headed for the hotel. He suddenly froze when he saw her.

"Catherine!" he cried.

Catherine turned to face him. She did not want to believe her ears

238   A Passage to Siam

or her eyes. She felt as if she was about to faint, but when she began to lose her balance, he hurried to steady her.

"Catherine! Are you alright?"

The voice she had not heard for five years filled her ears.

"Thank God, I found you," he stammered. "Welcome home."

Five years had changed Arthur and, even though his face was not that different, his countenance and his clothing made him difficult to recognize. He had gained weight, and his hair was now the colour of straw. He had long sideburns and a neatly trimmed moustache, while the lines at the corners of his eyes gave him the appearance of a man of thirty-five rather than of someone not yet thirty. All in all, in his manner, there was no trace of the young officer she had known before. He appeared well-to-do, Catherine thought, noticing his dark brown coat with the velvet collar and his gold-tipped cane.

"I wasn't expecting to see you here," Catherine whispered.

His reply almost made her faint.

"Charlotte Palmer sent a telegraph to my office telling me you were here."

"Charlotte…" she repeated. "But why?"

"She knew where to find me."

"So you're still in contact with her."

"We exchange letters at Christmas. It's the only way for me to get news from…Siam."

He paused before the last word, revealing that he had meant news about her.

"Charlotte never told me she was still in contact with you."

They sat in the hotel's sitting room, which was warm and cosy.

"It's lucky I was in London. I'm often back in England at this time of year. I stay for Christmas with my family. At other times of the year, I'm usually travelling."

"Where do you travel?"

"I'm the sales representative for tea from the East. Alfred made me a partner. Business is going very well. I'm travelling for six to eight months of the year. It's no trouble since I don't have any family commitments."

"And why did Charlotte have to send you a telegraph when…"

She stopped, realizing that whatever she said would hurt his feelings.

The Wind from the Past 239

"When we've separated," he finished for her without any resentment in his voice. "Well, the thing is, even though I'm not your husband, I'd still like to be your friend."

"Oh… Arthur," Catherine cried, the words becoming strangled in her throat.

Arthur gazed at the figure wrapped in a dark blue shawl and noticed that she was shivering.

"Are you alright?" he asked with concern.

"Yes…I'm fine," she forced herself to reply. "I just…I just didn't expect to hear you say that."

"If you don't reject my friendship, then I'm happy," Arthur asserted. "Can I ask you something? I know from the telegraph that you came back alone, but perhaps there's…"

"I came alone. There's no one else."

Arthur leaned back in his chair and exhaled.

"Are you going anywhere? I mean…are you going to London, or…"

"I'm going back to Longstock."

"That's what I thought. Have you written to tell your mother?"

This was a problem that Catherine had still not resolved.

"No. I don't know what to tell her. What did you tell her?"

"I never told her anything."

"What do you mean?"

"Like I said, I never told her we'd separated. I thought you'd tell her."

"Wait. You mean my mother doesn't know we separated," Catherine cried, trying to contain herself. "What will she say when I suddenly return and…"

Arthur was unperturbed.

"I don't see why it would be a problem. You go home and…little by little you tell her what happened. It won't make any difference now."

Catherine put her head in her hands, and in her agitation, did not notice that Arthur was watching her intently.

"I…I thought she knew…I don't know where to start. In truth, what happened between us isn't as difficult as the matter of…"

"You and the prince?" Arthur finished for her.

"It's over between the prince and I, but…"

Her throat was dry as she continued, "I don't know how to tell

240 A Passage to Siam

her about this."

She stood up and unbuttoned the loose-fitting coat, which concealed her figure completely. Up to his point, she had intentionally kept it on, so as not to reveal her condition. But by now, she was too weary to hide it anymore.

"My God!" Arthur cried in shock.

Catherine buttoned up her coat and sank back on the chair.

"I expect my mother will have the same reaction."

Arthur came to his senses and stood up suddenly before moving towards her. She felt his strong hand clasp hers as he knelt in front of her. He spoke in a low voice that was filled with fury.

"Catherine, how could he do this to you?"

Catherine looked at him and felt a stab of pain as she did whenever her thoughts turned to Justin. But she was ready to protect his honour with all her remaining strength.

"You think he turned me out? No…" she began, trying to steady her voice. "I left of my own accord. He didn't know I was pregnant. I didn't even know myself. Please don't mention him again…"

"Then it's finished. The past is behind you. If you're ever in trouble, you're not alone. I'll do everything in my power to help you…I promise."

Arthur stayed in the same hotel, but in a different room. Understanding her awkwardness in meeting him again, he tried to ease the tension by asking her to join him for dinner in the hotel dining room.

"We have a lot to discuss, but let's not talk about the past. Will you join me?"

"Yes. Thank you for asking."

If she had refused him, it would have hurt his feelings, and she was relieved that he had promised not to talk about the past. And besides, having dinner with Arthur was better than staying all alone in her room. She noticed many changes in him. He was no longer the impetuous young man she had known before and was now a confident and determined businessman who treated her like an old friend.

"I've been thinking about how to help you. It isn't as difficult as it seems."

"What do you mean?"

"In fact, it would be much easier if you didn't tell your mother about what has happened."

"I can hardly hide it. At least I'll have to tell her whose child it is."

"Then tell her it's Arthur Lindley's."

Catherine felt as if he'd dropped a bomb on the table and her knife and fork almost slipped from her hands.

"Arthur! I can't do that…"

"Listen, Catherine," he said softly. "You can't leave your child fatherless. In a small community like yours, he or she will be a target for gossip. You'll have to invent a father, so why don't you just say the baby is mine?"

"Thank you."

Catherine put down her knife and fork and tried to steady her hands and her voice.

"But I can't. It wouldn't be fair for you to sacrifice your reputation for my sake."

Arthur was adamant.

"I wouldn't be sacrificing my reputation. Let me come with you to Longstock. When your mother sees us together, she won't suspect a thing. And the neighbours won't ask questions."

Catherine could see that Arthur was right, but there was still another problem.

"But how will we hide the fact that we've separated? If we say we're still together, what will we do next?"

"I'll go back to London."

"To London?"

"We'll simply tell everyone in Longstock that I have to travel again, and that, after we'd been living in the East for five years, you became pregnant, so I brought you back to have the baby at home."

"Thank you, Arthur. Let me think about it before I give you an answer."

"If you agree, I'll take you home as soon as you're well enough to travel. You can stay there, and I'll say I must get back to London, and that I'll come and visit from time to time before I go abroad."

"I appreciate it more than I can say."

242 A Passage to Siam

The next morning, as Catherine was packing her things before leaving for Longstock, Charlotte knocked on the door. She was dressed in travelling clothes with a green cape, and her red hair was tied back neatly under her hat.

"I'm goin' to London today," she announced. "I don't know if we'll 'ave a chance to meet again, so I've come to wish you all the best."

Catherine caught her breath. Over the past few months, Charlotte had become a trusted friend.

"I wish you all the best, too," she said sincerely. "And thank you… for being so good to me."

Charlotte grinned.

"That's a relief! I thought you'd be up in arms that I told Arthur. There's nothin' goin' on between us mind. We're just friends."

"If you and Arthur were to get married, you'd have my blessing."

"Me? Get married?" Charlotte exclaimed. "Not on your life!"

Catherine wrote down her address in Longstock on a piece of paper and handed it to Charlotte.

"I'd like you to visit me, Charlotte. I hope I can see you again."

Charlotte smiled again. Then her face fell.

"Oh, Catherine!" she cried, hugging her. "You take care. I don't think we'll meet again…"

And she released her grip and walked quickly towards the door.

***

When Catherine opened her eyes, the pale golden rays of the morning sun were shining through the window onto the quilt that covered her in her old upstairs bedroom. By this time of year, the roses that climbed up to the window had shed their petals and leaves, leaving only the dark thorn-covered stems.

I'm home at last!

Catherine slid out from under the warm quilt and slipped a shawl around her shoulders before walking towards the window. She looked down at the ground beside the house and across the grey street at the red brick houses opposite as if to make sure that she was not imagining the picture before her.

She felt a lump in her throat and could not say if it was because she was happy or sad.

Catherine got dressed and went downstairs to find Arthur sitting in the front room reading a newspaper.

"Good morning. Did you sleep well?" he asked, smiling. "You're looking well."

"Morning. I haven't slept so well for days."

In fact, she hadn't slept so well for almost a year until she had almost forgotten what a good night's sleep was like.

She had not slept well since Justin had left her bed in the night to see his other wife.

Her mother opened the door and entered the room, telling her with a smile, "I thought you'd be tired, so I didn't wake you. Come and have breakfast."

Emma had aged over the past five years. Her hair was specked with grey, and she was slower on her feet, but she was still a fastidious housekeeper.

Catherine was relieved that her mother's only reaction to her youngest daughter returning home was excitement. All Arthur had told her was that, after setting up home in the East, Catherine was not well enough to make the journey back, so she had remained in Siam while Arthur had returned to England, and he had been so concerned to get back to his wife that he had not had time to visit his mother-in-law.

"When Catherine found out she was with child, I thought it best that she came home," he explained. "Then when I travel again, I won't need to worry about her."

"Do you still need to travel?" Mrs Burnett asked with concern.

"I'm afraid so," Arthur replied, glancing at Catherine. "But I'll try to travel less."

Arthur explained that, since Catherine had become pregnant, she had had difficulty sleeping, so they had been sleeping in separate rooms to prevent him from being disturbed. This was not a problem since Pauline's room was empty, so Arthur slept there.

Although Emma Burnett was concerned that Arthur would be

away for months at a time, she was relieved when he assured her that he would leave Catherine with a reasonable amount of money to live on during his absence.

"I'd rather you didn't mention the subject of money to my mother." Arthur's feet stopped for a moment before he continued walking alongside Catherine down the path through the trees that had changed their colours to orange and gold, the ground covered by crisp brown leaves. "I must, so that she won't worry. You need money to live on."

Catherine had invited him to go for a walk that afternoon so she could speak to him without the presence of a third party.

"I appreciate your concern, but I can assure you I have some savings of my own."

"You should keep your assets from Siam hidden from your mother, or you'll arouse her suspicion."

"My assets are in sterling, so she won't suspect a thing. The second king of Siam gave me money for the journey, and I still have some left."

Arthur frowned as he always did when she spoke of her life in Siam.

"Let's not talk about that," he said abruptly, and pointed his cane towards the River Thames that lay ahead of them. "We'll walk as far as that willow tree, and then we'll stop and rest. This is where we walked before we got married. Do you remember?"

She had forgotten. Her memories of her time with Arthur were like a blank sheet of paper.

"I met your uncle in London two or three years ago, and he invited me to stay at his house. We should go and visit him."

She did not want to face General Burnett's questions, so she gently evaded the topic.

"I think it would be better to write to him. My aunt's so inquisitive, she'd be bound to find out the truth and, anyway, I wouldn't know what to say about Mary. I feel awful that I didn't know for over a year."

"George Rowland's coming back to England for good. He's remarried. I don't expect you knew."

"Oh! I had no idea."

The Wind from the Past 245

"It's difficult for a man to stay alone in India. I met his wife once. She's the widow of an English officer. She's a good woman. I'm sure you'd like her."

Arthur knew as well as she did that in reality she would be unlikely to have an opportunity to meet her, and that the only people she would be meeting were the people of Longstock.

They stopped to rest under the willow tree. After a while, Catherine said softly, "We should go back. It's getting chilly, and I'm still not used to the cold."

As they walked back, they were both silent, each engrossed in their own thoughts.

* * *

The raft was shut tight, and every room was empty, since all the furniture had been taken to the main house. Prince Vijjuprapha closed the bedroom door and put a chain across it before walking away without looking back. He went up to the main house to the part where his father had lived in a separate building to his mother.

The spacious room was comfortably outfitted with furniture from Europe, and the prince did not allow anyone, except his attendant Won who brought him his meals and the person who cleaned it, to enter, not even his wife.

Most of the time, Bua would keep herself to herself in her house, and only went to the main house to supervise her husband's breakfast preparations before he went to the Front Palace. In the afternoons, she would go to attend to Mom Yad as usual. She would also wait for him to return in the evenings with his evening meal because he never visited her house.

Even so, there was no tension between them as he would always ask after her health, since she was now heavily pregnant, before returning to his room alone. Mom Yad could only look on in frustration. By this time, she had become wary of him, having noticed his short temper since his foreign wife had left.

When she had mentioned the raft, he had snapped, "I won't be going back there alone. Keep it locked."

Khun Chom had been the one to reassure her when she went to the Front Palace to tell her what had happened.

"Don't you worry. In time, Saifa will forget her. Tell Bua not to take offense. It isn't good for the baby."

At least Bua was compliant, Mom Yad told herself with relief. She had not uttered a word of complaint or made any fuss whatsoever. It was because of this quality that Mom Yad hoped her son would not abandon her.

It was not that Bua did not know what was going on. Even though she said nothing, she was not so foolish that she could not guess. Unlike everyone's assumptions, she knew what it was to be in love. Even though she had not had any physical contact with her beloved, she knew from his eyes, and from the way he spoke to her when she went home to visit, that he had been desperate to see her.

When they had had to part, he had been so distraught that he had entered the monkhood and clung to the Buddha's teachings to find relief from the pain of his broken heart, unable to bear the sight of her in another man's arms.

"I can't bear to lose you. This way, I'll never have to hear any news."

When Bua had become the wife of Prince Vijjuprapha, her only motive was to show gratitude to her elders. Her heart belonged to her sweetheart, but her life belonged to her parents and Khun Chom Klee. She feared for her future but was relieved when she discovered that the prince was kind and had never tried to hurt her.

Her husband was a good-looking man – even better looking than her sweetheart, who had been considered handsome by the villagers. He was also charming with a dulcet voice, and she soon found herself falling in love with him. Nevertheless, there was still a barrier between them.

Her mother was not happy about her marriage to the prince, but she could not defy Khun Chom Klee. Everyone knew about the prince's affection for his forbidden foreign wife, and it was not unexpected that a more suitable wife would be found for him.

When Bua knew of her fate, she had not been jealous of the foreign teacher, but she had been uncomfortable because it was not possible to get close to her. But now that Catherine had left, instead of the matter

The Wind from the Past 247

being resolved as everyone had expected, the prince had demonstrated that there was no woman in his heart except for his first wife. At night, when she lay alone in her room with no sign of her husband, she would stroke her pregnant stomach and feel the child stirring.

"My child," she would whisper with joy tinged with sadness because she foresaw the future.

"I hope you're a girl, so I'll be able to take you back home and we'll stay together until you grow up, just the two of us."

Prince Saifa returned to work in the palace as soon as his health had improved. He immersed himself in his work and, at the end of each day, he went to see King Pinklao, sometimes not returning home until it was almost dawn.

A few days after conducting military training, the prince became ill again and had to rest, but he still received visitors, both Siamese and foreign. If they were Siamese, he would see them in the Throne Hall, but if they were foreign, he would meet them in his study, where they would be able to talk in private.

That day, his guest was Captain George Knox.

"I heard you were ill, Your Highness," he said.

"It's nothing," he replied wearily. "The day I trained the soldiers it was very hot, so I got a fever."

Captain Knox studied him, knowing full well that the prince had been out of sorts since his return from Singapore. His eyes inadvertently wandered to the desk that the prince had just stood up from and he noticed that, besides stationary, there was a porcelain doll with blonde ringlets as if it was there as a constant reminder of a certain young woman.

Knox caught himself and averted his eyes from the doll. When he turned back to the prince, he noticed his face was drawn and there was an expression of sadness in his dark eyes. The prince nodded, and a look of understanding passed between the two men.

"Yes, I miss my wife," he admitted. "Ever since she left, there hasn't been a single night that I haven't missed her, or a single day that I haven't thought about how to bring her back because…I can't go after her myself."

248   A Passage to Siam

Knox knew the reason was that king had cancelled his trip to Singapore due to ill health.

He said, "I realize that you're not able to travel wherever you please, Your Highness."

"I know you understand."

Knox knew that the king had decreed that none of his ministers or his relatives were allowed to leave the city of Bangkok without his permission. This was to ensure that none of them used their power to intimidate people, but it also made it impossible for Prince Vijjuprapha to leave the country and, if he left to go after his wife, his mother and his siblings would suffer the consequences.

Knox had been aware of the problems that the prince's forbidden love would cause from the beginning and, for the past five years, he had held mixed feelings about the matter. On the one hand, he disapproved of the partnership but, at the same time, he sympathized with the young couple. So when the prince explained his dilemma, Knox found himself listening instead of trying to stop him.

"In all of Bangkok, there's only you who I can talk to. How can I send news to Catherine, so that she sympathizes with me and comes back to me?"

Knox wanted to tell him that he needed to resign himself to the fact that it was over, but instead he said, "It depends on what you can offer her in return. While the problem remains, she won't come back."

"If you mean I did her wrong, then I admit it. I had no excuse."

The fact that the prince took responsibility for his actions endeared him to Knox.

"I was wrong because I was arrogant and presumptuous. I assumed that Catherine loved me and would accept it. I wanted to be well-thought of, and I thought I could have it both ways. But I was wrong."

Knox listened in silence.

"I realized when I read Catherine's letter, and my world came crashing down. I felt as if my life had no meaning any more. If I had lost Catherine for another reason, I wouldn't feel so ashamed. She gave up everything for me, and I drove her away because I broke my promise to her. My mistake destroyed both our lives. There's nothing I can do to amend the past…"

If he was only telling Knox because he wanted to get it off his chest, Knox would simply listen. But…he probably wasn't.

"…but I can amend myself for the future."

There it was, as Knox had predicted, and so he repeated, "While the problem remains, what are you going to do to bring your wife back? I doubt she'll come back while things remain as they are."

The prince stopped pacing and stood still at once.

"That's exactly what I want to tell you. I've decided to divorce Bua. It might sound harsh but, like you say, it's better than leaving things as they are. I'll solve the problem before Catherine returns."

Knox had lived in Siam long enough not to be puzzled by the prince's solution. He had noticed long ago that Siamese husbands were not what he would have called romantic, particularly the upper classes because most marriages were arranged by the couple's elders, but the marriages lasted, and couples rarely divorced.

Prince Vijjuprapha had been accustomed to the narrow social circles of the British in India where he had undergone military training, but in his free time he had liked reading literature, so it was not unexpected that he would have been influenced by notions of romantic love.

Knox wondered to himself if the literature and poems he had been exposed to, all of which described English beauties, had caused him to fall in love, not with a petite golden-skinned Siamese girl, but with a rosy-cheeked blue-eyed blonde.

Knox could not resist warning him, "Now that your wife has returned to her homeland, don't you think it would be better for her to remain there, Your Highness?"

"We were husband and wife for five years, Captain. No matter how far away she is, Catherine can't just cut all ties with me."

Knox could not help wondering if that were true, since she was still young and beautiful, and it was still possible for her to start over. He was also aware that it would be difficult for a young woman like Catherine to survive by herself. She could not work in a factory like working-class women and did not have the means to survive by herself without income. A middle-class woman like herself needed a husband to provide for her.

"Then what are you going to do, Your Highness?"

He had already prepared his answer.

"I'm going to write to Catherine. I'm asking you, as a friend, if you know of a way to make sure my letter finds her and, if possible, I'd like you to ask one of your friends in England to bring me news of her. I'm almost certain she's gone back to Longstock."

Thomas George Knox had no other choice, but to answer, "I'll send a letter on behalf of the British Consul in Siam. It will be certain to find her. And I can think of no one more suitable than Colonel George Rowland. I had a letter from him a few days ago informing me that he's retired from the military and will be returning to England."

* * *

Catherine did not hear any news from Arthur, and she did not try to contact him. Having stayed in Longstock for a week, Arthur had returned to London. After that, he sent a short note telling her that he was about to set sail and that he hoped she was well.

Catherine read it out loud to her mother, and Emma asked, "Is that all he wrote? Did he say when he'd be back?"

"Arthur doesn't like writing letters," Catherine replied. "It takes months to get to the East. He won't be back until next year."

"I hope he's back in time for the birth."

Pauline gave her a wicker cradle, and Catherine crocheted a white bed skirt to hang around it. She spent most of her time preparing for her baby to keep busy so that she wouldn't start worrying about the future. At some point, she would have to tell her mother that she and Arthur had separated.

"Have you thought of a name yet?" her mother asked one day, seeing that her daughter was close to giving birth.

"If it's a girl, I'll call her after me. I like the name Catherine," she replied softly.

"And if it's a boy, will you call him after his father?" Emma asked. "Arthur Lindley's a nice name."

Catherine was silent for a moment before replying firmly, "If it's a boy, I'll call him 'Justin.'"

13
New Life

That year, there had been heavy snowfall, and a blanket of white covered the ground. A few days before Christmas, the snow stopped, leaving traces of white on the window frames. The sky was clear, the air was still, and the crispness outside made Catherine not want to stay indoors any longer. As she was walking outside the house, Catherine saw a carriage pulled by two horses, gliding along the snow-covered road and, instead of going straight past, it stopped in front of the house. A man in a cloak got out.

Catherine could hardly believe her eyes as she hurried down the path to open the gate for him.

It was George Rowland!

"Colonel…I mean…George," she stuttered. "I wasn't expecting you."

The colonel's cheeks were ruddy, and he appeared older than he had five years earlier, but the kind expression in his eyes was unchanged.

"I'm glad you're in Longstock, Catherine. I came to see you."

Fortunately, Catherine's mother had just left the house to meet the vicar's wife, since they were sorting donations of Christmas gifts for orphans.

"Please come in," Catherine said.

Colonel Rowland knew Catherine had returned to England and did not seem surprised to find her heavily pregnant, which set alarm bells ringing for her. She invited him inside and took his cape before boiling a kettle for a pot of tea.

"When did you get back from India?"

George sipped his tea and explained that he had arrived back in England three days earlier and that his wife was staying in London. He was spending the night at the home of Colonel Burnett in Breamore,

252   A Passage to Siam

which was only a short distance from Catherine's.

"How did you know I was here? Did Arthur's brother tell you?"

"No. I wrote to Colonel Burnett, and he wrote back to me that he'd had a letter from your mother telling him you and Arthur had come back from the East. She said you were back home because you were with child and that Arthur had gone overseas again. What on earth's going on?"

As he spoke, George Rowland pulled something out of his coat pocket and handed it to Catherine.

Catherine's heart began to race the moment she caught sight of the cream envelope with the British Consul of Siam's stamp on the front alongside the handwriting she knew all too well.

Catherine, wife of His Serene Highness Prince Vijjuprapha

Her hands trembled as she took the envelope before Colonel Rowland drew his hand back abruptly as if he had just let go of something hot and was glad to be rid of it.

"The British Consul of Siam sent it to my battalion in India. The prince wrote to me telling me what had happened and asking me to find you and give you this letter."

Catherine clutched the letter tightly as conflicting emotions warred within her. At first, she longed to simply see Justin's writing, but a moment later, she did not want to open it, knowing that it would only cause her pain.

"Aren't you going to open it?" Colonel Rowland asked gently.

She did not answer, and he sighed.

"Catherine…Even though Mary's no longer with us, you're still like family to me and I was very close to the prince, so I think I have the right to ask. How on earth did things end up like this?"

Catherine took a deep breath and looked at him squarely.

"I didn't know I was pregnant until I was at sea, and I met Arthur in Dover. He offered to say he was the father, so my child wouldn't be fatherless. He's gone back now. I'll wait until after the birth before I tell my mother we've separated."

"Why don't you tell her the truth now?"

"I don't know how to tell her my child's fatherless…"

"Your child isn't fatherless," Colonel Rowland cut in at once.

New Life 253

"If you decide to go back to Siam, you can go after the birth. I'll make all the arrangements for you."

"I'm not going back."

"You're not going back?" he repeated. "Even when you have to raise the child alone?"

"Yes, George."

"Even when you know how much the prince loves you? He wrote to me begging me to find you because he's not allowed to leave Siam. He doesn't even know you're with his child. If he knew, he'd be more desperate for your return than ever."

"I'm not going back to him. It's over between us. If I can't choose the best thing, I'll choose the least awful."

"I'm sorry," he said. "I was forgetting you have your reasons but, from his letter, I can see he's been beside himself since you left."

Catherine clenched her fists and struggled to maintain her composure.

"You can sympathize with him, and yet you ask me to suffer as a sacrifice for his happiness. Are you saying that, because I'm his wife and I'm carrying his child, my only place is in his house in Siam?"

George's face fell.

"It isn't like that. You haven't read his letter yet. It isn't as bad as you think. The prince has decided to finish with his other wife. They're no longer living as man and wife."

"The Siamese don't believe in divorce. A man's allowed several wives. He doesn't have to give one up for another."

"He said that if his other wife remains in the palace, he'll provide for her as if she were his own sister, but if she wishes to leave and remarry, he'll release her."

"And you call that the best solution?"

Colonel Rowland shifted awkwardly.

"Well, I can't think of an easier one," he confessed. "It might not be a fairytale ending, but the prince knows you won't return to Siam if he has another wife. If he must choose between the two of you, he'll choose you with no hesitation."

"And do you think that's fair to his other wife, George?"

Colonel Rowland shifted uncomfortably again.

"I can't say I'm in complete agreement, but I lived in the East for

254 A Passage to Siam

many years, and I know the women there don't have a say. When they're children, they depend on their parents, when they grow up, they depend on their husbands, and when they get old, they depend on their children. If a woman's given permission to remarry, she's fortunate. She might be pleased. She won't have to stay with a husband who doesn't want her."

"And what about her child?"

"Her child?" Colonel Rowland repeated. "Well, according to Siamese custom if the child's a boy, he'll stay with his father. I doubt you'd be so cruel as to throw the child out, but if he bothered you, his paternal grandparents would take care of him."

Catherine did not answer and looked down at the envelope in her hand, which was creased because she had been clutching it so tightly.

Colonel Roland stood up and glanced out the window.

"I understand you need time to think about it, but when you're ready, you can write to me in London. I'll leave my address."

He looked for a piece of paper, so Catherine took her notebook and opened a clean page for him to write on.

"I should return to Breamore before dark. I'll write to the prince to let him know I've given you his letter."

Catherine led him out through the front door to see him off.

When they had walked as far as the gate, she said, "George. Can I ask you something?"

"Of course," he replied as he put his hat on.

"Please don't tell the prince I'm pregnant, or that Arthur's letting me use his surname. Will you give me your word?"

Catherine, my love,

I pray that this letter will reach you. As I write, I know that you are somewhere in England. Sometimes my mind runs wild, and I worry if you're still alive. I just hope George Rowland finds you. The first letter I sent to you in Columbo was sent back because you weren't there.

Come back, my love. I don't know what else to say. Since you left, every day and night has tormented me more than the flames of hell. Hardly a moment passes that I don't think of you, knowing you are somewhere out of my reach. If you're in danger, who will protect you, and if you're upset,

New Life 255

who will comfort you when you have abandoned the only person who loves you with all his heart?

I'm not trying to bring you back without thinking of your feelings. I know I was wrong, and I had no excuse, but that doesn't mean I can't put things right.

When I got back to Bangkok, I made up my mind. I told both my adoptive mother and my birth mother that my relationship with Bua is over. If my mother wishes her to stay, I will treat her like a sister, so that my mother has a daughter to take care of her, but if she wishes to remarry, I will give her my full consent, and she will have no obligations towards me, except that if she has a son, he will be raised by my mother. This is the best solution. I will not allow our situation to cause suffering to the two of us, and perhaps even to Bua, any longer.

I am writing this letter on our raft. It has been shut since I came back because I couldn't bear to stay in a place where your shadow is everywhere. I moved into my father's house, but I was miserable there, especially during the long nights when I slept in an empty bed without you next to me.

Today, I've come down to the raft so that I can be alone to write to you because I miss you too much to stay in my father's house any longer. You are all around me. I see your golden hair in the sun's rays that shimmer on the surface of the water. I see your blue eyes looking down from the sky above the Chao Phraya River. I see your smile in the flowers that bloom on the banks. When I see the river flowing past the raft, I see a beautiful water nymph letting her silky golden hair down, her skin as radiant as a rose, as I did when we swam together in the clear water at night, away from prying eyes. I'm starting to feel as if the memory was just a dream.

Catherine, my love. The reason I'm still alive is because I'm waiting for the day when I wake up with you by my side again. Until then, this is the longest nightmare of my life.

I hope that George finds you, that you read this letter, and that you know your husband is waiting for you with every breath he takes. Don't let him wait for the rest of his life.

I love you as much as my own life,

Justin

* * *

Prince Vijjuprapha returned to the house late as normal. The only difference was in his mood, which for the past few nights, had been unusually bright. Won was waiting with his evening meal, and two female servants were there to serve him but, otherwise, the house was empty and silent.

Although he noticed, he didn't ask any questions because he was preoccupied with other matters, even when he saw that Kham appeared restless.

He did not ask about Bua, who had not been to the house for the past month since she was now heavily pregnant.

After he had finished eating, he asked Kham, "Has my mother gone to bed yet?"

"She's been at your wife's house since afternoon, sir," Kham replied dutifully.

"And she's still not back? What's taking her so long?"

Kham hesitated before answering, "Your wife's in labour, sir."

The prince froze for a moment, then signalled for her to clear the plates away before he stood up.

When he reached the house, with Won following behind, he told his attendant, "Won, ask the servants to find out if Bua's given birth yet, and if the child's a boy or a girl. Then come back and tell me."

"Yes, sir," replied Won softly.

Behind a screen next to the house, Won filled a bowl with water so that the prince could wash and change his clothes. The water was fragrant with damask roses, just as Catherine had instructed the servants when they had lived on the raft, and his night clothes were set out for him. Instead of going to bed when he had finished bathing, the prince sat at his desk and pulled a letter out of a long envelope, which he had received from the British Consul two days earlier, and he reread it as he had done every night since getting it.

Your Royal Highness, Prince Vijjuprapha,

I have arrived in London, and I have been to Longstock to meet your wife, Catherine, to give her your letter.

As far as I can see, Catherine is in good health and is staying with her mother. I told her that whenever she returns to Siam, I will make the arrangements for her.

I expect she will write to you herself. I hope everything works out for the best.

Yours truly,
Colonel George C. Rowland

It was a short letter, which did not give him any of the details he had been waiting for, but it gave him hope, nonetheless. He carefully placed the envelope back in the desk drawer and stood up before walking over to the window from where he could see the raft. Up until now, that window had been shut tight.

The moonlight shimmered on the roof of the raft, giving life to the house that had stood empty and silent for the past few months. The prince smiled to himself as he mused that – soon – the raft would be lived in again. At last, George had found her. She had not wandered off but had gone home just as he thought. He had learnt that nobody could have it all. If you gained something, you had to lose something, and after he had been careless with his love, he had lost his love. Soon, she would be back. The days were brighter and passed more quickly than they had done for the past few months when they had been long and dark.

There was a polite knock on the screen that separated the prince's bedroom from his study to rouse him. The prince saw the dawn light coming in through the window and heard the birds singing in the trees. It was earlier than usual to wake him.

"What is it, Won?"

Won hurriedly crawled inside and told him the news.

"Your wife's given birth, sir."

"Is it a boy or a girl?"

"You have a son, sir."

The prince suddenly felt as if the sun was shining brighter than it had for the past few months and that the birth of a son would help to ease the tension that had clouded the atmosphere.

"And how is Bua?"

"The midwife says she's healthy, sir. Your mother says you can see her shortly."

Although he had only had a few hours' sleep, he did not feel sleepy and washed his face before changing his clothes and setting out for Bua's house, which was joined to the main house by a long, covered walkway. Her house was full of bustle and the veranda was crowded with female servants, while the male servants, who were not allowed inside, milled around outside waiting excitedly for news.

Mom Yad came out from the bedroom, followed by a female servant, and, when she saw her son, she said, "Oh, here you are. Come and sit down inside. I haven't slept all night. I'm quite exhausted. I'm going to have a lie down in a minute, but I couldn't leave Bua. The first birth is always difficult."

Although she was tired, she was clearly elated to have a grandson as she led her son eagerly to the sitting room.

When she sat down, she took a quid of betel and popped it in her mouth before saying excitedly, "Bua's contractions began in the evening. She didn't even know she was going into labour. Luckily, I had someone watch over her, so she called the midwife. It was almost morning by the time the baby came."

"And did Bua…" he asked reluctantly, "have a difficult birth?"

"The first birth is always difficult," Mom Yad replied at once. "And Bua's so slender. My heart ached for her. But she didn't cry until the baby was out…"

He was silent for a moment.

"Was she in a lot of pain?"

"They say when a woman gives birth, it's equal to a man going to war."

A moment later, the midwife, a sturdy elderly woman, brought out a tiny baby wrapped in white cloth and the prince carefully took his son in his arms. The gentle rays of the morning sun illuminated the baby's ruddy complexion, his chubby round face, and his silky black hair. A feeling of joy that he had all but forgotten came back to him once more. Since he had lost Charles, his happiness had disappeared and, out of the blue, it suddenly returned.

Although it was not the same as when he had held Catherine's son, since this child was not born of the woman he loved, he instinctively felt a father's love and tenderness for him.

His mother observed him with satisfaction and said, "Just look at him! His mother's so slight, and he's so chubby. No wonder it was a difficult birth."

"And where is Bua? Can I see her?"

"Of course, you can," Mom Yad said eagerly. "She's been sleeping, but I expect she's awake now. She'll have to stay by the fire soon. You can help bring Bua next to the fireside."

He started.

"How can I take her? I've never done it before. Let the servants do her."

He knew full well that it was a husband's duty to carry his wife to the fireside, but since he no longer considered her his wife, he did not want to do it and rekindle their relationship. Mom Yad realized this, but feigned ignorance.

"The servants' hands are rough. They'll hurt her."

"Let the midwife and the servants take her, Mother. If you're going to make such a fuss, I'd better go."

Not wanting to aggravate him any further, Mom Yad quickly changed the subject.

"Oh, stay now that you're here. Hurry up, girls! Get everything ready! He's going inside! Who's going to help me to my room? I'm so tired, I need to lie down."

The servant girls hurried to take Mom Yad to her room and, although she had said she was tired, she appeared more agile than ever. The prince waited for Bua's servants to come back before he stepped inside his wife's bedroom. The scent of herbs and smoke from the fire permeated the room. Bua lay awake on the bed but was still obviously weak. When she saw him, she shifted as if to sit up, but did not have the strength.

"Stay as you are. There's no need to sit up."

She did not answer, but looked at the midwife, who had brought the baby inside, and held out her arms as if to take the child, so the midwife gently placed the child beside her. Bua hugged the child to her, and at that moment, her lips began to quiver, and tears started to roll down her cheeks.

The prince looked on, feeling both awkwardness and sympathy, and said, "Don't cry. It's bad luck. The child's healthy. What are you sad about?"

260   A Passage to Siam

The midwife and the servants dutifully crawled outside, and when Bua saw that they were alone, she said in a trembling voice, "I wanted a girl."

The prince was silent, knowing full well what she meant. If it had been a girl, Bua would have been able to take her away with her and they would not have to be separated, unlike a boy. Although she had never mentioned it, her reply indicated that she understood her fate and had no choice but to accept it without complaint.

All he could think of to say was, "Don't think too much. A boy or a girl is still your child. Go and lie by the fireplace. I'll call the midwife and the servants to lift you."

* * *

Winter passed by slowly for Catherine as her stomach grew gradually larger, but she continued to do housework as usual to keep herself busy.

She received Arthur's letter around Christmas, informing her that he had arrived in Columbo and would be staying there until his business was finished when he would return home in time for the baby's birth. Catherine had to read Arthur's letter aloud to her mother who was eagerly awaiting news from her son-in-law.

"I'm so glad Athur will be back in time!" Emma grinned. "I was afraid he wouldn't make it."

Catherine folded the letter quietly, feeling agitated by Arthur's good intentions of returning in time for the birth, since it would make telling her mother that they had separated more difficult. And even worse than the letter was the fact that Arthur had sent her a gift, telling her in the letter that he had bought it in France and sent it to Alfred, asking him to send it to her at Christmas.

When Emma saw the gift, she exclaimed, "What a beautiful lace collar!"

Catherine passed it to her mother, who turned it over admiringly. A moment later, Catherine got up to continue with the housework, not wanting to talk about Arthur any more than was necessary.

Even though she hid her grief, she could not bring herself to be cheerful, realizing that the pain of unrequited love was nothing compared to the pain of separation when both sides still loved each other with all their hearts and knew that, not only was their own heart broken, but they had broken the heart of the one they loved.

Sitting next to the window in the bedroom, her hand resting on her stomach and feeling the growing life inside her, her spirits were suddenly lifted, and her sadness was chased away. At least her decision to renounce her heart would give her full rights to her child, and he would grow up in his mother's homeland, safe from tropical diseases and customs that might confuse him when he was grown.

She pressed her head against the frosty window as if it would be able to cool the burning agitation in her heart. On the other side of the world, what was Justin doing she wondered. Whether he was working in the front palace or sleeping alone, and whatever the time of day, he would be anxiously waiting for her letter. He did not know that Catherine was stretching out the time to test her own endurance before she decided to give him the answer that would break both his heart and hers.

"You've lost weight. You seemed to be getting better and now I'm worried again," Mom Yad greeted her son as he was preparing to go to the Front Palace one day.

She looked him over and affirmed, "You've got thinner. If you work too much, you'll be ill. The king's much better now, isn't he?"

Prince Vijjuprapha avoided mentioning himself.

"His condition's stable. He doesn't travel as much as before, but he worries about his duties, so I need to meet with him until late so I can report things to him."

By now, King Pinklao's failing health due to chronic illness was acknowledged by everyone in the Front Palace, but he continued with his duties unperturbed.

Mom Yad turned to signal for the wet nurse, who was carrying her grandson on a white cushion, to come closer before changing the subject.

"Look at my grandson! He's already a month old! It's almost time for the head-shaving ceremony.

Prince Vijjuprapha gazed at the tiny frame of his son, wriggling and gurgling as he looked up at him with clear black eyes, and the

262   A Passage to Siam

stern expression on his face softened. He held out a finger and the baby clutched it as Mom Yad looked on and smiled with satisfaction.

"Look at him! He knows who his father is! Where's Bua? She normally comes to see me at this time of day."

As soon as she had finished speaking, Bua's dainty frame appeared on the veranda that connected her house to the main house. She started a little when she saw the prince before kneeling and crawling inside as usual. She sat down, slightly apart from him and asked the wet nurse to bring the baby to her.

Mom Yad observed the couple, as she always did, and heard her son speak.

"Are you here to see Mother? She was just asking for you."

"Yes," Bua answered quietly. It was impossible to know if she felt awkward, resentful, or neutral because she was always composed and kept her feelings hidden.

The prince took his leave and did not say another word to her. Mom Yad signaled for the wet nurse to go and, when she was alone with Bua, said, "I can see he's relenting, Bua. Just now he was playing with his son. He'll soon forget that foreign woman."

* * *

Prince Vijjuprapha's job was to train the soldiers from morning until afternoon, and after he had finished lunch at two o'clock, he would supervise the construction of the new Throne Hall. After that, he would deal with paperwork in his office next to the king's study and have dinner at the Front Palace before going to meet with King Pinklao until late.

His many duties helped the days to pass more quickly, but not quickly enough for him to forget the long and silent nights when he would leave the Front Palace in his boat along the dark canals, the dim silver moonlight glinting on the ripples of the water that parted on either side of the boat when everyone on both sides of the riverbank had put out their lamps and gone to bed.

Each day and each night had turned into a month and the glimmer of hope that had been sparked by the news from Colonel

New Life 263

Roland gradually began to dim. Until now, he had still not heard from Catherine. He racked his brain trying to figure out what might have happened, imagining that the letter might have been lost, or that Catherine was secretly coming back to surprise him, or that she had been taken ill and could not write to him.

It had been three months since he had heard from George Rowland, and he had still received no news from England.

Or was she not coming back?

In the silver moonlight, as his boat docked at the pier, Prince Vijjuprapha turned his face away from the raft that was enveloped in darkness and stepped onto the bank where he passed the jasmine trellis and started, jolted by memories of the past.

Once he used to place the white flowers on Catherine's pillow each morning until one day she had opened her blue eyes and gazed at the flower before asking, "Do you like this flower?"

"I like the smell. I thought you'd like it too."

"Jasmine is beautiful like Siamese women, but English women are compared to roses."

It was because of this that he had searched for a rose in the palace gardens and asked for a branch from the large rose bush to plant in a pot for her, nurturing it until beautiful flowers had bloomed. But after she had gone, the roses had been left to wither, having no one to care for them.

If you come back, I'll build a house like the one in Singapore and I'll plant roses, so you won't be homesick.

***

He returned to the house, where Bua was waiting with his meal as she did every evening, but she did not sit next to him, remaining a few feet away as she waited for Won to serve him. That evening, Won had news for him.

"Just a moment ago, Captain Knox's servant brought a letter for you, sir. He said it's a letter from England."

The prince asked at once, "And where is it?"

"I put it on your desk, sir."

He rushed into his study at once, ignoring the meal in front of him and not noticing that Bua had moved out of the way for him. Bua understood that 'a letter from England' meant that her husband had received a letter from Catherine.

She could not help feeling that all the servants' eyes were turned towards her in sympathy, but no one knew that beneath her calm composure, she was telling herself, *'I won't abandon my son. If he has no mother, who will take care of him? His grandmother is getting older every day. If the foreign teacher comes back, I'll endure the humiliation of staying here for the sake of my son.'*

Justin, my love,

I know you are missing me with every breath you take, just as you are never out of my thoughts for a single breath that I take.

When I wake up in the morning and I look outside the window of the house I have lived in since I was born and will probably live in until I die, I realize that my love for you is the most important thing that has ever happened in my life. I will never love any other man as much as I love you. There is no happiness that transcends being in your arms, and I have never tired of hearing your voice, your laughter, and seeing you at my side.

But at the same time, whether you feel it or not, there is no man I loathe as much as you, and there is no greater suffering than being a slave to your love.

Although we lived together for five years and were passionately in love, you still don't understand me. I loved you 'too much' and if I had loved you less, I would have realized I had a duty as Arthur Lindley's wife, and I would have said goodbye to you through tears and returned to England five years ago. I would have been filled with sorrow, but I would not have suffered this much. But because I loved you so much – too much – I was willing to go and live with you, and did not regret giving up everything for you, because everything I had – whether it was my husband or my home in England – had no meaning for me without you.

And now, you are asking me to go back to you. You have decided to renounce your culture in return for my love, and I want you to know I appreciate the fact that you are willing to demonstrate your love for me no less than I did for you. However, you can probably guess that I am going to tell you that going back to how things once were is just a dream, and the reality is that the bitterness will remain.

My love, no matter how much you love me, you must accept that your family will never accept me as they accept Bua. Don't forget that I knew Bua before you did. She is a good person. She was raised to do her duty, not to follow the desires of her heart. She calls her duty to follow her parents' wishes, gratitude; her duty towards her husband, faithfulness; and her duty towards your child, love. She will never follow her own desires and remarry for as long as these duties remain.

If I return to Siam, I will return to the same cycle as before. You will be the only person in the world I have to turn to, and I will be completely at your mercy. Although we might have other children, we might also lose another child and suffer more.

Your family still depend on you, your wife has done no wrong, and your child deserves to have both his parents. Don't put them in jeopardy because of me.

I want you to know that I am alone. There is no other man, and I can never love any other man as I have loved you.

I will live out the rest of my days to the best of my ability without the husband I love.

With love always,
Catherine

The letter slipped from the prince's hand onto his desk and then onto the floor, while he sat motionless as if he had been struck by lightning. A moment later, he came to his senses and bent down to pick up the letter to reread since he could not believe his eyes. After reading it over and over, his initial euphoria turned to confusion, and finally, a sharp pain seared his chest like a sharp knife. He could not accept that it was over between the two of them. Her letter reminded him that there was no other man but him and she still loved him with all her heart.

The night was cool. Mist hung outside the window and droplets of dew clung to the jasmine that climbed up the trellis. The scent of the jasmine garland that Bua had threaded and instructed a servant to hang on the bedpost wafted through the room, but to the prince, the damp air, heavy with the fragrance of flowers, was nauseating. He stood up and wrenched the garland of white flowers from the bedpost, causing it to break and scatter petals across the floor, before he hurled what remained of it out through the window.

Then he came to his senses and covered his face with his hands. He had only himself to blame. He sat down at his desk again and pulled a sheet of paper from his drawer before picking up a feather quill, dipping it in his ink well and beginning to write.

Catherine, my love.

* * *

The snow began to melt in March and the air grew palpably warmer. Gradually tiny buds appeared on the trees, the wind became calm, and the days grew longer. One day, Arthur quietly appeared while Catherine sat knitting a jersey for her unborn child in front of the fire. He knocked on the front door and when Emma went to open it, he walked inside casually as if he had only been gone a few days.

"Arthur!" Emma cried. "I'm so glad you're back. Catherine's almost at full term."

The ball of wool on Catherine's lap fell to the floor as she stood up to greet him. She stood frozen to the spot as Arthur came towards her and kissed her lightly on the lips.

"How are you?" he asked gravely when Emma had gone into the kitchen to make a pot of tea.

"I'm fine," she replied, glancing down at her swollen stomach, which had begun to drop. "How was your journey?"

"I bought tea in Columbo. We have an agent there, which makes things easier."

Arthur talked about his travels and Emma listened before excusing herself to go and prepare the evening meal. She told him, "It's such as relief that you're back. I hope you won't be going off again for a while."

"I'll stay until after the christening for certain," he replied cheerfully.

Catherine went upstairs to make the bed for Arthur in Pauline's room before coming back downstairs to help her mother set the table.

New Life 267

She noticed her mother was in unusually good spirits as she chatted to Arthur as if all her hopes lay in him.

Two days later, Catherine's contractions began after she had gone to bed, and Arthur went out to fetch the doctor who lived just two streets away.

This time, the birth was easier than the previous two times, and the child was born the next morning. When she caught sight of the ruddy round face beneath dark hair, wrapped in the white blanket, as Arthur carefully passed the baby to her, she could tell that the child was healthy.

"Your son's healthy," he said gently.

Outside the window, tiny green leaves and buds brushed the glass like hundreds of tiny faces coming out to welcome the new baby.

Catherine sighed in contentment mixed with exhaustion.

"Justin…" she whispered before closing her eyes and drifting off to sleep.

***

Baby Justin was healthy and easy to care for and, although he was occasionally fretful, for the most part, he was never sick, sleeping for most of the day, and waking when it was time to feed.

Their day-to-day lives went by smoothly and Emma was happy to do the housework herself, so that Catherine could take care of her child. Arthur adjusted well to his new surroundings, occasionally going to London on business, where he would stay a night before returning to Longstock the next day.

Arthur assumed the role of man of the house, picking the child up from the cradle, or taking Catherine for walks, because she was still not strong enough to do it herself. In this way as time went by, the awkwardness between them gradually diminished.

But Catherine did not forget that, eventually, Arthur would have to leave.

***

Justin was christened on a clear spring day. He was dressed in a white smock edged with lace, while Catherine wore the dress that she had worn on her last night in Singapore paired with a tweed cape.

She parted her hair in the middle, twisting a long braid into a bun at the nape of her neck. Her flaxen tresses sparkled in the sunlight, and she still looked no less radiant than she had five years earlier.

Arthur wore a black jacket over a dark waistcoat with a white shirt underneath. A gold watchchain hung from his waistcoat and his face beamed with pride as he stood beside Catherine in the church. Arthur held the baby in his arms as Reverend Riggs performed the ceremony, and almost every family in the village was present.

The baby was christened Justin James Lindley.

"Do you want to go for a walk, Catherine? The baby's asleep."

Catherine glanced at the sleeping child in the cradle, realizing that Arthur wanted to talk to her alone. Her mother was home that day, so the baby's grandmother would be there if he woke up.

"Good idea," she said.

They walked along the path towards the River Thames as they had done the previous autumn. By now, the branches of the large trees on either side of the path were heavy with leaves and touched in the middle to form a shady canopy as they walked alongside fields carpeted with daisies. As they neared the silver waters of the River Thames, Catherine spoke.

"I want to thank you for everything."

She knew it was time for Arthur to say goodbye. There was no need for him to stay.

He was quiet for a moment before asking, "What are you going to do now?"

"I'll stay here in Longstock."

"Will you be happy staying here for the rest of your life?"

His question brought a stab of pain, but she forced herself to answer, "Arthur, I'm not the naïve young girl I was five years ago. Happiness is found by accepting things as they are."

Arthur stopped walking, forcing her to stand still also, and an anxious expression appeared in his eyes.

New Life 269

"I'm happy to hear you say that. Neither of us are young like when we first met anymore. We're no longer dreamers. I can't go on adventures around the world like I dreamed of, but I still get to travel, and at least I don't have to sit in an office all day. I make a good living, but do you know what's missing?"

Catherine shook her head.

"A bachelor's life is alright, but now I'm thirty, I want a home and a family. Do you understand?"

Catherine was silent for a moment before asking, "What are you trying to tell me, Arthur?"

"I'm trying to say…I want us to start over. It isn't too late. I'm not being rash. I've been thinking it over for months. And when I held Justin in church, I realized I want to be his father. I've been there for him since he was born, and I want to be there for him in the future. You and Justin are the family I want."

Catherine did not know what to say.

"I'm going back to London tomorrow. I'll give you two weeks to think about it, and then you can write to me. If you decide to stay in Longstock, I won't come back, but if you decide you want to start a new life with me, I'll come back and take you to London."

Arthur left the next day. All he told Emma was that he had to return to London on business and did not know when he would be back. In the days that followed, the house was quiet again and Catherine busied herself taking care of her son and helping her mother with the housework.

Emma noticed that Catherine appeared quiet and tense, so one evening she asked, "Catherine, can I ask you something about you and Arthur?"

They were sitting in the living room beside the fire and Catherine had just rocked Justin to sleep in his cradle. Catherine knew at once that it was time to tell her mother that she and Arthur had separated.

"Is anything the matter? Arthur looked rather out of sorts when he left for London, and he didn't say when he'd be coming back."

Catherine crossed the room to sit on a rocking chair and did not look her mother in the eye.

270   A Passage to Siam

"We talked about the future. Arthur must go abroad again, but I don't want to go to the East with a small child, so I'm going to stay in Longstock."

Emma studied Catherine and sighed before sticking her knitting needles in a ball of wool, and muttering, "Do you mean you and Arthur have separated?"

"Well…" Catherine stammered. "It's the only way."

"He isn't going to the East for good. He'll be coming back to London."

Catherine sighed.

"I've made up my mind."

Emma gazed at her daughter knowingly.

"Don't assume I don't know. You two were having problems before you came home, I could tell. I don't know what happened in the East, but you and Arthur have been separated since before you came back. I've known all along, but I didn't like to say anything. What happened?"

She looked at Catherine, hoping for an answer, but when Catherine said nothing, she continued, "When I saw Justin, I was sure of it. Will you trust me enough to tell me who the father is? It isn't Arthur Lindley, is it?"

Catherine's lips began to tremble, and she fought back tears.

"I didn't mean to hide it from you, Mother. I just didn't know how to tell you."

There was no point hiding the truth from her any longer. Catherine took a deep breath and began to tell her the whole story. She recounted how she had met Captain Justin, their journey to the East, how they had fallen in love, how she had found out that Arthur had been cheating on her, how she had left him and chosen to become the wife of the Siamese prince, how she had lived for five years in Siam, how he had taken another wife, and how she had discovered she was pregnant after she had left him.

Emma listened without saying a word until finally, she asked, "Did Arthur leave of his own accord, or was it because you don't want him anymore?"

"He wanted to start over, but I'm going to write and tell him it's impossible. I'm going to stay in Longstock."

"Why is it impossible? Stop being so stubborn, Catherine. How can you survive by yourself when you're not yet twenty-five? And what about Justin? How will he survive without a father?"

Catherine sat down at her father's desk and put pen to paper.

Dear Arthur,
Since we spoke beside the River Thames...
That was as far as she had got before she heard the front doorbell ring, so she got up, wondering who it was.

The postman was waiting with a letter. In the corner of the envelope was the name Colonel George Rowland.

Catherine's hands began to tremble as she pulled a pin out of her hair and used it to open the envelope. Inside was a smaller envelope and a short note from the colonel.

"The prince was afraid his letter wouldn't reach you because you never gave him your full address, so he sent it to me to give you."

With shaking hands, she opened the envelope to read it.

Catherine, my love,
Although your letter was like a bolt of lightning, my love for you is unchanged. Just knowing that you love me keeps my hope alive.
If you're not coming back to Siam, then I'll find a way to leave Siam to see you in England. I'm not allowed to leave Siam without the king's permission, or unless the king sends me on a diplomatic mission to Europe. Since he is presently sick, I must wait until he recovers.
Until then, please wait for me, Catherine, my love. I ask nothing more of you. All I want is to see you again, so I can tell you how much I love you. You're the only woman in my heart, and you always will be.
The only thing that keeps me alive is the hope that one day I'll see you again.

With love from your husband,
Justin

Catherine read the letter over and over before forcing herself to return it to the envelope and put it in the drawer with his previous letter.

She sat motionless as she tried to collect herself before dipping her pen in the inkpot and finishing her letter to Arthur. With each word she wrote, she grew gradually calmer, and by the time she had come to the final line, she felt as if she had passed through a stormy sea and come through to the other side.

Dear Arthur,

Since we spoke beside the River Thames, I have come to a decision, but first I want to tell you how much I appreciate your generosity to me. You are a true gentleman, and you deserve a better woman than me.

I have told my mother everything. She has nothing but admiration for you and she thinks I would be a fool to turn down your offer.

However, I don't believe that two people should stay together simply because one of them is grateful and the other doesn't want to be alone, or they may end up hating each other.

I have learned that there is a thin line between love and hate. However much you love someone, you can be hurt by them just as much. I don't want you to be hurt again because of me.

Since I cannot guarantee that I will make you happy, we should not take the risk of living together as husband and wife for a second time. It would be better for us to remain friends.

I hope you will find love with another woman who loves you and will be faithful to you.

Yours truly,
Catherine

Catherine posted her letter to Arthur without telling her mother of her decision. She thought her mother would realize when Arthur disappeared and did not come back. Life in Longstock would go on as usual, and she was ready to face whatever problems arose.

But just five days after she posted the letter to London, as she was feeding corn to the chickens behind the house, her mother opened the back door and called out to her in a shrill voice, "Catherine, come inside and see who's here!"

The excitement in her mother's voice jarred on her, and when she

New Life 273

walked into the living room, she could hardly believe her eyes when she saw a man in a cloak look up from the cradle and turn to smile at her cheerfully.

"I didn't write to tell you I was coming. I wanted to surprise you."

"Didn't you get my letter?" Catherine asked in confusion.

"I did. That's why I decided to come back."

It had become a thing of custom for Catherine and Arthur to go for a walk to the River Thames whenever they had something to discuss.

Catherine asked him to walk over the old stone bridge across the river with her, and they stopped on the bridge to watch the river that reflected the shady green trees along the banks flowing beneath.

"What else is there to say, Arthur?" Catherine asked after a while.

Arthur gazed at her as if he had been waiting for that moment.

"There's something I need to decide."

"But I gave you my answer."

"No, you gave me a question. And I have an answer."

"I gave you a question?" she repeated.

"Yes, Catherine. Your letter asked a question, so I've come back to give you an answer. I'm not asking you for anything more than what you can give me, and you don't expect anything more of me than what I can give you. Is that correct?"

"Yes, but I meant…"

"I agree," he interrupted. "However much you love someone, you can be hurt by them just as much. If we're not in love, but we're content with each other and we don't expect anything more, then that's enough."

"Do you mean…" Catherine asked in confusion, "Are you asking me to be your wife, even though you're not in love with me and you know I can't love you like…"

She stopped before she said the name Justin to avoid hurting his feelings.

Arthur was undeterred and replied, "We're older and more experienced now. We're not impulsive like we were before. This might be for the best. After all, you have Justin to think of. Don't you think he needs a father as well as a mother?"

274 A Passage to Siam

* * *

Catherine opened the desk drawer and touched the cream envelope that lay inside. She hesitated for a moment before pushing the drawer shut again.

She picked up a sheet of paper and placed it in front of her.

Justin, my love,
This will be my last letter.
I believe that you will try to find me because I know how determined you are. Otherwise, you would not have broken with tradition and taken me as your wife. But even if we met again, I still see no future for us because I will not return to Siam, just as you will not come and live in England.
I don't want you to wait for me in Siam and I cannot promise that I will wait for you in England. All I can promise is that I will never forget you. I will never regret having loved you as I can never love any other man. We were destined to love each other, but we were not destined to be happy together.
I know that you must do your duty in your homeland just as I must do my duty in my homeland.
You will always be in my heart until my last breath.
Love always,
Catherine

Catherine noted the contents of the letter in her journal before folding the letter and putting it in an envelope. Then she placed her journal in the drawer and closed it carefully.

* * *

Emma beamed as she listened to Arthur.

"I'm going to London to find a house for Catherine and the baby. Then I'll come back to fetch them as soon as I can."

"Good," Catherine's mother said, taking no notice of Catherine's despondent expression. "It will be nice for the three of you to have your own home."

Catherine did not say a word, telling herself that Arthur had everything in hand. All the colours around her had vanished and her world had become like a black and white photograph from the moment she told Arthur, "Thank you. I'll…go to London with you."

Arthur was pleased, she could tell. In fact, he was so happy that he hugged her tightly and although she did not push him away, she showed no expression of happiness. That night, when they returned home, Arthur moved from the other room into her bedroom, and she did not resist when he took her in his arms.

Arthur slept like a baby, but Catherine lay awake until morning when she drifted into a light sleep, sensing the undulating waves of the Chao Phraya washing against the raft as moonlight sparkled on the surface of the water like fireflies and shone onto the strong brown arms that held her.

Catherine woke with a start in the cold bed, and even Arthur's sleeping body next to her did nothing to warm her heart.

* * *

The new house in London was in Knightsbridge.

Arthur had found a house quickly and came back to Longstock in less than a week.

"You'll like the new house," Arthur told her proudly. "It isn't as big as Alfred's house, but it's big enough for the three of us to live in comfortably. We can move in right away."

From the outside, the house in Knightsbridge was no different from the other four-storey houses in the area, but inside was spacious and lavishly decorated.

"How is it?" Arthur asked her as they stepped inside the drawing room for the first time. "Do you like it?"

The large room was elaborately furnished with a plush sofa and armchairs and several wooden chairs arranged on a patterned carpet. Above the large fireplace, a brass clock stood on the mantelpiece with a wide mirror above it, reflecting the glinting crystal chandeliers and the deep red velvet curtains, making Catherine feel small as she stood in the middle of the room.

Catherine turned around awkwardly.

"What do I need to do? It looks as if you've taken care of everything."

"You're the lady of the house. All you need to do is give instructions to the housekeeper and make sure everything's running smoothly. There are several servants, but you don't need to worry. I've found a good housekeeper. Hollis has an excellent reference from her previous employer. If you'd like a nanny, I thought you'd prefer to choose someone yourself."

"I don't need a nanny. I'll take care of Justin myself."

"In that case, we can wait until we have another child."

Catherine felt a pang as she remembered someone else who had once said the same thing.

"Whatever you say, Arthur."

14

On the Other Side of the World

The words, "Whatever you say, Arthur," became Catherine's stock answer from then on. This was her way of avoiding conflict and helped to smooth things over between them. The house in London had numerous rooms, which meant that she and Arthur did not have to spend too much time together, especially when Arthur was at work during the day and out socializing most evenings.

If he ever had to stay at home, Arthur would be busy doing the accounts in his study, while Catherine spent most of her time with Justin in the nursery, but she never forgot to call the housekeeper to check the menu for each meal, especially when he invited guests for dinner, and she would play the role of a good hostess.

Sometimes, Arthur took her to the theatre in a horse-drawn carriage, but he was never aware when she let out a long sigh of relief as the lights on the stage came on and she could let her thoughts drift into her own world.

On the way home, he would ask, "Did you enjoy the show?"

"Yes, it was fun," she would answer with a smile. "Thank you for taking me."

This pleased Arthur and he did not notice that she never mentioned the show again. He did not know that she had built a wall around her heart so that nothing could touch it. Catherine did not suffer as she had when she had been with Justin, but neither was she filled with contentment as she had been when she had lived in Siam with the man she loved.

***

278   A Passage to Siam

The harsh rays of the midday Siamese sun shone through the window onto the mahogany desk in the corner of the study and the jasmine on the trellis outside the window undulated in the breeze as the small white flowers fell to the ground. A gust of wind blew the letter that the prince was holding limply in his hand to the floor.

It lay still on the ground, the small, neat handwriting illuminated by the sun's rays as if they were trying to make sense of it in order to understand the sorrow of the man who was sitting there with his face in his hands.

"I don't want you to wait for me in Siam and I cannot promise that I will wait for you in England. All I can promise is that I will never forget you. I will never regret having loved you as I can never love any other man. We were destined to love each other, but we were not destined to be happy together."

"Bua," Mom Yad called out to her daughter-in-law. From her tone of voice, Bua guessed that it was a matter related to her son, so she put down the cucumber she was carving and crawled towards her.

"He's not eating again, and he's lost weight. Since that foreign soldier brought him a letter, he hasn't eaten or slept. I had to force Won to tell me it was from her."

Bua had known straight away without needing to ask, and she had noticed how many spoonsful her husband had eaten each day.

"I don't know why he's still pining for that woman," Mom Yad continued. "Instead of letting go, he's being obstinate."

Bua had been in a difficult position for over a year. She clung to a small glimmer of hope that never got any brighter while she remained in limbo, half-way between wife and relative, and everyone looked on her with pity. If it hadn't been for her son, Bua would have left and gone back to the Front Palace long ago. She heard Mom Yad continue.

"I think she's left him for good. That's why he's grown so thin. From now on, you must get close to him, and take your son to see him every day. If he sees his wife and son every day, he's bound to relent. Make yourself attractive, Bua, and when you have more children, he'll forget all about her."

All Bua could do was bow her head. She did not have the nerve to

On the Other Side of the World 279

tell Mom Yad she thought she was being overly optimistic.

* * *

Catherine learned that there was nothing her husband valued more than freedom. He enjoyed going wherever he wanted and travelling abroad every year, while still being able to return to his home and family.

This was the reason they never had disagreements. Whenever Arthur went out, Catherine never asked where he was going, even when she heard other women gossip that he had been seen with his friends in the company of young actresses. She never felt the slightest twinge of jealousy, telling them it was only natural, so the women never mentioned it again, applauding the robustness of their marriage.

Arthur travelled for about six months of the year, but due to his concern for his wife and son, he reduced the length of time he was away.

He did not know that each time he left, Catherine breathed a sigh of relief and slept soundly, undisturbed by anxious imaginings about where he might be. She was certain he was safe, which was enough for her.

* * *

"There's a woman here to see you, madam."

Peterson, the butler, had opened the door.

"A woman? Did she tell you her name?"

"Her name's Charlotte Palmer, madam."

Catherine had not seen Charlotte for almost two years, so she stood up, pleased.

"Bring her to my sitting room. I'll see her."

Catherine had her own sitting room where she would write in her journal, read or crotchet in private. When she went inside, she saw Charlotte Palmer. The sunlight shone through the white net curtains onto Charlotte's red hair, which was complemented by her slightly faded dark red dress.

"Mrs Lindley," she cried excitedly. "I'm so 'appy to see you. You 'aven't changed a bit."

Next to Catherine, who was dressed in a lace-trimmed navy dress that contrasted with her flaxen hair and rosy cheeks, Charlotte looked haggard. She had lost weight and the lines around the corners of her eyes were very apparent, although her smile was still as warm as ever.

Catherine went towards her and kissed her on the cheek.

"It's me that should be happy. I thought I'd never see you again… Please…sit down and tell me where you've been all this time and how you found me."

Charlotte sat down and Catherine rang the bell for the maid to bring them tea.

"I 'eard you were in London. I'm 'appy for you that everything's worked out for you."

Catherine was silent for a moment before replying.

"Thank you. And what about you, Charlotte? Do you live in London?"

"Not for much longer," Charlotte said casually. "I'm about to go back to the East, so I came to say goodbye…and to ask you if there's any news you want me to take back to Siam."

Catherine caught her breath but forced herself to speak.

"Are you really going back to Siam? I thought you'd come home for good."

Charlotte smiled sadly.

"Two years was enough for me. I've 'ad enough of London. I miss the East, and as it 'appens, I met an old friend who's goin' back to Siam, so I'm goin' with 'im."

Catherine did not ask any questions and Charlotte did not add any details, asking instead, "If the prince asks me about you, what should I tell 'im?"

The colour suddenly drained from Catherine's face.

"Tell him the truth."

Charlotte regarded her thoughtfully.

"'Ow much of the truth do you want me to tell 'im? Should I tell 'im about the son 'e doesn't know about? That you're still in love with 'im? That you got back with Arthur, so your son would 'ave a father?"

"Don't tell him about our son, Charlotte…please."

She squeezed Charlotte's hand as her heart sank.

On the Other Side of the World 281

"Don't tell Justin he has a son in England. It will hurt him even more, and he'll never be happy with his family in Bangkok. It's better if he doesn't know."

"I understand your reasons," Charlotte said wearily, "but I can't say I agree with you. If it was me…I don't know what I'd do…"

Charlotte glanced around at the comfortable room.

"At least Arthur provides for you. That's all you want, ain't it?"

"It's the best I can do…" Catherine said, pausing before she continued, "If you're going to Siam, there's something I'd like you to return to Justin."

"I'd be 'appy to if I can carry it."

"You'll be able to carry it. It's only small."

Catherine pulled out a chain with a gold oval locket hanging from it and when she opened it, there was a ring inside. She took it out and placed it on her palm. It had a diamond and eight other stones all along the band, and it glinted as the sun's rays caught it through the window.

She could not stop her voice from shaking as she whispered, "It's an eternity ring…Justin gave it to me…it was a gift from the second king of Siam, so it means a lot to him. He gave it to me as a symbol of our eternal love, but since it's no longer true, there's no point in me keeping it anymore."

"Why's it no longer true when you and the prince are still in love?"

"We've no right to claim we're in love when we're both with someone else."

"But you can keep your love for 'im in your 'eart," Charlotte argued. "And your son deserves to 'ave somethin' from 'is father."

Catherine hesitated for a moment before returning the ring to the locket. She sighed before forcing a smile.

"Right…Let's have tea."

Charlotte smiled back at her sympathetically before saying, "Is there anythin' else you want me to give the prince?"

Catherine looked puzzled. Then Charlotte turned to indicate a photograph in a silver frame that stood on the desk.

"Like a picture of you."

Catherine suddenly thought of a portrait miniature she'd had painted a few days earlier that was set in a silver frame. It was a portrait

282 A Passage to Siam

of her head and shoulders that expertly detailed her lustrous golden hair, her bright blue eyes, her long neck, and the curve of her bosom above the lace neckline of her white dress. Arthur had never seen it because he had left before she'd had it painted, so he would not miss it.

"I have something," she heard herself say. "Thank you, Charlotte. You're right. I do still love Justin…and I'll never forget him as long as I live. I hope this reminds him that, despite everything that's happened, I'll never stop loving him."

***

It was common for Prince Vijjuprapha to have foreign guests, and almost every English-speaking Westerner who set foot in the kingdom, whether they were diplomats, missionaries, or traders, had an opportunity to meet him.

However, this was the first time that a foreign guest had caused Won to feel so awkward when they asked permission to see the prince.

"I need to speak to the prince," the guest said. "It's important."

Won swallowed when he saw the red-haired woman with sunburned skin.

All the men in Bangkok knew of her, and his throat became dry.

"I understand, madam, but you don't have an appointment."

"Tell the prince I've just come from London, and I've brought news from 'is wife, Catherine."

Since his study was rather cramped, Prince Vijjuprapha had set aside a meeting room with Western-style furniture for receiving guests. A set of chairs and a low table stood on the polished wooden floor, which was covered with a Persian carpet, and an oil lamp hung above the table. Bua was responsible for making sure that the room was kept clean and tidy and for providing refreshments for Western guests.

Charlotte Palmer had never seen the prince's wife before, but when she caught sight of the petite young woman with butterscotch skin peeping out of the window of one of the houses, she smiled to herself, thinking that Bua must have mistaken her for the prince's new mistress. Her smile faded when she saw the prince hurrying out of another house and going into the meeting room, calling to her excitedly, "Miss Palmer, I hear you've brought news from Catherine."

Charlotte's heart sank when she noticed the anxious expression on his face. She had seen him before in Singapore and conceded that he was a handsome man, but now, he appeared thin and gaunt, his face tired and pale.

Her satisfaction that he had got what he deserved vanished in an instant, and she replied politely, "I've been in England for the past two years, Your 'ighness. While I was there, I met your wife."

"How is she?" he cried in agitation.

"She's fine. She asked me to give you this."

Charlotte pulled a leather box out of the small drawstring bag she carried on her wrist and gave it to him. The prince hurriedly opened it, forgetting himself, and froze when he caught sight of the tiny portrait in the silver frame. He gazed at the woman in the picture as if he were trying to see her on the other side of the world until Charlotte felt as if she and everything around them had suddenly become invisible to him.

When he looked up again, Charlotte expected to see an expression of either joy or sadness in his face, but instead he looked confused.

"This was expensive. Catherine must be wealthy."

"Yes, Your 'ighness," Charlotte replied. "Catherine's moved from Longstock to London."

He paused before asking, "Why has she moved to London? She has no relatives there as far as I know."

Charlotte had no choice but to tell him the truth.

"She's moved there with 'er 'usband."

He was silent.

She saw him grip the picture so tightly she feared it would break.

After an awkward pause, she continued.

"She's gone back to Arthur Lindley…"

He suddenly raised his hand and she stopped.

"Is there a child?"

"Er…" Charlotte stuttered.

"Tell me the truth, Miss Palmer."

His tone of voice became suddenly aggressive, and Charlotte was alarmed.

284   A Passage to Siam

"You must know the answer. Tell me if she has a child."

"Er…yes, Your 'ighness," Charlotte stammered. "She's got a son."

She feared the prince would suspect the child was his, thinking that the truth would hurt him more than not knowing, but when she saw the pain in his eyes, she hoped he would guess.

The colour drained from his face and there was a long pause before he came to his senses, remembering that Charlotte was still sitting in front of him, so he said, "Thank you, Miss Palmer, for bringing this token from Catherine. I'll..I'll…"

He swallowed before continuing.

"I'll write to Catherine to tell her I've got it."

Charlotte stood up and a flicker of sadness passed across her face. "Goodbye, Your 'ighness."

Catherine has a son…

The child we wanted more than anything else in the world is now Arthur Lindley's.

No wonder you couldn't promise that you'd wait for me. When you said we couldn't be together again, it was really because you'd gone back to your old husband.

You never thought he was better than me, so how could you go back to him? The five years we were together and the two children we had meant less to you than I thought.

How could you go back to him when you told me your love for me was unchanged? Did my letter do nothing to soften your heart?

Or do you prefer your comfortable life in England? From your portrait, I can see that Mrs Lindley is far from poor.

Or is it like you said that there's a thin line between love and hate and you hate me too much to forgive me, and the love you still have for me is not strong enough to erase the hatred you feel?

Prince Vijjuprapha had to admit that the name Arthur Lindley had hit him like a lightning bolt because the young English officer had not entered his thoughts for several years. The words he had spoken seven years earlier rang in his ears.

"Even if I wasn't her husband, I'd still say the same thing. An Englishwoman can't be kept in a harem, cut off from the world outside.

She wouldn't even be your only wife. Just one of many that must compete for the same man's affections. Catherine doesn't know how unbearable it would be. Love wouldn't be of any use to her then."

And he remembered how he had answered with the presumptuous confidence of his youth, unaware that life was more complicated than he had assumed.

"I can guarantee that Catherine wouldn't have to face that situation. Just because Siamese men are allowed to have more than one wife, it doesn't mean they have to. A man can have only one wife if he so chooses. If I marry Catherine, she'll be my only wife."

And now, Catherine had experienced the situation that Arthur had spoken of and had found it so unbearable that she refused to risk going down the same path twice.

The crowing of a rooster told him it was almost morning and the cool breeze chilled him to the bone.

***

The sun had gone down, and the trees cast long shadows onto the veranda, where it was pleasantly cool, so Bua often chose to sit there and thread flower garlands for prayer offerings, while her son played close by. The young boy was lively and as soon as his nanny put him down, he would not keep still. After a while, he crawled onto his mother's lap and his chubby little hands tried to pull the garland from hers.

A moment later, one of the servants came hurrying towards her along the covered walkway that connected Bua's house to the main residence. Then she got down on her knees before crawling towards Bua and stammered, "The prince is back."

Bua showed no sign of alarm, but let go of the garland, allowing her son to take it before she picked him up and passed him to the nanny. The nanny followed behind Bua with the boy in her arms as Bua hurried towards the meeting room where the prince was sitting on a rug next to a low round table.

When he saw his wife, he said, "There you are, Bua. Tonight, I'll be going to the Front Palace to stay with the doctor. Can you have a mattress and a blanket brought to me?"

Everyone knew that men were not allowed inside the Front Palace, except for a doctor in emergencies, and if a doctor had to stay the night, it was necessary for Prince Saifa to chaperone him.

"Is the king ill?" Bua asked with concern.

"I'm afraid so."

Bua crawled away to see that the mattress was ready for him before he left for the palace.

When she returned, she noticed that her son had crawled onto his father's lap, but a moment later, he rolled off. Then she heard him say, "He's almost three and we still haven't given him a proper name aside from Nu. I was going to ask the king to name him, but there wasn't the right opportunity, so I'll name him myself. I'll call him Inthanu. It means lightning, the same as my name, Saifa."

Bua repeated the name thoughtfully.

"What do you think, Bua?"

"It's beautiful," she said sincerely.

Prince Saifa motioned to his son.

"Come and see your father, Inthanu."

He picked him up and the little boy was still for a while. He looked up at his father and smiled, his golden skin contrasting with his clear black eyes. Although he had lost Catherine, Rosalind, and Charles, he had not lost everything, he thought to himself, and the son that Bua had borne him brought him immense comfort. The little boy put the flower garland that he had been holding tightly over his father's wrist, and Prince Saifa smiled for the first time.

He stood up with his son in his arms, noticing that Won had crawled inside to take his orders.

"Won, have you torn up the house on the raft yet?"

"Yes, sir," Won replied.

In that case, thought Bua with relief, the rumours that the prince was bringing the redhaired woman who had been to see him to replace his first wife were untrue. He was showing more affection for his son than he had shown previously, and Bua's spirits were lifted more than ever before.

On the Other Side of the World 287

15

The Sands of Time

In December of 1864, King Pinklao was taken ill, and King Mongkut ordered that the royal tonsure, or topknot-cutting, ceremony of his son, Prince Chulalongkorn should be postponed. However, King Pinklao wanted the ceremony to go ahead, fearing that he would not live long enough to see it if it were delayed, so the plans continued.

However, as the day of the ceremony grew closer, King Pinklao's condition deteriorated.

Prince Vijjuprapha arrived at Siwamokhaphiman Hall as he had for the past several months with several attendants in tow. The Front Palace was full of royal doctors, busy preparing the king's medicine. When they caught sight of Prince Saifa, as King Pingklao called him, they prostrated themselves, knowing that he had come to give the king his medicine.

The king had been unwell for over two years and the prince knew that the doctors had done everything they could to cure him, but now all that could be done was ease his pain. The king had grown painfully thin and had become mostly confined to his bed. The royal pages carried the medicines to the throne hall in procession and passed them to Prince Vijjuprapha who administered them to the king himself.

Today, he appeared visibly weaker and, after he had taken his medicine, closed his eyes. At that moment, there was a commotion outside the room, and a servant brought a screen inside, indicating that King Mongkut had arrived to visit his brother. All the servants left and only Prince Saifa remained inside the king's room on the other side of the screen.

The prince heard the two kings talking to each other in low voices.

288   A Passage to Siam

King Pinklao was talking to King Mongkut about the royal tonsure ceremony of Prince Chulalongkorn that was to take place in three days' time, and said, "We can count on your son."

Prince Saifa had known Prince Chulalongkorn since he was a boy and had been responsible for looking after the young prince whenever he visited the Front Palace when they would converse together in English. Prince Saifa had seen him grow from a small boy into a tall young man with a handsome face and a gentle and kindly manner, but he could not know that one day he would become one of the great kings of Siam.

On January the 7th 1865, after the royal tonsure ceremony had been completed, King Pinklao passed away at the age of fifty-eight. King Monkut decreed that the second king's funeral was to be no different from that of the king of the land except, aside from the Front Palace officials, the citizens would not be expected to shave their heads.

After his death, the Front Palace officials moved to the Grand Palace, but the army and the navy remained in the Front Palace.

King Mongkut appointed Prince Chulalongkorn as the Commander of the Royal Guards in the Front Palace, and Prince Saifa was made his secretary.

* * *

Catherine did not find out about the death of the second king of Siam until two years later when Colonel George Rowland came to see Arthur.

George and his wife had a house in London and were good friends of Arthur so, whenever he was home from his travels, they would be invited for dinner. Arthur was out and Catherine was at home with her children. By this time, Justin was four and was sitting on a rocking horse in the middle of the room, while Margaret was one and a half and had tipped the animals out of a Noah's ark and scattered them across the floor.

When the maid came to tell her that Colonel Rowland had arrived, Catherine told the nanny to wash the children's hands and faces

The Sands of Time 289

before taking them downstairs and went down to greet him. By now, his hair had turned grey, and he had grown stouter than before.

"Arthur's still not back from the office," Catherine said.

"I didn't tell him I was coming, but I was passing, so I just stopped by to bring a letter," he smiled. "Knox wrote to me. He's the Consul in Siam now, and he sent another letter for me to pass on to Arthur."

Catherine caught her breath and quickly invited him to stay for tea.

"If you're not in a hurry, won't you stay for tea, I want to hear news from…"

She paused to steady her voice before continuing, "from Siam."

George regarded her with understanding.

"The prince wrote to me," he began. "He told me the sad news that the second king of Siam passed away two years ago."

"I'm sorry," Catherine muttered.

Her heart sank when she remembered the king's kindness to her.

"He wrote to me, but I think it was really meant for you."

Catherine's heart began to race.

"What did he say?"

Colonel Rowland took an envelope from his coat pocket and handed it to her.

"You keep it," he said kindly. "You don't have to reply. I can write to him if you prefer just to let him know you're alright."

12th August 1867

Dear George,

Although I haven't written to you over the past two years, I still think of you. So many things have happened in Siam that I have not had time to write.

The first thing is the very sad news that the second king of Siam passed away on the 7th of January 1867.

After his death, the Front Palace officials moved to the Grand Palace. I am still with the army, but I am now under the command of Prince Chulalongkorn, who speaks English well and was taught by an Englishwoman named Anna Leonowens, who has since returned to England.

Bangkok is now a centre for trade with the British, the French, and the Chinese, and many of the young princes can speak English.

Some exciting news is that King Mongkut is an expert in astronomy, and he has calculated that there will be a solar eclipse in 1868, which is next year, and it will be visible from Wa Ko in Koh Lak. The king has calculated the exact day that it will occur and plans to take a party of palace officials there to observe it. I am pleased to tell you that I will be joining the party.

I am now in good health after recovering from my sickness five years ago. Khun Chom Klee is getting frail and can no longer walk, so she has come to live with my mother in my home. In this way, my wife can take better care of her. My eldest son is now five and my daughter is not yet one. I named her 'Maliwan' after the fragrant white flowers that bloom on the riverbank next to the raft where I used to live with Catherine.

I still think of Catherine and have never forgotten her. I have never loved anyone else as I love her. If you have any news of her, please let me know to put my mind at rest that she is safe and well.

Yours truly,

Vijjuprapha

* * *

Preparations for the trip to see the eclipse were made several months in advance, and the Front Palace was abuzz with excitement.

Bua listened to the news with interest, but all that Prince Saifa said to her about it was, "Make sure my clothes are ready and organize food for the trip."

Bua's face fell and she asked, "When will you be going?"

"Next month. Do you want to bring the children to see the eclipse?"

"No," she replied with a worried expression. "I'm afraid. They say it's unlucky. You must make merit before you go to ward off the bad luck."

"Do you really believe that, Bua? In the West, they know it's just the moon passing in front of the sun."

* * *

King Mongkut commissioned a pavilion to be built in Wa Ko at the place where he calculated the solar eclipse would be visible from.

A team of French astronomers had journeyed to survey the area, and asked permission to set up camp there, and Sir Henry Ord, the Governor of Singapore, had been granted an audience with the king in the pavilion. The foreign guests were given tea and the king's sixteen-year-old daughter, Princess Somawadee, was allowed to come out to greet them in accordance with Western customs.

At eight o'clock in the morning, the telescopes were set up, and at ten o'clock the king looked eastwards through the telescope, but found the sky obscured by clouds. A few minutes later, the clouds dispersed, and he observed the moon's shadow touching the sun's edge, so he announced that the eclipse had begun.

By twenty past eleven, the sky had darkened, and many stars and planets were visible. At eleven thirty-six precisely, the moon completely blocked out the sun and day turned suddenly into night.

The eclipse took place at the exact time and place that the king had predicted.

Bua was there to greet Prince Saifa when he arrived home, but her face became filled with alarm when she noticed how pale he was.

"I'm afraid I might have caught malaria. I've been feeling unwell since yesterday. Everyone that went has a fever. Wa Ko's hot and humid. The locals say malaria's rampant there."

Bua's shock increased, but she remained calm outwardly and said, "I'll have a servant fetch the doctor."

"Have them bring Dr. Bradley. He has medicine that cures malaria."

Although she had no faith in Western medicine, Bua did not argue. She no longer wanted to ask him about the solar eclipse, convinced that her husband's illness had been caused by the bad luck it had brought. Luckily his condition was not serious and, once he had taken the quinine and rested for a few days, he was well again.

Nobody could have predicted the event that would happen next because Prince Saifa had not told anyone that he had noticed the king had grown pale and was losing weight.

Five days after his return, the king was taken seriously ill.

On the 1st of October 1868, the king passed away at the age of sixty-five after reigning for eighteen years.

292   A Passage to Siam

* * *

25th December 1871

Dear George,

Season's Greetings!

It's been a few years since I last wrote to you. I am presently in Singapore with the new king of Siam. We will be travelling to Penang, Rangoon, and finally, Calcutta. I will be visiting the place where I used to live but will only stay there a few months.

I expect you are aware that, for the past three years, Siam has had a new king, and there have been many changes.

King Chulalongkorn is the first king to have travelled outside the kingdom and he has instigated many reforms. Today, Bangkok has roads with horse-drawn carriages, and the uniforms and hairstyles of the palace nobles are more like those of Westerners. There are also schools like those in Western countries and the king has plans to send his sons to school abroad.

My children are growing up. I now have one son and two daughters. My son is still too young to be sent to school abroad, but I have been teaching him English.

I hope that sometime in the future I will be able to visit you in England. When you reply, please send me news of Catherine. I hope she is still safe and well like before.

Yours truly,

Vijjuprapha

Colonel George Rowland placed the letter in Catherine's hand before telling her, "I expect you'd like to keep it."

Catherine thanked him softly. Outside the sitting room window, she could see Arthur walking back from the park at the corner, where he had taken Justin and Margaret. He had returned in time for his appointment with Colonel Rowland, unaware that the old soldier had arrived early to give the letter to Catherine.

Justin was eight years old and walked ahead of his father who was holding Margaret's hand. Catherine smiled at them and waited for them to come inside the house before she stepped outside the room to greet them.

* * *

"Did you know that George has moved to the country?" Arthur asked as he sat down to tea with Catherine and the children.

Catherine put down the teapot as she had just finished pouring the tea. The children turned to their father with interest, since they had both known Colonel Rowland since they were small. Now that Justin was older, he was at boarding school, and had returned home for the Christmas holidays. The following year, he would be starting university.

"I heard him mention it, but he didn't say where they were moving to."

"He's bought your uncle's house in Breamore. I thought your mother would have told you."

"My uncle's house?" Catherine repeated. "I didn't think my aunt would sell it."

Colonel Burnett, Catherine's uncle, had passed away the previous year.

"The house is too big for her," Arthur explained. "It's too expensive to maintain, so she's moving to something smaller. George used to be her son-in-law, so she preferred to sell it to him than to someone else."

Arthur smiled before continuing teasingly, "George said that once they're settled, we should go and stay with them. Did you know, children, that that house is where I met your mother and proposed to her?"

Margaret's blue eyes sparkled excitedly, her rosy cheeks flushing a deeper hue, while Justin looked at his mother questioningly, his dark eyes reminding her of someone else. Justin was studying for exams in English, German, Geography, Mathematics and Science with the intention of reading Geology at the University of Manchester.

* * *

The following June, Colonel Rowland stopped by to visit the Lindley's. Since Arthur was not at home, Catherine met him in her sitting room.

"I have good news," she said, smiling. "Justin has passed all his exams and has been accepted at Manchester. We're all over the moon."

"Congratulations," George grinned. "I knew he'd pass. He's a determined young man."

He talked about Justin and student life in Manchester for a while before changing the subject.

"I've finished repairing the house at Breamore. I'm moving in in a couple of days."

"I'm glad you chose Breamore," Catherine said. "But I'll miss not seeing you and Marion as often as before."

George fell silent for a moment as if he was trying to decide whether to say something or not, so Catherine looked at him questioningly.

"Catherine," he said softly. "Justin's a man now. Don't you think it's time he knows the truth?"

Catherine started. She was still undecided about what to tell him.

"It isn't that I haven't thought about it," she confessed, "but I don't know where to start, George. If I tell him the father who raised him isn't his real father, but his real father is from a country in the East that he's never even heard of, his world will come crashing down."

"I understand, but he has a right to know who his father is."

"And what will he do with that right? Cross the ocean to Siam to meet his father, who doesn't even know he exists? His father has a family of his own. How will he feel if he finds out he has another son?"

"You and I both know the prince has never forgotten you. What I'm trying to tell you is that Justin doesn't have to cross the ocean. If the prince wants to meet his son, he'll come himself."

"But Justin can't leave Siam…"

"Times have changed. The new king of Siam's very modern. He's even sent his sons to school in England."

"Do you mean there are Siamese people in England?"

"Young students," he confirmed. "The prince wrote to me about it. Here's his letter."

Colonel Rowland took an envelope out of his coat pocket and passed it to Catherine.

11th February 1880
Dear George,
I haven't written for several years, but I'm writing today because I want to ask your advice about a certain young man who will be going to England to study.

The Sands of Time 295

First, I should explain that there are already several Siamese students studying in England.

My son, Mom Rajawongse Inthanu, is now fluent in English, and even our old friend Knox, who is now the Consular General, commented on his fluency.

The king has generously chosen him to study in England but doesn't want him to go to military college as I did, because Siam no longer has any wars, so the king would prefer him to study something that could be applied to developing our country.

Knox suggested he study Engineering because Siam needs roads and railways. Please advise me on which university he should attend. He will stay in London for a while before starting university.

I am now a major general and my three children are all grown. Khun Chom Klee, my adoptive mother, passed away three years ago, and my mother is now frail, but my wife takes care of her.

England and Siam are no longer as far apart as before. I hope to come and visit you before I die.

Although many years have passed, I still think of Catherine. Please let me know how she is.

Yours truly,
Vijjuprapha

* * *

Arthur left for the East in November. He was reluctant to go, as since his brother Alfred had passed away that August responsibility for the office in London now rested on his shoulders. A few days before he left, he told Catherine, "This will be my last trip to the East, or there will be no one to take care of the office."

Arthur's face was lined, and his hair had grown thin. Catherine knew he loved to travel, but she accepted his decision.

"It's for the best," she agreed. "It's tiring for you, and it isn't as if we don't have enough money. You should take things easy now."

Arthur took her hand and smiled.

"Thank you, Catherine. I didn't use to like staying at home, but now nothing makes me happier than staying at home with you."

296   A Passage to Siam

* * *

Catherine sat at the desk in her sitting room, a blank sheet of paper in front of her. She had tried to put pen to paper countless times but had never got any further than her address at the top of the page. How could she tell her son the truth without hurting him?

She put the feather quill back in the inkpot and sat motionless for a while. She stared out of the window at the garden, gazing at the red maple leaves and the grey sky.

In three months, Arthur would be home. By now, he would be in the middle of the Mediterranean with his young assistant, David Bromfield, who had shares in the company. Arthur hoped to pass the task of travelling to the East to buy tobacco onto the young man.

After a moment's consideration, Catherine opened the drawer and put the quill and the paper back inside.

A few months after returning from his travels, Arthur became ill with a fever. It began as an ordinary cold, but when his temperature rose sharply and did not come down for three days, Catherine called for the doctor.

"It's pneumonia," the doctor pronounced after examining him.

Arthur was forty-six, the same age her father had been when he died.

* * *

15th December 1881

Dear Mother,

I was concerned to read about father's illness, but it's a relief to know he's starting to feel better. I'm sure having you and Margaret by his side will speed up his recovery.

My good news is that my second-year results were as good as for my first year, and I am expecting to attain an honours degree as I have set my mind to.

Before I come home for the Christmas holidays, I plan to visit Colonel Rowland in Breamore with one of my university friends.

My friend is from the East. He comes from a small country that I had never heard of called the kingdom of Siam. He is an Engineering student

The Sands of Time 297

and Colonel Rowland is supervising him, just as he supervised his father when his father was at military college in India.

His Siamese name is Inthanu, but the colonel has given him the name Ernest because it is easier to pronounce, and he is the son of a Siamese prince.

Ernest is one year older than me and he is a very agreeable fellow. He is every inch a gentleman, and he speaks English fluently. We have been friends since he gave me Colonel Rowland's letter of introduction at university.

Please give everyone my love. I'm looking forward to coming home at Christmas.

Love,
Justin

The letter slipped from Catherine's hand onto the desk. She did not have the energy to put it back in the envelope and sat motionless as a statue. It was fortunate that she had opened the letter to read while she was alone and not in front of Arthur as she usually did when she read Justin's letters aloud to him. Inthanu, the son of a Siamese prince and Justin, the son of a London businessman, had become friends.

She came to her senses when she heard Margaret calling her.

"Mother…Mother?"

Catherine blinked and saw Margaret standing in front of her with an anxious expression on her face.

"Are you alright, Mother? I've sent for the doctor. Father's struggling to catch his breath."

Arthur's condition had deteriorated since the arrival of winter and the cold seemed to exacerbate it. Catherine could not hide his illness from her son any longer, so she decided to write and tell him before he returned home for Christmas. She stood up quickly. For the present, nothing was more important than Arthur's health.

"I'll go up and see him right away."

Arthur grew steadily worse and began to lose consciousness as his breathing became increasingly difficult. Catherine remained at his side day and night, sometimes falling asleep at his bedside.

Margaret decided to send a telegram to Justin, asking him to return home.

Catherine remembered that day clearly. The winter sun was shining after the sky had been gloomy for several days, so she had opened the curtains to let the sunlight into Arthur's room.

She had been upstairs when Justin arrived with two guests. Margaret had learned of their arrival from the housekeeper, so she hurried downstairs to greet them. She hugged her brother before turning to greet Colonel Rowland and then glanced curiously at the stranger standing next to him.

"This is my friend, Ernest. He's from Siam, a country in the East," Justin said.

The young man had pale brown skin with black hair and black eyes, and he regarded Margaret with no less curiosity.

"I didn't mean to stare, Miss Lindley. It's just that I feel as if I've seen you before."

Margaret looked puzzled and smiled.

"I don't think so. I've never even been to Manchester."

"Not in Manchester," he said and thought for a moment. "Oh, I know. In a picture."

"What picture?" Justin asked, puzzled.

"A portrait miniature," he explained. "As small as a locket. It's a picture of a woman that looks just like Miss Lindley. My father's had it on his desk ever since I can remember. I don't know who the woman is, but if you saw it, Justin, I'm sure you'd think it was your sister."

Nobody noticed the strange expression in Colonel Rowland's eyes, but he placed his hand on the young Siamese man's shoulder, and said gently, "In a moment, you'll meet Mrs Lindley. Margaret looks just like her mother. You should tell her about it. She'd be interested."

A moment later, when the housekeeper announced that Justin and Colonel Rowland had arrived, Catherine hurried downstairs to greet them.

"Mother," Justin said, moving towards her anxiously. "How's father?"

Catherine hardly heard him. She was staring past him at the other young man who had stood up to greet her. Her heart almost stopped because he looked so much like his father, and she had to hold onto her son to steady herself.

The Sands of Time 299

"Mother? Are you alright?"

Margaret led her mother to a chair and explained to the guests, "Mother's been taking care of Father night and day. She must be exhausted. You sit here and rest, Mother. I'll take the colonel and Justin to see Father."

George Rowland understood Catherine's affliction better than the others, so he said, "Thank you, Margaret. Let's go up and see him. Ernest can talk to Mrs Lindley for a while."

The three of them went upstairs leaving Catherine alone with Prince Saifa's son.

Ernest was the spitting image of his father, but when she looked at him closely, she could also see Bua's likeness in his almond eyes.

He stared back at her, looking puzzled, before commenting, "Colonel Rowland said Miss Lindley looked just like her mother, and now I've met you, I see what he means if you don't mind my saying so."

"Not at all. Everyone says that," Catherine smiled.

"And you remind me of the woman in the portrait miniature."

"A portrait miniature?"

"Yes. My father keeps it on his desk. It's as small as a locket. He's had it there for as long as I can remember."

Catherine's eyes began to fill with tears, and she tried to speak, but no sound came out. The young man looked at her, puzzled.

"Are you alright, Mrs Lindley? You look pale..."

Catherine forced a smile, although her lips were trembling.

"I'm fine. It's just..." She swallowed, not knowing what to say, before attempting to change the subject.

"Tell me about your home in Bangkok."

His eyes widened.

"I'm amazed that you've heard of my country. Most of the people I've met don't even know where Siam is. You must have heard about it from Mr Lindley. Justin told me his father travels a lot."

"I used to live there," Catherine said quietly.

"You used to live there?" he repeated in surprise. "Justin never told me his parents used to live in Siam."

"It was before he was born. Arthur worked in the Front Palace for

300 A Passage to Siam

a short time, and I…" she said, trying to steady her voice, "lived in Bangkok for a while."

The colour rushed to Ernest's cheeks, revealing his excitement at meeting someone who had been to his country.

"Are you still in contact with anyone from Bangkok, Mrs Lindley?" he asked.

"Occasionally I hear news of them, but the person I know…will be old now."

"Who is it? I might know them."

Catherine's heart sank when Ernest explained that Dr Bradley had passed away a few years earlier and had been buried in a Christian cemetery next to the Chao Phraya River. He also told her that Knox had been made Consul of Bangkok.

She asked him about Charlotte Palmer but was disappointed to find that Ernest had never heard of her, and Catherine thought she might never know what had become of her.

"And what about your family?" she asked hesitantly.

Ernest told her about his two sisters, who lived with his mother, and had helped her take care of his two grandmothers before they had passed away.

"My father's a major general. He teaches English to the new officers. He must accompany the king, so he isn't home much."

Catherine wanted to ask him more about his family, but the door opened, and her son came inside.

"Mother, go and see Father."

She stood up hurriedly and excused herself before rushing out of the room.

***

2ⁿᵈ January 1882

Dear Father,

I expect you have already received the last letter I sent you in English two months ago. I am writing again because there is something I want to tell you.

The subject of this letter is not my studies like the last one because

I have already told you everything about university life. This letter concerns someone that I have met in England.

I have a friend at university who was introduced to me by Colonel George Rowland. His name is Justin Lindley, and he is a Geology student.

Justin Lindley was born in 1863, a year after me, but he is in the same year as me, and we are good friends. He took me and the colonel to visit his home in London just before Christmas, but I didn't stay overnight because I was staying with the colonel in Breamore.

While I was at his house, I discovered that Justin's parents used to live in Bangkok, but he did not know about it because it was before he was born.

His mother is a beautiful woman just like the woman in the portrait miniature on your desk and his sister looks exactly like her. I have never asked you who the woman in the picture is. Is it a picture of her, or is it just coincidence?

Mrs Lindley told me that she and her husband lived in Bangkok, but I did not have the opportunity to ask her if she knew you. She mentioned Knox and Dr Bradley, so I think she must have known you.

When I got back to Breamore, I asked Colonel Rowland if the Lindleys' knew you, and he said they knew you well, so I had to write and tell you.

Sadly, I did not have a chance to meet Mr Lindley since he was very sick. His son got home just in time to see him before he passed away.

I attended the funeral with the colonel and his wife, but I did not have a chance to talk to Mrs Lindley as I had to return to university in Manchester.

Please give my love to Mother and my sisters.

Respectfully yours,
Inthanu

* * *

Bua had just finished her prayers.

She was planning to go to bed as usual but was puzzled to find that her daughters were not sleeping on the mattress in front of her bed where they normally slept, so she stepped outside the bedroom and went to the front of the house. The two young women were sitting threading flower garlands and chatting, surrounded by several maids.

"Are you two still up?"

Mom Rachawongse Maliwan, the elder sister, and Mom Rachawongse Ladawan turned and smiled at their mother. The elder spoke first.

"May I just finish this garland for Father to take as a prayer offering?"

"You make him a garland every day. Why do you need to ask?"

"Father asked for an extra one."

Bua nodded and did not ask any more questions.

"Father asked you to go and see him," the younger sister added.

Bua started, and looked puzzled, wondering what he wanted to see her about, but all she said was, "Then I'll go and see him. Inthanu must have sent a letter from England."

Bua walked slowly down from the veranda of her house to the meeting room in the prince's residence. When she reached the meeting room, she noticed that the prince appeared agitated and was pacing the floor, so she asked, "Has something happened?"

She saw that her husband's face was flushed and his eyes, which normally had a solemn expression, were sparkling with excitement.

"I've had a letter from Inthanu. There's something you should know. He isn't ill or anything, don't worry."

He added the last sentence when he saw the alarm in Bua's face.

"He told me about his friend in England. It's Catherine's son."

They had not spoken her name for the past twenty years and Bua had almost forgotten about her.

"The foreign teacher's son?" Bua asked. "I didn't know she had a son."

Prince Saifa had not mentioned her since he had ordered the raft to be torn up.

"I believe he's my son. If he were the son of her former husband, she wouldn't have named him Justin, and he's only a year younger than Inthanu. She must have been pregnant when she left."

Bua shook her head slowly.

"I don't understand. If the foreign teacher was pregnant, why didn't she tell you?"

Her question hit a weak spot, and the colour suddenly drained from his face.

"She cut all ties with me. Why would she come back to me after what I did to her? I broke my promise."

Bua felt as if she had been slapped and stood motionless.

The Sands of Time 303

"I asked Colonel Rowland for news of Catherine, but he never told me. Why would Arthur Lindley allow his wife to name their son Justin if he were his own son?"

Bua sighed softly in resignation. As Bua had reached middle age, she had resigned herself to the fact that her husband would never regard her with anything more than brotherly affection.

"What are you going to do?" she asked softly.

"I'm going to write to Inthanu and tell him to ask Catherine. He's smart enough. He was saying that Mrs Lindley looks like the woman in the portrait miniature. He's probably figured it out, but he didn't like to say. Bua, I think I should tell him about Catherine. What do you think?"

Bua was silent for a moment because she wasn't used to voicing her opinions. It wasn't that she didn't have her own opinions, but simply that she had been taught to suppress them. In the past, she would have said, 'It's up to you,' to avoid having to decide.But now, after twenty years of letting others make all her decisions for her, whether it was Khun Chom Klee, Mom Yad, or even her husband, she realized that she was still responsible for the consequences of those decisions. And the worst part was that she felt an even heavier burden than if she had made the decisions herself. By now, she had realized that her husband's heart still belonged to his first love.

What was to be gained by standing in his way?

"Inthanu's a man now. What's the point of hiding the truth from him? You should tell him or write to the foreign teacher and ask her."

"If it's alright with you, I'll write to him and tell him the truth. I'll have to tell him that I broke my promise to Catherine when I married you to please my elders, so he'll understand."

In the past, Bua would have been hurt by his words, but by now she knew that his heart had never belonged to her.

She stood up, seeing her daughter bringing the flower garland on a tray, and said gently, "When you write to Inthanu, I'll prepare some dried foods for you to send him with your letter."

***

The house in Knightsbridge was quiet after Arthur's passing, and when Justin had returned to university.

However, the emptiness was mitigated by the frequent visits of David Bromfield, who had now taken on the sole responsibility for the business. At first, he came to discuss selling Arthur's shares in the tea company, since Justin had no intention of taking on his father's business, so David needed to find a new partner. As time went on, David became a regular guest, and within the space of a few months, he was like one of the family, routinely coming for dinner with Catherine and her daughter.

David Bromfield was twenty-six. He was well-mannered and clean-cut, but Catherine saw nothing special in him, and thought him no different from the thousands of other London businessmen whose life would follow the same path as Arthur and Alfred's.

Margaret, however, had a different view.

"Mr Bromfield's a nice man, Mother. He's just like Father."

Margaret was like Catherine in her appearance only. In other ways, they were quite different. She was talkative like her grandmother and aunt, and preferred staying at home doing embroidery or baking pies to going out.

David helped to ease her loneliness when she missed her father and brother and, being of a more reticent nature, let her do most of the talking, while Catherine sat knitting in the sitting room to keep an eye on the two of them.

It was not long before Catherine realized that David Bromfield had fallen deeply in love with her daughter. He met her alone one day, his face a deep crimson, and confessed his feelings for Margaret.

"I love Margaret, Mrs Lindley. She's my first love…and if you don't object…I want to marry her."

Arthur had left a substantial dowry for his daughter, which provided her with the opportunity to marry a man from a good family, and David's background was impeccable.

Margaret would get married the following year and move in with her husband, while Justin was soon to graduate and start a career. One day, he would have a family of his own. The task of raising her children for the past twenty years was complete, but her heart whispered that she had only felt truly alive during her five years in Siam.

***

"There's a visitor to see you, madam. It's Justin's friend from the East."

Catherine could hardly believe her ears when the maid brought the news as she was writing in her journal as she did every day. It was a Sunday and Justin was home from university for a few days but had gone out. David had taken Margaret for a ride in a horse-drawn carriage as he did every Sunday.

"To see me? Did you tell him Justin's not at home?"

"I told him, madam, but he said it's you he wants to see."

"Then ask him inside."

She could not imagine why Inthanu would want to see her, but her heart began to race all the same. He greeted her briefly with a solemn expression, and Catherine could sense the tension in the atmosphere before he had even spoken a word. He gazed at the middle-aged woman in front of him. The beauty of her youth was still evident, even though there were strands of silver in her flaxen hair, which contrasted with her black mourning dress.

Even after rehearsing what he was going to say over and over on the train from Manchester to London, he still felt inexplicably awkward.

"My father wrote to me…He told me about you and him, Mrs Lindley. He's just found out you have a son called Justin Lindley and…"

The moment had come. Twenty years of biding time had culminated in a single sentence. She collapsed on a chair as if her knees had turned to jelly. Inthanu started. It was not necessary for him to speak the words he had agonized over. Mrs Lindley's response told him that she knew full well what he was going to ask.

Instead, he pulled the letter that he had read countless times out of his shirt pocket and passed it to Catherine. Through her tears, Catherine saw only a few sentences written in English in the hand she had never forgotten.

"…go and see my first wife and tell her I've never forgotten her for a single moment and ask her if her son is Arthur Lindley's or mine.

I have no rights concerning my son since I did not raise him. All I ask is that Catherine tell me the truth about who his father is, so I can die in peace…"

306 A Passage to Siam

Catherine did not answer, except for the tears that rolled down her cheeks and onto the letter, leaving inky blotches as she bent her head and sobbed as if her heart would break.

"Mrs Lindley…" Inthanu cried, not knowing what to do.

He knelt in front of her, not daring to touch her, in awkward silence.

A moment later, the door opened, and he heard Justin's voice call cheerily, "Mother, I'm home. Hollis said Ernest is here…Oh!"

Justin froze, dumbfounded.

"What's happened? What is it, Mother?" he asked, hurrying towards her, and looking at Ernest questioningly.

Catherine managed to collect herself and wiped her tears with a lace handkerchief. In a low but steady voice, she told her son, "Sit down, dear. I have something important to tell you. Ernest, sit down next to Justin and listen together."

16

When the River Runs Backwards

The most difficult thing was knowing where to start. She had to start over three times before she could finally continue, since two pairs of eyes were staring at her intently.

She began by telling them how she had dreamed of seeing the world, as a bird hopes to fly to the end of the horizon, and how a young officer had made her dream come true, but his hastiness in leaving her behind when he went to start his new job had ended their marriage before it had even begun.

She told them how she had met another young officer from a small kingdom in the East and how they had fallen in love while they were at sea.

And how in the end, she had left Arthur when she had found him with another Englishwoman and gone to live with the Siamese prince for the next five years…

And how her happiness had been shattered when he had taken a wife that his elders approved of.

She had left for her homeland only to discover that she was pregnant, and then she had met Arthur who had helped her get back on her feet again.

Over the next twenty years, her anguish had lessened, except for the fact that she was hiding the secret of who her son's father was. While Arthur was alive, she had agonized over whether to tell her son or not and decided to remain silent for the sake of her family.

Now the moment of truth had arrived, and she was ready to face the consequences.

The room was silent except for the sound of Catherine's voice. As she ended, she whispered, "Justin, I hope you can forgive me for hiding the truth from you, but I didn't know how to tell you."

Justin stared at her before turning to Ernest, who put his hand out for him to shake and laughed gently, "My dear brother…"

Alone in the sitting room, Ernest paced the floor. A moment later, the door opened, and Justin entered. He stopped suddenly when he saw Ernest standing up and looking at him questioningly.

"Is Mrs Lindley alright?"

"She's gone to lie down."

The two young men stared at each other as if each seeing the other for the first time.

Justin spoke first.

"What's your father – I mean our father – like?

Ernest pointed at the letter that lay on the desk.

"You should read it for yourself," he said. "Mrs Lindley won't mind."

Justin picked up the letter hesitantly and bent his head to read it. There was silence except for the sound of him turning over the paper several times as he read it over and over. Ernest waited patiently until finally, Justin looked up and stammered, "He's never forgotten my mother…He said his world collapsed when she went away. He was left alone…"

"I didn't know about them, although I had wondered about the portrait, but I wasn't sure until I read the letter today and now, I'm certain. But one thing you can be sure of is that he's a good father and I'm proud to be his son."

Justin's taut expression relaxed.

"Didn't he ever search for my mother?"

"He wrote to her, but Mrs Lindley never replied. After that, he always wrote to Colonel Rowland. I think he gave up hope of ever seeing Mrs Lindley again. Colonel Rowland will know more than we do, but Father never knew he had another son. As soon as he suspected, he could hardly contain his excitement. Trust me, if he knows he has a son with the woman he loves, he'll be over the moon."

Justin was silent for a moment.

"No wonder…" he finally blurted, "I don't look like my father. I always wondered why I had dark hair when Margaret and my parents were all fair. But my father was such a good father I never thought…"

"I understand how you feel, Justin. Mrs Lindley should have told you but imagine how she felt carrying that secret for so long."

Justin sighed.

"Thank you, Ernest. It's hard to take in. Tell me about Siam and your family. I want to know about them."

***

Bua waited in agitation as her husband had accompanied the king to Bang Pa In and had been due to return since that afternoon. She waited until midnight when he finally returned. As he walked up the steps of the veranda to the meeting room where Bua had been waiting, she could discern his excitement from his flushed face and lively manner.

"Oh, good. You're still up, Bua," he said cheerfully. "I thought I'd have to tell you tomorrow."

"What's the…"

But before she could finish, Prince Saifa interrupted eagerly.

"Do you want to go to England?"

She swallowed her words and looked at him in disbelief.

"How can I?" she asked, puzzled.

Prince Saifa sat down.

"I'll tell you. I had an opportunity to talk to the king, and I told him I had another son in England, so he gave me permission to go there and to take my family. What do you say?"

Bua collected herself and said, "You want me and the girls to go with you?"

"Yes. I might be there for two or three years, or even longer. What will you and the girls do if you stay here all by yourselves?"

Bua was silent as if something was disturbing her, and when he looked at her questioningly, she explained softly, "Mom Prong came to see me yesterday."

Mom Prong was the wife of one of the princes and, although they both knew her, they were not close, so the fact that she had come to see Bua indicated that it was a matter of importance.

"She came to ask for Maliwan's hand in marriage for her son," Bua

310 A Passage to Siam

explained. After asking her a few questions, Prince Saifa could tell that Bua was satisfied that the young man was a suitable match, so he asked, "Do want her to get married before we go or wait until we get back? I'll let you decide."

Bua thought for a moment and answered assuredly, "She's a grown woman now. I'd rather see her married."

"Then you'll have to find an auspicious day before you come to England."

Bua considered again before replying decisively, "I'd rather stay here."

"What did you say?" Prince Saifa asked, puzzled. "Even if you don't go, I shall still be going, and I won't be back for a long time. What are you thinking, or is it that...?"

He paused to study her, but her expression remained neutral.

"You're not jealous because I'll be meeting Catherine, are you? She went back to her first husband ages ago. And besides, we're older now and our children are grown."

"Why would I be jealous?" she replied gently. "What good would it do? Jealousy only brings suffering. I got over it years ago and I don't want to repeat it."

"I don't understand, Bua."

"You don't understand?" she repeated. "I wish I'd had the courage to oppose our elders when they wanted me to marry you, but I didn't dare...I thought I was showing gratitude to them, and I was...because they died in peace...but I was miserable..."

Once Bua started speaking, it was as if a dam had broken.

"The Buddha taught that you suffer when you face something you don't want, and you suffer when you lose something you want...It's true...You've suffered no less than I."

Bua paused as if she was waiting for him to respond, and when he said nothing, she continued.

"I'd like to be released from that cycle of suffering and remain here with my children."

***

The bedroom was empty. Although the furniture remained, it no longer looked lived in. The stationary on the desk and all the prince's belongings had disappeared from their usual place and been packed into a trunk, which Won's son, Hom, was securing with a rope before he carried it outside ready to take onto the boat.

Bua surveyed the room, realizing that her husband's attendants were more familiar with his bedroom than she was.

"Have you checked that everything's been packed?" she asked the young attendant.

He nodded and fell to his knees in deference as the prince stepped inside the room.

"Ah, Bua," he said softly by way of greeting before turning to Hom. "You can take the trunks out now."

Hom carried the first trunk out and signalled to his colleague, who was kneeling in front of the door, to lift the second trunk, before shutting the door mindfully behind him.

Prince Saifa sat down on a chair, while Bua sat on the floor with her legs to the side as she was used to doing. They were silent for a moment before the prince spoke.

"Bua, in a short while, I'll be leaving. I don't know how many years it will be before I come back. Take care of the girls, and the servants, and yourself."

Bua bowed her head and pressed her palms together gently.

"I have something for you."

She turned and picked up a small silk purse that she had brought with her and placed it in front of him.

"It's lace, I made it myself. The foreign teacher taught me how to do it."

The prince was stunned for a moment before he bent over to pick it up doubtfully.

"I didn't know you knew how to make lace."

Bua had never shown anyone her work. She had not dared to show it to Mom Yad or Chao Chom Klee, fearing that it would remind them of the foreign teacher.

"I never showed anyone, but I had some free time, so I made it."

The silk purse contained something soft, and when he opened it, he found a delicately sewn small lace mat.

312 A Passage to Siam

"It's very fine," he admired. "You should teach the girls."

"Lek can crochet a little, but she needs more practice."

He picked it up again and turned it over approvingly.

"What's it for?"

"It's to stand the portrait of the foreign teacher on."

She glanced at his desk and saw that the portrait was no longer there, knowing that he would not be parted from it.

"The foreign teacher came to see me at the Front Palace when she found out about us...to ask me not to marry you...If you see her... tell her I didn't mean to hurt her. I sympathized with her, but I didn't have the courage to say no...I've regretted it ever since."

Bua accepted the fact that she had attained everything that Chao Chom Klee and Mom Yad had intended for her, including honour, status, wealth, and three wonderful children, except for the one thing she had never had from Prince Saifa.

And that was his love.

This made her realize that she had always been a third person who had come between the prince and another woman. As the prince looked at her, he asked himself why he had never been able to love her when she had been an exemplary wife and mother. The answer was the same as always. He had overcome numerous obstacles to be with his first love, whom he would not have lost if he had not taken another wife. Now he had a chance to make amends.

"What's done is done. Life's too short to live with regret. You've shown gratitue to your elders, you've been a good wife, and you've been a wonderful mother to our children. All the servants respect you. Thank you for being faultless in every way. I'm sorry we're not destined to be together any longer."

He placed his hand on Bua's head gently.

"I'll be gone for a long time, and I don't know if we'll meet again. May the gods protect you from sickness and harm and may you continue to follow the Buddha's teachings. If I've done you wrong, I ask your forgiveness. Don't be sorry that we have to part, because nothing lasts forever, and everything will pass away."

Bua bent her head and placed her palms together. Although there was a lump in her throat, she now realized that she had been released from the burden that she had carried for many years.

* * *

The veranda and the meeting room were lit up with coconut oil lamps and filled with relatives who had come to see the prince off, while the dirt courtyard below was packed with servants.

Prince Saifa was in front with Bua behind him. After saying goodbye to his relatives, he headed to the pier and boarded a small boat that was to take him to a larger ship bound for Singapore. Only Bua showed no emotion, unlike her two daughters whose cheeks were soaked with tears as they kneeled in front of their father. Nobody thought it strange that the prince's wife was not accompanying him to England, since she had made the excuse that she was not well enough to travel to Europe, and everybody thought he would not be gone for more than two years.

Only Bua knew that, whether he returned or not, it was over between them.

The evening mist enveloped the treetops like a white blanket, and as the small boat moved further away along the Chao Phraya, the lamps from the larger vessel became dimly visible through the mist.

Bua stood looking out from the pier, a pang in her heart, knowing that she would never see Prince Saifa again.

17
The Glowing of Such Fire

The strains of the organ flooded the church, signalling that the bride had arrived, preceded by an endearing young flower girl scattering rose petals down the aisle, and a pageboy carrying the rings on a velvet cushion.

The bride, in a long white dress, moved down the aisle, and through her tears, Catherine saw that she was smiling beneath her veil. A garland of orange blossom adorned her golden hair and decorated the bouquet of white flowers in her hands as she stepped forward in time with the music.

The groom was waiting in a black long-tailed coat with dark trousers, his face flushed with excitement and nervousness, but as the bride drew up beside him, he composed himself and moved next to her, so that the couple stood facing the vicar.

The vicar's deep voice resonated in the church as he presided over the vows for one of the biggest weddings in the church of that year. Catherine glanced at all the splendidly dressed guests packed into the pews and blinked.

The bride's brother sat next to her and, although his clothes were elegant, his face was solemn. She glanced at the young man with darker skin who sat beside him. Since all the guests understood that he was a close friend of the bride's brother, and was under the care of Colonel Rowland, his presence did not raise any eyebrows.

As the ceremony ended, one by one, the guests left the church and went on to the reception at the bride's house, which Catherine had been preparing for the past month.

Everything went smoothly, but Catherine did not breathe a sigh of relief until the bride and groom had changed their clothes and set out for their honeymoon, and the final guests had said goodbye.

The final two guests were George and Marion.

The colonel's wife squeezed Catherine's hand and told her kindly, "Catherine, you must be exhausted. If you have time, you should come and stay with us in Breamore. Justin and Ernest should come, too."

It was the summer holidays, and Ernest was staying in Catherine's house as a guest before he returned to Manchester for the new term in the autumn.

***

The house at Breamore was just as it had always been. As soon as Catherine stepped down from the horse-drawn carriage and looked up at the old grey building, it looked back at her through the ivy-framed windows like the same old friend that had greeted her twenty years earlier when she had been a young girl of eighteen.

Marion welcomed them warmly and, after a servant had helped them take their trunks upstairs, Catherine went downstairs to join her for tea, but was surprised to find that George was not at home.

"George sends his apologies. He had to go into the city at short notice, but he promised he'd be back in time for dinner. He'll be bringing a guest with him," Marion explained with a smile.

After they had chatted for a while, Catherine excused herself to go for a walk outside. When she stepped onto the extensive lawn behind the house, she turned to look for the rose garden from twenty years earlier and found that there was now a large greenhouse standing where it had once been. She peered inside and saw green ornamental plants interspersed with bright flowers in hanging baskets.

As she stood there gazing, the greenhouse vanished and was replaced by a lawn in the middle of a rose garden. A young man with blonde hair and a tanned complexion came hurrying towards her to confess that he had fallen in love with her. They had both been too young to know that fate would come between them.

A strange feeling suddenly came over her. It could have been nostalgia making her emotional, but she felt strangely dizzy. She walked towards the large maple tree that stood next to the lake, which was

316 A Passage to Siam

surrounded by a grassy bank, and stopped beneath it. The sun was setting behind the trees, casting shadows on the flaxen hair specked with silver strands of the slim forty-three-year-old woman.

In the distance, the spire of the ancient Anglo-Saxon church recalled the Shakespeare sonnet she had loved years ago.

That time of year thou mayst in me behold
When yellow leaves, or none, or few, do hang
Upon those boughs which shake against the cold,
Bare ruin'd choirs, where late the sweet birds sang.
In me thou see'st the twilight of such day
As after sunset fadeth in the west,
Which by and by black night doth take away,
Death's second self, that seals up all in rest.
In me thou see'st the glowing of such fire
That on the ashes of his youth doth lie,
As the death-bed whereon it must expire,
Consum'd with that which it was nourish'd by.
This thou perceiv'st, which makes thy love more strong,
To love that well which thou must leave ere long.

A feeling of inexplicable sadness washed over her. Now that Arthur was no longer there and her children were grown, the autumn of her life stretched out in front of her, empty and desolate. Silence engulfed her. There was not even the sound of the wind blowing through the leaves, or birds chirping in the branches of the trees, but Catherine suddenly felt as if someone was behind her, and something compelled her to turn around.

She saw a pair of eyes staring straight at her! They were as black as a starless night, and although they did not sparkle as they once had, dulled by the weariness of fifty years, they lit up distinctly when they met hers.

Catherine's heart almost stopped. Everything suddenly went black, and her knees buckled beneath her. When she came to her senses, the first thing she felt was a warm pair of arms as she heard a voice whispering in her ear.

"Catherine…my love. Are you alright? Tell me you're alright."

She found herself lying on the grass, her upper body supported by someone who was kneeling and clutching her hand tightly, his black eyes gazing at her anxiously.

"I didn't man to startle you. I'm sorry I didn't tell you I was coming, but I wasn't sure if you'd see me."

Although Justin's voice had grown deeper with the passage of time, she still recognized it as his. She lifted a trembling finger to his chin and stroked his cheek as she had done in the past.

The years had changed him in several ways, from the white hair at his temples to his weathered skin and the lines etched on his forehead and around the corners of his eyes, but he was still the same Justin.

"Am I dreaming?" she heard herself stammer. "Or have I died and met you in heaven?"

Justin lifted her hand to his lips. The neatly trimmed moustache above his lips was another thing that made him look different from the young man she had once known.

"It's really happening, Catherine. In the end, I found you. After I thought I'd never see you again."

Catherine slowly got to her feet as she held tightly onto his arm. The ground beneath her stopped swaying and became still once again.

"I never thought you'd be able to leave Siam and come to England."

When Justin stood up, Catherine noticed the changes in him more clearly. He was now a middle-aged man, portlier than before, but still fit and strong with a straight back. He was also gazing at her, and she looked down at herself disconcertedly.

Although her slender figure still gained compliments, there was no denying that the passage of time had left its mark. Her golden hair was streaked with grey and the rosy glow had faded from her cheeks Although her eyes were still as blue as a clear sky, the lines around them were evident and she was no longer as fresh as a budding rose.

And then Justin smiled at her. His smile was like a flash of lightning breaking through a gloomy sky and the old Justin returned.

"Are you thinking of someone you met right here for the first time?"

The colour rushed to her cheeks.

"You remember."

318　A Passage to Siam

His strong hand squeezed hers as he said in a deep voice, "I've never forgotten the beautiful young girl standing sadly by herself, and the shadows that the red maple leaves cast on her golden hair. I told myself I'd never seen a dryad before...and there you were. I fell in love with you the moment I set eyes on you. Before I knew you were already married. I loved you even though I knew I'd met you too late."

He lifted her hand to his chest.

"...And do you know what? I feel just the same right now."

* * *

Catherine sat down on the white cast iron bench on the grass beside the lake between two maple trees, where daisies dotted the lawn like white stars

Justin did not sit down next to her but stood regarding her.

"I don't want to forgive you, Catherine."

Catherine knew at once what he was referring to.

"You must have been angry when you found out about Justin."

He gazed at her for a moment, a hurt expression in his eyes.

"I suspected it ever since my son told me he had a friend named Justin Lindley. As if you'd name your son Justin if his father were someone else. If you'd hated me, you'd never have named your son after me. And for another thing, if he were Lindley's son, Lindley would never have allowed it. Waiting for Inthanu's reply to my letter was torment."

Catherine was filled with empathy as she realized that he had suffered no less than she had, and her voice trembled as she responded.

"If I'd hated you, I would have let you know about Justin. It would have been easy to write and tell you that I'd given birth to a child here in England, and that I'd gone back to Arthur, so he'd have a father."

Catherine paused and when he said nothing, she continued.

"If you'd known, think how much you'd have suffered, knowing you had a son and weren't able to see him. You'd have been miserable all the time you were with your wife and children in Siam."

The expression on his face relaxed and he smiled slightly.

"You're still as headstrong as you always were, Catherine. You're right. But only half right. If I'd known I had a son, and he was being

The Glowing of Such Fire 319

raised by another man, I might have lost the will to live."

"But you had everything that your mother and Chao Chom Klee wanted for you. You had Bua and children. Ernest's a fine young man. He's more like Bua than you."

When he heard her mention Bua, he put his hand inside his coat and pulled something out to give her. Catherine looked puzzled when she looked at the small delicately sewn lace mat on her palm.

"Bua crocheted it for me to stand your portrait on. She told me to tell you she sympathized with you when you went to ask her not to marry me. She's always regretted her decision. That's why I said you were only half right. Now Bua's made another decision. She's asked to separate from me. I'm free from her…and from my elders who've all passed away."

Her heart was suddenly flooded with warmth like the late summer sun bursting through clouds, after it had been numb for so long that she had almost forgotten what happiness felt like. Justin opened his arms as Catherine stood up and sank into his embrace. The past melted into the present as the wall of time that had stood between them came crashing down.

Catherine and Prince Saifa were reunited at last.

Although the wall had been destroyed, the remains of some bricks survived, making their path difficult to negotiate. The difficulty that bothered Catherine like a thorn in her heart was the fact that Justin had never met his father, who was from a different world, and she did not know how they would overcome the cultural barrier.

Her heart began to race as she and Prince Saifa walked into the sitting room of the house at Breamore. The two young men were sitting waiting. Justin stood up first as he saw his mother enter the room, but his dark brown eyes were not looking at her. Instead, he was peering past her at the man who had stepped inside with her. Noticing his awkward expression, Catherine's heart sank.

Prince Saifa gazed at his son and grinned.

"My son!" he said, extending his hand.

The young man put his hand out mechanically and Prince Saifa clasped it firmly before pulling him into his embrace without a trace of

320 A Passage to Siam

embarrassment as if it was the most natural thing in the world. Justin's awkwardness vanished as Prince Saifa took a step back and gazed at him in delight and Catherine noticed the colour rising in her son's cheeks.

Inthanu stood up and, when his father moved towards him, he got to his knees and prostrated himself before his father. It was a gesture that did not surprise Catherine, since she had seen it before, but Justin looked on in bewilderment.

"Stand up, son," Prince Saifa told his son in English with an ease that indicated that they were used to addressing each other in English. You look even more strapping than before. I'm proud of you, son."

Then he turned to Justin and said softly, "My son. We've only just had a chance to meet. I want to get to know you, and I expect you want to get to know me. Don't be vexed that we were born on different sides of the world because, even though we were far apart, from the moment I knew I had another son…with the woman I love, you've never left my heart."

Tears rolled down Catherine's cheeks and she did not bother to wipe them away as she gazed at the three men. Prince Saifa had one arm around Justin's shoulder and the other arm around Inthanu.

Her heart, which for the past twenty years had been like a parched desert, was flooded with joy once again.

＊＊＊

They all stayed in Breamore for a month before Justin and Inthanu returned to Manchester University that autumn.

Catherine enjoyed looking out the window at the wide lawn at the back of the house dotted with small green bushes and shady trees, and seeing the middle-aged man walking alongside the brown-haired young man who was several inches taller than him or watching them ride horses together across the lawn to the open fields and woods beyond. Sometimes, a raven-haired young man was with them.

Mostly, Inthanu would give his father and his half-brother a chance to get to know each other, going into the town or to London to meet Captain Rowland. It was strange how his easy-going and generous nature endeared him to Catherine as if he were her own son.

The Glowing of Such Fire 321

Catherine's happiness was complete on seeing the man she loved in the role of father to her son, and she was amazed because she was aware that, beneath his casual demeanour, the prince had been very worried that his son would not accept him as his father.

In the evenings, she would invite Justin to go for a walk with her, so that they could be alone together, and he talked about their son as if he knew she had been waiting to hear how they were getting along. Catherine's heart was filled with contentment when he talked proudly of their son's attributes, whether it was his love of learning, his responsible nature, his intelligence, or his keen powers of observation. Once Justin told her smiling, "He's nothing like me. You're lucky he's just like you!"

"What do you mean?" she asked, knowing he was only teasing. "He has to be like both of us or he wouldn't get along with you so well! I'm so happy."

"I'm happy too," Justin said thoughtfully. "I'm glad he's accepted me so quickly in case one day he comes to live in Siam."

Catherine froze.

"You're teasing, aren't you? How can he go to live in Siam when…"

Prince Saifa's old audacity rose to the surface, and he cut in.

"Justin's a nobleman just like Inthanu, He has a responsibility to his ancestors' homeland. When I was in India, I always knew I'd go back home to serve my country. You're the same, Catherine. When I've finished my business in England, we'll go back together."

The clear evening sky suddenly darkened, and the cool autumn weather chilled her to the bone. Her heart turned to ice.

It was true. Justin was half Siamese, but Catherine had never prepared him for life in Siam. She had never even imagined that he would have a chance to meet his father.

Once again, she felt like a tree shaken by a storm. What would happen to Justin if his father took him to Siam?

"What's the matter?" Prince Saifa asked, noticing her face was pale. "Aren't you happy to be going back? It won't be so different from England. I'm going to build you a house like the one in Singapore."

A house like the one in Singapore twenty years ago. Justin had planned to build her a house and he had not forgotten his promise. He was still just as determined as he had always been.

The years had made Catherine less impetuous, and she did not blurt out a refusal, knowing full well that it would make no difference to someone as strong-willed as Justin, and what's more, what reason could she give for not allowing her son to go with his father that would not hurt either of their feelings?

All she could do was to ask him carefully, "If Justin goes to Siam, how will he get by when he's been raised in England? He knows nothing about Siam."

"Justin will be with me."

The other issue that troubled Catherine was how she and Prince Saifa would be able to live together in England. They were still staying in separate bedrooms, since nobody knew about their relationship, but every night Justin would leave his room and spend the night in Catherine's room before returning to his own before anyone else was awake.

He had told her from the beginning, "Never mind the customs here. I won't be separated from you when you're my wife and you always have been."

She could not refuse him when her heart belonged to him, and for the first time since the birth of her son, she slept soundly and contentedly in his arms as she had done twenty years earlier.

***

"Justin! Oh, you're here. I thought you'd gone to London with your father."

The young man walked up the old stone steps of the terrace at the back of the house in Breamore and smiled at his mother who was coming towards him, so he changed his mind about going inside and offered her his arm to take. They walked down the steps together onto the wide lawn under the maple trees.

"Father's gone with Ernest. They won't be back until this evening."

Justin didn't say why they'd gone, but she imagined it had something to do with finding a place to stay for the princes who were coming to study in England the following year.

Arm in arm, they strolled beneath the trees, and Catherine decided to ask him something that had been on her mind for the past few days.

"How do you find your father, my love?"

"I respect him," he replied at once as if he had been waiting for her to ask. "At first, I was worried he might have had an agenda, but he doesn't at all. When he said he wanted to get to know me, that's what he meant."

Justin wasn't aware that his words had lifted a heavy burden from his mother's shoulders.

"I know he loves me and he's proud of me," he continued. "When I talk about the father who raised me, I know it hit's a nerve, but Father admits he did you wrong. He blames himself for driving you away. I told him it wasn't anyone's fault, and there's no point to keep bringing up the past. We should make the best of the present."

Catherine's eyes filled with tears, and she pulled out a handkerchief.

"I'm glad," she said, steadying her voice. "I'm glad you're mature enough to face the truth calmly. Now I know that whatever happens, you'll be able to handle it."

Justin stroked the back of his mother's hand that held his arm comfortingly.

"My father's determined to take me to Siam one of these days. With him by my side, you don't need to worry that I won't be accepted. And the Siamese are peaceful and tolerant of different religions. That's what Colonel Rowland told me. I don't mind travelling to the East, but I'll always come back home."

"I was the same when I was your age. I wanted to see the world, but it was just a dream…"

"Now you can make your dream come true."

"What do you mean?" Catherine asked, looking up into his dark brown eyes. "Your father and I met and then we parted ways as if our time together had been just a dream. I don't see a way for us to be together after I go back to London, but I'm happy that you've finally met your father. Are you really going to Siam?"

"I don't think it will be a problem, Mother. I'm old enough to make my own decisions and I told him I wouldn't be able to do everything

324　A Passage to Siam

he asks, but I didn't refuse him completely. I've found a compromise."

Catherine looked at him doubtfully.

"A compromise?" she repeated. "Where did you get that idea from?"

"From my father, Lindley," he replied. "He always told me he never wanted to be a businessman. When he was young, the only thing he wanted to do was travel the world, but when he was older, he found a compromise. He always taught me we should find a way to make our dreams come true."

"How do you do that?" Catherine asked.

"If you wake from your dream, you can make it come true," her son answered gently.

* * *

It was Justin's last day before going back to university with Ernest, and Catherine was preparing to return to London with Prince Saifa, who had found a house to rent on the outskirts of the city.

"My father has to find teachers and a place to live for the Siamese students who will be coming to England, and he also needs to find engineers to take back to Siam."

Catherine found out later that Justin and his father had agreed that, after finishing university, Justin would go to work in Siam to help with planning the first railway that would run from Bangkok to the northern part of the kingdom. This was one of King Chulalongkorn's projects to develop the country's transportation systems.

"Father says that Westerners will be employed in the beginning and that I'll be able to help. He's going to write to the king to ask his permission, but…"

The word 'but' made Catherine realize that it would not be as easy as it had appeared at first.

"But when the job's done, I told him I'd return to England."

"You mean you don't intend to stay in Siam?"

Catherine did not know if she was disappointed or relieved that her son had found a way out of his dilemma.

"Yes, Mother," he replied firmly. "I've found a compromise. I'll go to Siam with my father as he wishes, but when my work's done, which

The Sands of Time 325

might take several years, I'll return to England."

Catherine gazed at her son as if seeing him for the first time. Although he looked the same on the outside, there was a resoluteness and a calmness in his expression that she had never observed before.

"What about you and Father?" Justin asked. "He hopes you'll go back to Bangkok with him now that he's separated from Ernest's mother. As I understand, you were his first wife, so there won't be any problems. The decision rests with you."

"Justin," Catherine began. "Your father will stay in England for a while and then he'll return to Siam with Ernest. If I go back to Siam with him, I'll be considered his wife there, but here in England, I'm still Mrs Lindley. I can't allow him to come and live with me. What will Margaret and David say? And what will people think?"

"Do you care?"

"When I was eighteen, I didn't care. And look what happened?"

Justin smiled.

"I understand. Sometimes out hearts and the traditions that bind us go in opposite directions. If we follow tradition, our lives will be uncomplicated, but narrow and boring. Sometimes you're bored, aren't you, Mother?"

Catherine was silent for a moment. She had never once told Arthur or her children that she was bored.

"What makes you say that? I'm sure I've never said I was bored."

"I could tell. Sometimes you looked detached as if there was something missing, but now I've seen you with Father, I've realized it was him that was missing. Why would you let what people think stand in the way of your happiness?"

Her eyes brimming with tears, Catherine hugged her son tightly as she had done when he was small.

"Thank you for understanding me."

Justin squeezed his mother tightly before releasing her and walked to the window. The morning was misty, and he could just make out two lamps on the horse-drawn carriage parked outside the gate.

"Colonel Rowland has found Father a house not far from Knightsbridge. He'll be able to have dinner with you often. And don't worry about gossip. Father will find a way," Justin said, smiling as she looked at him in puzzlement.

"Father and I have found a way out. When you get back to London, he'll tell you."

* * *

Two days after she had returned to London, Prince Saifa came to dinner at the house in Knightsbridge along with Margaret and her husband David. Catherine had not intended to dress up, but she could not help studying herself in the mirror.

Although her waist was no longer as tiny as it had been when she was young, her navy silk dress with a bustle at the back accentuated her slim figure and complemented her flaxen hair and blue eyes.

She lifted her hand to admire the eternity ring on her finger, which she could not resist wearing for the prince's first visit to her house. When he arrived, he was wearing a white bowtie with a black suit, and he smiled when he saw the ring on Catherine's finger.

* * *

The next day, Prince Saifa came to visit her alone for the first time and, instead of meeting him in the large drawing room, she led him to her sitting room, but he stopped in front of an old photograph of Arthur in a polished oval frame that hung on the wall.

Prince Saifa looked up at the young man with long sideburns and a neatly trimmed moustache above his lips. The man in the picture looked back at him with a grave expression as if he were asking the visitor what business he had being there.

"Arthur Lindley," the prince said gravely as if he were addressing a living person. "It's taken me most of my life to find Catherine and my son in England. I admit that I broke my word to you when I vowed to take care of Catherine and I drove her away, but now I want to make it up to her. I hope you understand."

The prince's words melted her heart and a warm sensation spread through her being.

"I love Catherine," the prince continued as he reached for her hand.

The Sands of Time 327

"There's no one else in my heart, but I haven't forgotten that I snatched her away from you, and I won't hurt your honour again. This time, I'll do things properly. We won't live together until…"

As he turned to smile at her, his smile brought back the young man from years ago.

"Until the king of Siam gives his permission for me to marry her in accordance with English law."

"Justin…" Catherine stammered, her blue eyes sparkling like the morning sun rising over the horizon as brightly they had done twenty years earlier.

He placed his other hand on the eternity ring on Catherine's right hand before removing it and replacing it on her left ring finger, from which she had since removed Arthur's wedding ring.

"You took care of Catherine and my son for twenty years, Lindley. From now on, it's my turn. I intend to make Catherine my wife for the twilight of our lives. No one knows how much time we have left. I hope you understand and give us your blessing."

Catherine's heart glowed like the smouldering embers of a fire and, from somewhere far away, the words of the sonnet she had recalled when she had first been reunited with Prince Saifa drifted back into her consciousness.

> In me thou see'st the glowing of such fire
> That on the ashes of his youth doth lie,
> As the death-bed whereon it must expire,
> Consum'd with that which it was nourish'd by.
> This thou perceiv'st, which makes thy love more strong,
> To love that well which thou must leave ere long.

Epilogue

The story would not be complete if I did not describe what happened after Prince Saifa and Catherine started a new life together in the twilight of their lives.

Prince Saifa wrote a letter to the King of Siam, asking permission to take a widow by the name of Catherine Burnett Lindley back to Siam as his wife. The letter explained that they had previously lived together as man and wife and had a grown son who planned to travel to Siam to survey routes in the North for construction of a railway. The following year, Prince Saifa was appointed Siamese ambassador to the United Kingdom, and given permission to take his English wife back to Siam as he had requested.

* * *

The evidence that Jane gave me, which her father had saved, was Catherine and Prince Vijjuprapha's marriage certificate from the registry office in London, which was dated 1884, indicating that Prince Saifa and Catherine had lived together as man and wife. This confirmed the information I had, which was documented by Prince Vijjuprapha and had been passed down to his grandson, who was my great-grandfather and the eldest son of Mom Rachawongse Inthanu.

I worked out that Mom Rachawongse Inthanu graduated in 1886 and returned to Siam a few months later, but Justin Lindley did not go back with him, waiting for several more years until he travelled there with his father, Prince Saifa.

Although Prince Saifa lived to the age of seventy, Catherine only had the chance to live with the man she loved until 1887, since she died of heart failure at the age of forty-seven.

By that time, Prince Saifa was fifty-three years old, and was in poor health, so he resigned from his post as ambassador and returned to Siam, taking his son Justin with him. In his capacity as an expert in Geology, Justin surveyed routes in the North for a railway.

Prince Saifa never saw Bua again, just as Bua had predicated.

Two years after Prince Saifa had left for England, Bua's youngest daughter got married, so Bua became a nun and went to live in a temple in Nonthaburi, where she remained until her death at the age of sixty-five.

Justin worked in Siam for about six years before returning to England, but he and Mom Rachawongse Inthanu remained in touch until their old age, and when Justin retired, he went to live in his mother's house in Longstock. After the First World War, there was no news of him, and Inthanu did not find out about his death until a year later. Several young men with the surname Lindley died in the Second World War, but fortunately one of Justin's descendants had kept some documents, and that was Kenneth Lindley, whom I met by chance in Longstock.

My family had only documents recorded by Prince Saifa, but when Jane and I combined them with Kenneth Lindley's documents, I was able to complete Catherine's story.

I took the documents to England, where I wrote the story.

I can hardly believe that I'm staying in the house in Breamore. The old grey house with ivy around the windows has changed hands many times since it belonged to Colonel George Rowland, who died in 1888. It is now a hotel, and Jane's father, Kenneth Lindley, made reservations for Jane and me, so that we would get to experience the place where Catherine and Prince Saifa first met.

I went for a walk in the garden behind the hotel yesterday evening. The hundred-year-old maple trees were still standing by the lake, their autumn leaves red and golden, just as they were when Prince Saifa met Catherine.

I paused to gaze at the red leaves, glinting in the evening sunshine as they cast shadows on the flaxen hair of the lovely young Englishwoman standing next to me beside the lake.

She turned to smile at me.

"I thought I'd find you here, Asanee," Jane said as she put her arm in mine. "Have you finished the final chapter?"

"Almost," I replied, grinning. "I just have one question left to answer."

"What is it? Tell me."

I asked her if it had been a sad ending for Prince Saifa, who had spent the final years of his old age without Catherine and their son by his side, and whether the time that they had spent together had been worth it.

The first five years after they had fallen in love added to the five later years that they were together were likely to have meant more to him than if he had lived for a hundred years without Catherine, we agreed.

"If you knew that you'd only be with the woman you loved for another five years, would you still have travelled to England, or would you have stayed with Bua?" Jane asked me.

Understanding the meaning behind her words, I laughed and put my arm around her shoulder as we walked past the lake and around the garden. As the sun was setting, we strolled across the wide green lawn as Catherine and Prince Saifa had done a hundred years earlier.

"I'd choose to stay with you, of course, even if it was just for five years or even five days."

Our story had begun because we had been researching Catherine's story together. For two years, we communicated via email, and after that, Jane came to stay in my house in Thailand as a guest of my family while we traced the story of Catherine and Prince Saifa. In the end, a bond had formed between us that could not be broken.

Jane agreed to come and live with me in Thailand, and I couldn't help thinking that she had inherited the sense of adventure of a woman who had lived a hundred years before her.

I am more fortunate than Prince Saifa in that I have not had to experience the family pressures that he faced and, after reading Catherine's story, my father wanted to make up for what had happened to her by welcoming Jane into our family with open arms.

I shall endeavor to maintain the bond between us as Prince Saifa and Catherine did at the beginning and the end of their lives.

Asanee Vijjusena Na Ayuthaya

Background

'A Passage to Siam' is the author's fourth historical fiction after 'Rattanakosin', 'Song Fang Khlong' and 'A Night Full of Stars' but, chronologically, this novel comes after 'Rattanakosin', which closes at the end of the reign of Rama III, because it is set during the reign of Rama IV and at the beginning of the reign of Rama V.

The purpose of this novel is to explore Siam's relationship with Western powers during the fourth reign since, as far as I know, there have not been any Thai works of historical fiction set during this period that explore this idea. It took four years to research and two years to write.

I wasted time in the beginning because I started out on the wrong foot by planning for the female protagonist to be the daughter of an American missionary, since missionaries had a role in Thai society from the end of the third reign. However, as I began to write the outline, I realized that religion would have to play a part, which would have changed the scope of the story, so I had to stop and find a new idea, which was for the protagonist to be an Englishwoman instead. Therefore, I researched the relationship between Siam and England, as well as the way of life in Victorian England, and was able to finish the story outline without any difficulty.

Although I borrowed the names of real historical characters, such as Captain Thomas George Knox, Captain Dick or Luang Surawiset, Dr. Dan Beach Bradley, Robert Hunter, Charlotte Palmer, and King Pinklao, the male and female protagonists are entirely fictional. Nevertheless, the idea of a Siamese prince marrying a European girl was inspired by the lives of Prince Chakrabongse and his wife, Katya, who lived during the fifth and sixth reign, although the details of their lives are not part of this novel. In fact, I have never found documentation of any Siamese man marrying an English woman during the fourth reign.

The story's details are all based on historical sources and were not made up. The idea of the male protagonist going abroad for military training was based on real records of King Pinklao sending a Thai to India for military training so that he would be able to train the Front Palace soldiers according to European military traditions on his return. The officer in question was Major Luang Radaronayuth (Lek Chulanon), whose name appears in the writings of Prince Damrong Rajanubhab. Consul Hillier and Captain George Knox were also real people and, during the fifth reign, the latter was given a knighthood and was the British Consul in Siam.

The details about the Front Palace and King Pinklao were from a book by the late Khun Amphan Tanthawatana, who faithfully compiled information about the Second King of Siam, of whom relatively little is known about by the younger generation.

The solar eclipse, Siamese customs for receiving envoys, the route taken by envoys to Siam, King Pinklao's illness, the head-shaving ceremony, and other traditions, were all based on historical sources, which I combined to create the story.

If readers wonder why the story did not end with Prince Saifa and Catherine either living happily ever after or tragically dying together, it is because life is made up of both fulfillment and disappointment, so the outcome of Prince Saifa and Catherine having only a short time together at the end of their lives is a more likely scenario than the others.

About Khunying Vinita
(Vinicchayakul) Diteeyont

Khunying Vinita Diteeyont, the National Artist of 2004, is an author, academic, critic and translator under the pen names V. Vinicchayakul and Kaewkao.

Educational Background
Alumnus of 35th class of Mater Dei College
Alumnus of 26th class of Triam Udom Suksa School
Bachelor's degree from the Faculty of Language Arts, Chulalongkorn University, 34th class
EdD in Curriculum and Instruction (Literature) from the University of Northern Colorado, USA

Professional Background
She was a lecturer in the Faculty of Language Arts, Silpakorn University from 1970-1995 for 25 years. The year before retiring, she held the position of Level 9 Associate Professor.
She was a part time lecturer in Translation for graduate students of the Language Research Institute, Mahidol University from 1995-2010.
She has been in charge of the website www.reurnthai.com since 1999 until the present, proliferating knowledge of language, culture, literature, history and general knowledge under the name "Tao Chompoo" after the colour of the Faculty of Language Arts, Chulalongkorn University.
She has received 12 other honorary awards, namely:
1. The Thai National Heritage Preservation Award in 1994
2. The Thai National Culture Award in 1997

3 The Prakaew Thong Kam Award for Outstanding Alumni of the Faculty of Language Arts, Chulalongkorn University in 2001

4. The Angela Award of the Inter-Ursuline Student Community (Thailand) as an alumnus of Mater Dei College for Service to Society in 2004

5. The National Artist Award for Literature in 2004

6. The Democratic Family Example (The 'Diteeyont' family Sompan-Khunying Vinita Diteeyont) in 2005 from the National Identity Committee

7. She was the first foreigner to receive the Doctor of Humane Letters from the University of Northern Colorado in 2005 because her work received numerous national awards and she brought prestige to the university.

8. Outstanding Mother of Bangkok in 2007 for promoting Thai Arts and Culture and Performance

9. The Surintaracha Award for Outstanding Senior Translators in 2008 from the The Translator and Interpreter Association of Thailand

10 Honoured Alumna of the University of Northern Colorado in 2009

11. The Patokta Silpa Bhirasri Award in 2014 and the Silpa Bhirasri Medal of Honour

12. The Honorary Award for Literature of Bangkok Districts for her novels *"Song Fang Khlong"* (Khlongsarn District), *"Jak Fan Su Nirandorn"* (Ladprao District), and *"Burapha"* (Thonburi District) in 2014

She has received 24 awards for writing from both the government and private sectors, including awards for *Rattanakosin, Song Fang Khlong, Niramit, Ratri Pradap Dao, Burapha, Malai Sam Chai*, and others.

Of these, the novel, *"Rattanakosin"* has been acclaimed as national literature. She is a composer for the Suntaraporn Band. Most of her work was writing the lyrics for royal songs and songs for Suntaraporn concerts, such as *Tawaisaja* and *Dangsaifon*.

Examples of Past Work
1. Arbitrator for the Institute of the Department of Intellectual Property
2. President of the Board of Judges for the SEA Write Award Fiction Category
3. Subcommittee for Child and Youth Affairs of the Social Commission, National Legislative Assembly

Current Work
1. She is an advisor to the Suntaraporn Foundation.
2. She is on the subcommittee for publications in honour of His Majesty King Maha Vajiralongkorn in the field of sports of the Sports Authority of Thailand.
3. She is a member of the National Identity Foundation committee.
4. She is a member of the National Identity committee.

She has been awarded the following decorations of honour:
1. The Most Exalted Order of the White Elephant in 1991
2. The Knight Grand Cross (First Class) of the Most Noble Order of the Crown of Thailand in 1995
3. The Most Illustrious Order of Chulachomklao (Fourth Class) in 1998
4 The Most Illustrious Order of Chulachomklao (Third Class) in 2001
5. Companion (Fourth Class) of the Most Admirable Order of the Direkgunabhorn in 2006